Praise for Lorelei James's
Chasin' Eight

"...an awesome series...parts that were funny, hysterical, sad and yet it shows us what a great and talented author Lorelei James is."
~ *Fallen Angel Reviews*

"All in all, this book was great with fantastic world-building, hot sex, great characters and an intense roller coaster ride of a plot."
~ *The Romance Studio*

"In the mood for some zesty cowboy love? Then it's time to read Lorelei James. Chasin' Eight, book eleven in the Rough Riders Series, provides everything a reader needs and more: an alpha hero, a feisty heroine, and enough sexual tension to keep you turning the pages."
~ *Whipped Cream Reviews*

"All in all, James came through with another smokin' hot cowboy story, filled with tight wrangles, unbelievable sexual tension, incredible characters and a great love story."
~ *The Book Pushers*

"...the sex scenes are smokin' hot and will leave you hot and bothered, due to the fact those scenes are vintage Lorelei James. No one does it better."
~ *The Good, The Bad, The Unread*

D0931945

Look for these titles by
Lorelei James

Now Available:

Running With the Devil
Dirty Deeds
Babe in the Woods

Rough Riders
Long Hard Ride
Rode Hard, Put Up Wet
Cowgirl Up and Ride
Tied Up, Tied Down
Rough, Raw, and Ready
Branded As Trouble
Shoulda Been A Cowboy
All Jacked Up
Raising Kane
Slow Ride
Cowgirls Don't Cry
Cowboy Casanova

Wild West Boys
Mistress Christmas
Miss Firecracker

Print Anthologies and Collections
Wild Ride: Strong, Silent Type
Three's Company: Wicked Garden
Wild West Boys
Wild Ride

Chasin' Eight

Lorelei James

SAMHAIN
PUBLISHING

Henderson County Public Library

Samhain Publishing, Ltd.
11821 Mason Montgomery Road, 4B
Cincinnati, OH 45249
www.samhainpublishing.com

Chasin' Eight
Copyright © 2012 by Lorelei James
Print ISBN: 978-1-60928-597-5
Digital ISBN: 978-1-60928-491-6

Editing by Lindsey Faber
Cover by Scott Carpenter

This book is a work of fiction. The names, characters, places, and incidents are products of the writer's imagination or have been used fictitiously and are not to be construed as real. Any resemblance to persons, living or dead, actual events, locale or organizations is entirely coincidental.

All Rights Are Reserved. No part of this book may be used or reproduced in any manner whatsoever without written permission, except in the case of brief quotations embodied in critical articles and reviews.

First Samhain Publishing, Ltd. electronic publication: June 2011
First Samhain Publishing, Ltd. print publication: May 2012

Chapter One

There was nothing like live porn.

Chase McKay rested his shoulders against the cheap headboard, taking a long pull off his beer as he settled in for the show.

The naked blonde with the huge rack balanced on her knees, head thrown back as the naked brunette, with an equally impressive set of double D's, feasted noisily on her nipples. When the blonde—Lanae, or was it Renee?—grabbed the brunette's head, trying to force her to take more of her nipple into her mouth, the brunette—Leah, or was it Gia?—smacked her ass.

"Rhea," the blonde whimpered, "that hurt."

So the brunette was Rhea. Check.

Rhea fisted her hand in the blonde's mane, gaining her full attention. "Every time you touch me without permission, I'll stop what I'm doing, Janae. Understand?"

Ah, so that made the blonde Janae.

And people said he was bad with names.

Janae's nod of assent earned her a reward from Rhea. A kiss. A deep, openmouthed kiss, with lots of glimpses of flashing pink tongues and feminine moans.

Damn. That was freakin' hot.

But not as hot as watching Rhea's hand gliding down the center of Janae's body.

Chase's dick stirred—a happy surprise as he'd already received the duo's oral worship. Talk about a tandem effort—French kissing with the head of his cock between their warring tongues and lips. Then Janae jacked his shaft while Rhea's hungry mouth milked him to orgasm, but Rhea didn't swallow. He watched, panting and wide-eyed as Rhea kissed Janae, sharing his come with her.

Yeah, that'd been something new for him. But not for them apparently.

"We've been selfish," Janae cooed, adding a husky, "your turn."

As he sank into a blissful place where embarrassing buck-off times were a bad memory, and two sets of soft, talented hands caressed him, he heard the door open and then slam into the wall.

"Chase? Honey? Are you okay? I've been so worried..." A gasp. Then another. Louder. More horrified and theatrical than the first. "And to think I came here because..." The length and pitch of her sobs escalated.

Fucking awesome.

"What in God's name is going on here?" boomed an outraged male voice.

Chase's impassive gaze zoomed from Sheree Bishop—her triumphant eyes filled with crocodile tears—to her father, Lou Bishop, then to Winnie, his PBR publicist, and Elroy, his PBR liaison.

Hail! Hail! The gang's all fucking here.

"How did you get a goddammed key to my room?" Chase demanded.

"See, Daddy? He isn't even the least bit sorry for being caught red-handed with..." Sheree gasped dramatically. "Are there *two* of you?"

Janae waggled her fingers at Sheree as Rhea said, "Hey. What's up?"

Chase might've laughed if he wasn't so incensed.

Sheree burst into tears.

Lou Bishop patted his daughter's heaving back as she fell into a fit of hysterics. "I've heard rumors about you, McKay. And you've outdone yourself this time." Lou glared at Elroy. "The PBR condones this behavior from riders?"

"No," Elroy assured him, "but I think we all oughta take a deep breath and a big step back—"

"Yeah, feel free to take a big step right the hell outta my room," Chase snapped.

Lou stabbed his sausage-shaped finger at Chase. "Don't think I won't knock you on your ass, punk, for your smart mouth and for what you've done to my Sheree."

The absurdity of this situation was the only thing stopping Chase from leaping out of bed and laying Lou Bishop out cold.

"Daddy, please," Sheree sniffled. "Let's just go." In a calculated move that so perfectly defined the type of manipulation Sheree Bishop specialized in, she yanked a ring from her finger and threw it at him. "You can have this back, Chase McKay. We're done. For good." Wailing, she ran out, Winnie close on her heels.

Lou's fury pulsed through the room. Without taking his burning gaze away from Chase, he spoke to Elroy. "I want this handled. Tonight. You know what's at stake." After aiming one more death glare at Chase, he lumbered after his daughter.

Trying to remain calm, Chase picked up the ring and slid it to the first knuckle of his pinkie finger.

"McKay."

He glanced up at Elroy.

"Meet me in the parking lot. After you put on some clothes." Elroy glared at the women who were hurriedly getting dressed. "Alone."

Chase let his head fall back against the cheap headboard after the door slammed. "Fuck." This was the last thing he'd needed tonight. He never should've gotten mixed up with Sheree Bishop.

Or maybe you shouldn't have comforted yourself about your disappointing buck-off time by instigating a threesome.

Probably true. But it pissed him off that Elroy and his publicist had just burst in on him, like he was some delinquent kid who needed constant supervision. What he did off the dirt was nobody's business but his. No matter who they were.

Chase slid his jeans up his naked flanks. Zipped, buttoned and buckled, he reached for his shirt. "You ladies goin' someplace?"

"Don't you want us to go?" Janae said.

"Maybe they did, but I sure as hell don't."

"That woman wasn't your wife...or something?"

"Not even close." He jammed his feet in his boots without socks— God he hated that—and snagged his hat off the nightstand. "I'll be back."

"Promise?" they cooed in unison.

"Oh yeah." He ran his fingertip up the inside of Rhea's left arm, mirroring the motion on Janae's right arm. "I'm sure you two can find interesting ways to entertain yourselves while I'm gone."

Snagging a keycard from the dresser, he slipped into the humid night. The parking lot was nearly empty. He'd chosen this motel for its off-the-beaten-path location, which made him wonder if Sheree had planted a tracking device in his truck. He wouldn't put it past the psychotic broad.

Chase stopped ten feet from where Elroy paced in front of a big semi emblazoned with the PBR merchandise logo.

"No, sir. It's an extreme solution." Elroy gestured wildly. "Because sponsors shouldn't have that kind of power—" He hung his head. "I didn't say I *wouldn't* do it. I said I didn't agree that it needed to be done at all. Fine. Your call." He poked a button and let the phone dangle by his side.

Chase ambled across the asphalt. "Getting your ass chewed by the big boss?"

"Jesus, McKay. Ya think?" Elroy rubbed the skin between his eyebrows. "I can't fix this for you. Lou Bishop is threatening to pull every penny of PBR sponsorship money if we don't take action against you."

"What kind of action?"

"Lou wants you suspended from competition."

Chase's blood boiled. "I'm getting suspended because Lou Bishop barged into *my* private room and didn't like that he'd caught me in bed with two women?"

"Neither of the women in question was his daughter."

"So the fuck what? I'm not with Sheree."

Elroy cocked his head. "Does Sheree know that?"

"What the hell kinda question is that?"

"FYI, McKay, Sheree's been blabbing to every bull riding mag and pro rodeo blog that you two are practically engaged."

He never read those magazines. It pissed him off that some "expert" asshole gave commentary about how to improve a specific bull rider's riding percentage. Yeah, Chase had an idea how to improve too—stay on the damn bull for the full eight seconds. "That's bullshit."

"So why'd she throw the ring at you?"

"I have no idea." He held up his pinkie. "You think I gave her this ring? I've *never* given a woman a piece of jewelry in my life." Chase tossed the ring to the ground and pulverized the cheap piece of shit beneath his boot heel. "Besides, no one believes her."

"Her father believes her. That's our biggest problem."

Chase froze. *Our.* Not his.

Elroy started pacing. "I told you not to get mixed up with her, Chase. Told you not to take her to dinner. Told you not to encourage her. Told you whatever you do—don't sleep with her. But did you listen? No. Women like Sheree get what they want. Period. For some reason, she set her sights on getting you."

"Since she can't have me, she causes a scene with Daddy as a witness to get me tossed off the tour." He hadn't a clue a total lunatic lurked beneath the surface of polished Sheree Bishop, former Miss Rodeo USA. Sheree was on the hunt for a husband—a bull rider husband. His biggest mistake was ignoring her, believing she'd switch her affections to another rider once she got wind of his extracurricular sexual activities. But Sheree's determination had only increased.

"So this incident, coupled with the one in Lubbock last week..."

His thoughts rolled back to his last PBR performance. He'd bucked off at two point four seconds and decided to drown his sorrows at a local honky-tonk. Some dumbass redneck made a remark about the superiority of Texas bull riders. Given Chase's shitty mood and four shots of Chivas, he let loose on Texas cowboys being soft, jeering they wouldn't last a single winter day in the real West. Then he added a crack about butt-ugly Texas longhorn cattle not being good for nothing but trophy heads. Two Texas guys took offense. They dragged him outside, puffed up with Lone Star pride, intent on teaching a Wyoming sheep fucker a lesson.

Chase beat the living shit out of them.

Three other guys jumped in the fray. When Chase got control of his rage, five men were moaning in the dirt, mopping blood from their bruised faces, and he was still standing. Wobbling a little, but still standing.

Until the cops tackled him, cuffed him and threatened to arrest him for assault. But ten minutes later they released him, because not a single man came forward to press charges. They all claimed to be too drunk to remember who'd taken the first swing.

But the truth was no man wanted to admit that five-foot-seven-inch Chase McKay had taken on five Texas tough guys, all who topped the six foot mark...and won.

Luckily no one had uploaded streaming video to YouTube of PBR bad boy Chase McKay busting heads. But his ass smarted after Elroy ripped him a new one the following day.

And it was more of the same tonight.

Elroy said, "This attitude isn't helping you. And we both know this situation has been building for a while, because you, my friend, like to fight and fuck. Not necessarily in that order."

Through the haze of anger, he demanded, "How'd you guys get a key to my room anyway?"

"Sheree told the manager you were despondent about your bad ride and she feared you'd do something drastic like kill yourself."

"Bitch thought of everything, didn't she?" he muttered. "I get why the big bosses would be upset by what happened in Lubbock. I screwed up. In public. But tonight? I was in my private room. If Sheree lies believably enough to break in there, why wouldn't Lou suspect she was lying when she told him we were practically engaged?"

"No clue. But it changes nothing." Elroy sighed. "Bottom line: you're off the tour."

Fury lit his insides and Chase got right in Elroy's face. "This is bullshit and you know it. I have fans. Those fans bring revenue to the PBR. And what do you plan to tell the blogs and trade mags about my abrupt disappearance? Because if this 'incident' is presented to the public as I'm a discipline problem, then I'll fire right back about nepotism with the PBR's newest Daddy Warbucks corporate sponsor."

"First off, you signed a shitload of nondisclosure forms. Even if you're pissed—and between us, yes, you have a right to be—you can't violate the terms of the contracts. This is short term, Chase. Does this suck? Absolutely. That's why the PR arm will release news of a recurrence of your previous injury, which is a perfect excuse for why you rode so shitty tonight after being last year's defending champion. Fans should be happy to know you are recuperating until you're ready to ride again."

The PR spin machine thought of everything. "Tell me Winnie ain't gonna be involved in issuing the statement." He'd been taunting

Winnie, his assigned PR person, for the last year. The woman was too sharp, and saw right through his bullshit attempts to rattle and distract her. Plus, her comments, always softly spoken, grated on him, mostly because she was dead-on in her assessments. And he hated she saw things about him that he tried to hide from everyone else.

"Look at it this way. The PBR goes on hiatus for two months. So you're really only missing three performances instead of eleven."

Chase didn't exactly relax, but he realized if he was going to fuck up, he'd picked an ideal time to do it—because he might actually have a chance to fix it. "Can you guarantee I'll be on the roster come August?"

Elroy gave him a considering look. "Two things you need to do before I'll consider recommending you for reinstatement."

"Name them."

"Stay out of the damn spotlight. I don't wanna hear about you, I don't wanna read about you in the trade mags or see your naked ass on YouTube. No interviews, no drunken brawls, no excess of easy women, no Chase McKay sightings anywhere. You vanish. Understood?"

"Yes, sir." Chase exhaled the breath he hadn't been aware of holding. "What else?"

"In the meantime...try to remember how to ride a damn bull, okay? Practice, relearn, do whatever the hell it takes to get back to the professional level where you belong. Give me your word that you'll figure out what you've been doin' wrong and try and fix it."

Jesus. That fucking stung. He said, "You have my word, Elroy," and wondered how he was supposed to relearn something he'd been doing for over a decade.

"You do those two things. Prove to me you can do them and I'll push for you to get back in as soon as the season restarts."

Chase didn't bother mentioning the break would put him out of contention for the world title this year because he wasn't even close to contention. In fact, if he didn't get his shit together, he'd soon be off the PBR tour altogether.

Helluva mess you got yourself in, McKay.

"Try to behave, and I'll be in touch," Elroy said.

With nothing left to say, Chase started across the parking lot toward the motel. Lost in thought, he almost bumped into Winnie when she slithered from the shadows.

She blocked him like a sentry, arms crossed over her flat chest, her eyes strangely defiant behind glasses.

"You stick around to gloat?" he taunted.

Winnie sighed. "No, I don't enjoy this, but it's necessary to speak my piece while I have the chance."

"So go ahead and tell me I'm the Antichrist."

"There you go, putting words in my mouth." She held up her hand to stop his rebuttal. "And I don't need to hear for the umpteenth time that you'd rather put something *else* in my mouth."

"You've got me pegged, down to knowing exactly what I'm gonna say?"

"Yes. You aren't all that complex, Chase."

Low blow. "You calling me a simpleton?"

"Three things matter to you. Bull riding, sex and Chase McKay. That seems pretty simple to me."

"Bullshit," he spat.

"I understand athletes at the top of their game are self-centered. Privileged. I worked with a pro baseball team before I joined the PBR staff." Winnie sneered at him. "Betcha didn't know that. Know why? Because you didn't bother to ask. I never expected us to become BFFs, but I deserved your cooperation. I deserved your faith that I knew how to do my job just as well as you did yours. I deserved your respect. Whenever you called me—"

"Sugar tits?" he supplied.

"Nothing about you calling me *sugar tits* is considered remotely respectable," she snapped. "You know exactly where to strike to make me feel small, but that doesn't make you a big man, Chase McKay."

A flush rose up his neck. It'd been an assholish thing to say and he had no excuse for it, besides lashing out from sheer frustration. Before he could buck up and apologize to her for a change, Winnie lit into him.

"But here's the thing: It's my job to know all about you. Because of your natural riding talent early on, everyone in your ranching family cut you slack, believing you were destined for great things, and you accepted it as your due. Maybe you did work hard initially at being the best bull rider around, but I've seen none of that drive in the last year. Now you make excuses for your piss-poor riding averages."

She ticked off the reasons on her fingers. "It has to be the organization that's holding you back. Or the shitty bulls. Or the sponsorship commitments. Couldn't be that you've become a slacker. Resting on your previous laurels. Using charm and your good looks to keep your sponsorships rather than utilizing the talent that should keep you at the top of the standings."

"The PBR ain't the only game in town," he reminded her.

Winnie laughed. "Don't think the PBR isn't aware that you spoke to the PRCA folks about jumping circuits. We didn't address it because, given how you've been riding? Chances were high the situation would resolve itself and you'd get kicked off the PBR tour anyway."

Chase fumed but kept his mouth shut as another layer of harsh reality settled in.

"I tried to get you on track. Suggesting you focus on improving your average by going back to basics. By keeping distractions during the season to a minimum. And by distractions, yes, I meant women. You don't need me to tell you how good looking you are. But I'll point out that even the homeliest riders in the PBR are highly sought after. Those types of women want the thrill of riding a man who rides a bull. They dream of being the wives in the stands the cameras pan to when you get a hoof to the gut. They're star-fuckers. It's less about you personally than about the fact that you're on TV every week. Or you're talked about incessantly on the fan sites. Or your career is dissected in the trade mags. Oh, and let's not forget the potential for the top riders to make over a million bucks in a single season. That's mighty appealing to a woman who just has to show a little cleavage to garner your attention."

"Got a high opinion of the PBR fans, do you, Winnie?" he half-snarled. "Because I'll remind you, they're paying your salary."

She shook her finger in his face. "Do not twist this around, Chase. The fans are there to watch you ride. To get behind you in a good season. To stay behind you in a bad season. Ninety-nine percent of the PBR fans don't want to climb into your bed. So I find it ironic that you only give a crap about the one percent of fans that do."

Good thing the shadows hid the heat burning his cheeks and neck. He'd never had a dressing down like this. Ever.

You need it.

The fact it came from mealy-mouthed Winnie, who normally wouldn't say shit if she had a mouthful? That seemed to make everything about this nightmare situation a hundred times worse.

"You have so much potential. You're wasting it. I hope to heaven that you use this time off to pull your head out of your ass before you start that downward spiral."

"Are you really worried about me?" he asked with total sincerity.

"No, I'm worried about the image you project. An image the PBR doesn't need."

"What image is that?"

"Spoiled. You, Chase McKay, are a spoiled brat." With that, Winnie spun on her high-heeled boot and stormed off.

Smarting from the dressing down, Chase waited until he heard her car roar away before he moved and sat on a bench.

She'd called him a spoiled brat.

For Christsake, he was a twenty-eight-year-old man. He was too goddamned old to be a brat.

Wasn't he?

How'd you react tonight after getting your ass handed to you on an easy bull?

He'd taken off to indulge in a threesome instead of sticking around to talk to the fans.

Yeah. That was kind of bratty.

How did you respond after being caught in bed with two women by PBR officials?

He'd gotten indignant. Like he was being persecuted for his bad choices. Like he was being singled out.

Yeah. That was kind of bratty behavior too.

He scrubbed his hand over his face. This was all kinds of fucked up. But he wasn't too delusional or self-centered to admit the astute Winnie had a point. Several of them. He didn't have much farther to fall before he hit bottom.

And Winnie knew just where to strike the hardest blow—when it came to his family. Maybe his parents had indulged him, given him leeway with ranch chores. His brothers Quinn and Ben hadn't minded. Had they?

Even if they had complained, it would've been wasted effort.

What would he do if this "break" became permanent? Who would Chase McKay be if he wasn't a bull rider? What would he do?

Not go back to Sundance and ride the range looking for lost cattle with his brothers and cousins. He'd sold his portion of the ranch to the McKays who wanted to keep the legacy alive for themselves and their children. Chase hadn't seen a life in Wyoming as something he wanted.

He'd opted not to go to college or a trade school, but straight into the world of rodeo. He'd never developed a hobby. He had nothing in his life he was passionate about except bull riding.

So why had he allowed his riding skills to erode to the point he was standing on the brink of losing everything that mattered to him? For another nameless piece of ass in a cheap motel in another stop along the tour?

Fuck that.

He needed a plan.

He needed to get back to basics.

He needed to prove to himself he could get a handle on his own life.

He needed to make a decision and stick to it.

And he really needed to stay away from easy women.

Hell, he needed to stay away from *all* women. Swear off women. Forever. Okay, maybe not forever. For at least a month.

At that moment, a star tumbled from the sky, which he took as a sign.

No women for a month. No sex. No exceptions.

Chase had never seriously abstained. Oh sure, he'd bragged to his brothers and cousins he'd gone for four months without sex—but that'd been a total lie. He'd been too embarrassed to admit he had no

15

willpower when it came to offers of free and easy sex and he'd blown it within the first week. Not only that, he'd fucked up his chance of ownership in a prize bucking bull because he couldn't keep his damn Wranglers zipped. Not even his buddy calling him a fucking pathetic man-whore had changed his love-'em-and-leave-'em ways. Goddamn. His life had been careening out of control for the better part of a year. He hadn't hit rock bottom, but he sure could hear his boots scrabbling for purchase on that ledge from where he was teetering.

Enough. Focus on the here and now.

Mind racing, he trudged back to the motel. He opened the door and tried not to goggle at the two women indulging in a mutual sixty-nine.

Janae lifted her head from between Rhea's thighs and grinned at him. "Chase! You're back. We've been entertaining ourselves, like you asked."

"I see that. And as much as I appreciate your...efforts, I'm afraid, ladies, that I have some bad news."

Two weeks later...

Kane McKay answered the phone with a brusque, "Chase? Why're you callin' me?"

"Nice to hear your voice too, cuz."

"Sorry. Lack of sleep makes me cranky. What's up?"

"I need a favor. And it's gonna sound really freakin' weird, so just hear me out."

"Okay."

"I need a place to crash. I don't want anyone—and yeah, by anyone I mean my folks, my brothers and the rest of the assorted McKays—to know I'm in Wyoming."

Silence. "Ya ain't killed someone and are on the run from the law or anything?"

"No. I was suspended from the PBR. Mostly because of bullshit politics—" *Still in denial, buddy?* "—but I need time to figure out my next move. I can't do it with my family hovering."

"So it'd just be you?" Kane asked skeptically.

"Yep."

"No women?"

"I've sworn off women."

"Again? What is that? The fourth time this year?"

"You're fuckin' hilarious. That's another reason I need to get away. Too many temptations of the female flesh around me, and I'm willing to admit I'm a weak, weak man."

Kane laughed.

"So is anyone living in your old trailer?"

"Nope. Me'n Red hang out there occasionally when we need a break from the kids. I'll ask Ginger—"

"That's the other thing. Can we keep it strictly between us?"

A sigh. "I ain't gonna lie to my wife. I'll do this much. I won't tell Ginger you're comin', but once you're here, I'll let her know. If she suspects someone's squatting in our love shack, she'll call Cam. Wouldn't want our cousin to shoot ya on accident."

"That'll work. Thanks."

"Happy to help. Though, I'll point out your folks and brothers will be pissed if they hear you're around and hiding from them. So if it comes up, you keep me out of it. We just straightened out the last of the family drama."

"Quinn and Ben tell me the new arrangement is workin' great." The older generation had officially retired the last few months, forcing changes in the way McKay Ranches were run, leaving his brothers and cousins in charge for the first time.

"So far," Kane said.

"No fistfights yet?"

"Oh, I wouldn't say that."

Once again Chase was glad he'd cashed out his portion of the McKay Ranch with the change in ownership. The financial windfall provided him options and freedom. Yet...he half-wondered if not having a burning need for that prize money contributed to him slacking off on tour.

"When do you plan on bein' here?" Kane asked.

"I don't know. I'll call you after I get in."

"Fair enough. There's a key under the bottom porch step."

"Thanks, Kane, I really appreciate it."

"Glad to help. Drive safe."

Chapter Two

"Ava! Over here!"

Ava Cooper ignored the photographers snapping pictures as she waited for the valet to bring her Mazerati around.

"Come on," the photographer cajoled. "Give us something. Anything."

She recognized the fat, balding man, the most aggressive of the paparazzi. In the not-too-distant past she would've given him a sound bite. Now they circled her, waiting to swoop in and pick off the remaining bits of her dignity.

Fucking vultures.

"Ava. Open up to us. You know our readers are on your side. Don't you have anything to say to your fans?"

Her black sports car rumbled at the curb. She skirted the back end, colliding with the valet. "Pardon me, Miss Cooper."

"No problem. I'm ready to get the hell out of here." Ava peeled out, burning rubber before she even buckled her seat belt.

The traffic was light on the freeway this time of day as she headed...where? Home? Most paparazzi were on to fresher stories, but a couple persistent buggers detailed her comings and goings on a Twitter feed. If she didn't leave her house for a few days, rumors would fly she was too depressed, too drunk, too emotionally eviscerated to be seen in public. If she ran errands, or met with her agent, or visited her friends and family, or dined out, she'd put on a brave face through her personal heartache.

Ava wasn't sure when the ridiculousness of the situation occurred to her. She was a B-list actress. Why would anyone give a shit about her?

Because in the last month, her life, as she'd known it, had been turned upside down, and everyone gawked at a train wreck. She hadn't been in a state of denial as much as shock. It wasn't every day a woman found out via press conference that the man she'd been involved with for months was in a relationship...with another man.

Fucking Jake Vasquez. Talk about a double whammy—he'd betrayed her on both a personal and professional level.

They'd met while filming a low-budget independent romantic comedy in which they'd been cast in the lead roles. Jake was the most exquisite man she'd ever seen. Dark black hair, dreamy golden eyes, a killer body comprised of sinewy muscle beneath an expanse of luminescent olive-toned skin. Their attraction was instantaneous, and by the end of the film shoot, they were lovers. After the movie wrapped, the fall TV taping season started. Jake's popular TV show was filmed in Vancouver; hers was filmed in LA. But never during those months they maintained a long-distance relationship had she suspected Jake preferred men in bed.

The suspicion didn't even kick in the night Jake showed up at her place, half-liquored up, with his new friend Decker. Jake's increasing sexual aggressiveness with her in front of his buddy had gotten Decker all hot and bothered, so Jake spontaneously suggested a threesome.

Growing up in California, Ava had seen plenty of kinky things and even experimented with a few. But she'd shied away from a ménage, mostly because men wanted girl-on-girl action. The thought of kissing and touching another woman did nothing for her.

But two guys catering to her? That'd been a no-brainer. The three of them had spent all night and part of the following day in bed. Even now, Ava overheated recalling the erotic hedonism. Sandwiched between two hot men, bodies slick with sweat and pressed tightly together as they fucked to exhaustion.

At the time, she'd been blown away by Jake's willingness to cede control to another man. To do anything and everything Decker suggested. Or demanded. Watching Jake's beautiful face lost in pleasure as Decker fucked him. Seeing how expertly Jake sucked Decker off. Finding their stamina as arousing as their unexpected tenderness in the aftermath of such aggressiveness. In retrospect, she should've known Jake and Decker were too well attuned to each other.

The fact the paparazzi had caught Jake and Decker together in a full-body clinch at a gay club late one night in LA should've warranted a warning phone call from Jake. But no.

Before either of their publicity teams were informed, Jake held a press conference, admitting he could no longer lie about his true sexual orientation. Then he'd claimed both the movie studio and Ava had known their relationship was a sham to build buzz for the movie—which was a total lie.

She'd been completely blindsided. The movie studio scrapped the entire publicity campaign for the movie a mere month from release. The movie tanked. Her phone rang off the hook with requests for interviews. Paparazzi camped out around her house, forcing her to hire security guards to keep the press off her private stretch of beach.

How did she bounce back from this? Did she even want to? The brutal truth was she'd been frustrated in recent years with her acting career. Every role was supposed to be the vehicle for landing her a "big" breakout role. Hadn't happened. Now her years of hard work were overshadowed by events beyond her control. With the scandal simmering in the backs of directors' and producers' minds, she'd have to work twice as hard to prove herself.

To who?"

Her parents had never gauged her worth by her public success; they believed pursuing an acting career was a waste. As an heiress to the Cooper fortune, which included a string of hotels, a tire manufacturing business and a line of power tools, her mother had hoped Ava would join the family business. But Ava knew being a bottom-line businesswoman would stifle her creativity, regardless of the avenue she followed after this latest debacle blew over.

Maybe she should run away and join the circus.

As she waited in traffic, she happened to catch a glimpse of herself in the rearview mirror. Ugh. She looked like dog shit. She dialed her go-to guy for hair and makeup, cajoling him into squeezing her in immediately.

Hours later, when Ava exited the salon, she had an extra spring in her step because no one had recognized her.

Keeping up with her fab idea to run away, she needed to find someplace outside her normal haunts. Someplace nobody would ever think to look for her. Someplace remote. Unpopulated.

Hello, Wyoming.

Ava waited while the secretary patched her through to her long-time friend, the one person she'd always been able to count on to help her out of a jam.

"This is Ginger Paulson."

"I thought you were going by Ginger McKay?"

"Ava! I was just thinking about you. I'm Ginger Paulson while I'm at Paulson Law Office. But when it's me, Kane and the kids at home, I'm...ah, hell, I'm just mama. A frazzled mama."

"How are the McKay kiddos?"

"Hayden has developed a love of ranch work and has forgotten about his X-Box. Paul crawls as fast as a cockroach. Maddie is an angel, if you can overlook the death metal scream she's debuted in the last week."

Ava laughed. "You love it. And how is that smokin' hot hubby of yours?"

Ginger sighed. "Amazing. He can do physical labor all day, come home, diaper and care for two babies, help Hayden with school projects, play cards with my dad and still keep me purring like a contented kitten. So, amazing doesn't begin to cover how fabulous my

Kane is. Anyway, what's up with you? 'Cause, sweetie, you rarely call me out of the blue anymore."

"Sorry." She slipped out the patio door and gazed across the turbulent ocean. "I'm... I need to clear my head, Ginger. I thought this mess would blow over. It mostly has, but there's enough of it lingering I can't even have lunch in this town without being tracked down by the press. Which is why I need a break."

Ginger was quiet for just a beat too long.

"What?"

"Just thinking back to when your punkish seventeen-year-old self swaggered into my office. You had your career path all laid out. You couldn't wait to be the focus of the paparazzi."

Ava tilted her head to better catch the salty ocean breeze. "I was so cocky." She grimaced with bitter remembrance. "And I had no reason to be. No experience. Nothing but a solid belief in myself. If I'd known then what I know now..."

"You might've listened to your parents and gone into one of the family businesses?" Ginger supplied with syrupy sarcasm.

"Ha-ha."

"Come on, Ava. It hasn't turned out so badly for you. You've been in a critically acclaimed TV show and in a few movies. You've done it mostly on your own. You should be proud."

"But?" Ava prompted.

"But the smart, savvy girl I met had ambitions of being more than a mere actress. You were writing screenplays, studying directing and cinematography, planning to start a production company to showcase projects you loved."

"True. So what happened to me?"

"Sweetie. You got lazy. Rather than letting the money from the acting gigs fund those aspirations, using it as a stepping stone for bigger things, the last few years you've allowed complacency to wedge you into a place you don't want to be."

Ginger's ability to get to the heart of the matter was exactly what Ava needed. "Well, letting an in-the-closet actor come out and annihilate my career is a stepping stone I would've loved to skip."

Ginger laughed. "Sometimes what seems like the worst turn of events can turn into the best. And yes, I'm speaking from experience, as you well know."

"That's what I'm saying. I need new experiences. I need a change. I need to live something real." Ava breathed in the familiar scent of wet sand and exhaled slowly. "I want to come to Wyoming. I know your life is beyond busy, and I'd never presume to crash at your place. But a change of scenery will force me out of complacency. I need to stop being Ava Cooper for a while. Figure out who Ava Dumond is."

"I agree with you, but no matter what name you use, you are a celebrity. You will be recognized even in the small burg of Sundance, Wyoming."

"That's where you're wrong. Without makeup, designer clothes and my snazzy sports car, I doubt anyone would recognize me." She turned, checking out her reflection in the picture window. "My stylist reverted my hair to its original brown today. If his assistant didn't recognize me, and I've dealt with him for years, I'm pretty confident no one else will recognize me either. Besides, I'm not being snobby when I say I don't want to mingle with the Sundance locals. Luckily, Kane's old trailer is out in the middle of nowhere. Have you rented it yet?"

"No. Finding adult alone time in a house with three kids and my dad is impossible sometimes. And Kane and I need a place to connect."

"Could you put your libido on hold for like a week and lend me your love lair?"

"Let me talk to Kane—"

"No! I mean, I don't even want Kane to know I'm there."

"Why not?" Ginger demanded.

"Because your gentleman hubby would fuss over me, stopping by every day to see if I needed anything. I'd rather not put him in that position of feeling obligated."

"What am I supposed to tell him, Ava? I won't lie to him."

She'd forgotten cajoling didn't work on Ginger. "Don't tell him I'm coming, but once I'm there, I'll swing by your place and let him know I'm hanging out in Wyoming for a bit."

"But—"

"I didn't want to play this card, but you're leaving me no choice. You and Kane spent your honeymoon at my house for one entire week. You owe me a week in Wyoming."

"You shoulda gone to law school. Fine. I'll put away the spanking bench and the ceiling restraints before you get here. Which is...when exactly?"

Ava wasn't sure if Ginger was kidding about the marital aids. "I'm planning to fly into Denver and rent a car to drive the Wyoming leg. I'll call you when I arrive."

"All right. I'll make sure the trailer is unlocked that morning. And if you really don't want anyone to know you're there, park in the barn."

Ava sagged against the weathered siding. "This is exactly what I need. Thank you."

"Glad I can help. I know you'll figure it out, Ava. See you soon."

Next she called her dad.

"And to what do I owe the pleasure of a phone call from my beautiful daughter?"

"Hey, Dad. Just calling to see how you're doing."

"I'm sure you don't wanna hear about the modifications we've made to the latest test engine. So, as pleased as I am that charm school paid off, can the crap, Ava, and tell me what you want." He paused and puffed out air, which indicated he was outside on the patio smoking a cigar, which also meant her mother wasn't around.

Did she really only contact him when she needed something from him? Yes. But she'd deal with that guilt later. "I need to get out of LA for a while."

"Any idea where? The resort in Mexico? Or the chateau in France? I hear the new Barcelona property is inspiring."

"None of the above. I'm thinking about Colorado."

"The skiing won't be good this time of year in Aspen."

"Funny, Dad. I know that."

"I know you don't need money, so why you calling me?"

"I need to borrow the Citation."

Silence.

Ava blurted, "Please? The paparazzi are everywhere. They don't have access to the private air strip so I truly can just disappear."

Puff, puff. "How soon would you need to leave?"

"First thing tomorrow. That'd give me time to figure out a way to slip the tabloid guys who are determined to be the first to report my suicide."

Her father chuckled. "People are idiots if they believe you're still despondent over that cocksucker Jake."

"I'm hoping out of sight, out of mind will cure lingering curiosity."

"You really doing okay, Ava Rose?" he asked gruffly. "You've been awful damn scarce since this whole thing went down."

Switching her phone to her other ear, Ava rested her elbows on the railing. "The last thing I wanted was you guys getting swamped by my shit storm."

"Well, honey girl, that's what family does—sticks together and flips the world the bird. I'll remind you that your mother and I've been through a shit storm or two in the thirty years we've been married. We're tougher than you give us credit." *Puff, puff.* "Far as I know, your mom doesn't need the plane tomorrow. So I'll call and arrange it."

"Thanks, Dad."

"Keep in contact. You're a big girl and all that, but we worry, okay?"

Guilt swamped her. Her justification for shutting her family out was only partially true. They'd never understood her pursuit of a show business career, and when she failed so publicly in that career and her personal life, she felt like an embarrassment and a disappointment. "Okay. Love you."

"Love you too. Be safe, be well and—"

"Give 'em hell," she finished and hung up.

"I love the Dumond family motto," a dry, female voice intoned behind her.

Ava turned toward Hannah, her friend/personal assistant/gal Friday. "Hey, Han. I didn't know you were here."

"I gathered that. Now what's this bullshit plan about you hiding out in some godforsaken Western state?"

"Not like it'll be permanent. Just seeing the sights."

"For how long?"

"I don't know."

"Who are you going with?"

"No one. Just me."

Hannah lifted one eyebrow in her usual imperious manner. "Oh really? That's surprising."

"Why?"

"Because you never go anywhere by yourself, Ava. Never."

Ava bristled. "I do too go places by myself. I went to lunch by myself today."

"No, you met your agent for lunch." She raised her hand, stopping Ava's protest. "And please don't think that driving four miles to lunch in your car counts as by yourself."

Shoot. Hannah knew her too well. "I went to Madrid by myself last year."

"You *flew* to Madrid by yourself last year, in your parents' plane. As soon as your Manalos hit Spanish soil you had a translator, a stylist and a driver." Hannah cocked her head. "Come to think of it, that *is* a small entourage for you."

"Fuck off," Ava said crossly.

Hannah laughed. "I make your schedule, so I know where you've been and where you're going better than you do."

Maybe that was another part of the problem. Her decisions were all laid out for her. She hadn't done things for herself...well, ever. In addition to Hannah, she employed a housekeeper, a groundskeeper, a personal trainer, a stylist, a publicist, a part-time chef, a financial planner, an agent...and the list went on. Made her head spin. She curled her hands into fists by her sides and said, "Stop."

"Stop?" Hannah asked, alarmed. "Stop what? Stop you from doing this?"

"No. I need to stop. All of this. I need to stop being Ava Cooper. I need to know if Ava Dumond is capable of taking care of herself, because it's obvious Ava Cooper can't."

Hannah was dead silent. Then she smiled. "I know I should be worried about job security with your sudden identity crisis, but I'm not."

"Good. So you're not going to try and talk me out of this?"

"No. Besides, I know you'll be back by the first week in August." Hanna's eyes narrowed. "You are scheduled to start filming the new Lynch movie in Mexico that week. And given that the contracts were signed *before* this shit went down with the movie studio and Jake, you absolutely cannot fuck that up, Ava."

"I know."

"Do you?" Hanna pressed. "You know there's no warning when the casting director calls you in for a reading, so you'll need to be someplace where you can hop a plane at a moment's notice."

"Relax. I doubt I'll be gone that long. I just need a break." She watched the frown lines deepen on Hanna's forehead. "Are you rethinking that job security comment?"

"No. Since getting far away from here is your idea, I believe it's something you need to do. I just want you to be careful."

Ava hugged her. "I will. Thank you. You are the best, Han."

"You're welcome. Now will you at least let me help you pack and plan?"

She shook her head. "I need to do it all on my own. Like regular people do."

"With the exception of flying commercial like regular people do," Hannah inserted.

"Extenuating circumstances." Ava allowed a sheepish look. "Ah, can you tell me where I keep my suitcases?"

"Under the bed in the guest bedroom. I'll grab them."

As Ava flipped through her closet, she was torn. What to bring for clothes? Comfy. Casual. Weather appropriate. Did she own anything fitting that description?

Hannah set the luggage on the floor by the closet door. Ava's gaze strayed to the large duffel bag she'd never used. If she had to haul her belongings everywhere by herself, she'd need a manageable bag. She grabbed the gray duffel. "I'm taking this one."

"Ava. You can't even get your shoes in that."

"Ava *Cooper* can't get her shoes in that. Ava *Dumond* travels light."

"I need a glass of wine," Hannah said wearily.

"Help yourself." As Hannah left the room, Ava yelled, "Oh, on your way back from the kitchen, will you grab the box of condoms from the main bathroom?"

Hannah poked her head back in. "You don't care about packing shoes, but you're packing condoms?"

"Yep. I'm gonna find me a hot man and offer him unlimited, anything-goes sex—no strings, no regrets, just lots of getting naked and getting loose."

"So you're setting out to prove Ava Dumond is a sleazy ho-bag?"

"If that's what it takes to get my sexual confidence back where men are concerned? Then yes."

"Forget a glass of wine, I'm bringing back the whole damn bottle."

Ava laughed. Let her Wild West adventure begin.

Chapter Three

Chase could barely keep his eyes open. Disoriented, he slowed his truck to a crawl on the gravel road, braking at the cattle guard that denoted the turnoff to Kane's place.

He parked by the deck and stumbled out of his truck, taking a moment to stretch his legs and adjust the crick in his neck. But anticipation of falling face-first into a puffy mattress and sleeping a solid twelve hours put a spring in his step.

Once he'd unearthed the key and unlocked the door, he slipped inside the dark trailer and caught a whiff of flowers. Probably from cleaning supplies.

Too tired to shower, Chase stripped to his boxer-briefs in the living room and wandered to the kitchen sink to wash off the worst of the road grime. Rather than flipping on the lights, his fingers trailed along the hallway wall for guidance as he headed toward the back bedroom.

The bedroom door was closed. With as hot as it'd been, the room would be stuffy, but he was too damn whipped to even open a window. He flopped on the mattress and stretched out, but his arm connected with something solid. And warm. And soft.

And moving.

Chase leapt out of bed the same time the high-pitched shrieking started.

He fumbled with the light, blinking against the sudden brightness. He kept blinking because he didn't trust what he was seeing. There was a nekkid woman in his bed. A nekkid, pissed-off woman who'd jumped up and struck a Jackie Chan martial arts pose.

"Back off, perv! I have a black belt in taekwondo and I will fuck you up if you take another step toward me."

Chase raised his hands in surrender, trying really, really hard to keep his eyes on hers. "Whoa, there, crouching tiger. Let's just take this down a notch."

"Bet you'd like that, fuckface."

Fuckface? Christ. Just his luck he'd come across another psychotic woman. "Maybe you oughta tell me why you broke in."

"I didn't break in, you moron."

"Hey, enough with the name-callin'," he snapped. "Maybe I oughta call the deputy and let him deal with your lyin' ass."

"Hey, enough with the name-callin'," she mimicked flawlessly. "Go ahead and make the call."

Dammit. He had no guarantee Cam was on duty tonight. And did he really want to try and explain...this?

"Hah! Called your bluff, didn't I?" she sneered.

"Yeah, honey pie, you sure did. I'm just wondering if the rash of shit I'll get from my cousin—who is the deputy I'd call—is worth the hassle at two o'clock in the fuckin' mornin'."

She dropped her hands and studied him. "Wait a second. Your cousin is a local deputy?"

"Yes."

"What's his name?"

"Cam McKay."

"Oh fuck me. You're one of the two hundred McKay men Ginger always talks about."

That startled Chase. "You know Ginger?"

"Who do you think invited me to stay here?"

"Well, we have a problem because my cousin Kane said *I* could stay here." As Chase tried to stay focused on her eyes, he realized something about this woman was very familiar. His gaze wandered. Drool-worthy tits. Tiny waist. Curvy hips. Long legs.

"Eyes up here, buddy."

He didn't exactly hurry his gaze as it tracked her curvaceous body from the bottom up. Goddamn, the woman had it going on. "Do I know you?"

"Do I know *you*?" she shot back sarcastically.

"I'm serious. Were you in *Playboy*?"

"Is that your idea of flattery?"

"Yes, you're sporting a helluva centerfold body, sugar t—" Shit. He was supposed to stop saying stuff like that.

Not bothered at all by her total nakedness, she pushed up the pink satin eye mask that kept slipping down. "I don't remember seeing you at Ginger and Kane's wedding. Which McKay are you again?"

"Chase. I wasn't at the wedding. Mind tellin' me your name?"

"Ava."

"Ava...?"

"Ava Cooper is my stage name. Ava Dumond is my real name."

Stage name. With a body like hers and zero modesty she had to be a stripper. "Well, Ava, it appears we're roomies, at least for tonight."

Ava didn't respond. Her gaze was glued to his belly. "What the hell happened to you?"

Chase glanced at his stomach and touched the bruise beneath his rib cage. "That's what fifteen hundred pounds of pissed-off bull will do to ya."

"Bull? As in a male cow? Were you doing ranch work or something?"

"No. I was trying to ride the damn thing, but he didn't wanna be rode. Threw me on my ass and stomped on me for good measure."

"You do that a lot? Ride bulls?"

"That's my job."

Her eyes widened. "Really? That's an actual job? You get paid and everything?"

He scowled at her. "Really. And look, no offense, but I'm dead on my feet. I'll take the couch tonight. We'll talk about the rest of this in the mornin'."

"How do I know you're not a serial killer?"

"You don't." Chase offered a smug smile. "Sweet dreams."

When Ava saw the half-naked cowboy sprawled on the couch, snoring softly, she knew last night hadn't been a dream.

She rested her shoulder against the partition separating the hallway from the living room and looked her fill.

The man, quite simply, was stunning. And living in California, surrounded by the best-looking men in the world, she knew stunning. Sculpted cheekbones that emphasized the leanness of his cheeks. A broad, masculine jaw. Full, ripe lips. His nose was slightly crooked, but it worked centered among the rest of his perfect features. His dark eyebrows were drawn together in a frown, even as he slept. His hair, a striking shade of coal black, held a hint of curl.

Her gaze meandered south, over the flare of his thick neck, to his bare chest, packed with muscles. More dark hair highlighted his defined pectorals, trailing down to bisect his ripped abs. The damn blanket hid his lower half from his hip to his knee, but one bare calf and foot poked out.

Probably creepy to gawk at him when he was unaware, but he'd seen her naked body last night, so tit for tat.

He'd thrown his left arm above his head, which drew her eye to his—holy crap—mammoth biceps and meaty forearm. Her gaze dropped to his crotch. Chances were high he had a little dick. Beautiful men like him always had one physical flaw, and since she couldn't see any others...

Wait.

Her eyes narrowed and swept down the length of his body. His feet didn't reach the end of the couch. Which made him short. At least three inches shorter than her. Not that it made a damn bit of difference in her mind. They'd still be eye to eye when they were having sex missionary style. And it wouldn't matter at all when she was on top.

Stop gawking before he catches you, perv. You're acting like you haven't seen a half-naked man in years, not months.

She started a pot of coffee, lamenting the fact there weren't any Starbucks within two hundred miles, and turned on her laptop, shooting a glance at the still-sleeping cowboy. Last night he'd claimed to be some kind of...rodeo riding guy.

Hello, Google search.

Ava was shocked by all the links that popped up when she typed in Chase McKay. This guy was a big deal in the Professional Bull Riders world. He had a website. He had a fan page on Facebook. She scrolled down. Hey. Chase McKay had more "Likes" than she did. But she noticed no new posts since the announcement he planned to take time off to heal a recurring injury.

He didn't look injured.

She continued to cyber stalk him, fascinated by a world she knew nothing about. She found pictures of Chase McKay with mayors and governors. Other bull riders. Country singers. Stock contractors. PBR officials and sponsors. Close-up stills of his best rides and his worst wrecks.

But most of the pictures were of the hot cowboy with women. Lots of women—young, old, fat, skinny. Rodeo queens and other rhinestone-wearing women who weren't queens but sure looked the part. The other odd thing? Not a single woman was taller than him.

Ava followed a link that directed her to articles about Chase. Happy as she was to hit pay dirt, the consensus in the last year of rodeo sports experts? Chase McKay was washed up. His riding percentage—whatever that meant—was rock bottom. Rumors abounded about the trail of broken hearts he left across the country. A couple of snarky reporters dubbed him "Chase'n Tail McKay" since his personal life overshadowed his professional career.

Welcome to the club, bub.

The next series of articles, dated the last three months, hinted at Chase settling into a relationship with Sheree Bishop, daughter of Lou Bishop, billionaire owner of Bishop's Sporting Goods, the PBR's new sponsor. During one interview, Sheree admitted she and Chase were "serious" but Chase neither confirmed nor denied Sheree's claim. In fact, there were no pictures of Chase and Sheree together.

Were they keeping their relationship on the down low? Or was there nothing to report?

"Looks like you've found some interesting reading," Chase drawled behind her.

30

2305789

Ava jumped. Heat rushed to her face and she fought the urge to slam her laptop shut. "Can you blame me for being curious? Since you were sleeping in the next room and wouldn't confirm or deny you're a serial killer?"

"I guess not. But you coulda just asked me."

"You were asleep." She watched him pour himself a cup of coffee. He wore athletic shorts, no shirt, apparently perfectly comfortable half-dressed with a woman he didn't know.

Like you have room to judge. You were naked in front of him last night.

And wowza. With a slamming body like that? The man should waltz around naked all the time.

"So?" He pursed his lips and blew across his coffee. "Did you find proof I'm not a serial killer?"

"Yes. But it sounds like you're some kind of lady killer."

Chase rolled his eyes but didn't deny it.

"I'll plead total ignorance on what it means to be a bull rider, so I did some research. All the rest of this stuff popped up." Ava bit back a girly sigh when his beautiful blue gaze connected with hers. "Are you really off the PBR tour because of an injury?"

Chase held her gaze long enough to make her heart speed up. Just when she thought he wouldn't answer, he said, "Nope. I'm suspended indefinitely for inappropriate behavior."

"What'd you do?" Another one of his intense eye locks. But he didn't seem inclined to answer this time, so she tossed out, "I'm no stranger to PR nightmares. Regardless if I was the one at fault. If you're looking for someone to commiserate with? That'd be me."

He smiled. And holy fuck was it a smile that unlocked the gates of heaven.

Or the devil's door. Which quite frankly, she preferred.

"Short version? Two weeks ago I was caught in a compromising position with a couple of ladies. I ain't gonna make excuses, it was what it was, and I'm paying the price. I suddenly found myself with time off while I wait for the PBR to call me back. My folks and brothers live here, but I didn't want to deal with their pity, so I asked Kane if I could hang out and make plans."

"Sounds like you're reading a page out of the story of my life." Ava typed her name into the search engine and spun the laptop around. "Have a look."

Chase scooted out the chair across from her and sat. His fingers clicked on the keyboard. His eyebrows went up a couple of times. But he didn't speak for a few minutes.

She refilled their cups and braced herself when she sensed him staring at her.

"Your ex was gay?"

"Yes. It was quite a shock to me."

"It wouldn't have shocked me at all. He looks gay."

Ava bristled. "You can't tell that by looking at him."

"Sure I can." Chase spun the laptop around and enlarged the photo of Ava and Jake at an Emmy Awards after-party. He pointed at Jake's feet enclosed in white patent leather clogs decorated with brightly colored polka dots. "No straight man ever wears shoes like them."

"Shows what you know. Those are high-couture shoes."

"Those are highly *gay* shoes."

She wanted to laugh, she really did. It'd been ages since she'd met a man so willing to speak his mind. "Shoes are your gauge for determining sexual preference?"

"No, the best indicator is sex. How often did you have sex?"

"I don't see how that's relevant," she snipped.

Chase leaned closer. "It's the only thing that's relevant. Because if he wasn't dragging you to bed at least twice a day, the man was either a fuckin' moron or totally gay. Probably both."

That was kind of sweet...in a caveman sort of way. "Not everything has to do with sex."

"Oh yeah? If that's true, then this Jake guy wouldn't have left you to have sex with a dude, would he?"

Ava's mouth dropped open.

"Shit. Sorry. That came out wrong. What I meant—"

"No. Don't." She placed her hand on his arm. "I think you're the first person who's been totally honest with me."

He relaxed. Smiled again and she bit back another sigh. "So this is what sent you running from California?"

"I got tired of the paparazzi." Something kicked from what he'd said about his family. "I got tired of the pity. Of the trade mags making such a big deal out of it. I needed to get away and prove..."

There was that amazing grin again. "Don't clam up on me now, Hollywood."

Ava laughed at his impromptu nickname for her.

"And if you're afraid I'll judge you? Think again."

"You were dead-on with the sex question. One of the reasons I'm here? To find a guy I can get wild with. To prove I'm hot between the sheets. To prove I can keep a man sexually satisfied."

"Is that right?" he drawled.

Her brain slipped into seductress mode as she channeled the femme fatale she'd played on TV for two seasons. "Maybe...you're the man who can help me with that."

Bad karma is coming back to bite you in the ass, McKay.

Of all the times to have sworn off sex, this had to happen? Now? When the hottest woman on the planet sat right across from him? Burning him alive with her smoldering eyes? Oh, and she wanted to prove—with him—that she was a tiger between the sheets.

Fuck.

He wondered why God hated him.

He wondered if it was too early in the day to start drinking.

He wondered if Ava had any condoms because he hadn't brought any.

No, no, no. He would not break the vow he'd made to himself. He'd been making excuses for his behavior for far too long. This "break" was supposed to get him back on track, not drive him off the rails completely.

"Chase?" she asked softly.

He tore his mind from the image of her oh so curvaceous body twined around his as he fucked her blind. "Ah, well, that's the thing. See, after the last...incident, I swore off women."

She blinked with confusion. "Forever?"

"No. For a while."

"How long?"

He started to say two months to remove all temptation to get down and dirty with her, but amended it to, "A month."

"I take it that's a big deal for you, going without sex for a month?"

Chase nodded. "Go ahead and call me a dog. I deserve it."

"We're in the no-judgment zone, remember? But I've gotta admit..."

"What?"

"I'm disappointed."

His dick decided to show disappointment at the lack of recent activity by instantly going rock hard.

"I am too, Ava. More than you can imagine. Any other time in my life I'd be stripping you to skin right where you stood."

"That's not helping, Chase."

"Sorry. But we seem to be getting along. Can we be friends while we're both hiding out here?"

Ava said, "Absolutely," but her sneaky smile said, *Wanna take bets on how long you can hold out on that 'friends' thing, cowboy?*

His eyes narrowed. "I'm not kiddin', Ava. I am *not* sleeping with you."

"I understand."

"Seriously. We won't be getting nekkid together."

"Totally your call."

"I mean it. We will *not* be havin' sex."

"Fine. I get it. Hands off. No hugs, no kisses, no holding hands, no hot looks, no copping a feel. No chance for a hard, fast, sweaty, screaming, raunchy fuckfest against the wall, or on the floor, or in the shower, and definitely not on the bed."

For fucking Christsake.

"But I am curious as to how long you've been on this abstinence kick."

Tempting to lie. But he admitted, "I'm two weeks in."

She smirked. And Chase swore she was marking off the remaining calendar days in her mind with big red X's.

Change the subject. "Do you have plans for today?"

"Not really. Thought I might go for a walk. Take in the clean air and the big sky. Moo at any livestock I happened by during my nature stroll. Run from the bulls. They are easy to tell apart from cows, aren't they?"

He laughed. She was funny in that offbeat way that appealed to him.

"What are your plans?" she asked.

"I hafta make a call this morning. I figured I'd hop on a four-wheeler and take a spin later." He frowned. "But I'll have to be careful where I go, so as not to run into any of my family."

"Could I tag along? There's room for two riders on most ATVs, isn't there?"

New images unleashed in his brain. Ava's slim thighs gripping the outside of his legs. Ava's crotch nestled against his butt. Ava's arms circling his waist as they descended a steep slope. Ava's bountiful tits pressing into his back. Ava's breath teasing his ear. Ava's fragrant, windswept hair drifting across his face. Ava flat on her back in the mud as he hammered into her.

No way could they ride double. No way. So he was shocked to hear, "Absolutely," tumbling from his traitorous mouth.

"Great! I'll just get ready so we can go whenever you are."

Chase ended up dressing in the living room and brushing his teeth in the kitchen. When the shower kicked on, flashes of Ava's wet, naked body had him fleeing outside.

Chapter Four

He wandered behind the barn and gazed across the pasture. Heavy winter snow allowed for green grass, a boon in the cattle business. Even the sagebrush had lost the dusty silver shimmer and looked brighter. The scrub oaks lining the creek bed were leafed out with dark green foliage. A few patches of wildflowers dotted the landscape, hues ranging from brilliant yellow to soft purple.

Stop admiring the posies and make the call, chickenshit.

Chase blew out a breath and dialed. As he listened to the rings, he paced in front of the fence.

"Hello?"

"Hey, Cash. It's Chase McKay. Remember me?"

"Chase! 'Course I remember you. How you doin'? I heard you were on the PBR's injured list."

"Well, not really." He forced a laugh. "It's a long story. One we're keeping on the down low, if you know what I mean."

"So why you callin' me, hey?"

"I need your help."

A pause. Then, "Tell you what. You give me the truth about what's really goin' on with the PBR and I'll let you know if I'm willin' to help."

"Sounds fair." Chase let fly.

When he finished, Cash whistled. "Ain't nothin' the rest of us weren't doin' on the road, but things are different now. But I'm confused on how you think I can help you."

"I need to get my ridin' back on track. It seems I'm doin' everything the same way I always have, but that ain't the case or my scores would be better, or at least on par, not completely in the shitter like they are now. I wondered if you're still holding a bull ridin' school?"

"Now and again. Why? You lookin' to go back to school?"

"Yeah." Chase slumped against the barn. "And before you get pissy and think this is a joke, I'll tell you I'm dead-ass serious. I need an expert to look at my ridin' objectively and help me figure out what the devil I'm doin' wrong."

"Expert." Cash snorted. "But an old-timer like me ain't immune to such smooth bullshit."

Chase grinned. "You had a good run, what? Almost twenty years as a pro? With my buck-off average, I'll be goddammed lucky if I make it another two."

"So when you thinkin' you wanna get started?"

"Bein's I have time off and you've got a ranch to run, I'll work around your schedule."

"Sorry. I don't have another training session scheduled until the end of next month. That probably don't help you."

Not only that, Chase didn't want to train in front of rookies. Maybe it was an ego thing. A bratty thing. But he wanted one-on-one attention to his riding issues.

Before he could say thanks and hang up, Cash said, "But if you can get here in two days, I'll put you on as many bulls as you can handle."

"Really? That would be great. I wasn't sure if you'd...ah, take offense to me offering to pay for a private session."

Cash's laughter boomed. "McKay, if I didn't think you could afford it I wouldn't've suggested it, because it ain't gonna be cheap. But there's one other thing."

Seemed there always was a catch. "What?"

"I'm bringing your cousin Colby in on this. He's been off the rodeo circuit for a while, but he's still a pro to the core and I trust his judgment. Two sets of eyes would be better than one, doncha think?"

"Yeah. I guess." Of all his cousins, Colby was the second least likely to blab to other family members, right behind his cousin Kane.

"Good. There's a bunkhouse if you need a place to stay."

"That'll work. Thanks, Cash, I appreciate it more than you know. I'll see you in a couple of days."

Soon as he hung up, Chase let out a whoop and spun around.

Ava stood in the open space between the barn and the fence. Her hands jammed in the front pockets of her hoodie, sunshine glinting off her hair. Looking so drop-dead gorgeous he almost forgot to breathe.

"That was a pretty enthusiastic whoop," she remarked.

"I got some good news for a change."

Ava didn't ask him to elaborate. "You ready to rip it up on the ATV?"

Chase shook his head. "I've gotta eat first. Is there any food in the house?"

"Just the basic stuff I brought. Coffee, creamer, grapes, salad, bread and a couple cans of soup."

"That's what you call food? Please tell me you ain't one of them actresses who starves herself to look like a heroin addict."

"Do I look like I starve myself?"

His gaze might've lingered on certain curves longer than polite. "No, Hollywood, you look exactly like a woman ought to. Let's head to town. The Shell station has the best chilidogs I've ever tasted."

"Do they have tofu dogs?"

Chase's smile fell. "Oh *hell* no. You're not a vegetarian?"

"And if I was?" she intoned sweetly.

"I'd take it as my sworn duty as the son of a cattleman to send you packing off McKay land immediately."

There was that little sexy smirk again. "Relax, cowboy. I'm a carnivore to the core. I seriously doubt Wyoming can boast the best chilidog, but I'm willing to give it a fair shake." She pointed at him with her car keys. "You brag, you buy."

"Deal."

When Ava started to jerk on the handle to open the barn door, Chase gently moved her aside. He wasn't sure if he expected to see her ripping it up in a Ferrari, but the vehicle behind the door was a letdown. A black four-door RAV4. With Colorado plates. "You didn't drive here?"

"I flew to Denver, rented this and drove the rest of the way. So I really don't care if you spill chili and cheese all over the seats."

There was another glimpse of her bizarre sense of humor, which made her seem normal and not movie starish.

In Sundance, Chase pulled his sweatshirt hood over his head. "You'll have to go inside and load them up."

"Why can't you help?"

"Family. Fans. I'm on the down low, remember?"

"What exactly am I slathering on these dogs besides chili?"

"Mustard. Onion. A couple of squirts of that fake cheese." Chase dug a crumpled twenty from his front pocket and pressed it into her hand. "And anything else that strikes your fancy."

"Should I leave the car running in case you need to make a quick getaway from your adoring fans?"

"No, but I tell you what. I'll keep it running in case you do," he shot back.

She laughed. "We're quite the pair, huh?"

Chase slumped into the seat, trying to stay inconspicuous.

After almost ten minutes, the car door opened. "Careful, those are hot and oozing stuff out the sides."

"That means you did it right." Chase peeked inside the bag she'd dropped on his lap. Two bundles wrapped in white parchment paper, two single-serving packages of nacho cheese Doritos and two Heath bars. When she shoved two bottles of grape soda in the beverage holders, he gave her a dubious look. "How'd you know this is exactly what I would've gotten?"

"Lucky guess?" She twisted the top on a bottle of soda. "Or maybe there's an index card that lists *Sundance's own PBR bull rider Chase McKay's favorites!* on the wall by the hot food section."

"Are you serious?"

"Yep."

"Christ. That's embarrassing."

"Where to now?" she asked with a smirk.

"Follow the signs to Devil's Tower." They started the twisty ascent out of Sundance. After a few miles they entered a valley and he said, "Turn left and take the road until it stops."

"This is considered a road?"

"In Wyoming? Yes."

Once they came around the last bend, Ava said, "Oh wow. Look at that view."

Devil's Tower jutted up, the land surrounding it a rainbow palette of red dirt, dark green pine trees, a caramel-colored butte against the backdrop of a cloudless blue sky. "You like?"

"It's spectacular. I'll bet most tourists don't even know this view is here."

"Some stumble on it. But it's mostly a local secret." Chase tossed her a bag of Doritos and a hot dog.

As he slowly unwrapped his food, the familiar scent of spicy chili, creamy cheese, tangy mustard and onion caused a sharp pang, not of hunger, of homesickness. It'd been ages since he'd taken time to stop at the Shell station that'd at one time been a constant in his life.

Ava released a long, deep moan. A moan that sounded like a woman about to come undone by pure pleasure.

Chase shot her a sideways glance. Her beautiful face had a dreamy look best described as post-orgasmic. From sucking on a hot dog?

"That's the best chili dog I've ever eaten." Ava kept making throaty groans.

His brain overloaded. He imagined dragging her across the console and giving her another reason to moan. Pushing down her sweatpants and pressing her legs wide open. Burying his face between her thighs. Turning her moans into screams of ecstasy as she came against his mouth in a wet rush.

"Chase?"

He jumped at the closeness of her voice in his ear and snapped, "Jesus, what?"

"Are you okay?"

"Uh. Yeah. Why?"

"Oh, you're just squeezing that chili dog so hard I thought the meat might shoot straight out of the bun."

Dammit. He eyed the balled-up wrapper in her hand. "You finished yours? Already?"

"I was hungry," she retorted. "And for all your grumbling about being starved, you sure were looking at that hot dog like you wanted to eat something else."

You have no idea. Chase took a bite and chewed.

"Can we skip the ATV thingy today and check out the countryside?"

"I guess."

"Good. And will you drive so I can film?"

Thank God. Nothing he hated more than being a captive passenger on a trip without purpose. "Sure. You want me to choose our route?"

When her extraordinary aquamarine eyes lit up, Chase was nearly struck stupid by her beauty.

"That would be awesome! But I need footage of this spot before we go." She snagged her cameras off the backseat and hopped from the car.

Chase ditched his hoodie and exited the SUV. Slipping on his shades, he parked his backside against the front quarter panel and watched her.

She'd videotape, then grab her camera and click off a few still shots. The elegance of her movements, even simply crouching down in the gravel were naturally graceful. Several strands of glossy brown hair blew around her face, but she didn't swipe them away. In that moment, Chase wished for a camera to capture the loveliness of Ava's profile.

She smiled at him. "Bored yet?"

"Nope. It's a gorgeous day, I'm hauling around a gorgeous...ah, *friend*. What more could a man want?"

Her sultry look said a real man should want more. A lot more. Like hot kisses and frantic touches that led to bare skin rubbing on bare skin. Like bodies slamming together, hard breathing and moans of raw pleasure. But Ava didn't give voice to that image. She didn't have to. Every thought was right there on her beautiful face.

Movement on the edge of the ridge caught his eye. "Quick, get your video camera."

She picked up the equipment and said, "Where?"

Chase pointed to the sky. "There. Two red-tailed hawks are hovering on a thermal."

"I see them." They didn't speak, just watched the grace of the birds. Circling higher, swooping down, then floating, remaining so still they'd look like blots on the horizon to the casual observer. After the birds drifted away, she shut off her camera and faced him. "Thank you."

"For?"

"Being observant."

He didn't ruin the moment and confess if he hadn't been observing her, he wouldn't have noticed the birds. He smiled back. "No problem. You ready to move on?"

"Yes."

Seeing the long line of tourists at the Devil's Tower entrance, he suggested an alternative.

"How much of this is McKay land?"

"A lot of it." All of it for the last ten miles in fact. But he knew she couldn't grasp the enormity of McKay land holdings.

"I'm not sure how the ranch succession works. Do you, or will you own part of it?"

"Not since I opted out." He settled in the driver's seat and stole glances at her when she talked about expectations of family businesses. "How does the succession work in yours?"

"My mom was an only child, so she inherited everything. She's been at the helm of the Cooper Hotel chain and the other businesses in the Cooper conglomerate since before I was born. Since I've no interest in running it, my brother has been learning the ropes, but I still own a chunk of it by default."

She was an heiress to the Cooper conglomerate, which meant she was loaded. Like really fucking loaded. "This might sound weird, but as an actress, did you purposely use Cooper as your last name because of...?"

"Paris Hilton? Yep. Worked for her, didn't it? But while I'm on sabbatical, I'm Ava Dumond."

He drove, although it seemed they stopped every two miles so she could get out and film something new. Everything from gnarled fence posts to different breeds of cows, to clusters of scrub oak. She got a huge kick out of the frolicking calves and the bovine mamas mooing a warning at her.

Chase noticed the calves were awful young for the time of year. He squinted at the mile marker at the end of the gravel road. Near as he could tell they were near the Glanzers' place. He'd heard through the McKay grapevine the trio had increased their acreage the past five years and were experimenting with different breeds. He didn't want to stick around and find out if these late-born calves were theirs.

Ava put the video camera away. "How far are we from the closest town?"

"Why? Bored already?"

"No, Sundance, I'm not bored. Geez. Give me some credit."

"Sundance. Funny."

"I need to use the facilities."

"Okay." Chase stopped the car on the edge of the road. He pointed across the field. "See that tree? It'll offer some privacy, but be careful when you climb over the barbwire fence. Watch out for snakes."

Ava's eyes widened. "I've never... I don't even know..."

Chase burst out laughing. "You oughta see your face, Hollywood. It's too bad you didn't give me the camera so I capture your look of horror."

"Making a city girl feel like an idiot at first opportunity?" She sent him an accusatory glance. "Do you treat all your *friends* this way?"

"Yep."

"Then I don't want to be your friend."

Same goes, honey pie. "We're only about ten miles out of Moorcroft."

"Great because now I'm hungry too."

Chase parked up front at the C-Store and Ava jumped out. It occurred to him when he saw the familiar dark-haired woman lingering by the front door that he should've chosen the back lot.

When Ava slid back into the seat, Chase wrapped an arm around her shoulders, hauling her close, nestling his face into the base of her throat.

"What the hell?"

"Don't look, but my cousin Keely is standing by the door and she's awful damn interested in us. Just stay like this for a sec, okay? Looks like were making out and hopefully she'll trot her snoopy self into the store."

Ava angled her head until her lips brushed his cheek. "Don't know if you're aware, but I'm a method actor. Which means I prefer we make out for real so I can get into character."

Chase groaned. "You are the devil, you know that, right?"

Her low, sexy chuckle vibrated against his jaw. "That's me, Ava the evil temptress."

"Talk about tempting." Against his better judgment, he let his nose follow the sweetly scented arch of her neck. "Damn, woman, do you smell great right here."

"Thanks. I actually smell like that all over."

Before he stupidly demanded she prove it and strip down to skin, he kissed the hollow of her throat. Then he peered over her shoulder. "Coast is clear. Let's go while we can." He threw it in reverse and they were back on the road.

Ava waved a piece of red licorice at him. "Want some?"

"Not really a fan of licorice."

"What's your favorite sweet besides a Heath bar?"

Chase settled in now that Moorcroft was in the rearview mirror.

"Actually, I'm not a big sweets eater."

She jammed a piece of licorice in her mouth and reached for her camera. "So, friend, can I ask you a question?"

"Depends."

"On?"

"On who you plan on showing the answer to."

"Spoken like a man who's been burned by camera-phone video capabilities."

"Did you see that clip on YouTube?"

"Which one? The one where the blonde chick is riding you like a jockey while her friend is giving commentary and taping? Or the one where you're on the receiving end of serious oral worship?" She cleared her throat. "Not that I gave either clip more than a brief glance."

Chase scowled. "That's why I make sure no one's cell phone is within reach anymore."

"Ah. So it didn't change your *behavior* with the ladies, just changed your behavior with technology?"

Shrewd woman. "Getting off track here, Hollywood. My question was who gets to view this?"

Ava lowered the camera, but Chase knew it was running. "Me. It's a personal video diary of how I spent my summer vacation."

He grudgingly said, "Okay, but if any part of this video diary is made public, I will hire Ginger—or worse—to sue you."

"Ooh, that's mean. But understood." She fiddled with the camera. "My first question is, what's the best thing that ever happened to you? On a personal level or on a professional level."

"One and the same for me." Did that make him sound one-dimensional? "The best thing was when I won the Man of Steel competition last year."

"What about the worst thing that ever happened to you?"

"Getting kicked off the PBR Tour."

"Really?"

"Yeah, why?"

"I thought you'd pick something else. Something tragic."

"Not everyone has tragedy in their lives that defines them." And even if he did, he'd never share it. "Same questions back atcha."

"Best thing was landing a role on *Miller's Ridge*. Worst thing? When my Grandpa Cooper died. All people talked about was my inheritance. Like I was so greedy and entitled I'd blow every penny he'd worked so hard for on stupid shit."

"What kind of stupid shit?" Chase asked.

A beat passed. "I didn't realize my battery is low. Enough for today." She yawned. "I think I might take a nap when we get back."

Interesting how quickly she shut down his questions. He let it slide. This time. "Sounds good. I'm dragging a bit myself."

The remainder of the drive was quiet. At the trailer, Ava grabbed her laptop and retreated to the bedroom.

Chase was restless. He'd left his phone and saw he'd missed a call from Elroy. And from his former traveling partner, Justin Donohue. And from his brother Ben. None left messages.

Probably because they know you won't call them back.

With nothing else to do, he brought up the search engine on his phone and typed in Ava Cooper, just to see what shook loose.

Chapter Five

Ava downloaded her footage to her computer. Groggy from the heat in the trailer, she stripped, stretched out on the bed and fell sound asleep.

She woke at eleven o'clock at night feeling refreshed. After slipping on her clothes, she wandered into the kitchen.

Oh, looky there. The delicious dish known as Chase McKay sat on the counter, looking good enough to eat.

Why yes. I'd love to be your appetizer, entrée and dessert. One serving of hot, hunky cowboy coming right up.

Behave, Ava.

"I figured you'd gone to bed," Chase said.

"I'll admit I did crash for a while. Before that I had some things to catch up on. Takes a boatload of time to download everything from my cameras into the right folders on my laptop. Then I transferred the notes I jotted down so I don't forget things."

"Sounds tedious. Why are you doin' this again?"

"I'm trying my hand at having a hobby," she said sardonically. "And no, I'm not getting paid. Don't you ever do something just because you've always wanted to?"

"Can't say as I have. In fact, it's just the opposite. I find myself doin' stuff I don't wanna do all the damn time."

Ava's smile vanished. "You could've said no if you didn't want to squire me around today." She turned and walked away.

A thump sounded and then strong hands circled her waist, spinning her around. He got in her face, as much as he could despite her height advantage. "Will you let me finish? I wasn't talking about you. Or today. Today was great, Ava. I had a blast."

"But?"

"No buts. Seems I never do things like that. At least I don't take the time to do them because I'm so busy doin' other things I don't wanna do. These last two weeks off have shown me I'm not really living my life. I'm just killing time between bull ridin' events. And I don't make the best decisions on what to do with that free time."

Mollified and surprised by his honesty, Ava forced her hands to remain at her sides. She freely gave casual affection to friends and lovers alike, but something about Chase's body language cautioned her to hold back, afraid he'd misread her friendliness as a sexual come-on. Didn't mean she wouldn't flirt her ass off with him, but touching without invitation was a definite no-no. "Don't you have buddies you hang out with when you're not rodeoing?"

"Sometimes. Truth is, I'm a little low on friends. So, thanks for today."

Did Chase show anyone this sweet side? Probably not. Why that filled her with warmth was stupidly juvenile. "You are welcome. I'm a little low on friends myself, so I'm glad I didn't kill you with a karate chop to the head last night."

He laughed. "Death by nekkid ninja don't sound so bad."

Do not give me false hope you've been imagining me naked. "What have you been doing?"

"Nothin'. I sat outside and watched the sunset. You really oughta tape it tomorrow night. I was rummaging in the cupboards for food and found this." He reached around her and waggled a bottle of Maker's Mark whisky.

"Ooh. Liquid dinner? I'm all over that."

"Good. 'Cause there's really no food, but I did find a six-pack in the vegetable drawer."

Ava stood on tiptoe to reach two shot glasses from the top shelf. She spun around and Chase didn't bother to pretend he hadn't been ogling her ass. After they sat at the table, she said, "Let's have a toast."

"To what?"

To the sexy way your hat shadows your face. To your full lower lip that looks so succulent I wanna take a bite out of it. To your hands, big and scarred, and how that rough flesh would feel dancing across on my skin.

"Ava?"

She swallowed her escalating lust. "Oh, I dunno. We could toast to Kane and Ginger for allowing us to hide out here."

"Sounds good."

Ava poured them each a shot. They held the shot glasses aloft. "To Kane and Ginger."

He chinked his glass to hers and threw back his whisky.

She followed suit. The alcohol disappeared down the hatch, leaving a trail of fire, and she sputtered.

"The second one will be better." Chase refilled their glasses and passed out two bottles of Coors Light.

"Another shot?"

"Come on. I thought you were a wild party girl, Hollywood. Least, that's what the tabloids say about you."

"And I thought you'd have me tied to the bed with your bull rope by now, making me scream your name as you rode me hard," she retorted sweetly. "That's what the rodeo mags say about you, Chase'n Tail McKay." Ava leaned forward, gifting him with an excellent view of her cleavage. "Did you Google me while I was sleeping, cowboy?"

Took a second for his eyes to meet hers. "Yeah."

"And what did you find?"

"No juicy YouTube videos of you caught in indecent sex acts. But I did check out your website. I realized I had seen you in something a while back. A TV movie."

"Which one?"

"The one where you played a prep school girl hooked on...some kinda drugs and you sold your body to feed the addiction. Until a young priest rescued you, setting you back on the straight and narrow."

"Ah. *Naughty Girl by Night.* One of my first roles. I'm surprised you even know what Lifetime TV is, say nothing of catching the 'ripped from the headlines' drama every week."

"I was killing time one afternoon before a PBR event, and I distinctly remember I kept watching just to catch a glimpse of your legs in them short miniskirts."

"So you're a leg man?"

"Sugar," he said with a silky rasp, "I'm an everything man. Any woman I find attractive? Every single part of her is sexy to me."

"But you're still going to give this abstinence thing a whirl?"

His face turned somber very quickly. "I have to. My career is at stake. I've worked too damn long and hard to be forced out because I fucked the wrong woman."

"He says with a bitter edge."

"Funny. We've gotten off track. My turn to make a toast. But I'll warn ya, I'm not very original."

"Bring it."

"A toast to both of us reigniting that magic spark so we can continue to do what we love."

"Not original, my ass," she mumbled and sucked down the liquid in a single gulp, releasing a heartfelt, "Ah."

"Good stuff. If we keep this up, we'll owe Kane a full bottle."

"So let's keep going."

He raised both eyebrows. "You sure? It's kinda late."

"It's not like either of us has to get up early. And besides, I'm not tired. Are you?"

"Nope."

"Good. Since we're both licking our wounds from a lie in one form or another, let's play a game called Truth or Lie."

Chase looked at her suspiciously. "What kinda game is that?"

"I tell you something about myself, and you try to figure out if it's a lie or the truth. If it's a lie and you call it as such, I drink. If you make a wrong call either way, you drink."

"You aiming to get shitfaced tonight, Ava?"

She shrugged. "No one around here but us, Sundance. And since we've decided to be *friends*—" she emphasized the word with a hiss because it stung her pride this beautiful, rugged, manly man didn't want to take her for a test ride, "—I think we should get to know each other better. I'll even go first."

"I don't see how this is fair, you bein' a professional actress and all," Chase grumbled.

"You might as well have called me a professional liar, Chase."

"If the stiletto fits..." He dodged her kick under the table. "You can't deny bein' an actress gives you an advantage."

"Suck it up, cowboy. I'm betting your poker face is damn impressive when you're in pain and showing the fans and your sponsors you're feeling just fine."

He sipped his beer. "Point taken. Okay, Hollywood, dazzle and confuse me with a page from the book of Ava."

What to start with? "I posed nude early in my career and the photos caught the eye of a producer who ended up giving me my first acting job."

Chase cocked his head, studying her. "Lie. You might've had nekkid pictures done, but my guess is no one has seen them."

Ava couldn't believe she'd lost the first question. "Busted. Your turn."

He topped off her glass. "Before I ever got on a bull, I practiced my skills by ridin' sheep."

"I've heard the joke—Wyoming: where men are men and sheep are nervous. You're trying to trip me up, McKay, so I'm gonna say...lie."

"Nope. Truth. The rodeo event 'mutton bustin' is a kid's precursor to bull and bronc ridin'. That's where a lot of riders get their first taste of it."

"Shoot. I'm gonna be hammered in no time flat."

"I'll remind you this was your idea. But I'm thinking we should alternate beer with whisky."

Ava held the shot glass between her palms. Maybe Chase wouldn't notice if she didn't drink it right away.

"Drink up so you can ask your question," he drawled.

Dammit. She tossed the amber liquid into her mouth, suppressing a shudder. Time to put on her game face. "Truth or lie: my younger brother's name is Axel because my mother heard 'Sweet Child O' Mine' on the radio in the delivery room when she was in labor with him."

Chase was quiet for a moment, then he laughed. "Easy. Lie. I doubt your mother has heard of the band Guns N' Roses, let alone knows who the lead singer is."

She nudged the full shot glass at him. "Bottoms up. Truth. My brother's full name is Axel Rose Cooper Dumond. My mom heard the song, which is one of her all-time faves, in the throes of labor. And since my middle name is Rose, she believed it was a sign to name her baby boy Axel, after Axel Rose. FYI, Mom is a total rocker chick and a huge fan of '80s metal bands."

"I'll be damned." Chase drank his shot. "So, Ava Rose, what did your dad have to say about naming his son Axel?"

"Well, he is a mechanic, so it fits. But it was way better than the name he had picked out."

"Which was?"

"Festus Merle."

Chase frowned. "Is that true?"

"You tell me," Ava challenged. "Or are you afraid you'll have to drink again?"

A cocky smile spread across Chase's face and heat curled in her belly. Oh, she *so* didn't want to be just friends with this beautiful man. She wanted to taste that smirk on his lips. Suck the whisky from his tongue. And when he laughed? She could almost picture her head on his chest as she listened to that deep rumble.

"I ain't afraid because I call bullshit on that one too."

Ava splashed beer in his glass. "Have another. Because it's one hundred percent true. My dad wanted the name Marshall Dillon Dumond. Since my mother vetoes his first suggestion on anything, he came up with Festus Merle, knowing she'd be horrified. Then when he sprang Marshall Dillon on her, she'd agree it was much better and he'd get his way."

"Your dad is a big *Gunsmoke* fan?"

"Yes. We watched westerns every day after school."

"Your parents don't sound at all like I'd pictured them."

"How did you picture them?"

He stretched out in his chair. "Like the rest of them rich, slick, skinny plastic people on TV who live in California. No offense."

"I'll admit I didn't want for much growing up, but they kept a close eye on my brother and me. My dad is proud to be blue collar and refused to let us turn into rich-kid brats." She sipped her water. "What are your parents like?"

"My dad's a rancher, my mom's a ranch wife. They've been married a long time. But they almost didn't get married at all."

"Really? What happened?"

"My mom's dad was a preacher and didn't want his daughter runnin' around with one of them 'wild McKay boys' so he packed up their whole family and moved them from Wyoming."

"Seriously?"

Chase smirked. "You tell me. Or are you afraid you'll have to drink again?"

Fifty-fifty chance. She studied his face. Too impassive. The last thing he'd told her had been the truth, so this one had to be... "Lie. I'll bet your mom and dad were high school sweethearts and haven't been apart since they met."

"Wrong. Drink up."

She sighed and swallowed the beer in one gulp. "Okay. Now tell me the whole story."

"Evidently my grandfather thought my dad's family was a bunch of immoral heathens. He sent my mom away to a private Christian high school in Colorado when it looked like my mom and dad were getting too serious. As soon as he found a replacement preacher for his parish in Hulett, they were long gone."

"So how did your mom and dad get back together?"

"According to my dad, they'd lost contact and she just showed up in Sundance one day, four years later. He took one look at her and knew why he hadn't settled down. They were married within the week."

"That's so romantic."

"Romantic ain't the first word that comes to mind when I think of my folks. How about your parents?"

"My mom wrecked her car. She took it to a repair shop and my dad chewed her out for her casual disregard of such a beautiful piece of machinery. Sparks flew. Literally. Dad was welding. They disliked each other intensely, yet somehow they ended up sneaking off to Vegas a month later to get married. They've been together ever since."

"See? That's romantic."

"Ever come close to dropping to one knee and popping the question?"

Chase shook his head.

"Why not?"

"Haven't found a woman who doesn't drive me crazy after two weeks."

Ava lifted her eyebrows. "Your longest relationship has been two weeks?"

"Give or take." He gazed at her from beneath the brim of his hat. "What about you? Been planning your wedding since you were a little girl?"

"I'm all for a secluded beach wedding with no one around except the officiant and my intended."

"What's your longest relationship?" he asked.

At least they'd slowed down on the shots. Her head was getting muzzy. "Jake, the bastard switch-hitter, and I were together for six months."

"Together as in...living together?"

"No, he'd been in Vancouver for most the TV season."

Chase frowned. "So you had no idea what he was doin' when he was away from you?"

"Wasn't like I didn't see him. I flew to Vancouver or he came to LA. When he came back to LA, I was dealing with my show getting cancelled and didn't think anything of him spending so much time with his new friend Decker." She groaned. "Maybe the tabloids were right. How didn't I see they were so into each other? I'm such an idiot."

He curled his hand around hers. "Hey. Sometimes we see what we want to. Doesn't make you an idiot, Ava. In my mind, it makes you a victim. He lied to you. Used you. Set you up. It sucks that it was played out in public. You're handling it better than most would."

"You really think so?"

"Yep." Chase smiled and squeezed her hand, peering at her closely. "You still wanna play this game?"

For a second, she hoped he'd meant the game they were playing, pretending not to be wildly attracted to each other. But when he kept staring at her, she understood he was referring to the actual drinking game. "Ah. Sure. My turn, right?"

"Right."

Okay. Think, Ava. Something...sexy. "In an episode of *Miller's Ridge*, I shared a steamy onscreen kiss with my female costar."

"I told you I don't watch TV."

"Means you have a fifty-fifty chance of guessing...wrong." When she glanced up and saw his gaze focused on her lips, she knew he'd been imagining that girl-on-girl liplock. In full detail.

"True," he said hoarsely.

"Sorry. A total lie."

"Shit." He was a bit slower knocking that one back. But when he looked at her again, he had a glimmer in his eye. "My turn. First time I rode a bull, my cup damn near pinched off my balls."

She winced in sympathy. "Oh, I'll bet that hurt." Her eyes roamed his angular face, noticing the color spreading across his cheekbones. Talking about it embarrassed him. She permitted a small, smug smile. "True."

His wicked grin appeared and he topped off her glass. "Lie. Bull riders don't wear a cup."

"Dammit. I am so not playing poker with you." Ava sucked in a breath and held it while she slammed the whisky. She let out a stream of air that sounded like a hiss.

"Are you starting to feel the effects of your losing streak, Ava Rose?"

God she loved the husky way he drew out her whole name. "Losing streak? I believe we're tied." Or maybe Chase was right. Maybe she was losing because the shots were blurring together. Ava squinted at him. "Are you feeling the whisky at all? Or am I just a lightweight?"

"I'm feelin' it."

She tried really hard to concentrate on those tempting lips and smoky-blue bedroom eyes, but his handsome face kept swimming out of focus.

"Ava? You okay?"

Instead of admitting *No, I am totally wasted*, she offered him the charming smile she was known for. "Just thinking about the subject of lies."

"What about it?"

"What's the biggest lie you ever told?"

That I'm not gonna sleep with you.

Jesus. Where had that come from?

The booze, probably.

Ironic, they'd been talking about alcohol-fueled mistakes. No way would Chase let his whisky throw-down with her become an excuse to take her to bed.

Besides, Ava Cooper, TV star, was out of his league. Way out. The rich girl bombshell wouldn't have looked at him twice if they hadn't accidentally ended up hiding out at the same place. Plus, her feminine pride and sexual self-esteem had taken a blow because of her asshole gay ex-boyfriend, so naturally she wanted to prove her sex appeal to a man. Any man. He just happened to be convenient.

Chase didn't like being convenient.

"Hey, cowboy, are you ignoring me because I'm drunk?" Ava clapped a hand over her mouth and giggled.

"I think we oughta call it a night, Hollywood."

"Fine by me." She stood. Swayed. And would've hit the floor if Chase had slower reflexes.

"Whoa, there. Not so fast."

She inhaled deeply. Exhaled gustily. "You know today when you said I smelled great? Well, I'll bet you smell great all over too." She nuzzled the side of his head.

"Stop sniffing me. It tickles."

"Where else are you ticklish?"

"My feet."

Ava frowned. "Lie. I'll bet you're most ticklish behind your balls. I bet I can prove it."

You're on. Let's test your theory right now.

No. No. No. No.

"Ah, Ava, we're not playing the game anymore."

"Oh. Shoot. Everything is spinning anyway. I just really need to go to sleep now. Nighty night." She started down the hallway, stripping clothes as she bounced from wall to wall like a slow-moving pinball.

The seven—or was it eight?—shots hit him full force. The hallway became a tunnel-like funhouse mirror. Distorted. Sideways. He stretched his arms into a T and put one wobbly foot in front of the other.

He had to stop and grip the doorframe leading to the bedroom when he saw Ava sprawled face first on the mattress. *Would you lookit that.* He might be drunk, but he wasn't fuckin' blind.

The sweetest, tightest, most delectable ass he'd ever seen—and he'd seen more than his fair share of nice asses—just begging to be caressed. Kissed. Squeezing those perfectly round globes as he hiked her hips up and slid his cock inside her.

As he took another step, he tripped over a shoe, or his own damn feet, and went skidding across the carpet. The room spun as he rolled to his back, blinking at the ceiling.

The bed jiggled. Soft, fragrant strands of hair teased his chest and then an angel's face was suspended above him.

"Cowboy? You all right?"

"Uh. Yeah."

"Do you need help getting up?"

"No. I never need help getting it up. That's my problem." He laughed. Hard. No idea why because it wasn't particularly funny, but Ava must've seen the humor because she busted a gut right along with him. After wiping the tears from his blurred vision, he mumbled, "I'm actually pretty comfy. I might just crash here tonight."

"No. Come up on the bed. There's room."

Chase rolled to his knees. Clambered on the bed. The last thing he remembered before he passed out was Ava slurring, "Pillow fight!"

Chapter Six

"What in the hell is goin' on here?"

Ava didn't recognize the voice, the loud voice, reverberating in her skull like a jackhammer. She shifted on the mattress and felt the warm weight of something on her butt.

Turning her head required effort, but somehow she managed and found herself staring into Chase McKay's handsome face. Wait a second. How had she ended up in bed with the sexy cowboy? When he'd reiterated that he wouldn't sleep with her?

"Earth to Ava," a feminine voice trilled.

Now that voice she recognized. Ginger.

Ava reached down and removed Chase's hand from her ass and rolled onto her back. Bright sunlight from the window stabbed her retinas and she groaned.

Chase stirred. His leg repeatedly rubbed against hers, sending goose bumps dancing up her thighs.

"Chase. We have company."

"Get rid of 'em. Christ, I have a headache."

She poked him in the ribs until he turned over.

Kane was crouched by the bed, looking slightly amused. "Serves you right, Chase, for drinkin' all my goddamned whisky."

Chase jackknifed, and his hands flew up to cradle his head. "Ow. Fuck. Yell in my ear again, cuz, and I'll give the whisky right back to you in another form."

Kane laughed.

"So you've been here a day and you're already sleeping together?"

Ava finally looked at Ginger. "No."

Ginger arched an eyebrow.

"I know what it looks like. But Chase and I are just friends. Right, McKay?"

"Yeah, but you and me ain't never drinkin' together again."

Her answering laugh sent a spike of pain to her brain.

Chase scooted back to rest against the headboard and glared at Kane and Ginger. "Woulda been nice if you'd told us that we'd be roommates. Teenage Ninja Turtle over there almost killed me."

"Oh please." Ava yanked the sheet to her waist as she sat up. "Like it wasn't ten kinds of scary for a city girl to be out in the middle of nowhere, woken up in the dead of night by a half-naked guy wearing a big hat and carrying a duffel bag that has ropes in it."

"I sure as shootin' didn't have on my cowboy hat when I was headed for bed."

"That's not how I saw it."

"I don't know how you saw *anything* since your eyes were half-covered by a fancy piece of pink fluff."

"I call bullshit on that. You're just—"

Kane whistled shrilly and both Chase and Ava winced. "Enough. Don't be blaming me or my wife, because we kept your secrets. We only realized this morning what'd happened, which is why we're here."

Ava looked at Chase. She didn't like scruffy whiskers on men, but on him? A whole 'nother story. Gave him a harsher edge. Toned down his almost too-perfect good looks.

Why don't you just write the man a fucking sonnet?

God. What was wrong with her? She never got moon-eyed over a guy. Never.

Chase frowned at her. "Why are you starin' at me?"

Lie. "You've got a serious case of bedhead."

"You oughta talk. Your hair looks like you stuck your hand in a bug zapper," he shot back.

She reached for the ponytail holder on the nightstand and began to twist her unruly hair into a messy bun. "Better?"

But Chase's eyes weren't on her makeshift hairdo. His gaze was firmly glued to her breasts shifting beneath the tight tank top. He swallowed hard. But he didn't look away.

Aha. So the cowboy was a breast man. She'd live in cleavage-enhancing shirts if it'd make him rethink his "just friends" mindset.

"Maybe we oughta get dressed," Chase suggested, staring at her nipples. "In long sleeves. It appears to be cold in here."

Damn smartass man.

"Good idea," Kane said. "We'll be in the kitchen."

She'd forgotten Ginger and Kane were in the room.

Chase set his feet on the floor and scooped up his clothes. He muttered, "I don't remember getting undressed."

"Me either."

He squinted at her over his shoulder. "I take less time in the bathroom so I'll go first."

"Fine." Soon as she heard the bathroom door close, she jumped up. Ooh. Too fast. Made her woozy. She slipped on a pair of Capri-style yoga pants and her Santa Clara community college sweatshirt.

As she passed the bathroom, she paused. Her mouth tasted like ass. The shower was running and Chase probably wouldn't notice if she just popped in and grabbed her toothbrush and toothpaste.

Ava turned the door handle. Unlocked. She slowly pushed the door open and came face-to-face with a completely nude Chase. Her eyes followed the dark line of hair—his treasure trail—stopping when she hit the mother lode. Wow. Chase was aroused. And well hung. Very well hung.

"Jesus, Hollywood. Do you not understand privacy at all?"

Rather than reminding him the door had a lock, she said, "I need my toothbrush."

He stomped closer, which caused his dick to jump against his belly. "Get out."

"God, Chase, relax. It's just a penis. And here's a newsflash for you. I've seen other penises, so it's no big deal." *Such a liar, Ava.*

"It's a big deal to me," he snarled. "Get the fuck out of the bathroom and wait your turn."

"Let me grab my toothbrush and toothpaste and I'll go."

"Get your eyes off my junk and you'll see that I have your toothbrush and toothpaste in my hand."

Oh shit. She raised her gaze only high enough to see, yes indeed, Chase was holding her oral hygiene supplies. She snatched them from him and exited the bathroom.

The door slammed behind her. She heard the lock click and some pretty choice swear words.

She stopped outside the kitchen upon seeing Kane and Ginger in a private moment. His lower back rested against the counter with the front of Ginger's body pressed to his. He had one hand fisted in her hair as he kissed the side of her neck and he'd jammed his other hand in the back pocket of her jeans. Everything about the way they were entwined together screamed love, not just lovers.

Despite Ava's joy that Ginger found a man who loved her so completely, Ava felt a smidgen of jealousy. Would she ever find that total love and acceptance for herself?

She cleared her throat and the couple parted.

Kane grinned unrepentantly. "I tend to get carried away when I have alone time with my beautiful wife."

"I imagine," she said distractedly, staring at the section of skin where Ginger's blouse had slipped down. "Since when do you have a tattoo?"

Ginger's fingers brushed her left shoulder. "I got it after the twins were born."

"What is it?"

"The McKay brand." Ginger rolled her eyes. "Oh, don't look so appalled. It's not a symbol of ownership. It's become a tradition for the women who marry into the McKay family."

"Who started the tradition?"

"Keely. When she was the only McKay girl. After she married Jack Donohue, she insisted that he, like the other spouses who married into the family, should be tattooed with the McKay brand. Jack refused— not surprising if you knew Jack—and insisted Keely tattoo *his* initials on her body, since she was no longer a McKay."

"How'd that work out?"

"Keely had India put Jack's initials below the pair of lips tattooed on her butt." Kane shook his head. "And Jack thought once they were married she'd become docile. That girl is about as tame as a mountain lion."

Ava grinned. "I knew I liked her. Now if you'll step aside, I need to use the sink."

Kane squinted at her.

"What?"

"It's weird. Watchin' you on TV you always look so much smaller. I forget how tall you are in person."

"I look short on *Miller's Ridge* because my costar, Alex Summers, is six foot six. He's the first man who makes me look petite." *But he's not the first guy who made me feel small.*

Dammit. No negativity today.

After she washed her face and brushed her teeth, Ava started a pot of coffee. A jolt of caffeine would lessen the pounding in her head. She stared out the window, lost in thought, and only roused herself when she heard Chase join Kane and Ginger's conversation about other McKay family members.

Ginger sidled up next to her. "Sorry about the Chase mix- up."

"It's okay. I didn't give you a choice. And I really do appreciate you guys letting me crash here."

"Have you figured anything out?"

She gave Ginger a wry look. "Besides that I'm never drinking Maker's Mark again?"

"Smartass."

"Actually, I'm shooting things that interest me with my video camera. Don't know what I'll do with any of it, but that's the whole point. Trying to figure some of this out. Who I am when I'm not in Hollywood. What I want to do when I go back, right?"

"Right. I hope you're not factoring Chase into your plans for the time you're here." Ginger dropped her voice. "Chase is a great guy for the most part. A little too self-involved to the McKays' liking. But they're all so damn proud of him they'll forgive his neglectful behavior. That said, Ava, do *not* get mixed-up with him. Woman trouble follows him everywhere and you don't need that after what you've dealt with lately."

"Is Kane giving Chase the same advice? Don't get mixed up with Ava because man trouble follows her everywhere?"

"Shit, Ava, I didn't mean—"

"No need to worry because nothing is going on between us. I swear. We're just friends. We had a blast hanging out yesterday. And to be honest, Chase understands better than anyone what I've gone through with the press since he's gone through the same thing."

Ginger seemed surprised by Ava's observation. "I hadn't thought of it that way."

"That's because you still see me as the clueless seventeen-year-old girl who stumbled into your law office by mistake."

"That's where you're wrong." Ginger bumped Ava with her hip. "While you're contemplating life and your place in it...do something about that chip on your shoulder, eh?"

Ava laughed. But it felt forced, not that Ginger noticed. "So, tell me all about the McKay brood."

Kane and Ginger were enamored with their offspring but clearly exhausted. Maddie's temper was a testament to her red hair. Hayden had christened the corkscrew tufts on Maddie's head her "mean curls" and lamented the fact Paul was a climber and constantly pulled the chess board to the floor. Since Ginger's father lived with them, he was a big help to keeping some semblance of order in the house. But the way they described it, it sounded more like a zoo.

"Oh, before I forget, Ava, did you leave your car parked out front yesterday?"

Ava looked at Kane. "Only for about five minutes. Why?"

"Chase's brother Ben passed by and wondered if someone was staying here. He called this morning, so I had to tell him you were in town, but to keep it quiet." Kane looked at Chase when he opened his mouth. "I told them about Ava to cover *your* ass, cuz, so no complaints from you. But I suggest you keep your truck outta sight." Kane stood and held his hand out to Ginger. "Come on, Red. I need your help checkin' that gate before we head home."

Ginger looked confused. "What gate?"

"You know, the gate we talked about on the way over here?"

"Oh. Oh! That gate." She blushed. "Ah, sure. I'd be happy to help." Ginger paused at the door. "If you need anything, call."

"Will do."

As soon as the door shut, Chase snickered. "Fixin' a gate, my ass. Kane is fixin' to have his way with his wife in his pickup."

"Is 'gate' some kind of country euphemism for sex?"

"Nope. But I believe our bein' in their love nest has forced them to get creative for their marital activities."

She really had no response for that.

"Ever done it in a pickup, Hollywood?"

"No." *Don't ask.* "Have you?"

Chase's I-can-rock-your-world grin turned her knees weak. "I was born and raised in Wyoming. Never had any vehicle that wasn't a truck...so what do you think?"

"I think imagining you and me fogging up the windows and rocking the wheels until the suspension squeaks isn't helping get sex off my brain." Ava set her coffee cup on the table. "My turn in the bathroom."

He yelled, "Don't forget to lock the door."

Doubtful he saw her flip him off.

Later that evening, they were playing a rousing game of Go Fish when headlights swept the kitchen window.

"Were you expecting someone?" Chase said.

"I'm not from around here, remember? What about you?"

"No one knows I'm here, remember?" He pulled back the living room curtain and froze. What the fuck was his brother Ben doing here? He grabbed Ava by the elbow and dragged her out of sight.

"What the hell are you doing, Chase?"

"Ssh."

"Don't shush me. Who's here?"

Four insistent raps sounded on the screen door.

"Ava? I know it's late but I wondered if you were still up? It's Ben McKay, Kane's cousin. Don't know if you remember me, but we met at Kane and Ginger's wedding."

Ava smirked at Chase and yelled, "Of course I remember, you, Ben. Hang on, let me throw on some clothes and I'll be right there."

"Are you fuckin' serious?" Chase hissed in her ear. "You *cannot* let my brother in."

"Sure I can. And if you don't want to be found out as my dirty little secret, you'd better stay in the bedroom." Ava sidestepped him, slipped on her Juicy jacket and fluffed her hair. Then she made a shooing motion at him. "Go."

"I don't believe this," he muttered, stealthily snagging his duffel bag. He left the bedroom door ajar, hoping the hallway had decent acoustics.

"Ben! Wow. You look great. Thanks so much for taking the time to check on this poor city mouse."

"It's no trouble. Just bein' neighborly."

Bullshit. Ben lived twenty-five fucking miles from here. Maybe Ben would see Ava was fine and skedaddle on home. Chase just hoped

Ava wouldn't offer him a beer.

"Can I get you something to drink?" Ava asked with entirely too much cheer for Chase's liking.

"A beer would be great."

Dammit. They sat in the easy chairs, which meant Chase had no way to see them and could only hear his brother making charming small talk with Ava.

"Kane and Ginger swung by today, and told me you'd seen my car out front."

"Gotta admit I was surprised that we had a beautiful celebrity in our midst again."

Jesus. When Ben spewed that lame bullshit, he actually got laid? Unbelievable.

"More like a fugitive than a celebrity since I'm on the lam from my life."

"I read about that nasty business with your ex. You okay?"

"Getting there. Needed time to clear my head and there's too much smog in LA to do that, so I headed for wide-open spaces."

"You're not finding it too isolated out here?"

Why don't you just come out and ask to spend the night so you can keep her safe?

"Not yet."

"If you get bored or lonely, or hell, just hungry, call me. I'm a decent cook and I get tired of cooking for one."

"Thank you, Ben, I may do that."

Their voices dropped. All Chase could hear were Ben's deep murmurs and Ava's occasional trills of laughter. He fumed, wondering how Ben's impromptu visit had turned into an extended stay.

Then Ben's voice reached him, clear as a bell. "You might as well come out, Chase. I know you're back there. I recognize that damn cologne you bathe in. And your boots are by the door."

Chase wandered out of the bedroom and faced his older brother. Even as a kid Ben owned an air of fortitude. Since Ben smiled and laughed more than their oldest brother, Quinn, everyone assumed Ben was easygoing. Laid-back.

But he wasn't. Not by a long shot. Ben had a level of intensity that could be downright scary. Luckily Ben hadn't inherited the tendency to use his fists to solve problems, a trait some of their McKay cousins shared. He didn't mince words, didn't have time for bullshit or lies. When a man was defined by how hard he worked, Chase always thought of Bennett McKay first.

"Would you excuse us?" Ben asked as he stood. "I need to talk to my little brother outside for a minute."

Ava tossed off a breezy, "Sure."

Ben exited the trailer. He kept walking until they were by the barn. Then he faced Chase, hands on his hips, his tone as cold as steel. "What the hell is wrong with you? You come home and stay at Kane's place and don't let any of your family know you're here?"

Chase's brain started to form a lie, but his mouth wouldn't give voice to it. "Sorry."

"Sorry? You too good for us now? Do your country kin embarrass the big time PBR bull rider?"

Shame made heat flare in his cheeks. "Goddammit, Ben, no, I ain't that way, you know that. I got kicked off the tour and didn't want you guys to know because I don't want any of you to think less of me than you already do."

Ben stared at him. Hard. With such a mix of emotions swimming in his eyes that Chase couldn't look away. Then he said curtly, "The truth about what went down. All of it. Right now."

Chase relayed everything.

His brother walked to the fence. Gazed across the pasture. Walked back. "Okay. I believe you."

That stung. Ben's first thought was he'd been lying? Right. Ben had caught Chase in lies more times than he cared to admit.

"But you don't get to toss off the 'think less of you' bullshit comment because that's a total lie. We're all proud of you, Chase. But the fact is, you ain't proud of yourself. And I get sick and tired of us— your family—bein' dead last on your list of priorities. You should've come to us first."

"Really? Last time I came home, I ended up staying with Tell because Mom was having the entire inside of the house repainted, Quinn and Libby's kids were sick, and you had 'plans', so don't give me that I should've come to you first crap. You don't know what it's like not to have a home you can go to whenever you feel like it."

Ben seemed surprised by Chase's explanation. "Regardless. Mom is worried about you because of the injury announcement, and you weren't forthcoming about it." He pointed at Chase. "Then no one hears from you for two weeks? Beyond the 'I'm fine, more later' texts you've sent to all of us. That's bogus and you know it."

"Yeah, I suck, I'm sure that's a big fuckin' shocker," he muttered. "Are they pissed?"

"Not as much as they might've been in the past. A whole lot changed between them after Aunt Joan left Uncle Casper."

His aunt and uncle being Splitsville after so many years of marriage was hard to believe. "Like what?"

"I dunno, I don't..." Ben sighed and studied his boots. "It's like they're in a honeymoon phase. That sounds stupid, but whenever I see Brandt and Jessie, I realize Mom and Dad are acting just like them. Maybe it has to do with Dad retiring."

Not realizing things had changed in his family made Chase feel guiltier yet.

"As far as you sneaking into Wyoming because you thought I'd judge you? Yeah, I probably would've chewed your ass. Reminded you that when things go to hell you don't run from your family, you're supposed *to* run to them. Reminded you that we talked about some of this distraction shit last year. You didn't listen to me. Or Quinn. But I figure I'm entitled to givin' you what for now, bein's I'm the older, wiser brother and all."

Chase grinned. "Thought I saw some new gray hair on that stubborn head of yours."

"Bite me." Ben's smile faded. "I've said my piece. But there's one thing I ain't letting you off the hook for."

He expected Ben to bring up Ava and braced himself. "What?"

"You're gonna make a 'surprise' visit to Mom and Dad before you leave." Ben frowned. "I'd call first just to make sure they're not goin' at it on the living room floor."

"Thanks for that mental picture, bro."

"Hey, I got to see the live version, so consider yourself lucky."

"No. Way. Mom and Dad? Doin' the nasty on the floral rug we weren't even allowed to walk on?"

Ben nodded. "They didn't see me and I backed away quietly when I saw them. Then went home and drank until I passed out. Quinn wasn't happy I was worthless the next day. So I gave him a much more graphic version of what I'd seen than what I'm telling you. And while you're out and about, stop and see Quinn, Libby and the kids."

"I'm never gonna get outta town tomorrow," he grumbled.

"I'm glad you're leaving. I hoped you had a better plan than holing up in this trailer and spending the summer sulking."

He knew Ben was worried, and the way he showed concern was to provoke him. Weird, but it always worked.

"Where you off to?"

"Cash Big Crow is gonna help me figure out what I changed in my ridin' style. Guess I'll be getting on a lot of bulls to try and fix it."

"Smart. Then what?"

Chase couldn't tell his "don't lie" brother about his bogus PRCA card and his intent to ride as many bulls as possible in the next month. "Honestly? I don't know. I'm gonna try like hell to stay off the radar. Maybe the PBR will commute my sentence."

"Be interesting to see what happens. Just don't keep me outta the loop, okay?"

He had the sense there was more to it. Was Ben somehow...lonely? "So. You been winning at the McKay poker games?"

Ben shrugged. "Some. Dalton's poker face is for shit. Tell's been working on his professional face since he became a licensed rodeo judge. Truth is, the games have tapered off, despite our married cousin's claims they wanted to join in. Hell, even Brandt can't be away from Jessie for a night of cards."

"Whatcha been doin' with yourself?"

"This and that. Spending time in Gillette. Building furniture. Got a bed and breakfast joint in Jackson Hole that ordered eight complete bedroom sets. But they want eight different designs, so that's been a challenge."

Ben had turned his talent for building log furniture into a nice sideline. "That's great. But I know you ain't sawing logs all the time."

"Ha-ha. That's still not as funny as the first fifty times you said it."

"You seein' anyone?"

"I'm working with a couple of ladies. Won't be anything long term. Speaking of short term...What's goin' on with you and Ava?"

"There's nothin' goin' on because I swore off women."

"Again?" Ben rolled his eyes. "How long this time?"

"A month."

"Got any money or a share in a bull ridin' on it?"

"No. My career is ridin' on it."

That gave Ben pause.

"Look, Ava is beyond beautiful. She's got a body that don't quit. Yet she ain't at all the phony, snooty, rich TV star I figured she'd be. She's funny. And smart. Curious as a damn cat. And she's...real. I like her. We're friends. Which is why I ain't gonna sleep with her."

You trying to convince him or yourself?

A strange expression crossed Ben's face.

"What?"

"Well, she is taller than you, so according to your dating rules, she don't stand a chance."

"Fuck off," Chase shot back.

"In all seriousness, I've gotta admit, I already see some changes in you. I hope you can sustain them and get your bull ridin' mojo back. But I'd like to offer you a piece of advice when your good intentions with Ava go straight to hell."

His brother assumed he couldn't keep his dick in his pants, which only strengthened his determination to do just that. "And what's that?"

Ben locked his gaze to Chase's. "Be a man."

Chase bristled. "What the fuck is that supposed to mean?"

"I've seen you in action with women over the years. Pains me to admit this, but you're too damn good-lookin' for your own good and charming to boot. All's you gotta do is smile and the ladies fall at your feet and into your bed."

"And that's a bad thing...why?"

"Because you don't hafta work for a woman. Once you've got her in bed, I'm betting she'll do anything to impress you."

How had Ben figured that out? But in Chase's own defense, he wasn't the lazy dude who relaxed in a pile of pillows and let women service him. He was an active participant in sex. He was a good lover. Respectful. Made sure his partner got off. And he hadn't had any complaints.

The women aren't around long enough to complain.

"I assume this has a point?" he said brusquely.

"You have a sense of entitlement. You look at a conquest and think, what can she do for me?"

"Christ, Ben, that's normal. All guys are like that."

Ben flashed his teeth. "I'm not. I see a woman I want and I think, what can I do to her that'll give her what *she* needs? Give her what no other man has?"

That was too much information from his close-mouth brother. "You sayin' I need to be more...giving?"

"No. I'm sayin' you need to be more forceful in proving to Ava you can be the man that finally sees beyond the surface. As a Hollywood princess, she's also used to being worshiped and not having to work very hard at it. Ava doesn't need a man to pet her and stroke her. To wait for her signal. She needs a man to take charge. No excuses, no apologies, no holding back. In essence, be a man."

"You could be that man?" Chase asked a little testily.

"I *am* that man." Ben's gaze never wavered. "The thing is, you are that man too. As long as you're working on getting your bull ridin' mojo back, get that other male mojo back."

"Did you not hear me? I'm celibate. Sworn off women, remember?"

Ben laughed and clapped him on the back. "Lemme know how that works out for ya. In the meantime, just think about what I said, okay?"

"Do you hand out this advice often?"

"Nope. Only to those who need it. Like you. And Quinn."

"Quinn? Really?"

"I can't take the credit for him and Libby stayin' together, but I know my talk with him prompted a different way of thinking."

Huh. He'd wondered about the changes in Quinn. He seemed a lot more confident in recent years, especially when it came to Libby.

Ben walked to his truck and Chase fell in step beside him. "Say goodbye to the lovely Ava for me. And keep in touch, goddammit."

"I will. Thanks, Ben. For givin' me an ass kickin' when I needed it." He pulled his brother in and hugged him hard.

Ava wondered why Ben had spirited Chase away.

Some super-secret family discussion?

To warn him to keep his eyes on the prize and not on his accidental roommate?

While they'd been having their little he-man powwow, she'd crafted a list of reasons why Chase should let her come along with him tomorrow.

The screen door slammed. Ava looked up to see Chase grinning at her. Damn him and that funny tickle in her belly his smile caused. "Is everything okay?"

"Fine. Sorry to put you on the spot with my brother."

"No worries. But I'll admit, Ben is a little...forceful. In a quiet way. This is sort of embarrassing to admit, but one time when I looked in his eyes? I had this overwhelming urge to do whatever he told me. No matter what it was."

Chase froze. "Seriously?"

"Uh-huh. Ben is unbelievably sexy in that Tarzan, 'me man, you woman' way. Normally that type of blatant maleness has the opposite effect on me and I want to run. But I had the perverse idea that if I did run? I'd really enjoy having him chase me. And catch me." She thought back to the dark heat in Ben's eyes. His invasive look that let her know if he ever touched her, he'd get inside her head, push her limits, and she'd be grateful for every second of it. Talk about pure sexual power.

"Jesus, Ava, wipe that dreamy look off your face," Chase growled. "He's my fucking brother."

"And what? He's off limits?"

"Yes."

Ava sighed heavily. "You're off limits. He's off limits. What's a girl gotta do to get laid around here?"

His mouth opened. Closed.

"Chase. I was kidding." She patted the couch cushion next to her. "Please sit. I want to talk to you."

"Fine." He plopped down next to her. "Talk."

"I know you're leaving tomorrow. And I overheard your conversation about where you're going and what you're doing."

Chase scowled. "Ain't polite to eavesdrop, Ava."

"Says the man who practically fell out the door trying to hear what your brother and I were discussing," she pointed out. "Anyway, I know you're going to a private bull riding school. If I came along with you, we could help each other out."

"How?"

"I got to thinking while I've been taping other stuff that it'd be helpful if you had someone to video your rides so you can break them down, frame by frame, to see what you did right and what you did wrong. I humbly offer my services as your videographer, if you'll allow me to tag along."

"That don't seem like your thing, bein' behind the camera instead of in front of it."

How could she explain this without coming across as pathetic? Or worse, one of those hanger-ons she deplored? She pinched the piping in the couch seat cushion as she tried to find the best way to phrase it.

Chase sweetly clasped her restless hand in his and her belly jumped. "No judgment, remember? I'm listening."

Buoyed by his encouragement, she continued. "My offer to help isn't entirely selfless. I'll admit I've never done anything like this in my life—gone off on a road trip with a duffel bag, my video camera and no agenda with a man I hardly know. But God, it's something I want to do. I want to be a part of something real. To experience life as it unfolds. Unscripted. Where the corrals aren't on some sound stage and the rodeo contestants aren't stunt men. Where I'm just a woman on an adventure. Where I'm just...normal."

"Ava. Darlin', I don't know how to say this without you taking it wrong. But you're fucking hot as hell, you're a TV star, and you've been in movies, so I don't think incognito is an option for you. No offense, but I don't need to be worrying that people will recognize you. That'd put us both back in the spotlight, right where we don't wanna be."

Ava tried not to read too much into the continual stroking of Chase's ragged thumb across her knuckles. "What do you have planned? Because it sounds more involved than you heading to River Bend to test bulls for a few days."

"It is." He dry-washed his face and heaved a long sigh. "Remember during the truth or lie game when you asked me the biggest lie I ever told?"

Ava nodded.

"I didn't fess up because this one is huge."

"Did you kill someone?"

"God no."

"Did you make a deal with a crossroads demon to give you five years of success for your soul? And now the five years are up and he's coming to drag you to hell?"

Chase gaped at her as if she'd sprouted horns. "Jesus, Ava. Where do you come up with this stuff?"

"Uh, hello? I was on a TV show that dealt with supernatural beings and otherworldly issues. I always think along those lines. Anyway. Proceed."

"When I turned eighteen and started competing professionally, everyone commented I was a natural. One of the best rookies to come along in years. But the truth was I had two years experience. I'd been competing in bull ridin' in the PRCA since I was sixteen."

Ava's eyebrows drew together. "How?"

"By using another name. My buddy Jet lent me his older brother's birth certificate so I could register and get my PRCA pro card. Every weekend Jet and I raced to the closest event if I'd scraped up enough entry money."

"But doesn't everyone around here know everyone else? And aren't the McKays infamous in the rodeo world?"

"I kept a low profile. Plus, I sucked." He groaned. "Bad. I got the hang of it after a dozen events. Started putting some jingle in my pocket. But that wasn't the best part. The best part was I finally got to do what I'd always dreamed: ride bulls."

"What name were you riding under?"

He grinned. "That's the ironic thing. Jet's last name was Chase. His brother's name was Bill Chase, so we figured it was meant to be."

"So no one besides Jet knows you did this?"

"I didn't tell my family or my friends. Back then it was all about getting on as many bulls as possible and learning the basics. That's what I need to relearn now." He slipped his wallet from his back pocket and thumbed through a stack of cards until he found the one he wanted. "I'm still a member of the PRCA. So I figured it's time to bring out Bill again."

Ava angled closer and pushed up the brim of his hat. "Ah, hate to break it to you cowboy, but this face you got going on? Ain't exactly forgettable. I'll remind you that you've been on TV. And you've built a sizeable fan base. *You* are recognizable. You should worry about PBR fans recognizing your megawatt smile. And this beautifully chiseled face. And this remarkably distinctive hair."

"Easy fix. I'll frown all the time. I'll grow a goatee. I'll even shave off my hair."

"You're really serious about this."

"Yes, I am. Never been more serious in my life."

She removed his hat, setting it on the table—upside down, as she'd seen him do. She fingered the ends of his hair, then sifted her hand through the soft strands to stroke his scalp. "I'd hate for you to cut this. Even though the length reminds me of a swashbuckling pirate and not a cowboy."

He didn't back away from her touch. "It'll grow back."

"If you're sure about hacking it off, and if you own a pair of clippers, and if you'll let me come along on the road with you, I'll cut it for you."

Chase looked at her oddly. "You're a barber too?"

"Axel went through a punk stage and I got pretty good at trimming up the sides of his Mohawk."

"You close to your brother?"

"He avoids being seen with me in public these days because of the bad press." Maybe that's why Chase was dragging his heels. Ava slowly let her hands drop and glanced away.

But Chase grabbed her chin, forcing her to meet his eyes, and that little show of force thrilled her. "I'm not embarrassed to be seen with you, Ava. Far from it. But it will reflect badly on you in the press if I get caught impersonating another bull rider and you're with me."

"It's a chance I'm willing to take. What will happen to *you* if you get caught?"

"I don't know. Which is why I have to be damn careful that no one recognizes me." His eyes turned a hard. "This is more than an adventure for me, Ava. This is my life, my livelihood. My entire future is at stake. You understand?"

"Yes. I promise not to do anything to jeopardize this chance for you, Chase. But please, I'm asking for the same chance. Let me be someone else for a while too."

Just when she thought he'd remind her of his "no sex" decree, Chase retreated. "Fine. You're in. Before we take off tomorrow, I need to stop in and see my folks. And my brother and his family."

"Great. That'll give me time to burn a CD of road tunes."

He groaned. "I'm already regretting this and we haven't left yet."

"But this will be the soundtrack to our buddy trip. Like *Thelma and Louise*. Or those old Bob Hope and Bing Crosby movies."

"Or Mel Gibson in *The Road Warrior*."

Ava bumped her knee to his. "That doesn't count. He had no buddies. He just drove around killing people."

"Maybe we'll wanna kill each other after a few weeks on the road together."

"Highly unlikely because we are gonna be the best friends in the history of the world." She tacked on a fake smile. "How far is the bull riding boot camp?"

"About two and a half hours."

Something occurred to her. "Will the people putting you up have a place for me to stay?"

"I'm sure we'll figure something out."

"But—"

Chase grabbed her hand again. "You wanted an adventure, Ava. Part of that is learning to go with the flow. Things ain't always gonna be planned out to the letter. Can you do that?"

"I can try."

Chapter Seven

Chase suspected Ava would chatter the entire way to the Bar 9. But she was absorbed with the scenery and writing in her notebook. Occasionally she'd ask a question, or make an observation. Since Chase spent the majority of his time on the road alone, he appreciated her company, but also long stretches of silence.

They'd gotten a later start than he'd planned. His folks had been pleased to see him. Especially after he gave them a more information on his professional life and how he intended to get it back on track. Neither pointed out the errors of his previous ways, as they'd been prone to do in the past. Which was the first outward first indication they'd changed.

Chase about fell off his chair when his dad rose from the table to help his mom serve butterscotch cake. And he got a bit choked up when his father followed him out to his truck and talked about not allowing past mistakes to affect his future. How the true measure of a man was learning from those mistakes, not dwelling on them.

So Chase had been introspective when he dropped by Quinn and Libby's. Five minutes with the rambunctious Adam cured that. The kid talked a mile a minute. Ran everywhere instead of walked. Barked a stellar dog impression. Then Adam was in his baby sister Amelia's face, much to Amelia's squealing delight. Amelia had grown so much since the last time he'd seen her, that once again Chase felt a pang of guilt for not being part of his niece and nephew's lives.

After they'd dropped off Ava's rental car in Spearfish, they grabbed a bite at McDonald's. Chase had purposely chosen the always-busy restaurant as a test to see if anyone recognized Ava. A couple guys sent appreciative glances her direction, but that was it. Wearing workout clothes, her hair secured in a ponytail and a Devil's Tower ball cap on her head, she looked nothing like a glamorous Hollywood actress. That was a mark of true beauty in Chase's mind; dressed up or dressed down, Ava looked exactly the same—amazingly beautiful.

The landscape changed dramatically from the pine-tree-dotted hills, red clay and sweeping vistas. Here the land was flat until a deep rock-ridged canyon appeared. Scrub oak abounded, as did several different kinds of sage. The wooden snow fences scattered at random intervals, set at odd angles and varying heights, piqued Ava's curiosity. Chase pointed out one covered in tumbleweeds and told her the patterns of blowing snow were predictable across the high plains desert, so the snow fences were permanent fixtures across Wyoming.

About ten miles to the turn-off to Gemma and Cash's ranch, he said, "Almost there."

Ava stowed her notebook and faced him. "You excited? Nervous?"

"Both. I've met Cash a few times over the years, but I don't know him. My dad and uncles have dealt with Cash's wife Gemma, but I don't know her either. Here's where it gets tricky. My cousin Carter is married to Macie, Cash's daughter from a previous relationship."

"I probably met Carter and Macie at Kane and Ginger's wedding?"

"Probably. If there's a family celebration, all the McKays are there." *Except for me.*

"So this really is a friend of a friend of a friend situation for you? With the exception of your cousin?"

"Yeah."

"That makes me feel better."

Chase felt her studying him. "Tell me what's on your mind, Hollywood."

"You're showing up with me. How do we explain that? I mean, would it be simpler if we told them we're in a relationship?"

He'd considered that and shook his head. "Let's tell them the truth. We're friends, you've never been out West and I'm giving you insight you need for your project. In exchange, you're helpin' me out by taping my rides."

"I thought that would be best too. Just don't...ditch me, okay?"

Seeing her shy smile, and a glimpse of vulnerability, kicked some unknown instinct to protect her. And that confused the hell out of him. "I won't ditch you, darlin', but you'd better be prepared to spend a lot of time on the dirt."

Chase turned down the gravel road leading to the ranch. When they parked in front of the house, dogs raced down the steps.

As soon as he climbed out of the truck, a boy skidded to a stop. He wore beat-up boots, dirty jeans and a huge, toothless grin. "Are you really Chase McKay?"

"Yep, I really am. Who are you?"

"Ryder Big Crow."

Chase stuck out his hand. "Great to meet you, Ryder."

Ryder shook his hand and wouldn't let go. "I watch you every week on TV. I can't believe you're at my house!" He yelled, "Dad! Look who's here!"

Cash ambled over. "I see that." He offered his hand so Ryder had to relinquish Chase's. "Good to see you, McKay."

"Good to be here, Cash. I appreciate you fitting me in to your busy summer schedule."

"No worries." Cash's gaze strayed and Chase knew what—who—had caught his attention.

Chase smiled at her approach. "Cash and Ryder Big Crow, this is my friend Ava. She's here to help me out."

Cash's smile didn't falter, but something passed through his eyes as he offered his hand. "Ava. Nice to meet you."

"Man, my mama will be happy you're here," Ryder said. "She always complains there ain't never enough girls."

Ava laughed. "I can't wait to meet her."

"Let's see about getting you two settled in the bunkhouse."

"Come on, it's this way," Ryder said, taking off at a run.

"You sure it isn't an imposition for me to stay here, Mr. Big Crow?"

"Call me Cash." He slung Ava's duffel over his shoulder as they started to walk. "No. We've got room. Without sounding like a prude... Since our kids are around and curious as little monkeys, I'm afraid I'll insist you two stay in separate sides of the bunkhouse."

"That's fine," Chase inserted. "Me'n Ava are just friends."

"Yes, just friends," Ava reiterated. "I've never been out West and Chase is my tour guide in exchange for my videotaping skills."

"That's smart, havin' a record of your rides so you can go back and look at them," Cash said.

"Hey, every little thing helps, right?"

"Right. We'll get started in the mornin' after I finish chores."

"Sounds good. When is Colby coming?"

"Day after tomorrow when the stock is scheduled to arrive. Might be a long couple days for you, Chase, with the amount of stock I'd like you to test out."

"I can't wait. Seems I've been in a holding pattern for too long."

Cash nodded. "It'll be good to find your seat again."

Then Ryder was jumping up and down in front of them. "Can I help ya pick a bunk? Please?"

"Sure. But no top bunk, okay?"

"'Kay," and he was off like a shot.

"Ryder is a little enthusiastic about you bein' here, if you haven't noticed." Cash glanced at Ava. "Any questions?"

"One that I hope isn't too weird."

"Shoot."

"Does the bunkhouse have Wi-Fi?"

"Yep. Them young bucks that come here can't be away from the cyber world for two whole weeks."

A planked porch ran in front of the bunkhouse. Two doors denoted the two sides. One door was open and Ryder popped his head out. "Got it all picked out!"

"Cool beans." Chase ducked inside. The room was rustic. No air conditioning. No running water. A ceiling fan spun above and another fan placed in front of the window pulled cool air from outside. "This is a great place, Cash. Same set up on the other side?"

"Yeah. A communal bathroom with showers on the back side."

"You really have sixteen bull riders here at a time?"

"We're always booked, since I only have sessions four times a year."

Ryder sat on the bed farthest from the window. "I'm hopin' maybe my dad will let me sleep out here on this bunk tonight?"

"Nope." Cash held up his hand and Ryder's protest died before it began.

Chase wandered to the other side of the bunkhouse to see how Ava was faring. He doubted she'd ever stayed in a place like this.

But she'd picked a bunk and set the lamp on the table, closer to the window.

"How's it goin' in here?"

Ava whirled around. "Great! I feel like I'm at camp. I might sneak a flashlight and read under the covers tonight just to make the experience complete."

Cash stuck his head in. "Anything you need, Ava, just let Gemma know."

"I'll keep that in mind, Cash, thanks."

"I need to do a quick cattle check if you wanna ride along," Cash said to Chase.

"And open gates for you," Chase said dryly.

"Yep."

"Can I come?" Ava asked. "I'd be happy to open gates."

"The more the merrier." Cash patted Ryder's shoulder. "Come on, son, load up the dogs."

Ava asked a million questions, none of them the invasive ones ranchers hate, such as: how many head of cattle do you run, or what's the size of your acreage. She and Cash had been so engrossed in conversation Chase had gotten stuck opening gates. But he didn't mind. With Ava focused on listening to Cash, he could focus on her.

Beautiful, vivacious, funny, he wondered if she ever felt out of place. She slipped into any situation with ease. Although he tried to ignore the voice of reason that reminded him *Of course she adapts easily because she's an actress*, Chase couldn't discount it completely. Still, Ava seemed genuine. She hadn't batted an eye at crawling in

Cash's dirty feed truck. He'd even caught her ruffling the dog's ears as she'd talked to Ryder. The woman absolutely knocked him for a loop. She was unlike any woman he'd ever met.

Why was that? He'd been involved with beautiful women before. Did he find Ava so appealing because they'd agreed to just be friends? He didn't try to be charming just so he could get into her pants? He could really be himself? Chase had racked his brain trying to remember if he'd ever been just friends with a woman. Not in the last decade, that was for damn sure. Yet, he knew if he gave the signal, she'd be all over him and their budding friendship would end.

See? That's your problem. You automatically put her in the role of the aggressor—even when the choice to change the parameters of your relationship...is yours.

Was he really that passive when it came to sex?

Yes.

Ben's advice, *Be a man,* still rankled. Mostly because it was true.

Hard to swallow, that he wasn't as aggressive in all areas of his life as when he was on the back of a bull.

But right now, for the next few days, his time spent on a bull was all that mattered.

Later that night, a cool breeze drifting from the window, the sound of crickets and the occasional garbled hoot from an owl lulled Chase to sleep.

A series of loud knocks jolted him from slumber. The door creaked as he peeled his eyes open.

"Chase? Are you awake?"

"I am now," he grumbled. "What's up?"

Rapid footsteps on wood were his only warning before Ava jumped on him.

"What the hell?" She burrowed into him, shaking from head to toe. "What's wrong?"

"I'm scared. I kept hearing these weird noises. Things brushing against the side of the bunkhouse under my window. Then this spooky howling started, followed by the most god-awful shriek. And I thought, what if it's a mountain lion and it jumps right through the open window to attack me?"

"Hey now, take a couple of deep breaths." Chase tucked her into his body, pulling the blanket over them, lightly running his fingertips up and down her spine.

Her chest pressed against his as she inhaled. A soft puff of air teased his chest when she exhaled.

As she concentrated on breathing, her tremors slowed. And finally stopped. She snuggled into him and he couldn't resist brushing his lips across the top of her head.

They remained entwined for several long minutes.

She spoke first. "You probably think I'm a wuss."

"You? A wuss? Ain't you the woman who threatened to kick my ass just a couple days ago while you were buck-ass nekkid?"

"It was a bluff. I was scared out of my mind, seeing a strange guy in my room, and I blurted out the first thing that popped into my head."

His hand stopped the stroking motion on her back. "So you don't have a black belt in taekwondo?"

"No. I once played a character who rocked at martial arts. I trained the minimum amount so it'd look like a pro onscreen." She paused. "You really thought I could hurt you?"

"Yes. Damn fine actin' job, Hollywood."

"Well, I *am* a professional."

He chuckled.

Ava rubbed her cheek against his pectoral. "Thanks for not laughing at me, Chase."

"I'm not that kinda guy." He started caressing her back again. "That said, please don't ever use your actin' talent on this gullible cowboy, okay?"

She lifted her head and said, "I won't," then snuggled into him.

Chase closed his eyes, enjoying Ava's soft curves melting into him and smelling her orange blossom scented lotion. After he'd seen the bottle in the bathroom at Kane's place, he told himself he wasn't perverted if he picked it up and sniffed it a couple of times.

"So have you told any of your LA friends about your big adventure out west?"

"No one to tell."

"Really?"

"Sounds weird. You'd think I'd have a multitude of friends, right? Since I'm a Native Californian, a TV actress, a tabloid target. Ooh, and let's not forget a rich girl." She shifted slightly, almost as if she intended to get up.

Chase pressed his palm between her shoulder blades as a sign he didn't want her to run out, and surprisingly, that seemed to calm her. "So why are you rolling in dough but not friends?"

"It's complicated."

"I got nowhere to be, darlin', so why don't you help me understand."

She struggled for a minute before she spoke. "The girls I went to school with are all married with families or they're focused on their careers. It's gotten harder and harder to connect with them. Other actresses are so damn competitive that I'm never sure of their

73

motivations for befriending me because it's always—and I mean always—been for some shady reason. Not to mention the blatant remarks about how I don't *need* to work as an actress since I've got money in the bank, and I should just bow out and make room for them."

"Women say shit like that to you?"

Ava huffed out a sigh. "All the time. Which is why I love the camaraderie on movie sets. But that disappears after the film wraps. I doubt I'll remain in touch with any of the actors from *Miller's Ridge*, because it was just a job. That's the other thing. Shooting a weekly TV show is grueling. When we're wrapped up for the week, I usually fall comatose in my bed because I haven't been home and the last thing I want to do is to go out."

"But you do, right?"

"There are events I'm obligated to attend. Those aren't so bad. It's the industry after-parties that make me question people's honesty and their friendly intentions. Like, are they going to a club with me because they like me and want to spend time with me? Or are they going because they know I've got money and expect to party on my dime? Or are they hanging out with me hoping to wind up in one of the trade rags? I mean, my celebrity isn't worth a whole lot, but it's worth something."

"And that makes you question your worth?" he asked gently.

"Yeah." A pause and then she laughed softly. "I know I sound horribly neurotic. Or ungrateful for the advantages I have simply because of my birthright. I'm not that callous or jaded. It makes it hard to blindly trust people. I end up spending a lot of time alone, sort of trapped by my own mediocre success." Her fingers traced the ridge of his collarbone. "My so-called issues pale in comparison to what most people have to deal with in their lives, and I feel like a big whiny spoiled baby even talking about it. But I don't talk about it because I've got no one to talk to."

"I'm glad you're talkin' to me."

"So my blathering doesn't make you rethink being my friend?"

Not in the way you're thinking. "Nope. I'm glad we're friends, Ava."

"Same here. I'm relieved to have a break from all that crap for a while."

"How long is a while?"

"I start shooting a movie in Mexico in August. I'm on standby for readings, costumes, all that stuff."

Chase frowned. "What's that mean?"

"If they call me, I have to go back to LA immediately."

"So between me waiting for a callback from the PBR, and you waiting for a callback from a movie studio, either of us could hafta leave at any time?"

"Sounds like it. So we'd better make the most of our time together."

The old Chase would've suggested they spend all that time between the sheets. The new, improved Chase...kept his mouth shut.

"What are your friends like in the PBR?" Ava asked.

"Well, I wouldn't call them all friends. The majority are good guys, for the most part. Then there are the ones who act one way in the spotlight and after the cameras are gone, act totally different. They talk a good game about their religious beliefs and the cowboy way, and then they're out at the honky-tonks after every performance trying to rack up as many sin points as possible."

"Does it bother you?"

"Only if their bad behavior gets them more airtime than me."

Ava lightly punched him in the stomach. "I'm serious."

"I am too. I think who we are in public, to some extent, should be the real us, or at least the polished version of ourselves the PR people want us to project. But I also think the most private part of who we are shouldn't be out there. We should save that part so we have something special about ourselves to share with the people who matter most to us."

She didn't say anything, just lifted her head and studied him with those big, startlingly expressive eyes.

"What? You think that's weird?"

"No. I think it's actually poetic, Chase. And it's a good rule to live by."

Relieved she didn't find him a dork, he kissed her forehead.

That rarely seen shy, sweet smile lit her beautiful face a second before she burrowed back into him.

Man. He liked her. A lot. He could really fall for her. Hard. Even before they had sex.

Not that they were going to have sex.

Keep telling yourself that, buddy.

Chase began to drift off. A cool breeze and a warm woman—sometimes the best things in life were simple.

"I should probably go back to the girls' cabin, huh?"

"Maybe. I'd hate for you to get kicked outta camp for fraternizing in the boys' cabin on your first night."

"True. But it'd be worth it not to be scared."

"Ava, if you're still scared, you can stay here. But this is an awful small bunk. It'd be better for both of us if you were on top of me." Not what he meant. "On the top bunk."

She kissed his sternum and disentangled from him. "Thanks for the offer. But what kind of adventurer would I be if I let my fear of a mountain lion attack derail me?"

Chase smiled. "You really are funny."
"Night, Sundance."
"Night, Hollywood."

Chapter Eight

Ava had just finished her workout the next morning when she heard three raps on the bunkhouse door. "Come in."

Gemma poked her head in. Her gaze dropped to the yoga mat and the big balance ball. "Am I interrupting?"

"No. I just finished. Come in. Maybe downwind from me since I reek." Ava wiped the sweat from her forehead. "Thanks for letting me stay here. I hope it's not an imposition."

Gemma sat on the straight-backed chair. "We're happy to have you. Although I'm sure it's not what you're used to."

Ava mopped her chest and debated her answer. Gemma knew who she was. "It's like going to camp, which I never had the opportunity to do."

"So do you mind if a snoopy old ranch woman asks a question about your life as a Hollywood actress?"

"As long as you don't mind if a clueless Hollywood actress asks questions about life on the range."

"Deal." Gemma grinned. "Is it hard livin' your life the way you want when you have to worry that people are watching your every move?"

Ava pulled out the other chair and the table and sat across from Gemma. "It wasn't an issue until I landed the role on *Miller's Ridge.* Then I was this 'hot, new actress', even though I'd been doing bit parts on TV for a few years. The first time the paparazzi yelled 'Look this way, Miss Cooper' and snapped my photo? I thought I was freakin' cool. I could not understand why other actors complained about photographers following them everywhere. It seemed I'd hit the big time when trade rags sent a photographer to trail me as I was out running errands.

"I made a few missteps. Doing the walk of shame, which naturally, the paparazzi captured on film. Getting pulled over for a broken taillight, which the tabloids twisted into me being under suspicion for DUI. I started dating an assistant director for the company that produces the show. He insisted we keep our relationship on the down-low since he was a really private guy. So we got...amorous on the patio at my place, not thinking anything of it because it's secluded, right? I was in my own home, right?"

"This ain't gonna end well, is it?"

"No. Some douchebag photographer ignored the *Private property* warning and snapped pics of us getting naked and wild. The pictures were plastered all over the tabloids the next day. Granted, you couldn't see his face, but you could see mine. He broke up with me immediately. Said being with me was too much work."

Gemma winced.

"And don't get me started on the Jake debacle. I had to leave California to get away from it." When Gemma didn't ask specifics, Ava knew the bad press had even made it to rural Wyoming.

"Do you love acting so much you'll put up with that ugly part of the business to get to do what makes you happy?"

Ava sighed. "I thought I loved acting, but I'm not even sure of that anymore." Why was it so easy to blurt this stuff out to a stranger? She smiled at Gemma. "Enough about that. What about you?"

"I love my life. I'm truly blessed. I'm married to the greatest man in the world, we have the rugrats we both always wanted," she smiled softly, "and we get to raise them around family on the land we love."

Footsteps pounded across the wooden planks and a dark-haired girl and a younger dark-haired boy burst into the bunkhouse. "Mama, come on. Daddy's got the training bull out. Says he might need your help."

Gemma stood. "All right. Tell him I'll be right there. You comin' to watch Chase practice?"

"I'll be there in ten." Ava ditched her sweaty yoga clothes and slipped on a pair of jeans and a T-shirt. With her messenger-style camera bag, notebook, sunglasses and ball cap, she was good to go.

The wind blew like crazy, which lessened the sun's blistering rays. Chalky dust covered her shoes and clothing. She'd arrived in time to see Chase get whipped off a piece of equipment that resembled a gymnastics vault—except a gymnastics vault didn't spin and tilt.

Chase picked himself up off the thick gym mats.

"Five point nine," Cash called out. "Better. Go again?"

"Yep."

Ava moved next to Gemma and draped her arms over the top of the metal fence. "What's going on?"

"Cash is workin' Chase on the mechanical bull today. When a rider hasn't been on a bull for a few weeks, it helps to regain the movement and sense of balance."

"Is it like being on the real thing?"

"The guys talk about it bein' similar. Guess the machine is

smoother, even set on random intervals."

She watched as Chase used the rope wrapped around the center of the machine to hoist himself up. "Why is Chase wearing a vest, chaps and spurs just for practice?"

"Because the weight and constriction of clothing needs to be constant. If he gets used to practicing without, it'll change his balance and movement when he wears it during competition. They try to keep every practice session in line with the real thing."

When Cash yelled, "Ready?" Ava reached into her camera bag for her video camera.

But Gemma put her hand on Ava's arm. "No need to tape this. Just watch."

The mechanical beast jerked, spinning one way and abruptly switching course. The back end popped up. The front end lifted and slammed down. Chase's feet were flying; his left hand was straight up above his head. His body countered every movement. The next switch set Chase sailing onto the puffy mats.

Ava cringed. That had to hurt.

But Chase didn't lie there, moaning in pain. He was back on his feet, yelling at Cash for another go.

This went on for an hour until Cash insisted Chase take a break. They huddled in the corner, Cash gesturing wildly and Chase nodding his head.

"How did Cash get started training bull riders?" Ava asked Gemma.

"Cash rode bulls in the PRCA for twenty years. He never won a national championship, which is ironic because if he would've competed in the Indian Rodeo circuit, he probably could've had multiple championships."

"He wasn't tempted to switch circuits?"

Gemma shook her head. "He wanted to be judged on his bull ridin' ability alongside all other riders, not just those with the same skin color. Then Cash fell on some tough times and couldn't compete. After we got married, I encouraged him to share his expertise."

"So is he looking to turn your boys into champion bull riders?"

Gemma peeked at Ava over the tops of her sunglasses. "Over my dead body."

Ava laughed.

"I'm bringing sandwiches down for the guys in a bit. You want one?"

"Sure. I'll take mine on whole grain bread, with low-fat mayo, goat cheese and organic sliced turkey. And I'd like avocado, sprouts and cilantro on it too."

Gemma froze.

Ava burst into laughter. "Hah! Gotcha. Bet you thought I was showing my true Hollywood diva side?"

"Just for that, I'm making you peanut butter and jelly. And don't even ask me to cut off the crusts."

Chase had been scarce yesterday after tangling with the mechanical bull and helping Cash in the afternoon. Ava suspected he'd gone to bed early because his body hurt, but he claimed fatigue, not soreness, and she let it go.

Midmorning, Ava headed for the corral to start her duties as videographer and noticed more kids hanging on the rails. "So, Gemma, did you lock up your other kids in the woodshed yesterday?"

Gemma snickered. "These are Cash's grandkids. Thane—" she pointed to the older boy who looked about six, wearing a Colorado Rockies ball cap, "—and Parker." Parker wore a coonskin cap. Gemma whispered, "Parker is in his pioneer phase and refuses to take the hat off. It's about to drive his mother crazy. Which is probably why Macie sent the older kids along with their dad today." Gemma gestured to the chute across the way. "Their dad, Carter, is helpin' Cash load bulls."

"Carter," Ava repeated. "I think I met him at Kane and Ginger's wedding."

"Probably. He's married to Cash's daughter. He's also Chase's cousin."

"I'll never keep this all straight."

"Took me a while too. Don't know what the hell those women were thinkin' with all the C and K names in the McKay family." Ryder raced off and Gemma yelled, "Huh-uh, buddy boy. Get back here. Daddy doesn't want you by those bulls today."

"Aw, Mom, that's not fair."

"Tough. Stay by me or go in the house."

Ryder sighed. Kicked a clump of dirt and scaled the metal rails like a monkey.

"Looks like Chase's about to leave the chute. You ready?"

"All set." Ava's hat shaded the worst of the sun's glare.

A man inside the arena opened the gate. The bull erupted from the chute, all four hooves airborne. Chase's entire body jerked forward as the bull's front legs landed. Then the beast twisted its back end, trying to throw Chase off. Somehow he stayed on. But the bull's next spin sent Chase sailing into the air and he collided with the ground.

The neck strap caught the camera as Ava lurched forward, shocked at seeing Chase lying on the ground. Motionless. The gate opener was leading the bull out another gate, ignoring Chase completely. "Why isn't someone helping him?" She began to scale the metal corral.

"Hold on." Gemma tugged her back down, forcing Ava to meet her gaze. "You've never actually seen bull ridin', have you?"

"No! I thought it'd be like yesterday, with the mechanical thingy. Not like this. Not with him really getting hurt."

"Ava. Honey. Bull ridin' is an extremely dangerous sport. Bulls are highly unpredictable. There is no control factor. And these bulls that Chase is trying to ride? Real wild cards because most of them haven't been ridden. We have no idea how the bull is gonna react until it's tested out." Her worried eyes searched Ava's. "Chase knew that goin' into these stock trials. Didn't he tell you the dangers? What you might see?"

Ava shook her head.

"Didn't you watch any bull ridin' on TV before you agreed to tape him?"

"I saw a video on YouTube. But it's nothing like watching this live, with the horns and the hooves, and the sickening sound of his body smashing into the ground." Ava pressed her hand against her lower abdomen. "I...I don't have the stomach for this, Gemma."

"Sure you do."

"What if he gets hurt? Like really badly hurt?"

"That's a risk. That's also part of the appeal for men who do this for a livin'. You must understand that about Chase, Ava. This is who he is. Ridin' bulls is not only his job, but also his passion. He's reached the highest level of the sport and you don't get to that position without bein' a damn good athlete." She rubbed Ava's arm. "See? He's already up and goin' back for more."

As much as Ava didn't want to look, she couldn't help it. Sure enough, the fringe on Chase's chaps flapped as he hustled back to the chute.

The guy at the gate yelled, "I'm thinkin' that one's a keeper, Cash, if it threw boy wonder on his ass."

Male laughter echoed back.

"That's Colby," Gemma said. "Carter's older brother and Chase's cousin. He got here early this morning."

"Colby knows rodeo stock?"

Gemma nodded. "Cash and Colby competed on the same PRCA circuit for years. They quit around the same time, but the love of rodeo never really left them. They've been buying and breeding bucking bulls for a couple years. We're doing things pretty unconventionally regarding stock trials. Seemed a sign Chase needed help with his ridin' the same time Cash and Colby needed an experienced rider to test new bulls."

Male shouts competed with the loud clanks.

"That one's a chute fighter," Gemma offered. "Which is problematic. They'll let him fight until he settles down. But he could be too tired to buck and they won't have an accurate idea of his bucking ability. After Chase rides him today, they'll probably need a re-ride tomorrow to see how he performs. A bull that's a chute fighter is an extra danger to the rider. A lot of injuries happen before the gate opens."

"Does that thing he's wearing, a modified catcher's mask, prevent that?"

"Not all riders wear those protective helmets, but Cash makes them mandatory here."

More loud sounds of flesh hitting steel and male warning shouts.

"Is Chase on the bull right now?"

"God no. They're waitin' to see if the bull calms down." She pointed to the camera. "You oughta be getting this on tape."

Eventually the huge bull, an ugly two-toned yellowish white with splotches of brown, calmed down. Chase secured his hand, nodded to Colby. Once again, Chase didn't reach the eight-second mark before his ass met the dirt. A less forceful buck off than the last one, but the power when his body impacted into the ground had to rattle his bones and jostle his brain.

The idea of Chase constantly being subjected to skull fractures from a horn or a hoof to the head made bile rise in her throat. She bent down and retrieved the water bottle from her messenger bag. Sipping the lukewarm liquid slowly, half-afraid she'd toss her cookies, half-tempted to force herself to hurl so she had a valid excuse to leave.

Suck it up. You willingly signed on for this and you can't quit the first day.

Ella tugged on her pant leg. "Miss Ava? Will you play with the kitties with me?"

Sure, kid. Let's go right now.

Gemma squeezed Ella's shoulders. "Maybe later, sweets. Ava is taping Chase's rides so he can watch 'em tonight."

"'Kay." Ella raced to the old barn.

"How come she gets to go somewhere but I can't?" Ryder complained.

"Because she could care less about the bulls. You, my curious son, would be back there pullin' Chase's bull rope if you had the chance. Here we go."

Ava resituated the camera.

Come on, Chase. Ride this one.

The gate opened, the bull shot out like a rocket, zigging and zagging. Halfway across the arena, Chase bailed off, slipping sideways and landing on his hands and knees. Even from this distance she could see the hard set to his jaw, the stiff angle to his shoulders. He yelled, "Set 'em up again. A big one this time."

Gemma said, "You know, it'd help if we recorded the buck-off times."

"Good idea. There's a notebook in my bag."

Bull number five leapt out of the chute like a two thousand pound ballet dancer and Chase went flying like a trapeze artist from Cirque du Soleil. He rolled to his feet after he landed on his shoulder. Dust followed behind him, à la Pigpen from Peanuts as he moseyed to the fence. Ava snickered, until she zoomed in on Chase's pained face. He was hurt. But that wouldn't stop him.

How many more bulls would he get on today?

All of them, until he rode at least one.

Another hour passed. Then two. Chase stayed on bull number sixteen the full eight seconds. She didn't get caught up in the clapping and whistles from Gemma, the kids and the guys because she was too busy taping the triumphant look on Chase's face.

Did he quit after that?

No.

He climbed on three more bulls. Rode two of them. Bull number twenty was another chute fighter. By the time the bull settled down, she could hear Cash and Carter yelling at Chase to take a break. He shook his head, bounced around on the bull's back and nodded at Colby.

It was apparent how not ready Chase was when the bull turned sharply, kicking out his rear end so powerfully that the rope jerked from Chase's hand. Chase did a flip midair before he crashed into the corral.

But did the Man of Steel stay down, wallowing in pain? Nope. He staggered to his feet. Holding the metal fence rails for support, he limped across the dirt, waving off Colby's help as they disappeared into the barn.

"That'll do it for today," Gemma said. "You comin' up to the house to eat with us, Ava?"

"No. Thanks for asking, I'm sure it'll be great, but it takes awhile to edit this. I imagine Chase will want to look at the footage later, so I'd better get started on it."

As soon as Ava was inside the bunkhouse, she locked the door, shut the window, pulled the curtains and flopped on her bed. Blessedly cool. Blessedly dark.

The tears came before she could stop them.

And she wasn't exactly sure why she was crying. Wasn't like *she'd* gotten thrown around like a rag doll twenty times. Her occupation didn't lend itself to danger. Maybe she'd get a paper cut from script pages. Or possibly she'd burn her mouth on a cup of coffee. Or she might have an allergic reaction to makeup. But nothing remotely life-threatening.

Talk about being out of her element on so, so many levels.

She'd never dated professional athletes, so she hadn't ever

witnessed that mindset and mix of physical perfection and determination needed to push to the highest level. She witnessed that drive in Chase today. It scared her to death.

So did this desolate feeling stem from fear for Chase?

No. Hers was fear of the unknown.

Out here in the real world? People dealt with serious hazards every day. Hazards she never even considered in her tidy universe, where *out of sight, out of mind* wasn't just a saying but a way of life.

Ava let her gaze wander around the bunkhouse. She'd seen the wary way Gemma, Cash and even Chase had looked at her, expecting to see disgust on her face about the primitive accommodations. Right now, where she rested her head at night was the least of her concerns. For all her bold talk about experiencing real life, she didn't know if she could handle it.

And didn't that make her spoiled? She had the luxury of packing up her stuff and escaping if she so chose. These people didn't.

So what was the appeal to sustain this way of life? When it was comprised of backbreaking work, extreme temperatures, isolation and daily physical danger? There didn't appear to be monetary gain. Was it the satisfaction of besting the elements and the animals year after year?

The only way she'd glean the tiniest bit of understanding would be to stick it out. Figure it out. Maybe by doing that, she'd find her way. Because one thing she *had* figured out? She was more than a little lost in her own life, regardless of her physical location.

Her thoughts drifted back to her sleeplessness last night and her flash of understanding of how important it was for Chase to prove he could keep the "no sex" promise he'd made to himself. Who was she to try and change his mind? Just because she wanted to prove that she had the mad skills to keep a man sexually satisfied? Chase ought to fall into bed with her?

Talk about diva-ish expectations.

Needing to sort out her emotions, she snagged her notebook and flipped on the desk lamp. She scrawled random thoughts, suggestions, ideas. Gibberish mostly, but she finally felt a measure of control. She was being honest on the page, not writing snarkily, or trying to be hip, or funny, but being real.

Ava also realized she'd never really know Chase except on a superficial level unless she studied his obsession and profession from a different angle. Not from fear, but from curiosity. She turned on her computer and searched for Chase McKay's previous year's rides, creating a separate disk with those, so he could compare then and now.

Time got away from her as she edited, copied folders and burned a DVD, so the knock on the bunkhouse door startled her. Sweet Ella stood on the porch, bouncing with impatience. "You still wanna go see the kitties?"

She could use a mental break. "Sure."

They messed with the balls of fluff until Gemma called Ella for supper. When Ava returned to the bunkhouse, she noticed Chase was in the bathroom. Now was her chance to get the disks up to the house without running into him. She needed time to figure out how to deal with these conflicting feelings, whether the emotional price of ditching her normal life was worth it for the short term. She couldn't avoid him for long, but she intended to try.

Chapter Nine

As Chase dished up a helping of sausage and fried potatoes, Gemma said, "Ava dropped off the disks she made of your rides today. One of the disks has all your previous good rides in the PBR and your worst rides to compare against your rides today."

Chase's fork stopped halfway to his mouth. "She did? That's above and beyond."

"Maybe slo-mo can give an idea of what you're doin' differently," Colby said. "Something is off in your ridin', but I'll be damned if I could pinpoint exactly what it is."

"That's because there were too many things wrong to focus on just one," Cash said with a smile.

If Cash's kids hadn't been at the table, Chase would've flipped him off. Oh right. His arm hurt too fucking bad to even lift up. "I'm gonna blame some of my altered performance on the safety helmet."

"If you wanna train here, you have to wear it. The sooner you get used to it, the sooner we can get you back on track. Besides, you were havin' troubles long before the headgear switch."

Colby pointed at Chase with his butter knife. "I'm with Cash on this."

"So you'd wear the helmet without complaint to every performance if you were still on the road?"

"Yep."

Chase snorted. His big, macho cousin wouldn't have worn one. Period.

"My boys all wear helmets when they're competing at junior rodeo events. They don't know different since they've always worn safety equipment." Before Colby took a breath and continued his diatribe, his cell rang and he excused himself.

Chase pushed his food around on his plate. He was sore as hell, worse than he'd been in months. He didn't feel like eating. But that wouldn't sit well with Gemma, especially since Ava had bailed on supper.

Ryder chattered. Ella threw out random facts about cats. The youngest boy, Jansen, looked ready to fall asleep in his chair.

Gemma asked, "Everything all right?" after Colby returned to the table.

"Fine. Channing says it's so quiet in the house with all her boys gone she actually spooked herself."

That made Chase think of the first night they'd arrived and Ava's fear of unfamiliar noises. Seemed odd she'd be off by herself somewhere.

"I wish Gib and Braxton coulda come," Ryder complained.

Cash ruffled Ryder's hair. "You're full of complaints tonight, son. What's up?"

"It was boring standin' around today. I wanna help with the bulls tomorrow."

"No can do. But I'll tell ya what. I'll let you watch Chase's rides in a bit. After you get cleaned up."

"Aw, Dad. Do I hafta?"

"Yep," Cash said. "And you two," he pointed to Ella and Jans, "start makin' your way upstairs to the shower."

After the kids left, Colby sighed. "What is it about boys' bone-deep fear of soap and water? Drives my wife insane."

"I'll bet Princess Talia is sweet-smelling," Gemma teased. "I'll bet she's getting big too."

Colby's face lit up. He shifted to dig his wallet out of his back pocket and passed around a picture of his baby girl.

Since Chase hadn't seen the newest addition to Colby and Channing's family—hard to keep up with his prolific cousins' offspring—he dutifully checked out the dark-haired, blue-eyed child. Definitely a McKay.

"She's the most beautiful thing in the world. Takes after her mama," Colby said. "Even at six months the girl's already got her brothers wrapped around her pinkie."

"Sounds like she's taking after Keely," Chase said with a grin.

"Speaking of the latest McKay newlywed..." Gemma asked Colby, "How is the wild child?"

"Busy. Her business is good, and that's sayin' something in this economy. Our West cousins, Chet and Remy, started building her and Jack's house as soon as the ground thawed. Not that Jack or my cousins need my dad's input, but apparently he's over at the building site every day to make sure Keely is happy. Damn man still dotes on her."

"It's easy to do with daughters," Cash said. "No matter how old they get."

"I can't believe my folks took all four boys fishing. But it ain't like they're roughing it in Grandpa and Grandma's new RV, with air conditioning and satellite TV."

"At least if they're around a lake Carolyn can toss them in the water so she won't hafta put up with their stinky selves in a small space." Gemma stood. "You guys head on into the family room. I'll dish up cake after you're done watchin' the rides."

Chase tried not to wince as he rose to his feet. He plopped on the closest easy chair, but didn't relax, fearing his muscles would seize and he'd have to ask for help getting up.

Cash popped in the DVD. "Let's have a look-see."

The rides were painful to watch. Not because of the reminder of physical pain, but because it looked as if Chase McKay had never ridden a bull.

After they watched all the short test rides, Cash inserted the disk with Chase's winning rides, or at least the rides he'd managed to hang on for the full eight seconds.

He listened as Colby and Cash discussed everything, from the angle of his chin, to the height and position of his arm in the air, to his spurring technique, to his initial seat on the bull. Chase didn't comment, or defend, as he might've done in the past, but listened.

Then they started the disk from the beginning again.

Ryder raced in and dropped at Chase's feet. The kid didn't utter a peep; his focus was entirely on the successful rides. Cash switched out the disks to Chase's attempts today.

About bull fifteen, Ryder piped up. "Dad? Can I ask something? How come Chase's left shoulder is back? Not straight in line like the right one? It kinda hangs over his leg."

Chase looked at the kid and then at the TV. "Rewind that." Sure enough, Chase noticed the discrepancy immediately. "Can we go back and watch the disk where I actually rode some bulls?"

Cash swapped out the disks. Lo and behold, Chase's shoulders were straight.

Colby said, "I'll be damned. I don't think that's all of the problem, but it's a good place to start." He grinned at Ryder. "Gib'll be fit to be tied when I tell him your eagle eye caught that. He'll probably want us to start taping him so he can watch for mistakes in his ridin'."

"What mistakes?" Ryder scoffed. "Gib is gonna be world champion one day." He looked up at Chase with pure hero worship. "After you win the world title a coupla times."

"I sure hope so."

Colby pushed up from the floor. "How you feelin', cuz?"

Like dogshit. "Okay. Why?"

"I'd like to get you on that mechanical bull while this is fresh in my mind."

When Chase didn't respond, Cash said, "Unless you're too sore. We can do it in the mornin'."

Chase's gaze moved between the two men. They were sacrificing family time to help him out. He'd cowboy up no matter how goddamn bad he hurt. He withheld a wince as he eased out of the chair. "I'm game. Might need a shot or two of whisky afterward."

"I figure we all will."

Gemma leaned in the doorway. "So I should wait on the cake?"

"I'm thinkin' Ryder deserves the biggest piece for his help," Chase said.

She smiled at her beaming son. "I'll have a cowboy-sized slice ready when you get back."

Cash didn't ease Chase into the ride. He cranked it full blast. Colby wandered the perimeter of the mats. After Chase's fourth attempt, Colby walked closer to pat Chase's left thigh. "Turn your leg in and you'll stop leanin' back on this hip. If the hip is aligned, so will the shoulder."

He shifted to find the proper seat. "That feels weird."

"Good. Now make sure when you throw your left arm up that you don't change this alignment."

Chase raised his left arm. The mechanical bull kicked hard to the right and then spun to the left. Chase focused on keeping his upper body aligned. It worked. He bailed off after he heard the buzzer.

Both Cash and Colby grinned at him. But Cash whistled when Chase started to walk off the mats. "Huh-uh, McKay. One ride could be a fluke. I'll need at least two more."

"Sadistic bastard," Chase mumbled under his breath as he climbed back on.

Think. Align. Focus.

He ended up riding the next two. As sore as he was, as tired as he was, he couldn't wait to get on bulls tomorrow.

Back at the house, he shoveled in a piece of strawberry shortcake and knocked back a shot of whisky with Cash and Colby before returning to the bunkhouse. He took another shower, needing the hot water to dull the day's aches and pains.

Ava's door was closed and no light spilled from the window as he walked past her side of the bunkhouse.

He wanted to tell her about the breakthrough he'd had tonight. What did it say that she was the first person he'd thought of telling?

That you're still not focused on the main reason you're here.

When Chase lumbered into the bunkhouse, he saw Colby sitting on the bunk across from his.

Colby glanced up from poking buttons on his cell phone. "Hang on a sec, I gotta tell Cord I fucked up and forgot to check the drainage ditch on the east side of our folks place before I left."

Chase popped three aspirin and collapsed on his bed.

"How you holdin' up?" Colby asked and flipped off the light.

"Been better." He rearranged his pillow. "Did you ever hit a low spot when you were on tour?"

"Plenty of times. I can't believe I stuck with it for as long as I did. That lifestyle takes a toll on a man. But I loved it. The competing. The traveling. Hanging with the guys. The easy women." He chuckled. "If you'd asked me, I'da sworn the abundance of willing women was my number one reason for stayin' on the road."

Only a guy who'd been there could understand that appeal.

"But now? I suspect the reason I stuck it out was because I was waitin' for a woman who didn't want a rodeo cowboy, but me. Luckily I found her."

"Do you miss that life on the road?"

"At first. Then not at all."

Chase couldn't fathom that. "Really? So if you'd met Channing two years before you did, you'da gladly given up your wild rodeo ways to set up housekeeping with her?"

"I see your opinion on marriage ain't changed. I can't answer that, because as much as I'd planned to quit rodeoin' fulltime at summers end? My injury gave me no choice." His pause weighed heavily in the room. "Just curious about what your plans are if you aren't allowed back on tour. Or if you can't keep up the ridin' percentage to stay on tour. You considering the PRCA?"

"Seems I've had two choices in my life. Rodeo or ranch."

"Your payout from your percentage of the ranch sure gives you more than two choices now, Chase. What about that buddy of yours? The one who offered you a stake in a bull? Any interest in breeding stock?"

"No. I'll leave that to you and Cash." Chase sighed and stared at the bunk above him. "Alls I ever wanted to do was ride bulls. I've never looked beyond that."

"That's an easy mindset to fall into when you're young, on top, and believe you'll stay there forever."

"But?" Chase prompted.

"But bull ridin' isn't a forever occupation." Colby sighed. "Look, you've got enough on your mind right now. We're all damn proud of you."

If they were all so proud of him, why did he feel like such a disappointment? Or were they proud of him for the wrong reason? "Thanks, Colby, I appreciate the advice."

Chase was tired of Ava avoiding him. Especially when he had no idea if he'd done something to piss her off.

For the last two days she'd dutifully recorded his rides, made DVD

90

copies and handed them to Gemma every afternoon. But as far as a one-on-one conversation between them? Not once.

Maybe she's changed her mind about continuing this western adventure with you.

After supper, Chase tracked her down to the training paddock, her silhouette reflected as a shadow in the moonlit dirt below the mechanical bull.

Despite the ache from wrist to shoulder, Chase balanced on one arm and hopped the fence. When he stood in front of her, he said, "You gonna get in a little practice?"

She shrugged.

"Ava? You all right?"

"No."

"What's wrong? Are you hurt?"

Her gaze finally snapped to his. "Are you?"

"No, I'm—"

"Fine, right? Acting like it's no big deal you got thrown on your ass half a dozen times. Or that you got stomped on by a bull at least four of those times. Oh, and that's just *today.* That's not counting the first two days I watched. And taped. And wanted to..."

"Wanted to what?"

"Hide," she said softly.

"Why?"

"So I didn't have to watch you getting hurt over and over. Record you getting hurt over and over."

Chase wasn't expecting that. He climbed on the mechanical bull, so they faced each other, knee-to-knee with their legs draped over the sides. "All this fuss is about me? Really?"

Ava nodded, but still wouldn't look at him. "In my head I knew climbing on a bull was dangerous, but seeing it firsthand scared the living piss out of me, Chase McKay."

Such sweet honesty bowled him over.

"The last bull today that threw you into the gate? I was really glad you were wearing a helmet."

"Me too. I'm getting used to the damn thing. But I still got my bell rung pretty good."

"Were you scared?"

"To be honest, I don't remember."

"Don't brush my concerns aside, Chase. You almost—"

"Almost don't count in bull ridin', Hollywood. Staying on eight seconds is the only thing that does count."

"Watching you sometimes...? God. A couple rides seemed like eight hours."

Chase murmured, "Seems that way to me too sometimes."

Ava's eyes were filled with frustration. "Why do you do this?"

"Why do you walk onto a fake set and pretend to be somebody you're not?" he volleyed back.

"Not the same thing."

"Yes, it is. We both take risks in our jobs, they're just different types of risks. We're both professionals."

"But—"

"Ava. Stop." Even as Chase's conscience warned *No no no*, his body urged him closer with *Yes yes yes*. He slipped his hand around the back of her neck and angled his head until their lips were barely an inch apart. Kissing her jaw, her chin. Soft, teasing smooches. Dragging out the innocent kisses until the heat kicked in.

When Ava opened her mouth, and the warm flesh of her lips skimmed across his, he lost his mind. His intention to gift her with the most sensual kiss in the history of the world vanished.

Chase inhaled her, keeping her in place as he feasted on her mouth. When her hands inched up his arms, he made a low-pitched warning sound and her fingers curled into his biceps.

He drank in the taste of her. Feeding her hot kisses. Wet kisses. Sliding his tongue deeper to explore her mouth, then retreating to gently smooch her kiss-plumped lips.

During one of those tender, fleeting kisses, she murmured, "Chase?"

He recognized the question in her voice, it was the same one running through his mind: *What the hell are you doing?* Twining silky strands of her hair around his fingers, he rested his forehead to hers, breathing raggedly. "Dammit, Hollywood. I'm sorry."

"Are you really?"

"No."

They stayed like that for several blissful minutes, even when Chase knew he should pull away.

"Are you having second thoughts about hitting the rodeo trail with me? Especially since I just gave you the mother of all mixed signals by layin' a big, wet kiss on you?"

"My second thoughts had nothing to do with that." Ava pressed her lips to his. "Besides, one little kiss isn't gonna scare me off. You and me? We're friends. Pals. Buddies. Road warriors. Road dogs. We'll probably be prancing around each other naked by the time our adventure is up. Prancing around totally nude and we won't even bat an eyelash."

Not a snowball's chance in hell of that happening if Ava was nekkid. Chase tipped her face up to gaze into her eyes. "You'll be all right watching me compete?"

"I think so. It's gotten better."

"That's because my ass didn't hit the dirt as often," he said dryly.

Chase slid off the bull and held out his hand to help her down. "You comin' back to the bunkhouse?"

"In a bit. It's so beautiful here. Almost like I'm on a movie set and it isn't real. I want to drink it in."

"Not worried a mountain lion will sneak up behind you and carry you off?"

Was the wind playing tricks on him? Or did he hear her mutter, "I wish *you'd* sneak up behind me and carry me off."

Chase said, "Pardon?"

"I said I'll be fine. Good night, Sundance."

"Night, Hollywood."

Ava stretched out on the mechanical bull and stargazed. So peaceful. The profusion of stars reinforced that feeling of insignificance.

Seemed to be a theme in her life.

She'd almost told Chase she was leaving for LA as soon as possible. Ever since his breakthrough on the bulls, she'd been waiting for him to tell her, in that charming cowboy way, that he wouldn't need her help videotaping his rides. Maybe it was high schoolish that she'd intended to give him the brush off first.

But he hadn't rescinded his offer. Instead, he'd kissed her.

Had he ever kissed her.

Ava remembered how his hot breath drifted across her cheek. A non-kiss, a tease, but one that raised goose bumps down the entire left side of her body. She'd withheld a shiver, suspecting he'd take her reaction the wrong way.

And she might've succeeded in pretending his peck was just a friendly gesture if he hadn't kept inching those clever lips down her jawline. If he hadn't made that nearly imperceptible growling noise in the back of his throat. If he hadn't tenderly smooched the tip of her chin on his way to tenderly smooching her mouth. Once. Twice. The third kiss lingered. No hint of tongue, just a gentle press of lips on lips. Somehow his left hand had curled around her neck. Somehow, her hands ended up clamped onto his biceps.

Ava expected he'd keep the kiss slow and easy. So when Chase kissed the living shit out of her, she understood she didn't know this Chase at all. The Chase who trapped her face in his big hands. The Chase who ably slipped his tongue past her teeth and fried her circuits with a kiss that stirred something inside her she'd never felt with any man.

Lust with an edge of danger. Lust that had no boundaries.

Just as Ava was about to lose herself in the sensation of surrender, Chase broke the kiss.

And then he'd apologized.

So yeah, she'd had that girlish sense of glee when he admitted he wasn't sorry. She could work with that.

A clement breeze wafted over her. The warmth of the leather soaked into her back and she was lulled into total relaxation. She sighed and closed her eyes.

"Ava," he whispered, "Come on."

"What?" She scrambled up and looked at him.

"Scoot over." Using the stirrup, Chase vaulted onto the back of the mechanical bull.

Ava watched him get situated; it wasn't much different than when he readied himself to ride a real bull. He offered his hand and hauled her closer, laughing at her shriek of surprise as he draped her thighs over the top of his.

"I've been dying to do this," Chase murmured, and that sinful mouth lowered to her neck, bestowing hot, sucking kisses that set her blood on fire. His tongue traced her collarbone from her shoulder to her throat. "Put your hands on me, Ava."

Chase nearly purred when she thrust her hands through is hair. He nuzzled her cleavage while he unbuttoned her blouse and flicked open her bra so her breasts tumbled free. A low groan of male pleasure vibrated through her body as he sucked her nipples with single-minded devotion.

"So sexy." Chase scattered kisses up to her ear. "You ready to take a real risk?"

Head muzzy from his kisses, she mumbled, "Sure."

"Good. Hold on to me. I'm gonna turn the machine on slow."

"What? Oh no."

"Oh yes." The back end of mechanical bull lifted, sending Ava sliding forward. Her whole body tensed as her weight rested on Chase fully.

"See, that's why I'm on the bottom."

The bull spun to the left and she closed her eyes.

"Look at me."

Ava blinked at him. Then Chase's mouth was on hers. His hands were on her. His body moved with the rhythm of the bull, and he urged hers to do the same.

She fell into him, giving herself over to his gracefulness, his athleticism and his sensuality.

"That's it," he muttered against her lips. "Relax, baby, trust me."

The constant swoop of her stomach faded, mostly because Chase distracted her. And what sweet, hot distraction it was. His rough fingertips stroking the inside of her thighs. His blistering kisses. His sexy growl against her skin. The pressure of her clit pressing into the hard muscle of his abdomen with the bull's every downward drop.

His hot breath flowed over her ear, sending a shiver of anticipation through her when he whispered, "Are you wet for me, Ava Rose?"

"You kiss me once and I'm ready for you."

The bucking stopped. "Scoot back for a sec." Keeping his fiery blue eyes on hers, Chase unbuttoned his jeans, unzipped and pulled his cock out. He reached around to bring her back onto his lap. "You ride me. I'll ride the bull." He lifted her and all that male hardness filled her in one deep plunge.

After Chase turned the bull back on, he reconnected to the rhythm of sex. Feeling his muscles flow in accord with the machine brought another level of appreciation for his riding abilities.

The spinning apparatus added another dimension. When the bull slanted forward, she shifted her hips side to side, trying to create friction on her clit. Even as she impaled herself on Chase's cock fully, it wasn't enough.

"Chase. I'm close. I need..."

"I know baby. Me too." He stopped the bull at a steep angle. Kissing the upper swells of her breasts, he said, "Lie back."

When her spine met the hard surface, Chase hooked his feet in the stirrups and stood. His hands slid beneath her butt, raising her so he could thrust into her hard. His gaze winged between her face and the way her breasts bounced with his every thrust.

"Touch yourself," he panted. "I wanna watch you get yourself off."

Ava covered her mound with her hand, scissoring her index and middle finger over her clit, before sliding down to where Chase's cock plunged in and out, performing the same motion.

His molten eyes snared hers. "Teasin' me?"

She shook her head. "The second I touch my clit I'll come."

"Do it."

She dragged her middle finger up the wet seam of her sex. Once she reached her clit, she rubbed up and down and quickly unraveled. Blood pulsed beneath the pad of her stroking finger, tightening her pussy muscles around Chase's cock.

He whispered her name, and thrust powerfully, staying buried inside her on the last stroke as he came.

Then Chase angled forward, remaining imbedded in her body, trapping her hand between them, placing his forearms by her head as he kissed her. A kiss unlike any other.

Ava felt weightless. Boneless. Dizzy. Buzzed.

Buzz, buzz, buzz.

She batted away the annoying insect but it kept buzzing around her head. *Go away. I'm basking in afterglow.* She swatted one more time and her hand connected with a solid object.

Her eyes flew open.

Stars twinkled above her. She was still stretched out on the mechanical bull. But she was alone. No heat and stickiness between her thighs. No weight of Chase's body on hers as he kissed her sweetly in the aftermath of zealous lovemaking.

It'd just been a damn dream.

The truth was, she knew that for at least the next two weeks, the only place she'd get down and dirty with him was in her dreams.

Chapter Ten

Ava checked the guard on the electric clippers. Better to leave it a little long than trim it too short. She bent down, letting the ends of his dark hair tickle her cheek as her lips grazed his ear. "You ready?"

Chase released a shudder and she smiled. He wasn't the only one who could send mixed signals.

Standing above him, she wedged his knees between her thighs as she wrapped the fingers of her left hand around his jaw. Keeping his head at the proper angle, Ava warned, "Hold still," and clicked on the clippers.

The first strip of hair to go was dead center, front to back. Then she moved to tackle the right side and finished with the left side. She brushed the hair from his shoulders, wishing some had landed on his arms, giving her an excuse to feel those bulging biceps. "Have a look."

He stood and meandered to the mirror. Ava watched him smooth his hand over his scalp. "Wow. That looks different, huh?"

"Ever worn your hair that short?"

"Nope." Chase slanted this way and that.

"Is it good? Or bad?"

"Good, I guess." Chase's vivid blue eyes met hers in the mirror. "What do you think?"

I think cutting off your gorgeous black locks just increased your hotness by a factor of ten million.

"I like it."

He mugged in the mirror. "I like it, but I think I wanna go just a hair shorter—ha-ha."

"Fine. Stop admiring your handsome self and sit so we can get this done."

He plopped back on the chair.

Ava straddled his legs and held his head in place. The second trim didn't take as long as the first. She shaved the hair on the back of his neck. Her hands took one last lingering sweep over his shorn hair, down his beautiful face, to his broad shoulders. She scooted back. "You look good with short hair, Chase."

"Thanks. Do I look recognizable?"

"The goatee helps."

He snagged the broom from her. "I'll finish up. We need to get on the road so I can make my check-in time."

"How far is it?"

"Four hours."

Once they were cruising down the blacktop, Ava cranked her window open for fresh air. "Where are we going?"

"A one-night rodeo in Broken Bow, Nebraska. Then we'll hit smaller rodeos within driving distance during the week. Next Thursday, Friday and Saturday we'll be in Scottsbluff, Nebraska. At some point I'm thinking we'll head to Cody, Wyoming. Their rodeo is set up differently. During tourist season, they have a new slate every night, and hand out a new purse every night."

"What kind of purse? Because I'd like to win a purse."

Chase laughed. Hard.

"What's so funny?"

"You. In rodeo, *purse* means the amount of money paid out to the winners." He laughed again. "Ain't like a purse you can buy on Ro-day-o Drive in LA."

"You are getting a huge kick out of me being such a neophyte."

"Check you out, using fancy words to confuse a simple cowboy. What's a neophyte?"

"Someone who's inexperienced in a certain area."

"You mean a greenhorn. Or a tenderfoot."

"Of course you'd prefer old Western terms."

"As long as we're on the subject, we need to get a few things straight about this road trip. Traveling partners split the expenses fifty-fifty. The goal is to get to the next event as cheaply and quickly as possible. Sometimes that means no time to check into a motel and clean up, especially if the events are geographically spread out."

"Was it my imagination, or did you emphasize *cheaply*?"

Chase grinned. "Glad to hear you picked up on that. We ain't gonna be staying anyplace as fancy as the Cooper hotel chain."

"I sorta figured," she said dryly.

"Is that gonna be a problem?"

"Why would it be?"

"Because, Hollywood, you're rich."

"So?" Ava said a little abruptly.

"So your idea of roughin' it and mine are likely polar opposites." Chase took his eyes off the road and peered at her over the top of his sunglasses. "I ain't askin' this to be a nosy dick, but have you ever tried to live on a budget?"

She'd had no reason to. "What does that have to do with anything? I can pay my half of the traveling expenses, no problem."

"In cash? We ain't using credit cards at all on this trip. We're both supposed to be under the radar. Heck, we're even using fake names."

"Give me some credit, Chase. I actually know how not to leave a credit card trail."

"But that still doesn't tell me if you've ever made a budget and stuck to it? Do you know what it's like to be completely out of money?"

Ava fought a shudder at the very idea of being out of money permanently. "No."

"Didn't think so. How much cash do you have on you right now?"

"I don't want to discuss money with you," she snipped.

"Tough shit. How much?"

She debated on telling the truth, or lying and stealthily lining her pockets with cash from an ATM during their next stop.

Chase eased onto the shoulder. "Dump your purse and count out the money in your wallet."

"Why do we have to do this right now?"

He offered her a wolflike smile. "Because I don't think you'll play fair."

Ava gasped with total sarcasm. "You callin' me a liar or a cheat, McKay?"

"Both, I reckon." He patted the bench seat. "Lay it on me, baby."

I'd like to lay something on you—my lips, my hands, my whole body.

Friends, Ava, remember? Friends, buddies, pals. Focus.

Hiding her superior look because she had planned for using only cash, Ava unsnapped the billfold portion of her wallet. She counted out seventeen hundred dollars and dug in her purse, finding another two hundred dollars worth of crumpled and folded bills.

Chase took out his wallet and counted out twenty-one hundred dollars, then reached in the glove compartment, coming up with five hundred more.

Holy crap. He had more money than she did. Not fair. "Can we stop at a cash machine so we're even?"

He shook his head. "We'll never be even. Remember I hafta pay contestant entry fees outta that."

"But if you win...you'll have more money."

"I'm not keeping anything I earn. Don't know what I'll do with it yet." He shoved his money back in his wallet. "So I gotta know, Hollywood. You up to the challenge of living like those of us who don't have an easily replenished pile of cash?"

"If I say no?"

"Then I'll know you ain't serious about wanting to experience something real, 'cause living on a budget is as real as it gets for most people."

Ava understood why Chase was pushing her. Didn't mean she appreciated it, but if she said no, everything would end before it began. What was she out? Wasn't like the temptation for gourmet dining would be an issue. Or boutique shopping for designer originals. Or forking over big bucks for a mani-pedi at an exclusive spa. Or buying pricey cocktails at trendy nightclubs.

"Ava?"

She met his challenging gaze head-on. "I'm in."

"Now the real adventure begins." After gifting her with his dazzling smile, he returned to the highway.

She dozed off at some point. After she woke, to the sound of crunching sunflower seeds, she asked, "You'll be okay to ride with as sore as you've been the last couple days?"

"Ain't as bad as it was. I'll be stiff no matter what I do, so I might as well try making the buzzer."

"What's the entry fee?"

"Sixty-five bucks."

"Do you want me to drop you off so I can find a hotel?"

"Yep. But it needs to be under a hundred bucks a night."

Ava started humming the music from *Mission Impossible* and Chase laughed.

"Since you're dropping me off, you'll have to park in public parking since I won't have a contestant tag yet."

"They have a separate area for contestants?"

He nodded. "Timed-event competitors take their horses and horse trailers take up a shitload of parking space. The competitors who travel with their family have campers."

"Sounds like the contestant area is one traveling party town."

"You'd be right. When I first started competing and I didn't have a nickel to my name, I'd drag an old tent along. Some of the stuff I saw people doin'...gave me quite the sexual education at the tender age of sixteen."

"Give me the juicy details so I'm not shocked by what I see."

Chase smirked. "Shocked. Right. I bet you've seen wild stuff in wacky Cal-y-forn-i-ay, so the countrified version will probably seem tame."

"Still not an answer, Sundance."

He drummed his fingers on the steering wheel. "I went to the first overnight event by myself 'cause my buddy Jet couldn't get time off from work. I set up my pup tent. Had a couple of pilfered beers in my cooler, feeling like I was hot shit, right? So I'm sitting in my lawn chair, watching the goin's on around the campground after the event ended. I hear a noise and creep around my tent to see two guys and a girl at the picnic shelter. They're having a good time. One guy and a girl are clearly a couple 'cause they can't keep their hands off each other. I start to back away when the *other* guy grabs the girl and kisses her. I'm thinking his buddy is gonna punch his lights out for touchin' his girl, but he yanks the girl's top down.

"The chick starts rubbing herself all over both of them. The guy behind her lifts up her skirt and shoves his hand between her thighs. I see his arm moving and I wondered what he was doing to make her squirm like that. She starts moaning real loud and the guy behind her turns her head to the side and kisses her to keep her quiet."

Chase's retelling of the story was making Ava squirmy.

"I figure they're all done. Except this chick dropped to her knees. At sixteen, I knew what that meant even when I hadn't found a girl willing to...ah, perform that particular act on me yet. I thought she'd blow one guy at a time while the other one watched. But no, she worked them both at the *same* time. Switching back and forth. And I was shocked that they were moving, fucking her mouth, not standing there letting her do the work. Then the guys take a half a step back and jack off on her tits. I'd never seen anything like it live and in person."

Ava rested her shoulders against the door, surprised by his honesty. "Did it turn you on, Chase?"

"Mad me hard as a fuckin' brick."

"What did you do?"

His cheeks bloomed a charming shade of pink and he smiled guiltily. "I jacked off right there. 'Course, afterward I sorta felt like a pervert. But it didn't stop me from checking out the picnic shelter the next night to see if they'd come back."

She laughed. "So how did seeing that affect you, other than making you horny?"

"I wanted that type of experience for myself."

"I assume you got to experience that, or something like it?"

"Yep. Eventually."

That's when he clammed up. Ava waited a couple of minutes before she said, "Come on, Chase. We're friends. Friends share stuff like this all the time."

"Not me."

"Not even with your brothers?"

"Nope. So can we drop it?"

"No way." Ava put her hands in the middle of the bench seat. "To show you this friends sharing thing isn't one-sided, you tell me the rest of the story and I'll tell you a story about me."

"Christ." He lifted his ball cap off his head and yanked it back down. "Is this the way the trip is gonna be? You nagging me?"

"Nagging? Really?"

"Bad word choice. What I meant is, are you gonna keep pestering me to blab personal shit that no one else on the planet knows about me?"

"Yes, Chase, it's really too fucking bad that I want to get to know you on more than a superficial level, because God knows I don't have enough of those fake friendships and relationships in my life."

"Ava—"

"I know it's harder for you to be my *friend*—to trust me, to talk to me honestly—than it would be if you just jumped my bones and fucked my brains out. But you're the one who set the friendship parameters, not me. And friends talk."

"Can we please just fucking drop it?"

"Not a chance." She crossed her arms over her chest. "Who isn't being real now? You're expecting me to change and yet you don't have to?"

"Didja ever think I don't wanna put myself in a bad light in front of you?"

Such a self-protective macho man. Chase was so different from the sensitive West Coast guys who constantly shared every emotion, every thought, every bad and good deed. He was more of a loner than she'd first suspected. He held himself at arm's length—a trait she recognized because she was the same. To get to the real Chase, she'd have to lay herself bare for him. The very thought caused her pulse to skip, but she'd do it.

"Great. First you wouldn't shut up and now you're giving me the silent treatment?"

"No. I'm trying to find a way to convince you to trust me. That whatever bad light you shine on yourself, I plan to do the same."

Silence.

Ava watched the mile markers go by. After they'd passed the fourth one, Chase spoke.

"I wanted that type of experience, hell, any type of sexual experience, but I knew..." He puffed out a breath. "Look, truth is I was a short, scrawny, sixteen-year-old kid. I hadn't added any height to my frame in over a year. Trust me. I measured every week. And every week I came up lacking. You've met my brothers. And my cousins." He reached for his water bottle in the cup holder and took a long drink. "More than one person asked me if I'd been adopted by the McKays because I sure didn't 'measure up' to them. Probably thought they were bein' funny, and I didn't have the life experience to give 'em what for.

"The first summer I started sneaking off to rodeos, I figured out I needed weight training. Not only to build my strength as a bull rider, but to change my physical appearance. I convinced myself if I was muscle bound, then maybe girls wouldn't care so much that I'm short."

Ava's stomach muscles knotted at his admission, but she didn't speak.

"In addition to ranch work, I lifted weights and added daily cardio. The change to my body came pretty fast. No steroids, in case you're wondering. By the following summer, I'd bulked up and was no longer a skinny teenage boy. After the physical transformation...well, I finally had my pick of the ladies. So I've kept up a weight training regimen for the past twelve years, half afraid if I don't, I'll revert to that ninety-pound weakling sitting in the shadows with my cock in my hand, just watching."

Knowing he needed a moment before she responded, she dug out a protein bar and offered him half, surprised when he took it. Maybe he thought it was a peace offering.

"No comments?" he said lightly.

"You took charge of your body because you wanted to. And it changed your life. That's admirable. I can't say the same. I let other people's perceptions and expectations change mine." She leaned across the seat. But this time she cupped her breasts. "These? Not real."

Chase's eyes wandered over her cleavage and up her face. "Seriously?"

"Seriously. I had a boob job two months after I turned nineteen. Wanna feel them?"

His mouth dropped open. "What? No."

"Sure you do." Ava snatched his hand and curled it around her left breast, holding it in place. "Because I know you're a tit guy."

"Jesus Christ, Ava, what the fuck are you doin'?"

"I'm providing a visual aid with my show and tell." When he attempted to move his hand back, she circled his wrist with her other hand. "I'm not trying to turn this into something sexual. I'm showing you what I gave up in order to have the perfect Hollywood body and a rack that makes men weep with want."

"What did you give up?" he asked hoarsely.

"I have very little sensation in my breasts. I went from flat-chested to busty in three hours and as soon as the incisions healed, I went out on casting calls."

"Did the ah...enhancement work?"

"Yes. I got the first role I auditioned for. And the second. But by the third cattle call, I realized I looked like everybody else. We were clones. Interchangeable. Blonde hair, big boobs, tanned, toned bodies, collagen lips. The only differences were our eye colors, but that could be changed too." Ava gently removed his hand.

"Your parents...?"

She closed her eyes. "My parents were appalled I'd 'maimed'

myself. It was awful. Not having their support hurt me so I lashed out, reminding them it was my body, my choice, my life, all that crap. We had limited contact for almost a year. That's not the worst part."

"Hey. Ava darlin', look at me. Talk to me."

Ava looked at him. "The first time I ended up in bed with a guy after receiving my new gigantic breasts? I felt nothing when he touched me."

"Could it've been operator error?"

She actually laughed and saw his quick smile. "I'd hoped...until the same thing happened with the next guy to come along. And the next guy. Stimulation by my own hand or a lover's hand rarely does anything for me. So I just..." An honest to God blush heated her cheeks because she'd never admitted that to anyone.

"Come on, *friend*. Don't hold out on me now."

"Well, I *am* an actress. I learned to fake my response when guys went crazy over my tits." She scowled. "Wasn't something I had to worry about with Jake. The fact he wasn't enamored with my chest should've been a tip-off."

Chase grinned. "Yep. Them shoes and him not bein' all over you twenty-four/seven were clues you missed." He reached over and traced the outline of her jaw. "Sad to say, most of the women I've been with over the years are interchangeable and unmemorable, so I know clones. And you, Ava Rose Cooper Dumond, are not a clone. Not even fuckin' close."

That was one of the sweetest, most heartfelt compliments she'd ever received. "Thank you."

He refocused on his driving. "We're about ten miles outside town."

"Do I go to the contestant area and they'll let me back there to find you?"

Chase shook his head. "The contestant area is for contestants only. They're strict about it and have security guards to keep non-authorized people out."

"So how am I supposed to get close ups of your rides?"

"Doesn't your video camera have a zoom?"

"Yes, but the footage will be better if I'm closer." She really couldn't believe there wasn't some way around the security rule. "No one gets back there?"

"Authorized people. Stock contractors. Event coordinators. The media."

That gave Ava an idea. Might take a few days to execute, so she said nothing.

Chase seemed distracted and didn't speak until they parked at the main entrance to the fairgrounds. "Hang out at the grounds and I'll find you when the rodeo ends." He grabbed his equipment bag from behind the seat. "Will you be all right driving around here?"

Ava snatched the keys from him. "I'm from LA, remember?" She squeezed his biceps. "Be careful tonight, Sundance."

"Always. See you later."

Chapter Eleven

Chase repositioned his equipment bag, trying not to smack into bystanders as he made his way to the registration table. The long line indicated he'd found the right place.

He automatically lifted his hand to adjust his cowboy hat, a nervous habit he'd had his entire life, but his fingertip connected with the curved bill of his ball cap, not his Stetson.

Everything about being here felt damn weird. He glanced around. Looked like the chutes were well maintained. The spectator stands were covered to keep out the worst of the midday heat and the occasional cloudburst. A brand new electronic scoreboard anchored one end. All in all, a nice county rodeo.

The line moved ahead a few feet. When Chase reached for his duffel bag, something struck him in the left shoulder. He glanced up sharply to see the young kid in front of him, backing away, a look of alarm on his face.

"Sorry. I lost my grip and it slid down... I didn't m-mean to..."

Christ. The kid was barely eighteen and looked scared Chase was going to beat the crap out of him. Chase shrugged. "No big deal. I'm still standing." He thrust out his hand. "Bill Chase."

The kid dropped his equipment bag so quickly it missed Chase's foot by barely an inch. "I'm Ryan, Ryan Ackerman."

"Well, Ryan, Ryan Ackerman, what event are you competing in?"

Ryan's face lit up like a firecracker. "Bull ridin'."

"Yeah? Me too."

"I'm official and everything." Ryan fumbled for his wallet in his back pocket and whipped out a PRCA card.

Chase took it, checking the date. The card still smelled of new plastic, as it was only a week old. "Congrats are in order."

"Thanks. I'm really excited to be here."

No lie. The kid fairly bounced from boot to boot. Chase grinned. "You have been on a bull before, right?"

He nodded. "I was on the high school rodeo team. Ended up fourth in the county semifinals, but third place is the cutoff for finals so I didn't get to go to state."

"You're here now, that's all that matters."

The line moved and Ryan kept a firmer grip on his bag even as he turned around to talk to Chase. "How long you been ridin' bulls?"

"Officially? About eleven years. Off and on. Off, mostly lately. I decided to hit rodeos this summer to try and get back on track."

Ryan's gaze briefly dropped to Chase's belt buckle, which was the fastest way to figure out if you were in the presence of a champion. But it wasn't like Chase could wear his Man of Steel belt buckle at these events, so he'd opted for just a plain belt and buckle.

"That's what I'm trying to do too. In between when I'm working construction for my mom's boyfriend."

"A man's gotta make a livin'. So is your mom here, watching your debut?"

He shook his head. "She's workin' this weekend."

Ryan was at the head of the line. He showed his PRCA pro card, and when the lady said, "That'll be sixty-five dollars," Ryan opened his wallet and froze.

Chase stealthily peered around the kid's arm. He held two twenties, a five and four singles.

Ryan stammered. The woman manning the registration was sympathetic, but Chase knew she wouldn't let the kid compete without paying the entry fee. Chase took a twenty out of his pocket and let it fall on the ground. Then he tapped Ryan on the shoulder. "Is everything all right?"

When Ryan turned, Chase noticed the kid's face was fire-engine red. "Ah, sorry, we're just tryin'—"

"I think something fell outta your pocket when you took out your wallet."

Relief swept over Ryan's face when he saw the twenty dollars behind his equipment bag. "Gosh. Thanks. I thought I had enough."

"No problem." Tickled Chase to no end to see Ryan's excitement when the lady handed him his contestant number.

Ryan grinned at Chase. "Nice meetin' you."

"See you behind the chutes." Chase handed over his PRCA card and entry cash to the secretary.

"Ma'am. Is there a section reserved for family?"

"Yep. Section F, first six rows. Seating is first come, first serve."

"Thanks. I'll let her know."

"Good luck."

He glanced at his cell phone. Two hours before the performance started. He texted Ava the family section info and cut around the contestant entrance. Normally he loved being behind the chutes trash talking with the other riders. But he feared he'd give too much of himself away, so he opted to stretch out, warm up and get his head in the game by finding a remote corner by the pens.

As team roping started, Chase paced along the back fence until he heard a noise that sounded like...retching. He turned the corner and found the rookie, bent over, hands on his knees.

And Chase thought he was nervous? Poor kid. He'd been there. He leaned against the rail and waited until Ryan pushed himself upright. With his pasty-white complexion, the kid resembled a zombie. Chase didn't say anything, merely handed him a bottle of water.

Ryan slumped next to him. Took a drink, swished it around in his mouth and spat it out. "Thanks, man."

"No problem."

"Did you ever...?"

"Barf before I rode? Yep. 'Course, I always told myself it was from something bad I ate or drank and definitely not from bein' scared shitless."

That earned Chase a wan smile.

"It's normal. In fact, I'd think you were abnormal if you weren't shaking in your boots."

"Yeah?"

"Uh-huh. But the trick is to use that fear and control it, not let it control you. Make sense?"

Ryan nodded.

"What number you ridin' tonight?"

"Fourteen."

"I'm ridin' sixteen. If you want, I can help pull your rope."

"You'd do that?" Ryan asked with total surprise.

"Ain't like we're competing against each other. We're tryin' to best a bull, and in my mind, that puts us on the same side."

"You're right, I guess."

Chase nudged him with his shoulder, or tried to, but the kid was a solid six inches taller than him. "I'm always right. Now come on, let's get ready to ride us some bulls."

Barrel racing ended. Most competitors were behind the scene, willing to lend a hand to whoever needed it. Chase watched as three of the first eight riders covered their bull. Then three more.

The kid was quick getting his hand in position and a wrap. An older guy stayed to help and released his hold on Ryan's vest when the kid nodded his hatted head.

The gate opened and they were off. First thing Chase noticed:

Ryan wasn't spurring much, but he remained on the bull, matching his upper body movements to every jerk and twist. When the buzzer sounded, Chase whooped and hollered with the rest of the riders.

The score boomed over the loudspeaker. "How about a ride of seventy-eight for the PRCA debut of this Nebraska cowboy?"

Not a bad score for a rookie. Not bad at all.

Chase wandered down to his chute and performed a couple of stretches before he secured his headgear. Funny thing was, for as much as he'd initially bitched about wearing the helmet during the training with Cash, he'd gotten used to it.

"Here. Lemme hold it for you," Ryan said. Once he was set, Chase slipped in the mouth guard and ran through his final mental checklist.

Good seat. Check.

Hips parallel. Check.

Chin up, arm up. Check and check.

Ready to rock and roll.

Chase nodded at the gate man.

They exploded from the chute, dirt flying. Chase didn't hear the crowd. He kept his focus on adjusting to each minute maneuver the bull made, and somehow, everything clicked into place.

The bull wasn't a jumper, but a spinner. Or so Chase thought until the animal nearly went vertical. But he gritted his teeth and held on until the buzzer sounded. As soon as he jerked his hand free, he sailed off and whipped off his helmet, squinting at the scoreboard. Nothing yet. The bullfighter jogged over with his bull rope and high-fived him.

Finally, as he reached the side gate, he heard, "Folks, we have a new leader. Let's hear it for an eighty-one point ride from Wyoming's Bill Chase, on the rank bull, Gnarly Dude, brought to you by Jackson Stock Contracting."

Chase waved to the crowd and disappeared into the contestant's area, switching out his helmet for his battered ball cap. He leaned against the railing to catch his breath. To replay the ride while it was fresh in his mind.

Isn't that Ava's job as a videographer? To provide you with instant replay?

Ava. He hadn't thought about her in hours. So when someone poked him in the chest hard, three times, he half-expected he'd look up into those stunning aquamarine eyes of hers.

No such luck. Ryan jammed his finger in Chase's sternum twice more. The kid looked furious. Before Chase could speak, Ryan bit off, "I need to talk to you. In private. Right now." He stomped over to the corner by the empty pens.

Chase followed. "What's up?"

Ryan loomed over him. "I've wanted to be a bull rider since I was

109

nine years old. So like any kid who discovered a dream, I became obsessed. I watched every bull-riding event on TV. Including spending the last five years studying the riders." His voice dropped to a fierce whisper. "Did you really think no one would recognize your ridin' style, *Chase McKay*?"

Shit.

"I've studied your form more than any other rider, including the reigning champs. You're like my hero...and instead of bein' happy I finally get to meet you, I'm pissed off that you're running around here lying to folks. Are you doing this for kicks? You don't get enough adoration ridin' in the big league and bein' on TV every week?"

Chase tamped down the immediate flare of temper. "I understand why you're upset. But if you truly know my percentages and how I ride, then you also know how bad I've been sucking it up. Not just in the last few months, but in the last year. I've had a boatload of distractions. Made some piss-poor choices that affected my ability to concentrate." He sent Ryan a questioning glance. "When was my last good ride?"

"Besides winning the championship at Man of Steel last year?" Ryan scratched the tip of his chin. "I'd have to say Tacoma. On Bad Reputation. You covered all your bulls, and if not for that single low score of eighty, you woulda won."

"But I didn't win. It's been a struggle. Almost like I forgot how to ride a goddamn bull. You have no idea how frustrating it's been for me." Chase blew out a slow breath. "Look, it's not my intention to trick anyone. I just wanna get on as many bulls as I can. So I'm asking you, Ryan. Please don't turn me in. My entire career depends on no one knowin' it's me."

"Sheesh. I ain't gonna snitch on ya." He sighed. Dug the toe of his boot in the dirt. "I can't imagine what it'd be like, bein' you but having to pretend you're someone else. Someone average. Someone less successful. Don't it feel weird?"

"A little. But mostly it feels good to ride."

"You looked better than you have in a long time."

"Thanks. Think anyone else recognized my ridin'?"

"Maybe. Most folks will chalk up the similarities to coincidence, kinda like I did at first. 'Cause no one would ever believe Chase McKay would be competing in a PRCA rodeo in Broken Bow, Nebraska."

Chase chuckled. "True. That's why I'm keeping a low profile around other riders and with the public."

"That'll be hard to do since you won," Ryan said.

The officials herded them back into the arena for the winners' presentation.

The older guy who helped Ryan in the chute said, "Great ride, kid." He offered his hand to Chase. "Taz Lashlee."

"Good to meet you, Taz."

"I ain't seen you around the circuit."

"Been off doin' other stuff. Thought I'd give it a go again." Chase folded his arms over his chest. "Sorry I missed your ride."

"I was last out. So I covered my bull. Not pretty, like you done, but I'm good with finishing third."

"How long you been rodeoin'?"

Taz's smile was missing a few teeth, which wasn't unusual in the world of rough stock riders. "Longer than is smart, that's for damn sure. I got a whole lotta try in me for bein' so long in the tooth." He grinned again.

"Taz also rides bareback," Ryan inserted. "And he's being modest. He's made it to the world finals three times. Twice in bareback and once in bull riding."

"That's awesome, Taz. Congrats," Chase said. "Where's home for you?"

"Here and there. I spend most my time on the road. Seen a lot of this great country. Met a lot of fine folks."

Then Chase understood. Taz was part of a dying breed, men so obsessed with rodeo they'd given up anything resembling a normal life. The lure of a championship buckle proved too strong, and like an addict, Taz couldn't separate himself from his fix of possible rodeo glory. Being a rodeo cowboy was all he knew. All he wanted to know. Chase remembered being at an event with Colby, and the late night conversation at the campground about old timers competing on the circuit. Both Colby and his traveling partner, Trevor Glanzer, swore they'd quit before they gave their entire lives up to the sport.

Being a new competitor at the time, Chase hadn't understood ever giving up the thrill of riding. But the longer Chase stayed in the business, the clearer his future became. He never wanted to be that guy—the grizzled fifty- or sixty-something rodeo dog—living out of his truck, with nothing to show for his life except aches and pains and stories about life on the road.

So how many more good years did he have left? What would he do with his life? His future?

"Got awful quiet there," Taz said. "You okay?"

Chase offered him a smile. "Yeah. I just realized I've gotta meet someone."

"A female someone?" Taz asked, elbowing Ryan and winking lewdly.

"As a matter of fact, yes. Nice meeting you guys."

"You gonna be ridin' around here again?"

"I'll be outta Nebraska until the two day event in Scottsbluff next weekend."

Ryan's face lit up. "Awesome! We'll be there too."

"See ya then." Chase snagged his equipment bag and exited the contestant area. He'd no more than cleared the gate when three women surrounded him. The old Chase would've smiled charmingly, flirted outrageously, made plans with one or all of the buxom buckle bunnies. The new Chase kept his head down after the "Nice ride, cowboy" comments, and sidestepped them.

But the determined ladies followed him, chattering like crows, apparently not caring that he had someplace else to be. He looked up to see how far he was from the stands and saw her.

Ava.

Christ, she took his breath away.

Chase had about three seconds before the lovely Ava launched herself at him. He wrapped her in his arms and squeezed.

"What a great ride! You were amazing. You looked totally in control."

He released her, but snuck in a quick peck on the mouth before he met her gaze. "You liked seeing me in control, huh?"

A soft blush stole across her cheeks. "I taped it, but the angle wasn't that great, so I don't know how it turned out."

"I'm sure it'll be great." That's when Chase noticed the hostility flowing from the buckle bunnies. He tugged Ava to his side before addressing the trio behind him. "Ladies. Have a great evening." Then he led Ava away, stopping beneath the stands.

Ava pushed him against the concrete wall and got right in his face. "It's always like that for you? Doesn't matter if I shaved you bald, you grew an ugly-ass ZZ Top beard and dressed like Charlie Brown, women of all ages would still line up for a shot at you, wouldn't they?"

Unsure how to answer, he squirmed.

Her eyes searched his.

"What?"

"And you kissed me again. Out of the blue."

Closing his eyes, Chase let his head fall back against the wall. "You caught that, huh." *Great response, McKay, especially when you have no excuse.*

Then Ava's warm, soft lips pressed against his. He bit back a groan. Fought the urge to spin her around, pin her to the wall and kiss her until they couldn't see straight.

She eased back and Chase opened his eyes.

Ava smirked. "Be warned. If you steal a kiss, so will I. Anything you do to me? I'll do right back to you."

Goddamn, she was hell on his good intentions. "Then no more kissing."

Something like resignation flitted through her eyes. "We're back on the road early tomorrow?"

"Yep. We've got one-nighters for the next week."

"Sounds like you're back in familiar territory."

Chase stopped and stared at her. "Was that a shot at me?"

She lightly punched him in the arm. "Friends give each other shit all the time. Suck it up, cowboy. Let's get you fed so you're not so cranky."

Chapter Twelve

An afternoon rodeo allowed the rare night off. He'd just slipped on his last clean pair of Cinch jeans, when two knocks preceded Ava opening the door and waltzing into the bathroom. Damn good thing he hadn't been standing around in his skin.

"Hey, Chase, oh, sorry..."

She didn't look particularly sorry as she stared at his chest. Before he backed off to grab his shirt, Ava traced a fresh bruise on the bottom curve of his rib cage. His skin beaded beneath her tender touch.

"Is this the only bruise you got today?" she asked softly.

"I guess. I didn't really look."

"So it doesn't hurt?"

"Nope."

Her beautiful, skeptical eyes connected with his.

Chase covered her hand with his on his stomach. "I'm not bein' a tough guy to impress you, Ava. I get the shit beat outta me by bulls on a weekly basis, so I've usually got pain one place or another." He stepped back. "You hungry?"

"Yes, and please tell me you've got a real restaurant in mind and not just a stop at the Qwickie Mart for more sunflower seeds and licorice."

He grinned. "There's a glimpse of that snooty California girl, but as a matter of fact, I've heard about this supper club called Steak'n a Claim."

"What, pray tell, is a supper club?"

"You eat on one side and there's entertainment and a bar on the other side. Something you'd be interested in?"

"Aren't you afraid we'll be recognized?"

He probably deserved that, since he'd purposely made them keep a low profile this first week on the road. "If you don't wanna go, Hollywood, just say so."

Ava rose to her three-inch height advantage and crowded him. "I just asked a question, McKay, so don't get snippy."

"Men don't get snippy. Men get pissy."

She poked him in the chest. "Fine. Don't get pissy."

"Fine. So is that a yes or a no?"

"Yes. What am I supposed to wear?"

Her long legs were encased in tight jeans. She wore a fluttery top with silver and blue swirls that reminded him of the ocean. "You look great right now."

Ava rolled her eyes. "I don't have a bit of makeup on, my hair is in a clip and I'm wearing flip-flops."

"You're tryin' *not* to call attention to yourself, remember? You get all fancied up, looking like the Hollywood star you are, and we'll draw more notice." He pushed up on his toes and kissed her forehead. "Besides, you don't need none of that junk anyway. You always look beautiful."

"Such sweet bullshit," she mimicked. "How soon before you're ready to leave?"

"As soon as I get my boots on."

"I'll change shoes too."

Chase shoved his wallet in his back pocket, and maybe for the first time he'd gone out with a woman, he hadn't double-checked his condom supply.

The place was jam-packed and they scored the last table. Pretty basic menu. Several different cuts and sizes of steak. Fried chicken. Pasta. Seafood. The house specialty was the chicken-fried buffalo steak, served with mashed potatoes, gravy and a cold broccoli salad.

"It all looks good. I'm too starved to pick one thing."

"Trust me to order for you?" Chase asked.

Ava folded her menu and set her elbows on the table. "Please."

The waitress dropped off two glasses of peach iced tea and Chase dumped in three packets of sugar.

"This is a cool place."

"Pretty standard for a small Midwestern town. I try to find joints like this rather than eating at another chain restaurant when I'm on the road."

She mumbled something as her focus followed someone's movements across the room.

"See someone you know?" he teased.

"I see someone I'd *like* to know," Ava purred. "Some fine, fine specimens of cowboy in here."

Jealousy had Chase cranking his head to check out which man had caught her eye. "Where?"

"Never mind. He's gone."

"Maybe you'll get lucky and run into him next door at the bar." Jesus. What the hell had possessed him to say that? He glanced up to see Ava looking at him skeptically. He said, "What?"

"I realize we're just friends, Sundance, but you have no problem with me slow dancing with another guy? Right in front of you?"

Chase hoped his shrug came across nonchalant.

"What if the sexual chemistry was off the charts and I wanted to go home with him?"

The thought of some random guy touching her in all the ways Chase imagined touching her made his teeth clench and his eyeballs pulse. He ripped open two more packets of sugar and angrily dumped them in his tea, violently stirring the liquid.

"That much sugar isn't good for you."

"Neither is an STD you might pick up from some loser bar rat."

"Really? Chase'n Tail McKay is going there with me?"

He glanced up. "No. Sorry. Obviously I can't tell you what to do, besides warning not to bring some strange dude back to the hotel room."

"I don't want to argue with you, but I'm not gonna lie either. While this road trip is fulfilling some of my needs, it's not fulfilling them all."

I can fulfill your every need and then some.

When Ava leaned across the table, Chase could see so far down her shirt he swore he caught a glimpse of nipple.

"I haven't had sex in four months, Chase. I didn't realize how much I missed something until I haven't had it. It's like my brain is on a continual loop—imagining rough hands stroking my skin, craving sweet and lazy kisses, or hot and hard kisses, needing an intense body-to-body connection."

"What exactly are you tryin' to do to me here?" he half-growled, hating—and loving—that she'd put such graphic images in his head.

"What? We're friends. I'm sharing my frustrations with you." Ava blinked innocently. "Oh wow. Sorry. For a second I forgot that you are captain of the USS Abstinence... Well, anyway, your lack-of-sex situation is self-imposed, mine is not. And I don't think I should have to suffer for your choice."

The food arrived. Chase watched Ava devour every bite, and tried to ignore the happy little humming moans that reminded him of sex.

Hell, everything about her made him think of sex.

Ava shoved aside her empty plate. "You're right. It'll be fun to hang out at the bar for a little while."

Yippee. He was such an idiot. Now he'd spend the rest of the night watching her entice the local yokels.

"Excuse me?"

They both glanced at the young woman at the end of the table.

"This might sound strange, but me'n my friends we were wondering if you are..."

Chase braced himself. Here it was. He should've known better than to show up in public place, even a rural dive, with the radiant Ava Cooper.

"Sure, I'd be happy to take your picture," Ava said pulling Chase from his worrisome thoughts. "Isn't it great that her friends took her out to celebrate her birthday?" Ava prompted Chase.

Hugely relieved, he offered the birthday girl a genuine smile. "While you're taking pics, I'll pay the bill." Grabbing the check, he stood and tossed a ten on the table for a tip.

Ava rose from the table. Even with the two inches his dress boots added to his height, Ava towered over him by five inches. She bent forward slightly and put her mouth by his ear. "Fess up, cowboy. You were worried one of us had been recognized."

Her hot breath sent a tingle straight to his dick. Resisting temptation of turning his head and pressing a kiss at the base of her neck, he sidestepped her. "See ya over there."

Chase secured a high-topped table in the middle of the room with both the bar and the dance floor in view. One thing he'd noticed over the years; patrons in small town bars were a diverse mix of people. Old-timers mingled with the younger set. No one was trying to act hip, cool or aloof. Or wear trendy clothes, although single ladies had done themselves up in tight clothes and rhinestones for a night on the town.

He purposely sought out places like this, as a reminder real cowboy country existed. Where small town values, hard work and integrity were as prized as a college degree. Where boots, jeans and hats were worn for both everyday and formal attire. Where no one looked at you funny for ordering cheap beer because most folks were on a budget. Where your neighbor would make sure you got home safely if you imbibed a little too much.

Would Ava see that? Understand it? Find it quaint? Or rural?

Ava slid next to him with a husky, "Hi."

"Hey. What would you like to drink?"

"I don't know. I'll wander up to the bar and see what they've got."

He lifted a brow. "You sure you're goin' to the bar to look for a...drink?"

"Yes. But it wouldn't hurt to check out my other options."

"Ain't a lot of options. It's a slow night."

"So you've been screening me for me?" she asked doubtfully.

"A guy checking out other guys in a joint like this will get your ass thrown outta here faster than you can say 'Brokeback', trust me."

Ava laughed.

He loved to hear her laugh. So sweetly melodic and yet completely unaffected.

The cocktail waitress stopped and Ava conferred with her in low tones before she ordered.

"What'd you decide on?"

A secretive smile bloomed and then she focused her attention elsewhere. "See that guy in the red plaid shirt? To your left? What do you think of him?"

"Him? Seriously? He's too old for you." Chase let his gaze wander, acting like he was playing along with the find-Ava-a-fuck-buddy game, when in all likelihood, he'd fuck up any man who laid a hand on her. "What about the dude in the bright blue shirt?"

"Eww. He's got a ZZ Top beard. And I think there's food in it."

"You don't like beards?"

"Only on Abraham Lincoln, Van Gogh and the aforementioned little 'ol band from Texas."

"You coulda told me you hate the goatee I'm growin'," he said a little shortly.

She reached over and tenderly stroked the bristly hair. "I didn't say that. I like it. Your lips are perfectly framed and look so kissable. I wondered if it'd be soft or scratchy."

Chase didn't move. Hell, he didn't breathe as her fingers repeatedly smoothed over his face, his whole face, not just the part with excess hair.

"I can't believe how much it's filled in. God. How many times a day do you have to shave?"

"When I'm on tour? Usually twice. Can't stand how razor stubble feels on my face."

"I'd like to feel your razor stubble on my face," she murmured.

Maybe she hadn't meant to say that out loud.

Or maybe she had.

The cocktail waitress floated a napkin on the table and placed a lowball glass in the center. "Took the bartender a minute to figure out how to make this." She grinned. "Don't get a lot of requests for that drink in here."

When Ava opened her purse to pay, Chase put his hand over hers. He pulled money from his front shirt pocket and dropped it on the tray.

Ava didn't speak until the waitress left. "I can buy my own drinks, Chase."

"I know you can. You can also open your own door and pay for your supper, but that ain't happening tonight, so deal with it."

Surprisingly, she didn't argue. She took a healthy sip of her drink and said, "Wow. That's good."

"What is it?"

"Tie me to the bed and fuck me."

Chase choked on his beer. Choked hard enough Ava had to pat

him on the back. "What the hell did you just ask me to do to you?"

"I didn't ask you to do anything to me, because I knew you'd say no. The name of my drink is called *Tie me to the bed and fuck me*."

His eyes narrowed. "Bullshit."

She held up her hand in Scout's honor pose. "It was the drink du jour at my friend Bella's bachelorette party. And if you don't believe me, ask the waitress."

Right. Ava just wanted to hear him say that drink name out loud. In a honky-tonk bar. Not a chance.

They watched the dancers for three songs. Ava leaned closer. "See that older couple with matching blue shirts?" He nodded. "How long you think they've been together?"

"Probably their whole adult lives. Why?"

She released a wistful sigh. "They're beautiful. So in tune with each other. I can't imagine what it'd be like to have that solid connection every day. I wish I had my video camera so I could capture their happiness."

Maybe Ava did understand more than he credited her.

"By the way, when are you planning to teach me to two-step?"

"I'm not."

"Do you dance?"

"Yep."

She frowned. "But you don't want to dance with me?"

"Drop it, Ava."

Of course she didn't. "I'll only put up with so much high-handed behavior, and you're pissing me off. Answer the question. Why don't you want to dance with me?"

"Because I'm short," he snapped.

About twenty seconds passed before she was in his face. "That's it? *That's* your reason for not dancing with me? Here's where I tell you that is not a valid reason. That's a sucky reason."

"It's a valid reason to *me*. Christ, Ava, you're a good three inches taller than me when you're not wearing them three-inch fuck-me heels. I will not make a goddamn spectacle of myself with you towering over me like I'm some kinda midget, getting my jollies burying my face in your chest, no matter how much the latter appeals to me." Dammit. Not a good time to spout that confession. "You wanna talk about drawing attention to us? Trust me, that'd do it."

"Chase. I didn't mean—"

"You're gorgeous and perfect and a California goddess, okay? You never have to deal with the 'less than' issues the rest of us mere mortals do."

"That's not fair."

He drank, refusing to get sucked into this with her.

119

"So if I wore flats and you wore the heeled boots you've got on now? Then would you dance with me?"

"Why you all fired up to dance with me, Hollywood?"

Ava opened her mouth. Closed it. "I like to dance. Dancing with my girlfriends at the clubs in LA isn't like close dancing with a man. I just thought it might be fun. Guess I was wrong." And she was gone.

Way to be a dickhead.

As Chase was formulating charming apologies, a female voice said, "Hey, I know you."

The woman was probably mid-thirties. Teased and sprayed blonde hair. Heavy glittery makeup. A low-cut tight T-shirt that outlined hard nipples. His first thought? She was a clone. Interchangeable with ninety percent of the women he'd been with in the last decade. Heck, he might've actually been with her. And didn't that make him the worst kind of man-whore? Chase shook his head. "Sorry. You've confused me with someone else."

Her mouth, thickly coated with frosty pink lipstick, curved into a smile and she rested her tits on the table. "I know my rodeo cowboys. Bull riders are my specialty. Even a hottie like you can't hide out in Pine Bluff, Wyoming without expecting fans to recognize you. You're Chase McKay."

Dammit. Chase took a drink to wet his suddenly dry mouth.

"Don't worry, lover, your secret is safe with me."

"What secret?" Ava cooed, possessively sliding her hand across his shoulders. "Sorry I was gone so long, baby. What'd I miss?"

He grinned at hearing Ava's precisely mimicked honey-smooth Southern drawl. "Nothin'. A case of mistaken identity."

"I am not mistaken," the woman retorted. "You are Chase McKay, the PBR bull rider, right?"

Ava tittered, "Oh, honey, I wish he was. This is just my boring old Bill. Who is such a Mr. Grumpy Pants tonight."

Mr. Grumpy Pants? What the fuck?

Tipping his hat back slightly, Ava kissed him four times, each kiss a little longer. "We've only got the sitter for another hour, Billy boy. What do you say we head out to the truck? I know what'll put a smile on my baby daddy's face."

The woman said, "Sorry, my mistake," and hustled away.

Ava's eyes lit with triumph. "If you want to pull this off, we'd better go right now. And for Godsake, act like you can't wait to get me naked and fuck me."

Chastised and yet turned on, Chase stood, keeping Ava's arm draped over his shoulder. Gritting his teeth against the stares about their height differences, he curled his arm around her waist and directed her outside.

After he'd climbed inside the truck cab, Ava said, "Are you still a

Mr. Grumpy Pants?"

He groaned. "Christ. Seriously? Did you have to call me Mr. Grumpy Pants?"

"I had to set the scene. Besides, it worked, didn't it?"

"Yeah."

"Well, one good thing came from her flashing her tits at you and me running interference to protect your virtue."

"What's that?"

"It kept me from asking you if the big chip on your shoulder about being a short man weighs you down when you're riding a bull as much as it does the rest of the time."

Ouch. Direct hit.

"Then again, I might've just said 'thank you for a great dinner' and left you to brood while I trolled the excellent selection of Wrangler butts. Not that I got to do that either, since I was too busy saving you from yet another one of your adoring female fans."

"Look, I'm sorry—"

"Save it." Ava yawned and turned away, giving him the cold shoulder he deserved.

Chapter Thirteen

Ava had a great time with Chase last night at the supper club despite his refusal to dance with her. It hadn't occurred to her the outwardly confident bull rider would be self-conscious of his height, or lack thereof. She loomed over many of the men she worked with. And Chase was so damn good-looking, so muscular, so charming, he seemed larger than life.

Probably a smart call on his part, keeping them from being plastered body to body as they swayed on the dance floor. Ava had behaved herself, following his friendly lead, even playing along when he'd started picking out potential conquests for her. But it quickly became apparent that no man in the joint held a candle to Chase McKay. It also became apparent that women who wanted the eye-catching cowboy were not cowed by the fact Chase was out with her. No wonder he could bed a different woman every night if the ladies constantly subjected him to come-ons. What red-blooded man wouldn't take every kinky thing that was freely offered?

Except he's not taking anything from you after you've offered. Several times. In several ways.

Like she needed that reminder. She was no different from any other woman; she regularly suffered from self-confidence issues, body issues, dating issues. People assumed that since she had a high profile career and a supposedly glamorous life she'd have hordes of men vying for her company. But the opposite held true; she rarely got asked out on a date. Maybe invites to dinner weren't issued because men were afraid she'd turn them down flatly and cruelly. Maybe men assumed she'd already have exciting plans with other celebrities. Maybe men were scared off by her bank account. Maybe men thought she was stupid because she hadn't finished college. Maybe men associated her with the man-eating character she played on TV. Maybe her real personality was too weird. Maybe her real personality was too abrasive. Or worse, maybe she didn't have a personality at all.

Wow. Insecure much?

Problem was... once those self-doubts surfaced, they multiplied. Maybe men were leery of becoming tabloid fodder if they publicly dated her. Maybe men were sick of big-boobed blondes. Maybe she should lose ten pounds, buy a whole new slutty wardrobe and then she'd have men falling at her feet.

Maybe you can wave your magic wand from the prop department and generate world peace. This negativity and second-guessing is not helping. You've never needed a man's approval to feel secure or to define you on any level—personally or professionally.

That wasn't true. She'd managed to fake that self-assured air so many of her peers owned—at least when it came to her career. But she failed miserably when it came to presenting the *I'm-so-hot-don't-you-want-me-baby?* attitude around men. Give her a script and she could act brash and sexy. Not so easy in the real world.

Sad thing was? Even the small scrap of relationship confidence she'd gained after being Jake's girlfriend had vanished after the tabloid story broke. For those months she'd been half a couple, she'd felt good about herself, knowing a beautiful, desirable man like Jake was attracted to her. Didn't that make her beautiful and desirable too? Which afterward, sort of made her feel pathetic, that she'd needed validation badly enough she overlooked the warning signs in their relationship. Before Jake had entered the picture, she'd sworn to herself she'd step out of Hollywood and find a man who wasn't in the entertainment industry. Like most single women she was mortified at the idea of asking her parents for a fix-up. So she'd been *this close* to signing up for a private dating service. She'd spent way too many weekend nights alone in her pajamas watching TV, eating ice cream straight out of the carton. Wouldn't that make a great tabloid headline? *Actress Ava Cooper—why are Ben & Jerry the only men in her life?*

Dammit. For the first time in years Ava felt totally comfortable being herself around a man she was wildly attracted to. Yes, she'd been fun and flirty, sexy even, but it didn't feel like acting. She'd taken a chance and shown Chase the real Ava. He hadn't run away calling her a freak, yet he'd still relegated her to the "friend zone" probably permanently. She could tell herself over and over that his refusal to become her lover was nothing personal, but that broken, feminine part inside of her took it very personally. Problem was, she didn't know what to do about it. Did she move on to another man in hopes he'd burn up the sheets with her? That idea held little appeal for her now, even when many of the cowboys she'd crossed paths with had made it very clear they'd love to take her for a ride.

Wanting what you can't have will only make this trip miserable. And this trip isn't only about getting down and dirty with Chase McKay.

Also true. Disgusted with herself for wallowing, she focused on the task at hand for today—finding a motel within their budget.

Chase wandered to check out the contractor's rough stock.

Ava wasn't content texting him; she called. "Hey, I found us a room. I actually comparison shopped. This place isn't as nice as the first one I checked out, but it does have free Wi-Fi."

It amused the hell out of him that she sounded so damn proud of herself. "It's less than a hundred bucks?"

"Of course. Be nice if you had a little faith in me, Sundance. Anyway. I'm starved. I'll probably try to find something healthy before I head to the rodeo grounds. Did you want me to pick you something up?"

"If it's healthy? Hell no. I noticed a couple of tempting treats as I wandered past the vendor stands."

"We are talking about *food* treats, right?" she said sharply.

"Be nice if you had a little faith in me, Hollywood," he shot back.

"Trusting lot, aren't we?"

"Goes with the territory for both of us."

"This goes with the territory as well. Please, please be careful tonight, Chase. Promise me."

Touched by her genuine concern, he said gruffly, "I promise."

"Good. And I expect you to share your idea of a tempting treat with me after the rodeo ends."

No way could he confess she was the most tempting thing in his life right now. Imagining her beautiful form stretched out nekkid on his bed as he worshipped every millimeter of her body. With his hands. His mouth. His tongue. At least twice.

"Chase? You still there?"

"Just thinking about the treat I'm gonna offer you."

"Can you give me a hint?"

"It's long and hard and filled with sweet white cream."

Ava sighed dreamily. "Am I perverted for admitting I can't wait to wrap my lips around it and taste it?"

He chuckled, even as he inwardly groaned at the sexy mental image she provided. "Are you in for a big surprise. See you later."

"You do realize you're supposed to stay on the bull a full eight seconds and not hop off at six point nine," Ava said after he'd cleared the contestant's area.

"Funny." Chase tried not to limp, but he'd taken a real ass buster. "It sucks I can't go behind the chutes."

"So you've said. After every performance," he said dryly. "You're shit outta luck unless you can miraculously prove you're a stock contractor, a promoter or a member of the media."

Ava stopped and looked at him. Her eyes narrowed. "Have you been snooping on my computer?"

Why the hell would she ask that? "No."

"Have you even looked at any of the rides I emailed to you?"

Probably not wise to admit he'd fallen behind watching the rides she'd so painstakingly taped. But he was riding a hundred times better than just two weeks ago. He carried enough rodeo superstition that he feared watching it might jinx his run of good luck. So he deflected. "Come on, sweet thang. It's time for that treat I promised you." He towed her to a food booth by the carnival grounds. "We'll take two fried Twinkies."

"That is not what I was expecting from your description, Sundance."

"I gathered that, Hollywood." Chase paid and handed Ava the stick, warning, "Careful. It's hot."

"Maybe I'll just blow on it a little." She held the phallic-shaped object close to her pursed lips.

This was a bad idea.

"Or, maybe it'd be better if I sucked on just the very tip. That's always the best part." She opened her mouth and those lush pink lips enclosed the end. Her cheeks hollowed as she sucked and emitted throaty groans of satisfaction.

Then she licked all the way around the head. The tip. No, the top of the Twinkie.

Dammit. Chase could not tear his eyes away from her avid mouth, nipping teeth and flashing tongue.

"Oops. I'd better be careful not to let that sweet, hot cream explode and coat my lips before I have a chance to swallow it all."

This was fucking torture and she knew it.

Keeping her eyes on his, Ava opened her mouth and the entire Twinkie disappeared inside.

Holy fuck. She was deep throating it.

Then she slowly, sensually, slid it back out, a little at a time. She licked her lips. "Mmm. You were right. This is delicious."

Chase had to turn away when she noisily started sucking again. He was hard as a fucking post just from watching her. He counted to one hundred before he chanced a look at her.

Mistake. She'd eaten down to the middle of the Twinkie and she'd dip her tongue inside before licking the outside rim. Her eyes danced with pure mischief. "Something wrong with your Twinkie, Chase?"

Time for a little payback. "Not at all. Just waiting for it to cool down. See, my favorite part is the warm, juicy center. I like to taste it slow, licking from bottom to top a few times before I bury my tongue deep."

She froze.

Chase held up his Twinkie and traced it from top to bottom with the tip of his index finger, creating a small crack in the batter. Then he spread the two sections apart, bent his head and licked straight up the slit and back down. Three times. Stopping at the center to suck with gusto. He lifted his mouth and growled, "God I love this. Love having my face covered with stickiness. Love to feel that sweetness sliding down my throat."

Ava drew in a sharp breath.

"So warm. So soft. So tasty." He locked his gaze to hers as he lapped up every bit of the filling.

Oh yeah. With the way her body shifted from side to side, look who was all hot and bothered now. "You all right? You stopped eating."

"Umm. I'm full." She walked to the garbage and tossed away the last half of her Twinkie.

Chase ate the rest of his quickly because he really did love the damn things.

When Ava sauntered back to him, his eyes zeroed in on a white dot by her mouth.

"You're staring at me. Do I have something on my face?"

"Yeah. You missed a spot."

Ava rubbed her fingers across her lips.

"Come here. I'll get it." Chase should've used his thumb to wipe it clean. But some primal instinct urged him to use his mouth. He curled his hand around the side of her face, letting his tongue follow the bottom arc of her lip. He nibbled at the corner of her smile, tasting the sweet cream filling and the sweetness of her mouth.

This woman turned him inside out. Everything about her tempted him in ways he'd never been tempted.

They stayed like that for several long moments, neither willing to break the tenuous connection.

"Thanks," Ava said softly. "It would've been embarrassing to walk around with a white spot on my face."

He murmured, "Especially when we both know what it looked like."

"Think people would've checked to see if I had dirty knees too?"

"Probably discreetly. Then they'd be checking me out to see if I was wearing a big ol' grin."

"But you probably wouldn't have been so eager to lick that spot away if it was...?"

Seen-it-all, done-it-all, kinky California chick couldn't even say the words? Interesting. Chase whispered, "Would I lick my come from your mouth after you finished blowing me? In a fuckin' heartbeat. I'd love to taste myself on your tongue, Ava. It'd be hot as hell."

Her breath caught.

"I shouldn't have said that. I didn't mean—"

"Don't lie to me and tell me you didn't mean it," she sniped, "when I know damn well you did."

Enough. This had gotten way out of hand. He stepped back. "Look. We're both tired. A little punchy. Let's just forget it and head to the motel."

Chapter Fourteen

Ava parked in front of the orange door of room 116 at the Westward Ho Motor Inn. Schlepping her duffel bag, Chase's bag and her assorted electronic bags made her long for a bellhop.

Inside the clean, small room, she picked the bed by the wall just to be ornery, because she knew Chase didn't like sleeping by the window. Which served him right. He'd been standoffish the last day, insisting she leave him at the Scottsbluff rodeo grounds, even when no official bull riding events were scheduled.

She flopped on the bed, turned on her computer and messed with the mockup websites for an hour before she called Hannah.

"If it isn't Wyoming's newest cowgirl," Hannah said drolly.

"Hah! The joke is on you. I'm not in Wyoming."

"Where are you?"

"Nebraska."

"That's actually worse because I'm from Nebraska. Anyway, you calling to rub it in you've gotten laid by a smokin'-hot cowboy or two?"

"I wish. The sex part of my summer vacation hasn't happened." Yet. "I'm calling because I need you to do something for me. Something that might be...well, not illegal per se, but a little on the shady side."

"And what's that?"

"I need you to make me a couple of press passes."

"Okay. I'll bite. What for?"

"So I can get access to the rodeo contestant area to videotape bull rides. It's manned by security, but media is allowed. So I thought, Hannah deals with media passes all the time, she'd know exactly how to fake a couple of good ones."

Hannah sighed. "Ava. I love you, but I'm not going to jail for you."

"Jail schmail. Seriously, this will be a piece of cake. Alls I need is the name of the magazine, my picture and my name laminated on an official badge."

"And no one will check to make sure you're legit?" she asked skeptically.

"Of course they will. Are you by a computer? Sorry. Stupid question. Go to *Faces of Rodeo* dot com."

"I'm there. What is it?"

"A new magazine I created," she said with pride.

"Seriously, Ava, this is your brainchild?" Computer keys clicked in the background. "The *Check back for more details* on the main page is vague."

"Which is perfect for my purposes. Anyone who checks it—and me—will believe this is a brand-spanking-new magazine, still working on a web presence. Ooh, now go to *Behind the Chutes* dot com."

"Why do you need two fake magazines? Why not just one?"

"So I have options."

"You're scaring me. You did all this?"

"Yep. Thank God for cheap, quick and easy websites."

"*Behind the Chutes*—all the news and current standings of the stars of the PRCA. Now that is a great magazine tagline."

"Thank you." Filled with nervous energy, Ava hopped off the bed. "So what do you say? Can you get these made up this afternoon and Fed Ex them to me by tomorrow?"

"I should say no, but I haven't heard you this excited about anything in a long time. What name are you using for these? Ava Dumond?"

Ava paced to the window and peeked out the curtain. "No. How about just initials? A.R. Dumond. I'll take a picture and email it to you. You can use it for both IDs." She picked up the guest services guide and rattled off the address. "I know this is last minute, but I really need to have these in hand by tomorrow, because we won't be staying anyplace this long for at least another week."

"Who's 'we'?"

As much as Ava trusted Hannah, she hedged on divulging Chase's identity. "A bull rider. He's showing me the sights in exchange for me taping his rides."

"Ava." Hannah heaved an exasperated sigh. "Did you hit your head or something? You're never this trusting. How can you be sure this dude isn't taking you for a ride as a smooth-talking con artist?"

"Because he's related to Ginger's husband. I'm being careful. And I'm having fun."

"Fine, but I'd appreciate you keeping in contact with me."

"I will. Oh, and one other thing? Can you grab three pairs of jeans out of my closet and send those too?"

"Why don't you just buy new ones?" When Ava didn't answer right away, Hannah demanded, "What the hell is going on, Ava?"

"He put me on a budget, okay? I only brought two pairs of jeans and I'm conserving cash because I have to kick in for food and gas and other traveling expenses."

"Wait. This...bull rider put you, the heiress who lives the high life, the shopaholic who doesn't bother checking price tags...on a strict budget?"

Damn embarrassing to admit. She bit off, "Yes." Hannah laughed so hard that Ava was tempted to hang up on her.

Hannah regained control, managing to only let a few giggles escape. "Oh man, Ava, I like this guy already."

"Why? Because he won't let me spend any money?"

"No, because it sounds like he's a taskmaster, and God knows, you need someone to teach you restraint."

Ava would like it entirely too much if Chase would restrain her. "I'd appreciate it if you'd keep this to yourself."

"Now I'm insulted."

"Sorry. I know I can trust you. You're about the only one I do trust. And not just because you work for me."

"I'd stay on the line just to hear you groveling, but I have press credentials to fake."

"Thanks. I'll owe you one."

The following morning Ava decided the next time she saw Chase she'd cluck at him, because he was being a chickenshit. He'd gotten up early again because he was obviously avoiding her.

She took advantage of the time alone and rolled out her yoga mat, sliding into her morning workout routine—a mix of yoga, Pilates and kickboxing. Maintaining a daily workout was the one thing she did for herself no matter what.

Ava showered and dressed. She scrutinized her face in the mirror, cursing the fluorescent lights. Bridget, her facial consultant would throw a hissy fit when Ava returned to LA, because she hadn't followed through with her normal skincare routine. But there was something freeing in applying the minimum amount of makeup and being oblivious to the size of her pores.

She sat cross-legged on the bed and checked her personal email. Not much. Ava waited for a feeling of homesickness to wash over her, but it never came.

What did that mean?

Two knocks sounded on the door.

She peered out the peephole. A FedEx guy. She opened the door and signed off on the packages. She ripped into the box first, unrolling three pairs of jeans and shoving them in her duffel. Two laminated press passes, complete with different colored lanyards, tumbled out from the cardboard envelope. Ava grinned. "Hannah. You're a genius."

"ID," the man blocking access to the contestant entrance demanded.

Ava gave the beefy cowboy a once-over after handing him the *Faces of Rodeo* media badge.

The guy squinted at her. "Never heard of this magazine."

"It's new. First issue won't hit the stands until November," she lied cheerfully. "We're still working on the website. Check us out if you have a chance."

"I'll do that." He jerked his chin toward the gate in a "go on" motion.

Ava kept her cool rather than doing a fist pump. Once she was among the mix of contestants, she wished she'd asked Chase specifics about where to go. She noticed an older gent with a steno pad jotting notes as his interview subject yammered. A cameraman from a TV news crew had set up in the closest corner, taking the best spot. She marched over anyway. There was room for two.

"Hey. Great night for a rodeo, huh?"

The guy rolled his eyes and returned to fiddling with his camera.

So much for Midwestern friendliness.

Ava draped the strap of her video camera over a fence rail and held the Nikon. She'd intended to only snap a few pictures to keep up her cover, but her lens kept coming across fascinating subjects on the periphery and in the arena.

Time sped by so quickly she was surprised to hear the announcement for bull riding. She switched out cameras and zoomed to the action in the chutes. Chase and a young kid were helping an older guy get set to ride. She hadn't thought of Chase as a team player, so seeing him in that role was a little shocking.

Rather than focusing on the bull and rider when the chute opened, she kept her lens on Chase and his young buddy. Both guys were rapt, hands circled around the top metal bar, lips moving with silent encouragement. They whooped when the ride ended successfully and high-fived each other.

Ava grinned right along with them.

The kid was up. Chase and the older guy helped situate him, holding the bull rope, dropping a booted foot into the pen, forcing the bull to stand up. For the hundredth time Ava was grateful for the days she spent at the Bar 9 with Gemma sharing her knowledge of the sport.

And once again she left the camera on Chase. He seemed tenser watching his young friend ride. More relieved than happy when the kid reached the eight-second buzzer and scored eighty-three points.

Then Chase was all business. With the zoom function when she zeroed in on his face. His fierceness, concentration and ruggedness were absolutely mesmerizing.

She shifted her position after Chase slipped on his helmet. Her heart raced when he climbed into the chute. Would she ever lose her fear for him in those seconds he tried to master a fifteen-hundred-pound beast?

Her lens panned the surrounding cowboys as Chase readied his bull rope. Few paid attention. How different would their attitudes be if they realized Chase McKay was set to ride?

The gate banged open. She literally held her breath as Chase and the bull exited the chute in an explosion of dirt. Chase countered the animal's every twisting maneuver. Staying strong. Keeping his seat. Maintaining his fluidity. His control. His mastery. He made it look so effortless. He was sheer physical perfection. Grace and flow.

No wonder Chase had buckle bunnies dogging him after a performance. Seeing him move like that on a bull, they imagined how he moved while riding them.

Don't pretend you haven't imagined it.

Ava watched him tug off his helmet and squint at the scoreboard. The announcer drawled, "You just watched the ride to beat, folks. Let's give Bill Chase a hand for his ninety point ride!"

That was his best ride and score yet.

That caused contestants to look at him differently. Her lens tracked his progress as he accepted handshakes and pats on the back. But his young buddy showed his excitement by picking Chase up and spinning him around. For being self-conscious about his height, Chase took it with humor. Then he knocked the kid's cowboy hat off his head and strode away.

You could be in big trouble, falling for this man, Ava.

No. She was in lust with him. His "just friends" edict made him more appealing because she hadn't been just friends with a guy since high school.

Something caused Chase to look her direction. He aimed a smoldering stare at her. A stare that seared her body right through the lens. A stare packed with so much raw sexual power Ava bobbled the camera. Her pulse pounded as Chase took his own sweet time sauntering toward her, but his posture wasn't the least bit casual. "That was some ride, Sundance."

"Thanks. Felt good." Those stunning blue eyes searched hers carefully from beneath the brim of his ratty-ass ball cap. He blurted, "Will you leave the contestant area with me tonight?"

"Need me to bat away all those bunnies for you?" she teased.

His jaw tightened. "Yeah. Seems to be a lot of them at this event."

"So you're done avoiding me?"

"Why would you say that?"

"Because you haven't been around since we arrived in Scottsbluff."

"I've gotten up early to work out. I met this rookie kid last week. After I rode, he cornered me, calling me out as Chase McKay." He smiled sheepishly. "The little shit promised to keep my secret if I gave him bull ridin' pointers."

"Which you did."

"Not that he listened to me. Kid is such a greenhorn. And stubborn? He won't turn his foot out, refuses to wear a helmet, won't consider a trying a different wrap. So I gave up talking to him about bull ridin' and we watched the slack competition. What did you do—" his knuckles grazed her breasts as he reached for the lanyard around her neck "—besides craft fake press passes?"

"I had my assistant whip them up. Realistic, don't you think? I needed access behind the chutes so I can video you from a closer angle. It's made a huge difference. You won't believe the footage I got today."

His rough-skinned hand enclosed hers. "Ava. We need to talk."

The lanky, shaggy-haired young rider inserted himself between Chase and Ava. "Man, that ride was epic. Textbook. I—"

"Ryan Ackerman, I'd like you to meet Ava," Chase inserted.

"Oh. Sorry. I didn't realize..." Ryan wiped his hand on his leg before he offered it to Ava. "Good to meet you." His gaze dropped to the press credentials. "Wow. You're a reporter?"

"Of sorts. Were you happy with your ride tonight?"

"Well...I...ah...I..."

Ava touched his arm. "This isn't an interview, okay?"

"Sorry." Ryan blew out a breath. "I pretty much suck at that kinda stuff."

"The longer you do it, the easier it gets," Chase said. "You goin' to get your bag? 'Cause I was headed that way myself."

Chase and Ryan returned as she finished stowing her video camera. Chase placed his hand in the small of her back, guiding her around groups of people. He paused before they exited the gate. "So, Ryan. Got a girlfriend at home?"

"No. Why?"

"Just making sure you're free and clear since we're about to stroll through the buckle bunny beltway. Got a preference? Blonde or brunette?"

Ryan blushed to the roots of his sandy-brown hair. "Don't matter. Them kinda girls never look twice at me anyway."

Chase flashed a devious smile. "That, my friend, is about to change." He let his gaze fall to Ryan's duffel bag. "You carrying condoms?"

"What the...? Why would you...?" Ryan glanced nervously over his shoulder to see who was within earshot.

"Simple question. Yes. Or no?"

"Yes," he hissed. "Happy now?"

"Not as happy as you're gonna be." Chase put his lips on Ava's ear. "Feel like snapping a few pictures of the PRCA's newest up-and-coming bull rider?"

The warm rasp of his deep voice in her ear sent an electric tingle down the right side of her body. She automatically leaned into him. God he smelled good. Like leather and man.

"Ava?" he murmured. "Did you hear me?"

No. Whisper it again. At least ten more times. "Sure."

As soon as they cleared the gate, a half-dozen women descended on them—mostly on Chase. Although Ryan topped Chase by six inches, Chase clapped the kid on the shoulder, pushing him front and center. "Damn good ridin'. You keep that up and I'll be watching my back the rest of the season." Chase discreetly nodded to Ava.

"Ryan, could I get a couple of pictures of you? Maybe leaning against the railing?"

"No problem." Ryan dropped his duffel bag and struck a pose. "How's this?"

"Tilt your chin up, sugar," Ava drawled. "We want a clear shot of that handsome face of yours, not your ratty old hat."

Ryan grinned goofily and Ava was completely charmed by this sweet man-boy.

She tested the flash twice after Chase moved to stand next to her.

A bold buckle bunny inserted herself between them—breasts first. "Who's he?"

"Ryan Ackerman. A bull rider." Chase confided, "Wasn't that eighty-three point ride tonight something? Now he's sittin' in second place."

"Really?" The busty brunette offered Ryan a jaunty little finger wave and a come-hither smile.

The poor kid didn't know what to do besides blush.

Ava cajoled, "Come on, Ryan. A couple more shots. Then you can charm all these lovely ladies who are waiting on you."

Ryan swallowed hard as his eyes darted to the women who'd formed a semi-circle behind her and Chase.

Click, click. "See? All finished. I'll be in touch about release forms."

"Ah. Good. Thanks."

Chase crowded her, setting his hand on her lower back, above her ass, showing everyone she was with him. "Great ride. See you on dirt tomorrow night."

None of the bunnies bothered him—just as Chase predicted.

And that bothered Ava. Big time. She felt used.

Frankly she was tired of Chase running hot and cold, gazing at her with lust and then acting like an offended monk when she responded to his blatant sexuality. What happened to her intent to reclaim her own sexuality?

You set it aside because that's what Chase wants.

But what about what I want?

What about it? You want a change, you'll have to make it or take it, not wait for it.

Ava huffed out a frustrated breath. It was annoying to realize that once again she'd shelved her intimate needs and followed a man's lead.

Enough. It was past time she took control.

"You're awful quiet," Chase said when they reached his truck.

"Just thinking about how thoughtful it was of you to look out for Ryan. Especially helping him get laid."

Chase's hand froze on the door handle.

"I've gotta admit jealousy, though. We've been friends longer and you haven't gone out of your way to help *me* get laid."

"Jesus, Ava."

She hip-checked him—not playfully—and opened her own door, then slammed it in his stunned face.

Music filled the truck cab as they exited the fairgrounds. They didn't speak. Ava rolled down her window, breathing in the humid night air. It smelled different here. Warm. Earthy.

Once they were inside the room, Chase stripped off his chaps. "I'm hitting the shower."

Ava waited until she heard the water turn on before she poked her head into the bathroom. "Chase?"

"Christ Almighty. What do I hafta do to get some damn privacy around here?"

"Learn to lock the door?" she intoned with fake cheer.

A growling noise bounced off the tile walls.

"I'm going out. Don't know when I'll be back, so don't wait up."

The shower curtain snapped open and he blinked the water from his eyes. "Where you goin'?"

"Won't know until I get there."

"Just lemme finish my shower and I'll come with you."

"Nope. I'm flying solo."

"Why?"

"Do I really need to spell it out for you?"

"Yeah, Hollywood, and use small words so the dumb cowboy don't get confused," he snapped.

"Don't be an ass."

"Don't be a diva," he shot back.

Ava stomped closer to the shower and purposely didn't allow her

135

gaze to drop below his eyes. "While I appreciate your friendship, you can't fault me for looking for something more, even for one night. Especially since I've told you I won't live like a nun just because you've decided to act like a monk."

"So because I won't nail you right goddamn now, you're goin' out to find some random dude to fuck just to prove you're as hot as sin?"

"How is that any different than you using me as a shield to prove you can abstain?"

That shocked him.

Good. "I'll see you later."

"Ava. Wait."

She didn't.

After grabbing her purse, she sailed out of the room and made tracks to the pub she'd passed earlier in the day. Although the place seemed crowded, Ava found a seat at the bar and ordered a draft beer.

The jukebox spewed country tunes. A few couples were dancing. Maybe she'd find a smooth-moving country guy to teach her to two-step, since Chase had refused.

Fucking Chase McKay. Damn man was intruding on all her thoughts.

An older guy took the barstool next to hers. She recognized him—he'd helped Ryan and Chase behind the chutes tonight. She smiled. "Great ride tonight."

He smiled back. "Thanks." He offered his hand. "Taz Lashlee. I saw you with Bill Chase and Ryan earlier. Ryan tells me you're a reporter?"

"Yes. Ava Dumond."

Taz looked around. "Am I in Bill's chair?"

"No. He's not here."

"Huh." Taz ordered a beer.

"So can I ask you a few questions?"

"You planning to put me in the hot seat?"

"Only if you want a chance to shitcan PC chit-chat and blow me away with your nitty-gritty, down-and-dirty stories about life on the road as a rodeo cowboy."

"Careful what you wish for." Taz held nothing back.

Ava wished she'd brought her video camera—Taz's life was the stuff of legends. She made a mental note to get footage of him riding. The variances between a grizzled old veteran, a competitor at the top of his career and a rookie in the beginning stage of learning the ropes made a fascinating dichotomy. After an hour passed, she felt as if she'd known him for years.

Taz said, "You expecting Bill to show up?"

"Nah. He was tired. He's probably crashed in the room."

"So you're traveling together?"

Ava nodded. "I'm new to the world of rodeo. He agreed to show me the inside scoop. That's all."

"Dollface, that surely ain't all. Not even close. The man has it bad for you."

Not bad enough to act on it.

"I seen how he's been lookin' at you."

"And how's that?"

"Like you're a hot, sweet fried Twinkie and he'd like to lick you up one side and down the other before devouring you completely."

"Except the man seems to be on a sugar-free diet," she said wryly.

Taz chuckled. "Maybe. But I reckon he's just trying to keep from gorging himself."

"Such an overactive imagination, Taz."

"I try. Better to be one of them colorful characters folks talk about than an average Joe."

The conversation drifted to Ryan. Upcoming rodeos they'd all be attending. Other events. Then Taz took off, leaving Ava alone. It was enough to give a girl a complex about men.

Right. She already had enough complexes, although she doubted anyone would look at her and believe that.

A guy paused behind the barstool on Ava's right side. He smiled. "Is this seat taken?"

"No. I was just—"

"Good. I'm Brad."

Brad was decent-looking. Tall. Mid-forties, with brownish-red hair, his smile nearly hidden by a mustache. "Nice to meet you, Brad. I'm Ava."

When she offered Brad her hand, he lifted it to his lips. "Enchanted, Ava."

His calculated charm set off her warning sensors.

He ordered a slow screw up against the wall, Mexican style. Another warning bell pealed. Ava decided to skip politeness and bail on this low-rent lothario.

"You're giving me the 'I need to get the hell outta here' vibe, Ava. What is it about me that's sending you running? The polyester shirt? The porn star 'stache?"

She couldn't help but laugh. "Busted."

"FYI: I'm not trolling."

"Maybe I am."

His thick eyebrows lifted. "That old dude your type?"

"No. He was offering me advice."

"On men?"

"On my career," she lied.

"Huh. That's interesting. You compete as a barrel racer or something?"

"Why would you ask that?"

"Because he's a circuit cowboy. I've known guys like him my entire life. Salt of the earth type. But his career is rodeo. He lets his life be measured eight seconds at a time."

Ava chewed that over, wondering if Chase would end up the same way. Living event to event, trying to recapture former glory. Chasing the buzz and the buzzer.

"So, he wasn't really giving you career advice, was he?"

"No. But I was going with the old adage about divulging things to a stranger that you wouldn't discuss with your closest friends."

"I'm a stranger. Talk to me."

She scrutinized him. "All joking aside, why should I trust you?"

"It's a gamble. But life is a gamble, isn't it?" He sighed. "Confession time. The instant I saw you tonight? Even with the darker hair? I knew exactly who you are, Ava Cooper. I'm a huge fan."

She froze.

"Don't worry, I'm not a stalker." Brad sipped his drink. "In fact, a mutual friend sent me."

"Chase," she hissed.

Brad frowned. "No, Hannah."

"How in the hell do you know Hannah?"

"She's my niece."

Ava gave him a cool once-over. "And you just happened to conveniently be in Scottsbluff, Nebraska? Tonight? Bullshit."

"Nothing convenient about it since I live over three hours from here," he muttered. "Look. Hannah was more than a little worried about you and this bull rider you've hooked up with. She knows I still enjoy a good rodeo, and I'm a lot closer than she is in California. So she called me after you had her make those press passes and asked me to double-check that this cowboy didn't have you shackled to his pickup or something."

Her eyes welled up. Damn Hannah. The woman was such a good friend.

"I wasn't supposed to contact you, but after that last text you sent her? She feared you might do something rash, so here I am." Brad leaned closer. "I'm trustworthy, Ava, I promise. Talk to me. Imagine I'm Hannah, if that helps."

She considered it and threw caution to the wind for a change. "All right, Uncle Brad. You've convinced me to give it a whirl." She swigged her beer and shared the basic run down of the situation with Chase. His "just friends" spiel. His mixed physical signals.

After she finished, Brad said, "No wonder you're confused. But I believe there's an easy solution."

"Which is?"

"Bring another guy to your hotel room. Or better yet, be half-naked with another guy when Chase walks in. He'll either rip the guy limb from limb or he'll leave until you've had your fun. Either way, you'll know how he feels."

Simple. Effective. But for all her bold talk...could she really do it? Push Chase to take action with her by making him jealous? Her every insecurity hit her full force. What if Chase was playing the friendship card because he really wasn't interested in anything more? What if he didn't like fake breasts? What if he'd never want her because she was taller? What if her less-than-glamorous appearance turned him off?

But what if he just needs a nudge? What are you out?

Not a damn thing. Nothing ventured, nothing gained. No more waiting in the wings. Time to let *her* sexual needs take center stage for a change.

"Is this idea gaining ground?"

"Maybe. The problem is—" *I don't know if he's attracted to me,* "—I haven't found a guy I could even pretend I'd want to bang, let alone finding the real deal."

"Does Chase know that?"

"No." She huffed out a frustrated breath. "I don't know. See why this is driving me crazy?"

He spun toward her on the barstool. "How far you willing to take this?"

All the way. "Why?"

"Let me be the guy you drag back to the room." When she frowned, he leaned closer. "Then it's a controlled situation. You don't have to worry about some strange guy taking things too far."

"Why would you do this, Brad?"

"I'm a sucker for this type of romance stuff. And I get to help out my favorite niece's friend. Plus, it'll be a hoot, acting with you."

"How well can you act?"

Brad bestowed a smoldering look of pure hot need. Invading her space, he stared directly at her lips. "You have a mouth made for sex. As much as I'd like to kiss those pretty pink lips for hours, and watch them wrapped around my cock, I'd really like to see them soft and open as I'm making you come for the fourth time."

Holy. Shit. Then Brad's eyes met hers and there was no sexual heat whatsoever.

"How's that?"

"Ah. Wow. Damn. That was a really great way to set the scene."

He chuckled. "Good to know I can still pass for straight."

Ava's mouth dropped open. "You're gay?"

"Since the day I was born," he said breezily.

Her gaydar wasn't just rusty; it was completely fucking broken.

"So what do you think?"

Brad didn't cajole her as she weighed the pros and cons. But the bottom line? She was desperate to do this. "Deal. But part of the deal is you can't tell anyone. Ever."

"You have my word." He rested his forearms on the bar. "What's the plan for tomorrow night?"

Ava smiled. "Why wait for tomorrow? Let's get started tonight."

Chapter Fifteen

Maybe faking sleep when Ava returned to the room last night at 1:04 a.m. made Chase a total pussy. He'd decided pretend slumber was preferable to beating the tar out of whoever Ava flirted and giggled with outside the motel room door.

She hadn't attempted to be quiet when she finally deigned to enter the room. That chapped his ass. It was almost as if she'd been...taunting him.

Sending the still-sleeping Ava a cursory glance, Chase slipped out. Three hours later, after running five miles and completing a full weight training session at the gym, Chase opened the door only to be greeted by Ava's crotch.

Her feet were spread wide and her legs were splayed open. The remainder of her body was bent back over the big blue ball. Ava's body was twisted so he couldn't even see her face—only the area between her thighs and the flat arc of her belly.

Goddamn if his mouth didn't water when he fantasized about dropping to his knees and burying his face against her tempting mound. Or testing the bounce factor of that exercise ball as he slammed his cock into her.

Ava sat up and rested her hands on her knees. She smirked as if she knew every lewd thought that'd crossed his mind. Her eyes flicked over him, head to toe. "Morning, roomie. Seems we're on the same wave length."

"Oh, I highly doubt our thoughts are even close to parallel, Hollywood." Chase drained his water bottle. Then he yanked his tank top over his head, mopped the sweat from his face with it and tossed it on his bed. His gaze returned to Ava. He wasn't imagining things this time; Ava actually licked her lips as she eyeballed his chest. He didn't hide his smirk as he gestured to her. "You about done doin'...?"

"My yoga practice? Yes. Why?"

"Just wondering who gets the shower first?"

Ava hopped off the ball. "Go ahead. I planned on staying around the room the rest of the day, trying to get some...ah...work done. I figured you'd be going to the fairgrounds with Ryan and hanging out until the rodeo started."

That vague comment got his back up. Was she trying to get rid of him? Just to be ornery, he said, "I hadn't planned on goin' anywhere today. Thought I'd stick around the room and rest up. Hang out with you, my *friend*."

Panic darted through her eyes. "Oh. Obviously since you're paying for half the room that's your prerogative. But I was hoping..."

"Hoping for what?"

"To have a few hours of quiet time so I can get your rides separated from the other footage."

Quiet time his ass. She wanted nookie time. And he'd be goddamned if he'd just fucking walk away and make it easy on her to bang a total stranger in his hotel room. "I'm not exactly loud, Ava."

"I know, Chase, but I need quiet. Complete silence. No TV. No talking. No cell phone conversations. No fighting."

The sneaky-ass woman knew that lying on his bed, counting the flaws in the ceiling tile for hours would drive him bonkers. But the idea of any man, in here—the private space Chase shared with Ava—touching her, kissing her, fucking her on that lumpy damn mattress—made Chase crazier yet. So he offered Little Miss Liar-Liar-Yoga-Pants-On-Fire a somber nod. "Understood. There's online work I've been putting off. I promise to be as quiet as a church mouse." By Ava's expression, she expected him to tuck his tail between his legs, exit the room and leave her alone.

Like hell.

Chase smiled at her. "I'm glad we can sort this stuff out so quickly."

After he was scrubbed and freshly shaven he wandered out of the bathroom with a towel loosely secured low around his hips. As he dug in his duffel bag for clean clothes, he felt her checking out his package, and then his butt, although she didn't utter a peep.

It was a long, quiet afternoon.

An hour before the finals performance at the fairgrounds, Chase checked out his bull, stretched his quads and hamstrings and tried to mentally prep himself. He was leaning against the corral, watching the last rays of sunshine through the clouds of humidity, when he heard, "Bill Chase. You're lookin' good to win this tonight."

He turned toward Taz. "I hope so. Be nice if we all came in the money, huh?"

Taz spit a stream of tobacco juice through the fence rails. "Yep. Be a boost to the boy if he could place."

"He's doin' better than I did. Took three events before I even rode one for eight seconds. I damn near gave up."

"Been there myself more times than I care to admit. Started the junior events at fifteen. Got my pro card at eighteen. I'll be fifty-one next month. So a long damn time." Another brown stream landed in the dirt.

"You get tired of it?"

"There are days. But it ain't like I got other skills. Ridin's all I know."

Sobering for Chase to admit that he might be Taz in a few years.

That's when Ava sauntered into view. Smiling at assorted cowboys as she shooed them aside and set up her video camera. Fuckin' hell, the woman was something else.

"She sure is," Taz said.

Shit. He hadn't meant to say that out loud.

"I saw her last night at the bar on Main Street."

He'd been too pissed off and filled with pride to track her down after she'd left. "Any guy in particular catch her notice?"

"Hmm. I believe one did." Taz snorted. "If I were twenty years younger, I'da given that guy a run for his money. Man. he was all over her."

Chase wanted to demand what the guy looked like. If he was tall. If Ava and the putz had danced together. Or whether they'd snuck off early. They could've gone back to his place right after they'd met. She could've ended her sexual drought and he wouldn't know it. That thought turned his vision a dangerous red and he wanted to rip something to pieces with his bare hands.

"Didn't see Ryan last night until late neither. Kid still had a grin on his face this mornin'. You got time to have a beer at the campsite tonight after the event?"

"I'll swing by. It'll be an early night since I'm hitting the road tomorrow mornin'." He clapped Taz on the shoulder. "Gotta get my head on straight about this ride. See you in the chutes."

He'd gone about fifty feet when Ryan tracked him down and blurted, "I need your help, man."

"You nervous?"

"Like you wouldn't believe. I don't know—"

"You'll be fine. You're in the home stretch. Just treat it like any other ride. Concentrate on staying on, ridin' hard, and that's it."

Ryan shot him a baffled look. "Huh-uh. I've heard guys talking and I know there's more to it than that. I've got the basics down, but I need...ummm...advice with the fancier stuff I ain't tried before."

"Fancier stuff?" Chase frowned. "Explain that."

His cheeks turned cherry red. "You know. Like usin' my mouth on

143

her and different positions."

"Whoa." Chase stepped back. "Whoa, whoa, whoa. You ain't talking about ridin' in the final go-round, are you? You're talking about ridin'...a girl."

"Ssh." Ryan glanced around, owl-eyed. "Sheesh. Of course I'm talking about a girl. I know how to ride a bull. I need to up my game with Allison tonight. You know, do some different sex stuff to impress her."

"For the love of Christ, Ryan. Seriously? You want my advice on sex?"

"Come on, everyone knows your reputation with the ladies. It's been all over the rodeo magazines and the fan sites."

"Don't believe everything you read."

"I don't see you denying it. Chicks still line up to get with you, even after that video, maybe especially after that video, so it's gotta be true." Ryan crossed his arms over his chest. "Besides. You owe me."

Of all the... Chase counted to ten. "How do you figure I owe you?"

"You threw me to Allison last night. And she... Well, she was all over me. Tonight I wanna show her that I can do more than just lie there with a stupid grin on my face wondering how I got so lucky to get naked with her."

That comment hit home on many levels. Chase sighed. "You ever gone down on a girl before?"

Ryan shook his head.

Fucking awesome. "Okay. Take your time getting down there. Don't just dive in. Especially not the first time. Use your mouth and your hands." His eyes searched Ryan's. "You do know where a woman's clit is?"

"Yes. I'm not stupid," he said sullenly.

"Well, you'd be surprised how many men are. Take your cues from her. If she's moving and getting wetter, then you're doin' it right. If she acts bored, she probably is bored, and you need to try something different. When she says 'Don't stop', for Godsake, don't stop."

"How will I know when she's about to..."

"Come? You'll be able to feel it. Trust me."

"Some guys say they don't like it."

"Then they're fuckin' idiots."

"But women like it, right?"

Chase grinned. "Women love it."

Again, Ryan briefly looked over his shoulder. "What about different positions? We did it the regular way once, and then she blew me, and then she rode me."

"It's more important she's hot to be nekkid with you than it is to try every position you see in porn."

"Oh. Okay. That makes sense." Ryan grinned and punched Chase in the shoulder. "Thanks, man. I wish I could tell my buddies I got sex advice from Chase McKay." He bounded off.

Yeah. Sex advice from the guy who currently wasn't getting any. That was something to brag about.

Somehow, Chase put sex out of his mind. At some events, the leader rode last, but this one he was scheduled to ride fourth. Helmet on, mouth guard in, a good wrap, a good seat and he was ready to hit it.

The bull went crazy, three jumps and then into the wildest spin Chase had ever experienced. Gritting his teeth, he held on by sheer strength. Soon as he heard that buzzer, he released his hand and hit the ground flat on his back. Luckily the bad dismount didn't knock the wind out of him, but he was so damn dizzy he could barely stand. The bullfighters helped him stagger to the fence as he awaited his score.

Eighty-eight. He'd won. No other rider could catch him. Chase allowed a smile as he waved to the crowd.

Ryan finished third, Taz not in the money. Ava taped the prize handout, but then she disappeared.

He had a single beer with Taz and lumbered across the grounds and highway to his motel room. He hadn't taken off his chaps, vest or even his spurs. Pausing in front of the room, he dug his keycard from his duffel bag and opened the door. It hadn't occurred to him that Ava might have made plans—nekkid plans—until he saw her stretched out on the bed in her birthday suit.

"Chase?" Her feet kept slipping on the cheap nylon comforter as she scrambled up the bed. "What are you doing here?"

He dropped his bag to the carpet absentmindedly. Holy hell, did she have a rockin' body. Golden skin that boasted curves, curves and more curves. As he took a step toward her, he noticed panic in her eyes—not heat or even that tempting sexual challenge he'd never be immune to. His gaze tracked her mesmerizing body, from the flare of her hip, to the contour of her belly, across those glorious tits and the graceful line of her neck.

Seconds after Chase noticed a full box of condoms, bottle of lube and two bandanas on the nightstand, a dude wearing chaps and a cowboy hat sauntered out of the bathroom with a hearty, "You ready for the ride of your life, toots?"

What the fuck?

After his shock wore off, Chase snarled, "Jesus, Ava, *this* is the type of douchebag you came up with? A wannabe cowboy with a fake drawl who calls you *toots*?"

"Who are you?" Douchebag demanded.

"The guy tellin' you to get the hell outta my room."

The douchebag looked at Ava. "I thought you said this was your room."

"Hey, fuckface, eyes on me, not her." When douchebag turned, Chase stabbed his finger at the clothes by the bed. "You're done. Grab your shit and get gone."

"Nuh-uh." Douchebag gestured to Ava. "I get gone when she tells me to, not you, little man."

Ava said not one word.

Chase's anger hit the boiling point. Instead of yelling, his voice dropped lethally low. "Get. The. Fuck. Out."

"Or what? You gonna throw me out?" Douchebag sneered. "You'll have to eat your spinach and grow some first."

Faking calmness he didn't feel, Chase scooped up the man's belongings, opened the door and dumped the pile onto the walkway.

"What is wrong with you?" Douchebag loomed over Chase.

"You have fifteen seconds to get out of my room and out of my face or I will beat you bloody. You're not the first asshole who's tried to take me on, believing a short man is a weak man. But by all means, I'm more than willing to offer you proof that's a mistake." Chase locked his cold gaze to the man who had six inches and a good fifty pounds on him. "Get out. Right. Fucking. Now."

Douchebag glared, but ultimately retreated. He sent Ava a dark look before he muttered, "No piece of ass is worth this bullshit," and stormed out.

Chase slammed the door, locked it and engaged the safety chain before he faced Ava.

Immediately she started babbling. "Chase. I'm sorry. I don't know what I was thinking."

"Oh, I know what you were thinking, sugar tits." He shucked off his vest as he ambled toward the bed. "You don't mind if I call you sugar tits, do you? Because, I gotta say, it's a whole lot better than toots."

"Very funny."

"You were thinking you wanted to get laid." Chase popped the buttons on his shirt. "But that douchebag was the best you could do? In an arena filled with real cowboys, you picked...him?"

"He wore a hat. And boots. And chaps."

Chase laughed. "He wore a Toby Keith party hat. His boots were brand spankin' new. And the chaps? Hell. Them I can't even explain." He toed off his boots. Unhooked his chaps and let them fall to the floor in a dusty *whoosh*. The fact Ava's eyes never wavered from watching him strip prompted him to bare it all. He unbuckled his belt. Once the zipper loosened his jeans, he slipped them off along with his briefs. He grabbed the back strap of his chaps. Felt goddamn stupid putting them back on nekkid, but he did it anyway.

He thought about what his brother Ben said about being a man. Being in control. Reading what his lover wanted and acting on it. He felt almost as clueless as Ryan tonight.

"Chase?"

Man up. "If you still want to get laid by a cowboy, just say the word. Say the word and I'll give you a night you'll never forget."

"But what about your self-promise to abstain? I don't want you blaming me afterward that I enticed you into fucking me."

"You've been enticing me since the moment I laid eyes on you. I consider it a personal victory that I held out as long as I did with you, Ava, because you are something else. Beautiful. Smart. Funny. Sexy. And in case you haven't looked at a calendar recently, the month is up."

"Is that the only reason you're doing this, Chase? Because I'm convenient and the calendar is giving you the all clear to revert to your love-'em-and-leave-'em ways?"

Chase climbed on the bed, straddling her hips. "Not even fucking close." He bent his head, studying the turbulent emotions in her beautiful eyes before he pressed his mouth to hers. Lightly teasing her sweet, warm lips. Sucking in her rapidly expelled breaths deep into his lungs. Fueling the need, building the sexual buzz.

When Ava playfully sank her teeth into his bottom lip and tugged, Chase shuddered. He thrust his tongue inside her mouth and intensified the kiss until she thrashed beneath him, attempting to force full-body contact.

He ripped his mouth free, panting as if he'd just climbed off a bull. Resting his forehead to hers, he said, "Damn. A man could lose his head just kissin' you." Chase smooched her plump lips twice more before following the curve of her jaw up to the sweet spot in front of her ear. "You're mine tonight, Hollywood. All night. Any way I want you. As many times as I want you. Make no mistake: I want you. And it doesn't have a goddamned thing to do with you being convenient, or any fucking calendar, understand?"

Her rapid-fire, "Yes," caused him to growl against the pulse beating wildly in her throat.

"You always smell so damn good." He nuzzled below her earlobe. "Girly. Like summer flowers." His tongue traced the shell of her ear. "And sugar."

"It's my lotion. Orange blossoms."

"Mmm. Good enough to eat." Chase let his lips drift down the center of her body between the deep swell of her cleavage. But he didn't stop to tongue those tempting nipples, or rub his mouth all over her succulent curves, he kept moving south. He felt her thighs clench between his when the very tip of his tongue circled her belly button. He swept openmouthed kisses from hipbone to hipbone. Then he brushed his goatee across the damp path his mouth had made, using his warm breath and the rough texture of his facial hair to make that delicate flesh quiver.

But he stopped mere inches from the rise of her mound. Her completely bare mound. "I like you so silky-smooth." He placed a tender kiss on the section of skin right above where her sex parted like a flower.

"Chase. Please. It's been so long..."

His gaze snapped back to hers. "So long since a guy went down on you?"

Ava nodded.

"How long?" he demanded.

"Since right after Jake and I started dating. He did it once and..." Her laugh resembled a groan. "Didn't like it."

Chase scooted back until he was between her thighs. "That shoulda been your first sign the man was gay." His tongue trailed down the seam of her sex and he licked back up to her clit.

Ava whispered, "Thank you."

That response did him in. No teasing her endlessly this time. A primitive growl rumbled free and he roughly pushed her legs apart, baring every glistening pink inch of her sex. He lowered his head and inhaled the aroma of pure Ava before he plunged his tongue inside her pussy. Hot and wet. Spicy sweet.

She bucked, but his grip on her legs held her steady, keeping her in place as he tasted her thoroughly. He flattened his tongue, lapping the honey from every hidden fold. As he sucked her pussy lips into his mouth, the tip of his tongue sought her clit. Flicking that little nub over and over until it plumped.

"Oh. Yes. Like that."

Chase narrowed his oral worship to just her clit, suckling softly but firmly until she arched against his mouth. Ava's fingernails dug into his scalp as her orgasm overtook her. Her sexy, low-throated groan escalated into gasps. Her entire body trembled and Chase didn't relent.

As soon as she finished coming, she attempted to scramble back, attempted to close her legs, attempted to regain control.

But Chase wanted her wild. Writhing beneath him as he made her come again. He grabbed her hips and jerked her back down where he wanted her. "Don't move."

"But I—"

"I'm not done with you. Come on, baby, one more," he murmured against the rise of her mound as he nuzzled her satiny skin.

"I can't. I never have..."

"Then you will with me."

After a tiny beat of hesitation, Ava rolled back onto the mattress, giving herself—her pleasure—over to him completely.

With that small act of surrender, Chase finally understood what Ben had meant. In that single defining moment, he shed his habitual sexual selfishness and became the lover Ava needed.

Mindful of the sensitivity of her clit, Chase used teasing breaths, fleeting kisses and soothing caresses. On her belly. On her hipbones. On the tops of her thighs. Everywhere but on her pussy. When Ava began to shift restlessly, he slipped two fingers into her, wiggling the digits, but not sliding them in and out. He continued the randomness of his kisses, memorizing her body's response to every lick, nibble and gentle bite.

Before Ava could beg, Chase let his mouth wander to where she wanted it most. Lapping at her clit instead of concentrated sucking, while his fingers fucked in and out of her wet heat. He couldn't wait to plunge his cock in and feel that hot velvet clamping around his shaft, but he didn't want to hurry this.

"More," she panted. "I need your mouth..."

Chase firmed his lips, pulling at the throbbing flesh and pushed another finger deep into her clenching channel, trying not to grind his aching cock against the sheet. That'd be damn embarrassing, spilling his seed before he even got inside her.

Ava released a wail as she came again.

Her sweet juices coated his mouth and he licked his lips before pressing openmouthed kisses on the inside of each thigh. While she caught her breath, he ripped open the box of condoms.

She lifted up to rest on her elbows and watched as he slipped one on.

God. She looked even more beautiful flushed with color, her eyes heavy with pleasure, her lips fuller from his kisses. He couldn't wait another second to have her. He said gruffly, "Roll over."

Something resembling wariness flashed in her eyes, but she didn't argue.

Chase hiked her hips and moved in behind her. He placed a single, tender kiss between the dimples above her ass. Then he took a taut cheek in each hand, aligned his cock and surged inside her.

Oh fuck yeah. Every goddamned bit as good as he'd imagined.

He was too far gone with need to take this first time slow. That'd come later. Much later. After he'd dulled this sharp edge of lust.

She pushed her hips back, meeting his every hard thrust with a soft grunt. The fringe on his chaps swung forward, the leather connecting with her skin.

Even as his cock plunged into her fully, even as his balls drew up, aching for release, even as his legs shook and sweat coated his skin, he planned for the next time he fucked her. The next hundred times.

Chase closed his eyes; his hands yanking her body back to meet his escalating thrusts. *Faster, harder, deeper,* the only words echoed in his head as primal need roared. Impossible to hold off his orgasm, no matter how much he wanted to prolong the sensation of sinking into her soft, wet, flesh.

He threw back his head, groaning as his cock emptied in hot pulses. Groaning louder when he felt Ava's pussy contracting around his dick as she came again.

Heart thumping, mouth dry, lungs lacking air, Chase fell forward onto Ava's back, bracing himself on his hands. Although this rendezvous was supposed to've been a dare, a fun, wild slap and tickle to ease the sexual tension between them, he felt he'd shared something of himself with her that he'd never shared before.

Chapter Sixteen

Three times.

The man made her come three times.

In an hour.

Just thinking about it and Ava's pussy clenched.

"Christ. Do that again and I'm never moving off you."

She did it again.

Chase lightly sank his teeth into her shoulder. Then his voice rumbled in her ear. "Just for that, I oughta stay inside you until I'm hard again and fuck you until you scream."

"My vocal cords could always use a good workout."

He lifted up, eased out and pinned her flat on her back with his mouth on hers. Kissing her with wild abandon. Making a mockery of any kisses she'd ever shared with another man.

This is what she wanted. His hunger. His mouth. All the muscular, sweaty weight of his body plastered against hers. His decision to take her from behind their first time half-shocked her. She'd never enjoyed that position.

Chase gradually slowed the avid stroking of his tongue, switching it up to tease her mouth with firm-lipped nibbles, turning passion into tenderness. He pressed his lips to her ear. "I ain't surprised it's like this between us, Ava."

"Like what?"

He mumbled something, kissed her and murmured, "Be right back."

Ava stretched contentedly, wondering what was next. Would he want another round or was he done for the night? Made zero sense she felt disappointment at that prospect, especially after three outstanding orgasms.

But Chase swaggered in, stopping at the foot of the bed, shucking his chaps, bestowing the devilish grin that turned her nipples hard. "That took the edge off. Now, after the appetizer I'm ready for the main meal."

She shrieked when he jumped on the bed.

He put a knee on either side of her hips. "Relax. I just wanna touch you. Seems I skipped a few crucial places in my rush to get nekkid with you."

Ava smoothed her palms up his muscular quads, inching toward his groin. "Oh, I don't know. You focused on one very crucial spot pretty good. Twice."

"Liked that, did you?"

"Mmm-hmm. I'd also like equal time." She licked her lips and stared at his cock. "So why don't you scoot that bad boy closer to my mouth so I can—"

"Huh-uh, Hollywood. You don't get to set the scene on the mattress. I do."

The intensity in his tone sent a shiver through her as his thumbs continually, idly stroked the lower curve of her breasts. His blue eyes teemed with sexual heat. "I can't wait to see your lips wrapped around my dick. But it'll be on my timeframe, not yours. Understand?"

So he was a little bossy in bed. Normally that'd be her cue to leave. She preferred to...top from the bottom as it were. But Chase wasn't having any of it. And that turned her on more than she'd thought possible. Her pulse skipped. Her breathing grew erratic as he held her gaze.

"You like me takin' charge," he murmured.

"No I don't."

"Yes you do and I'm more than happy to oblige you." He slid down her body, sucking her right nipple into his mouth while his fingers plucked the other.

Ava panicked a bit and squirmed. Not because it felt good, but for the first time she feared he hadn't been listening when she'd confessed about her desensitized breasts. How long would he play and tease, awaiting her response? Would he get pissed off when his attentions elicited no reaction? Or if she told him to stop?

A sharp pinch on each tip simultaneously had her crying out in total shock.

"You sure felt that," he drawled and returned his eager mouth to her nipples, delicately licking. Sucking forcefully. Nipping with his teeth. His rough-skinned hands continually caressing and squeezing the fleshy part of her breasts as his mouth worked the softened tips into rigid peaks.

This was okay. She relaxed slightly. She could handle him taking his own sweet time.

But as soon as she loosened up he moved. He stopped nuzzling and laving her chest and scooted down her torso. Kissing her stomach. Tracing each of her ribs with his hot mouth. Tonguing her belly button.

Rubbing his warm, soft lips over her hipbones. Letting his goatee skim the sides of her torso. Turning every inch of her skin into his personal playground. Never focusing too long on one area. Keeping her on edge until her body vibrated inside and out, wanting more than just his erotic caresses.

"Tell me why you got that panicked look when I told you to roll over when I had you the first time," he asked as if his mouth wasn't hovering over her mound.

Ava's face heated and the flush spread down her entire body. She looked away.

His tongue made a slow pass up her slit and he commanded, "Ava. Look at me and answer the question."

She blurted, "Because Jake always fucked me doggie style. Didn't register why until after." When guilt shone in Chase's eyes, Ava reassured him, "So I figured I shouldn't be greedy and ask if we could do it face to face since I'd already gotten off twice and you hadn't gotten off at all."

Chase's eyes iced over. "Taking one for the team, were you? Just goin' along with it because that's the way I wanted it?"

Yes. "No. Maybe. I don't know."

"Which is it? And don't tell me what you think I wanna hear. Tell me the truth."

Why was he pushing her on this now? And why, rather than putting on an easygoing front, distracting him with a kittenish purr, did she find herself snapping at him? "Here's the truth. I wasn't thrilled, okay? I never get off when a guy fucks me from behind. So go ahead and give me that cocky cowboy smirk because you know exactly how hard you made me come that way."

Chase pushed to his knees between her legs, tugging her into a sitting position so he loomed over her. "I'm not keeping a goddamned oral sex or orgasm scorecard, Ava. Christ." The tender way his big hands slipped up her neck to cup her head belied the fierceness on his face. "After all the nights I spent fantasizing about you, forcing myself to keep away from you, even when I know it hurt you, the last thing I wanna do is fight when we're finally nekkid together."

Made her go all gooey inside, how he balanced his gruff side with his sweet side—and he wasn't even aware he did it. She curled her fingers around those impressive biceps and whispered, "Me either."

His posture relaxed. He let his thumbs draw a slow arc over her cheekbones. "I still see questions in your eyes and that stubborn tilt to your chin, darlin'. Talk to me."

"I realize you like to be in control, but I want to touch you too. And it's sort of selfish, to be honest, that I can't run my hands and my mouth all over this incredible body."

"Selfish?" He laughed softly and kissed her nose. "That's a new one. I'll play along. Or I'll let you play. But I've got two rules. First, no touching my feet because they're so damn ticklish."

Ava smiled, surprised he'd admitted that weakness.

"Second. No touching my cock."

Her smile vanished. "That's not fair."

Chase cocked his head, studying her.

"What?"

"If I gave you full access to my cock, you wouldn't touch me anywhere else, would you?" He let his hands fall to her breasts. "Kinda like them other guys you've been with only wantin' to get their hands on these. I don't want that for us. Ever. Maybe that is selfish. But it's been the same story for me. Women I've been with have gone straight for my dick. I want you to feel your hands on me, on my body, not just between my legs. I want that more than you can imagine."

Ava's heart flipped over at his raw honesty. When she struggled to find a response that wasn't trivializing the situation, he sighed.

Then he retreated, stretching out on his back on the bed, folding his arms behind his head, spreading his legs.

She wanted to touch him in a way no other woman ever had. Physically. Emotionally. She straddled his hips, watching his face as she angled across him and freed his right arm. Starting with his hand, she outlined each thick finger from the ragged tips to the webbing, loving the rough texture of his knuckles and the hard calluses, built up from years of riding bulls. She placed a soft kiss in the center of his palm and curled his fingers into a fist. Next she followed the corded muscles in his forearm, marveling at the strength. When she reached his massive bicep, she sighed. Her fingertips traced every bulge and deeply cut section of muscle. She kissed the bend in his elbow and lowered it to the mattress before reaching for his left arm.

Instead of using her fingers to acquaint herself with this side of his rippling, muscular flesh, she used her tongue. The "damn, woman" uttered under his breath made her smile against his tricep as she mapped his muscles with her mouth. After she released his arm, her mouth wandered from the cup of his shoulder, up the column of his neck.

Chase groaned and turned his head, granting her full access.

She loved his reaction to the scrape of her teeth, the sucking kisses, the feather light placement of her lips in random spots on his neck. Goose bumps spread across his arms and up his nape. He shifted on the bed, not thrashing, but wiggling enough she knew he liked what she was doing to him. She reveled in this immense power of worshipping rather than being worshipped.

Ava immersed herself in him. The scent of his skin. The tangy taste of his sweat. The way his muscles strained beneath her tongue. She kissed, licked and nibbled her way down the center of his throat, from his square jaw to his breastbone. And could she get a halleluiah that he had chest hair? Talk about manly, masculine goodness. She rubbed her face over the dark patch of hair, breathing him in, listening to the pounding of his heart, warmed by the heat from his skin, and knowing his body's response to her was echoed in her body.

Bracing herself on all fours above him, she watched his face as she tongued his nipple.

The man actually arched up.

She sucked the flat disk until it became a stiff point and then she used her teeth on the hard nub. Alternating nipples, forcing herself to focus only on this part of his torso, even when her hands wanted to wander.

His breaths came in short bursts. When she blew a stream of air across his wet nipple, he moaned, "I...damn. I like that."

It'd been a long time since she'd indulged in foreplay. She also wanted to get to the good part, the hard thrusting, interlocking body parts of sex. But seeing Chase's reaction to the way she touched him made her burn hotter, made her want to drag out this exploration so she could know every dip and hollow of this magnificent body. She outlined his pectorals with her lips, looking up at him when she reached his sternum. "Your body is a work of art, Chase. Beautifully sculpted. Strong. Supple. You work it with pride and it shows."

His face filled with satisfaction. And pure male heat.

She planted kisses down the center of his torso, following the sexy dark trail of hair. When her chin bumped against the wet tip of his cock, she glanced up at him again. "Hold your cock off to the side, since I'm not supposed to touch it."

Chase quirked a brow, managing to look both menacing and obliging. He fisted his hand around the root and stroked upward a few times, never breaking their eye fuck. Finally he pulled his shaft aside and held it by is hip. "Happy?"

"Very. Because I've been wanting to get my mouth on your eight pack abs since I saw you naked in Ginger's bathroom." And yes, indeedy, she gloried in exploring his ridged, yet flat abdomen, dipping her tongue into the defining grooves. He tasted different down here. Muskier. More like sex. And again, she rubbed her face against his taut skin like a contented feline.

Well, not completely contented. She wanted more. She peered at him and saw he'd closed his eyes.

Perfect.

Ava reached between his legs and cupped his balls, squeezing gently as her nails scraped up the inside of his right leg, brushing the coarse pubic hair, then traveled back down to his knee.

Chase jerked back. "What are you doin', Hollywood? No touchin' my cock, remember?"

"Ah. But I'm not touching your cock; I'm touching your balls." Smiling—smirking really—she rolled the taut globes between her fingers, letting her thumb stroke the shiver-inducing skin right behind the sac. Holding his gaze, seeing him torn between wanting her to continue touching him, and denying her because she'd... sort of broken his rule.

He grabbed her wrist and flipped her on her back amidst her surprised shriek. He growled, "Don't move."

"Are you going to punish me?" She stretched her arms above her head, loving the way his eyes devoured her body. "Fifty lashes with your wet tongue, I hope."

"Nope. I have some very specific punishments in mind and I can't wait to try every fuckin' one of them. But it'll keep." He grabbed another condom and covered himself. Then he braced his forearms by her head, and lowered his body over hers.

She couldn't help but touch him. This man unlike any she'd ever met, who made her feel things that scared her and thrilled her.

His eyes regained their earlier intensity. "Know why I took you from behind? Besides me wanting to put my hands all over your fantastic ass?"

Say something flip and totally male. Don't be more sweet and loving than you've already been or I might fall for you.

"I knew I wouldn't last because I've wanted you for too damn long." Chase kissed the corners of her mouth. The apples of her cheeks. Her temples. "But this time? I'll be looking in your eyes, feeling your body wrapped around me, your nails scratching my back, your mouth on mine everywhere. I intend to make it last a good, long time."

And...Ava felt herself cartwheeling her arms, trying desperately not to tumble straight into the daunting place she'd never been. "Chase..."

"It's okay." Chase kissed her. Rocking against her. "You know what I like best about this position?"

"What?"

"That lying down we're the same height." Chase pushed into her fully.

Ava almost knocked him off balance she arched so sharply from his hard thrust. "God."

"No kiddin'. You—this—feels amazing." He pulled out slowly until just the head of his cock rested in her opening.

She waited, expecting he'd plunge back in. But he gave her a long, slow glide of his flesh into hers and stopped when he'd filled her completely. He did that exact same move twice more and stopped again.

"Am I hurtin' you?"

"No. Why?"

"Because you're holding your breath."

Damn. She exhaled. "Sorry."

Chase placed a soft smooch on her mouth. Then another. Until the kisses became longer. More intense. With hardly a breath between them. But still he didn't rush the joining of their bodies. Keeping the rhythm slow and steady.

Ava's hands were all over his slippery skin. She couldn't touch him enough—from his straining arms to his strong shoulders and back, down to his muscular ass. She arched and wiggled and squirmed against his rock solid body, urging him to get a move on.

He broke the kiss and murmured, "The more frantic you get, the slower I'm gonna go."

"Why?"

"Because I can." He softly blew in her ear, educing a whole body shudder. "Because I really love the sexy way you're grinding your whole body on mine and if I move faster you'll stop."

She trapped his face in her palms and looked into his laughing eyes. "You always going to be this controlling in bed?"

"Nope. Sometimes I'm gonna be worse." Then Chase raised his body up enough so his chest hair abraded her nipples with his every upward stroke. "Wrap your legs around my hips and grab the headboard."

Ava told herself it was his sexy growl that did it for her, not his command. But as soon as she reached up, he picked up the pace and she understood the appeal of surrender. This was heady stuff, ceding her pleasure to him. Becoming mindless in the friction of damp skin rubbing on damp skin. Anticipating the heat and hardness of his shaft plowing into her tender pussy. Destroying her wits as his mouth eked out every shiver and moan with hot, wet sucking kisses on her neck.

"That's it," he whispered fiercely. "Let me take you there."

"Yes," she hissed, her back bowing as his cock hit her G-spot. Over and over. He'd changed the angle of his hips so he wasn't bumping against her clit, but this felt so damn good she didn't care.

Chase took her mouth again as he drove into her, so in tune with what she needed that Ava swore they'd made love a thousand times before instead of just once.

Then he adjusted his position again, hitting both spots with each hard, deep stroke.

Ava seemed to splinter into a million pieces when she climaxed. She knew Chase wasn't far behind as his thrusts intensified. When he groaned and started to bury his face in her neck, she released her grip on the headboard and cradled his face in her palms. "Look at me. Show me what I do to you."

Chase whispered, "God, Ava," and shuddered as his orgasm rolled over him in a long wave that left him groaning and her stunned by the intensity.

Panting, they just held onto each other, trying to unscramble their brains. Finally Chase mumbled, kissed her, pushed up, pulled out, and got up to ditch the condom.

Ava rolled over, deliciously sore, but unsure what would happen next.

When he crawled back in bed, she pushed up on her elbow, intending to give him space. He said, "Where you goin'?"

"Umm. To my bed?"

"Like hell." He dropped his top leg over hers, holding her in place. "You don't get to fuck me and run. I suspect that's been both our habits in the past. We both know this ain't a one-night thing." He scooted behind her and planted a kiss on her shoulder. "So get used to sharing a bed with me."

Touched by his unexpected affection, Ava turned and rubbed her cheek over his. "Sounds good. I prefer a king-sized bed anyway."

"But the room's still gotta cost under a hundred bucks."

"Such a taskmaster."

"Someone's gotta keep you in line."

Chase was a hard sleeper. So Ava found it easy to slip free from his arms in the early morning hours.

She wished for light but didn't dare risk waking him by turning on the one in the bathroom. But it was handy that they'd slept naked. She paused at the foot of the bed, her eye on the prize. Although they'd had sex three times last night, Chase hadn't allowed her direct access to his cock, even one time, which was why Ava was helping herself to it now. It was a new day. Last night's rules no longer applied.

She knew she'd only have limited time before Chase woke up. Bending her head, she inhaled this warm, intimate scent before she sucked the soft cock into her mouth. She loved how the skin grew taut and the flesh expanded with every suctioning pull.

He stirred, moaning as his cock hardened. Lengthened.

When Ava started sliding his shaft over her tongue, his hand landed on her head.

Immediately it snapped back and Chase scrambled upright. "Ava? What the devil are you doin'?" He inhaled a sharp breath through his teeth when she tongued the tip. "Hell. I thought it was a dream."

She pulled off his shaft long enough to say, "Nope. I want to make this buff body to squirm." She licked him like a lollipop.

"Oh, I've no doubt you can make me squirm. You probably could get me to beg." He brushed her hair back from where it'd fallen in her face. "But—"

Again, Ava eased off and met his gaze in the near darkness. "But nothing. You don't get to direct this."

If she thought he'd lovingly pet her, agree, and murmur encouragement, she was mistaken. Chase's big hands were on her face, gripping her jaw. "Yes, I do."

His answer turned her panties damp. As did his explicit command, "On the floor. On your knees."

As Ava moved, so did Chase. He perched on the edge of the mattress, making space for her between his legs. Then he stroked her cheek. "Better. Now I can watch you workin' me and you ain't gonna choke when you swallow."

No mincing words there.

"Take me in your mouth again, Ava."

God that low gravely morning voice loosened something primitive inside her. She bent her head, letting her hair fall against his thighs, feeling his muscular quads quiver in response to the soft strands teasing the muscles. She suckled the tip, tracing the shape of the plump head with the inside of her lips, taking time to flick her tongue over the sweet spot below the cockhead with every wet swipe.

Tease. Retreat. Acquainting herself with his reactions, licking away the little pearls of pre-come. Then Ava moved in for the kill, needing to taste him fully. She made a fist around the base, sliding her hand up and down the length, bobbing her head to meet her fingers.

He stayed rigid, hands propped on the edge of the mattress, watching her. But Chase wasn't completely motionless. His body trembled. His chest rose and fell rapidly. His toes curled.

Something about seeing that odd vulnerability made Ava ache. Made her want to assure him she'd never exploit this part of him that he was bold enough to share with her.

Her hand slid down to fondle his balls as she worked that long shaft, rubbing the plump cockhead against the roof of her mouth before opening her throat. Breathing through the gag reflex, she swallowed him fully.

"Holy. Christ." Chase's palms covered her ears and he pushed her upper body back. Then he thrust past her lips, lodging his cock into her throat, staying there until she swallowed. He pulled out and did it again.

Ava had no control. Chase held her head, keeping her in place. "Ava. Look at me. See what you do to me."

Her gaze connected with his. Such lust. Such hunger in his eyes. Such need. She felt it all flowing between them, felt her body responding to the call of his. She hollowed her cheeks around the thickness filling her mouth and he groaned.

"Watch those teeth, darlin'," he warned, "but don't stop."

She switched from deep throating him to shallow bobs of her

head. Her senses were fine-tuned to the wet sucking sounds of his cock shuttling in and out of her mouth. The gentler grip he maintained in her hair. The shag carpet digging into her knees. His low murmurs of approval. The wholly male scent of his sex. And his entire body twitching with anticipation.

More more more. Give it all to me.

He swore and went motionless.

Ava moaned around his cock as he came and his taste exploded on her tongue. She swallowed each hot spurt and his pleasure rolled over her in a warm, satisfying wave. When the tremors ceased, she released his softened cock little by little, dragging out the moment for herself.

After his eyes opened and he seemed to remember where he was, he stroked her hair. Ran his thumb across her swollen lips. Then he granted Ava that cat-who'd-gotten-cream smirk. "Much better than an alarm clock."

As much as she'd loved blowing him, now in the aftermath, she felt shy. Exposed. She ducked her head, letting her mouth connect with his thigh, loving the way that coarse hair felt on her sensitized lips.

He continued to pet her, soothe her, trailing his fingers across her shoulder and down her spine. He only allowed her to hide from him for so long before he forced her to meet his gaze. "I don't want you to go back to LA now that we've scratched the itch. And before you go getting that mean glint in your eye, this has been way more than just sex for me. Way more."

For me too. But she couldn't say it. Instead she said, "But how does this—" she gestured to their naked bodies, "—change things between us?" She braced herself for a noncommittal answer, but Chase's next words blew her away.

"Ava. It changes nothing and it changes everything. We're friends. I can't imagine losing that part of you. But now I see us getting nekkid together as often as humanly possible, until we're both exhausted and grinning from ear to ear. So what does it mean we've gone from friends to lovers?" He bestowed that sweet, hot, naughty grin. "I believe that means we're havin' us a bonafide summer romance."

Ava watched from the shadows of the bleachers as Chase strode out of the medical tent. He stopped and talked to a couple of riders.

The man was magnificent. Not just his physique. Not just his face. Not just his cowboy charm. Not just his way with people that put them at ease. All those things by themselves were pretty impressive. But were powder-keg potent wrapped up in one package—a hunky cowboy who defined resilient.

She felt the other men's eyes on her, but she only had eyes for him. "Can I talk to you for a second?"

"Sure. Excuse us."

Wanting privacy, Ava wandered to the far corner, away from the contestants and rodeo officials.

When she turned around, Chase rested against a section of the metal corral.

"You still pissy with me for insisting we book a room tonight instead of heading to the next rodeo?"

His bad dismount last night affected his right side, his knee, his hip and his shoulder. She'd cringed this morning, seeing his bruised and battered body. He'd turned pissy and told her to quit staring at him like a circus freak. Then he'd grabbed his clothes and headed to the bathroom on stiff legs.

His blue eyes trapped hers. "Maybe." His big hands curled around her hips, but he kept their bodies apart. "But I'll let you make it up to me."

Chase's stance gave Ava additional height advantage. He didn't seem to mind, which was another big change in his attitude since they'd started sleeping together. "And what do you have in mind?"

He pressed a hot kiss on the center of her chest. Then those oh so talented lips traveled up the arc of her throat to her ear. "Guess."

"A blowjob."

Chase's chuckle against her neck caused goose flesh to break out. "Tempting, but no."

"You wanna bend me over a hay bale and spank my ass?"

"Wrong again. But you are givin' me some great ideas." His wet tongue flicked her earlobe like he was working her clit, which sent a spike of heat straight to her core. "I want a kiss."

"In public?"

"Yep. Right now."

She lowered her lips to his in a slow slide of mouth on mouth. Gradually shifting the kiss from sweet to fiery. Kissing him with passion, tempering it with tenderness. A languorous meeting of tongues, a communion of need.

He placed soft smooches on her mouth. "Thanks for caring about me, Ava."

"You sound surprised I do."

"Maybe I am. I'm not used to it because I've kept relationships casual. I wasn't joking about my threshold being two weeks." He twirled a piece of her hair around his finger. "I haven't answered to anyone for years. I find I like answering to you."

"I'm glad. I don't like to see you hurting. You don't have to be tough in front of me, Chase."

"It's a hard habit to break." He quickly changed the subject. "Are you taping me tonight?"

"Yeah. Unless you don't want me to."

"I want you to. I just hope it's not the same as last night."

His injury was causing him more pain than he'd let on. She'd be surprised if he rode any bulls tonight. "Good luck. I'll see you after."

Chase stuck it out on both bulls. But he wasn't in top form and finished in fourth place, out of the money.

First thing he did at the motel was shower. For thirty minutes. When they'd first started traveling on the road, she hadn't understood why it took him so long to shower. But now she knew he needed that long to get rid of the aches and pains from riding.

He dropped his towel and crawled in bed, twining himself around her like her own personal anaconda. "I'm not up for sex games tonight."

"So much for my nefarious plan to play nekkid Parcheesi with you."

Chase laughed softly.

"Seriously. Can I give you a massage or rub some ointment on the sore spots?"

"Thanks. But this is good. Your warm body is like a magic heating pad. Makes all my aches and pains go away. Makes me all tingly."

"Ooh. You're good."

"Mmm. You know it, but I'm at my best when I'm with you."

Ava melted just a little.

"Now, we done talking so we can see who gets tossed off *America's Next Top Model*, or what?"

Chapter Seventeen

Chase wasn't claustrophobic. But if he had to spend another fucking minute in the truck cab with Ava, surrounded by the scent of her lotion, the sight of her pink-tipped toes tapping on his dashboard and the porn queen way she sucked on licorice, he'd go insane.

In fact, he figured he deserved a medal for his ability to withstand the temptation of pulling off on the closest dirt road so he could fuck her inside the truck cab, or against the truck door, or in the truck bed. He'd been so lost in fantasies of the many, many ways he intended to take her, he'd missed the damn turn off.

He'd known the second he touched her he was done for. Ava needed him in a way no other woman ever had. He was a different man when he was with her, regardless if they were naked. So maybe that's why he couldn't freakin' wait to get naked with her again, day after day after day.

Seemed to take forever to check-in. He ditched the bags in the corner of the room. In the mirror above the sink, he saw Ava flop on the bed and heave a huge sigh.

"Before you get too comfy, maybe you oughta see if you got the door shut."

She popped to her feet and resituated her skirt as she crossed the room, those fucking sexy little pleats teasing the back of her legs.

When he'd gotten a look at her outfit this morning—short plaid skirt, plain white blouse, black ballet shoes—his cock had been hard all day as his head conjured up bad-schoolgirl-needing-a-spanking scenarios.

Ava tested the door by pushing on it. "I don't know why you were worried it wasn't shut—"

"Lock it." He put his mouth below her ear and pressed their bodies together.

The lock clicked.

"Hands on the door." He nuzzled her neck, whispering, "Want you."

She turned her head to catch his temple with a kiss and a soft, "You have me. What are you going to do with me?"

Chase let his breath tease her damp nape. Making her wait for a response.

"Chase?"

He licked the shell of her ear. "What do you want me to do to you?"

"Fuck me."

Made him hot as hell when crude words tumbled from that pretty mouth. But Chase knew it made her equally hot when he talked dirty right back to her. He curled his fingers around her hips and tugged her butt into his groin. "Grind this sweet ass against me. Make me want it. Make me want to touch it. Make me want to run my mouth over it. Make me want to fuck it."

He wondered if she'd balk, but she shimmied her hips and swung those perfect mounds of flesh into his groin like a pro.

Chase had a condom on two seconds after his jeans hit the floor. Dragging his cock up and down her sweet slit, he wasn't surprised how easily his cock slipped inside her welcoming heat. Ava was always ready for him. As much as he wanted to pound into her, he didn't.

Not at first. But her breathy whimpers and the tight clasp of her pussy when he drove in hard and deep shattered his strategy.

"Yes. I like that. God, I *love* that."

Hips pistoning, he set a plunge-and-retreat rhythm that felt so good he never wanted to stop. Each thrust pushed him to that elusive point, but Ava reached it first. Her cunt clamping down around his cock had him grunting, sweating, swearing as he fucked himself into an orgasmic stupor.

When he returned to earth, he muttered, "You all right?"

"I think I made claw marks in the door with my fingernails."

"Now that's a compliment."

Ava leaned back and wrapped her arm around his neck. "If I don't say it enough, you are an amazing lover, Chase."

"Same goes, sugar tits."

She laughed. "I know I shouldn't consider that a term of endearment, but I do."

"You're beautiful. Talented. Sexy. Smart. Sophisticated. Funny. Sweet." He kissed the back of her neck. "Are those better terms of endearment?"

She smiled against his throat. "Actually, I prefer sugar tits."

As they straightened their clothes, she said, "Now that we've got that out of the way, I expect you'll be looking for food next?"

"Out of the way?" Wearing a wicked, determined grin, Chase stalked her until the back of her knees hit the bed. "Just for that smartass crack, sugar tits, I'm gonna eat my fill of you. And darlin', you know how much I can eat."

Chase looked far too comfortable, far too sexy lounging against the passenger door, camera in hand. "Smile."

She scowled at him. "Why are you taping me?"

"Because you're driving and I'm bored out of my fuckin' mind."

At least if his hands were occupied he wasn't crunching on sunflower seeds. Or touching her. If the man put his hands on her while she was driving, she'd wreck his precious truck.

"Besides, what's good for the goose is good for the gander, right?"

"I'm from California. I don't even know what the hell that barnyard saying means."

"It means I answered your questions over the last few weeks, it's time for you to answer mine. Pains me to admit it, but your Gestapo tactic worked."

"Yeah?"

"You know stuff about me I've never told anyone."

But I want to know everything about you. I'm as obsessed with you as you are obsessed with riding bulls.

Chase fiddled with the camera. "Whoa. You can get really close with this."

"Are you getting shots of my nose hair?"

"Nope. I've zoomed in on your nipples. Think cold thoughts, baby."

"Chase."

"Think of what I did to you last night. That was pretty hot."

Her grip increased on the steering wheel even as her toes unconsciously curled. Chase's hungry mouth sucking on her clit. His fingers tweaking her nipples. Proving his mastery over her body, restraining her arms, denying her release, and building her to a frenzy with each lick. Each touch. Each whispered promise of ecstasy until she shattered with an epic orgasm that made her scream. Then he'd made love to her with such exquisite tenderness she'd melted.

"See? It worked. You've got that dreamy look you get right after I fuck you."

And so much for the basking. "Ask your damn question."

He chuckled. "Least favorite food."

"Eggplant. Slimy, nasty stuff. No matter how it's cooked it tastes like dog shit."

"I'd hafta agree."

"Same for zucchini. Our cook used to try and hide it in other dishes, but I always could taste it. Blech."

"You had a full-time cook, growing up?"

"Maria wasn't live-in help, but she came every day. Sometimes she cooked lunch, but most the time it was dinner. Why?"

"Most people I know don't hire out for them kinda domestic jobs. To be honest, you don't act nearly as spoiled as I thought you would."

"I think there was a compliment in that somewhere. Anyway, my mom worked a lot, expanding the hotel business. Cooking dinner and cleaning up the kitchen was the last thing she wanted to do after spending fourteen hours at the office."

"Gotta ask this, Hollywood. Did you have a nanny?"

She shook her head. "My dad stayed home with me and my brother when we were little. He jokes he can change a tire and a diaper in ten seconds flat. I told you he's a mechanic, right?"

Chase lowered the camera and squinted at her. "Wait a second. Dumond. Is your dad the Dumond in DRT—Dumond Racing Team?"

"Yeah. He started the team in our garage."

"Holy shit, Ava. DRT is my favorite NASCAR team. Darby Janeville had an amazing season last year with that second place showing in Darlington—"

Ava held up her hand. "No offense, but you might as well be speaking Chinese. I don't follow NASCAR. Haven't much cared for racing."

"Ever?"

"Ever."

Chase didn't say anything, but obviously he wanted to.

"What?"

"How is it you know all about your mother's position as CEO of Cooper Hotels, but you don't have any interest in your father's business? Especially since he built it from the ground up and he was around more during your growing-up years than your mom."

That jarred her. She'd never thought of it that way. Her dad used to ask her to come to races. She always refused. When had he stopped asking?

Why hadn't you noticed?

Chase's deep voice startled her out of guilty thoughts. "So your brother chose the hotel business over the racing business?"

"Axel is involved with DRT, mostly from the Cooper Tires side. He attends all the events with Dad." Again, it struck Ava, how much she'd cut herself off from her family in recent years since she'd "made it" as an actress. Was that why Axel acted so curt with her? Because she blew him off, he was mirroring her behavior?

When had she gotten so selfish? So stingy? Unwilling to share any of her free time with her family?

She knew Chase had taken a rash of crap about his emotional and physical distance from his family. She'd felt sorry for him, but come to find out, she'd been acting the same way.

"Ava?"

"Sorry. Spaced there for a second. I'm a lot like my mom in that I don't do domestic things. My housekeeping service keeps my house tidy. They take my dirty things to the laundry once a week. Then clean clothes are miraculously returned to their proper places. I don't have to do anything. So that makes me as useless as teats on a bull, doesn't it?"

Chase smiled. "Nice barnyard reference, Hollywood."

"If the horseshoe fits... Anyway. It's embarrassing to admit I'm so helpless."

"Shouldn't be. You lead a different life than most folks. Doesn't mean it's wrong. You have what most people work so hard for. You shouldn't apologize for it."

How was it this man knew exactly what to say? Not in a suck-up way, but with total sincerity?

Such a sucker for this man, Ava. Write it on your forehead—s-u-c-k-e-r.

"Okay, back to the hard-hitting questions. What's the most personal thing anyone gave you?"

"You go first this time, McKay."

"A bronze my cousin Carter sculpted of me ridin' the bull Chicken on a Chain that scored me a ninety-two point ride."

That was a very personal gift, which caused Ava another pang of sadness when she thought about the loss of hers.

"What's wrong? Your face changed."

"The camera showed you that?"

"Ava. I don't need to look through a viewfinder to see you're upset."

Damn intuitive man.

"The camera is off. Talk to me."

"My grandfather commissioned a necklace for my sixteenth birthday. A tiny beautiful Swarovski crystal rose with a gold stem artfully twisted into an 'A'. The one time I didn't take it off before I jumped into the ocean? I lost it. I don't know if the chain broke or what, but I was devastated because it happened about a month after he died."

"Aw, sugar, I'm so sorry."

Evidently Chase had enough taping. He returned the camera to the case and faced forward, wiggling to get comfortable.

"Before you nod off, tell me why we're backtracking. You planned a route through Montana and now we're back in Cornhusker territory."

He rolled his eyes. "South Dakota is not Cornhusker territory. The reason I'm not goin' to the event in Billings is because Ryan told me a former PBR bull rider who switched to the PRCA circuit will be competing. I don't wanna run into him."

"Why didn't you tell me this?"

"I did."

"When? Because I'd remember something like that."

"You were pecking away on your computer, and I told you about it as soon as I got off the phone with Ryan. You said, and I quote, 'Sounds like a good plan' so don't blame me that you tuned me out again."

Before she could apologize, Chase said, "I'm whupped," and wedged himself between the passenger door and the seat, pulling his hat down over his eyes.

Ava had just walked out of a truck-stop bathroom, when her phone rang. Her belly tightened at the caller ID: Marnie Driscoll. Her agent. "Hello?"

"Ava, dear, it's Marnie. I'm so happy to hear your voice. That secretive assistant of yours wouldn't tell me where you've been hiding yourself."

Thanks, Hannah. "I'm taking a vacation at an undisclosed location. Why? What's up?"

Marnie sighed. "Well, I'm afraid I have bad news. The movie shoot in Mexico has been postponed indefinitely."

"What happened?"

"Something with illegal permits and the production company's insurance carrier refusing to cover people and equipment in that part of Mexico due to previous issues. It's all very complicated, and evidently Lynch is incensed enough to completely rewrite the screenplay with an entirely new location. With as slow as that writing process is for him, you could be in limbo on this project for at least a year."

She slumped against the concrete wall. "Damn. I really looked forward to that role and working with Lynch."

"I understand. But to be perfectly blunt, dear, I'm not terribly unhappy about it. I know everyone is vying to work with Lynch because he's on his way up, but the pay was total crap. You'd signed on for slave wages, with less-than-decent living conditions in a dangerous part of Mexico for several months. And we both know the backend profit deal I negotiated for you wouldn't amount to much without major distribution, which Lynch still lacks with his small production company."

Marnie had lobbied hard for Ava not to take the part. But Marnie's bottom line wasn't Ava's—Marnie looked solely at dollar signs. That trait made her a great agent, but caused friction on occasion. "So what now?"

"This is actually very happy news for us. Since you were committed to that movie, I couldn't suggest you to casting agents for any new mid-season TV productions. Now that stumbling block is out of the way and I can let everyone know you're available."

Maybe it made her a diva, but Ava couldn't muster much enthusiasm for signing on for another series. Yes, it'd been upsetting when *Miller's Ridge* had been cancelled, but without being tied to a weekly TV show, she'd finally had the chance to branch out. "I don't know what to say."

"Say yes. Say you're excited." Marnie sighed again. "Look, Ava, I know you've mentioned that five years of working on television was enough. But sweetie, that was before this thing happened with Jake. You'll be lucky if anyone shows an interest in hiring you, even for TV."

That stung.

"We need to rebuild your name. It might take a couple of years, but you've given your all to your career, we both know it'd be suicide to stop now. I'll make the rounds. Throw out a few hooks to see who bites. Does that sound reasonable?"

"Yes. Thanks, Marnie."

"It's my job. But just so we're clear, if we do get lucky and land you an audition, I can count on you to be there, right?"

"Meaning, drop everything and fly to LA on a moment's notice."

"Exactly. I can't imagine your little vacation is more important than your career. I'll be in touch." Marnie hung up.

And Ava feared this was the beginning of the end of her Wild West adventure.

Hours later Ava's head was screaming. A thick haze settled behind her eyes, making it hard to see.

She hated to wake him, but she had no choice. "Chase?"

"Yeah." He stirred. "I'm awake. We already there?"

"No. We're about thirty miles out. But I can't drive anymore."

Chase was immediately upright. "What's wrong?"

"Is there a metal spike sticking out of the top of my head? Because it sure feels like it."

Now silvery fishlike lines were swimming in her peripheral vision, adding a layer of nausea to the pain and dizziness.

"Pull over," he said sharply.

"I'm sorry. I know you're hurting—"

"Ava. Ease off the gas and pull over before you cause an accident. You're driving down the middle of the damn road."

She slowed. By the time she stopped, her stomach was in full revolt. Ava let her head fall back into the headrest and muttered, "Give me a minute and we'll switch places."

Chase hopped out his side and opened the driver's side door. "Hold tight." His hands slipped beneath her legs and he picked her up slowly, taking extra care not to jostle her.

What a sweet, attentive man. But still it caused a spark of paranoia, imagining how many times he'd done the soothe-and-calm routine with other women. Ava managed to last fifteen seconds in the passenger side before she bailed out, falling to her knees on the rocky ground and dry heaving. Her belly roiled and she felt clammy sweat plastering her hair to her head.

Chase's hand rubbed circles on her back. "Better?"

"Some." She pushed back on her heels.

"Let's get you out of the heat." He helped her back into the truck. Once they were moving, he threaded his fingers through hers. "If you feel barfy, lemme know and I'll pull over."

Every bump in the road sent a shaft of pain into her skull. Finally, the truck stopped.

Chase said, "Be right back."

The truck cab heated, her whole body dripped sweat. Then blessedly cool air wafted over her. She opened her eyes and noticed they were in a motel parking lot. "Where are we?"

"A place where you can take it easy today. How often do you get migraines?"

"I don't get migraines," she said irritability.

"Ava. Sweetheart. I know what a migraine looks like and you need some damn—"

"I'm hot, sweaty and my brain feels like it's in a pressure cooker, so please don't yell at me, Chase, and give me an on-the-fly diagnosis."

He smoothed his hands up her neck to cup her face in his palms, wiping away her tears. Those blue eyes showed concern, not anger. "Got a great opinion of me, Hollywood, if you think I'd yell at a sick woman."

"I'm not sick." More tears leaked out before she could stop them. "I'm upset because I lost my job." The last word caught on a pain-filled gasp.

Chase went perfectly still. "Run that by me again?"

"My agent called when I stopped for gas. The movie shoot in Mexico has been called off."

"Oh, baby. I'm so sorry. I know how much you wanted that. No wonder you've made yourself sick. C'mere."

Ava didn't hold back the sobs. Her thoughts were so muddled, she couldn't tell him the rest. She'd probably have to leave any day and that made her sick to her stomach.

"Hey, now, come on, let's get you fixed up."

Ava gripped his hand as he started across the parking lot. But the shimmering mirage images were back in her peripheral vision and she stumbled. Chase caught her and gently lifted her into his arms. She whispered, "Sorry."

"Don't be. I've got you."

Inside the room, Chase settled her on the bed. "Lie back and close your eyes."

The dizziness didn't go away, but it didn't get worse.

The bed dipped. "This might be cold."

A cool cloth covered her forehead and eyes. She sighed. "You must think I'm a baby for—"

"Ssh. Relax. Breathe nice and slow, yoga girl."

She focused on forcing air in and out.

"That's it." His rough-skinned fingers trailed up and down her arm, soothing her, his touch more effective than any over-the-counter headache medicine.

"Chase—"

"Ssh." The last thing Ava remembered were his warm lips pressing against hers, and his whispered, "Rest."

Her stomach rumbled so loudly it woke her up. Disoriented, she opened her eyes and saw Chase lying next to her. Her stomach did a little flip, not from sickness, but from seeing those beautiful blue eyes first thing.

"Hey. How do you feel?"

"Hungry. Thirsty. Confused. Like I was in a time warp. What time is it?"

"Seven a.m." Chase handed her a bottle of water. "This'll help."

"Thanks." Ava sat up and drank all the water. "So I crashed for over twelve hours. Guess I missed the rodeo last night. How'd you do?"

Chase wore a stoic expression.

"What? Did you have like a ninety-nine point ride or something?"

He snorted.

"Seriously. What happened?" Her gaze swept over him. "Did you get hurt?"

"Nothin' happened, Ava. I didn't compete last night."

"What? Why not?"

"Do you really think I'd just leave you here alone when you were so goddamn sick?"

She froze.

Chase grabbed her hand and rubbed her knuckles against the razor stubble on his cheeks. "I was freaked out about you. I wasn't exactly sure what to do. I'm not...well, I don't have much experience taking care of sick people. My first response has always been to get the hell away, so I sort of winged it." A sheepish smile curled the corners of his mouth. "You don't look too worse for the wear."

"I can't believe you didn't compete last night."

"There are more important things in life than bull ridin'."

This tough man had given up a chance to ride some of the best rough stock around to play nursemaid. Just when she thought she had the one-track mind bull rider down cold, he bowled her over with something completely unexpected.

"Thank you."

"You take such good care of me, Ava, I was more than happy to return the favor."

She smiled until he got right in her face. "And I'm also happy to return the favor of nagging you into telling me exactly what your agent said that got you wound so tight." He flashed his teeth. "No dodging me either, because *friends* share stuff like this, remember?"

Somehow she'd known that comment would come back to bite her. But she wasn't an actress for nothing. She'd lie her ass off so Chase didn't put an end to their adventure right now.

Chapter Eighteen

The bad thing about driving all night? Trying to find a motel at six in the morning with available rooms. When they finally located one, they agreed paying seventy dollars over their budget was worth it.

As soon as they dropped their bags, they stripped, crawled between the cool sheets of the king-sized bed and conked out, twined together. Even in sleep Chase kept Ava close. He'd never imagined he'd like waking up with the same woman wrapped around his body every morning.

He woke around noon and showered. He didn't bother dressing because his priority was getting Ava nekkid. Immediately. But first he grabbed his supplies from his duffel bag and piled them on the nightstand.

Chase started at her pretty toes peeping out from beneath the comforter. She'd insisted on foregoing lunch for a pedicure. He hadn't understood why sporting pink toenails vastly improved her mood; it just had. And after how worried he'd been while she'd had that vicious migraine, he would've done anything to see her back to normal.

He nibbled on the top of her foot and pressed a kiss on her instep. His mouth wandered past her ankle, and he slowly zigzagged just the very tip of his tongue up her shin. God. She had such satiny smooth skin everywhere.

Ava stirred and murmured, "I'm liking this morning wake-up call, cowboy."

He threw back the covers and continued his northward progression, using his right hand to lightly stroke her right leg. "And just think, I'm only half-done."

"If you're getting tired you could stop at the midpoint and...rest."

"Rest...by putting my face in your crotch?"

"Yes. And you could leave it there as long as you wanted."

"Oh really?"

"Really. I'm an accommodating woman."

"Lucky for me." He lightly sank his teeth into her hipbone and snapped the stretchy string of her cherry-red thong. He peppered kisses down the sexy sweep of her belly to the rise of her pubic bone, but rather than continuing south, he dragged openmouthed kisses straight up her torso. Paused to tongue the rhinestone charm dangling from her belly button piercing. He lifted his mouth from feasting on her skin long enough to say, "Unhook your bra."

Ava twisted the front snap until it released. She tugged it down her arms and tossed it aside. Then her hands were on his head, sensuously rubbing her palms across his bristly hair. "I love how this feels."

"I love when you put your hands on me, but right now, I want them above your head."

"I really love it when you get all bossy," she said with a husky purr.

He kissed her sternum. "I know you do." Humbling, how readily Ava accepted it his aggressive side. She turned herself over to him without hesitation. Without restriction. With absolute trust that he could give her what she needed.

Which was why he was going to push her a little farther today than he usually did.

While letting his facial hair tease the underside of her breasts, Chase said, "Ava, do you trust me?"

A beat passed before she answered, "Yes."

"Be very sure of that answer."

"Why?"

"Because I wanna try something with you. But I hafta know you're on board. That you believe I'd never step far over the line."

"That does scare me a little." She squirmed. "But I'll admit my interest outweighs my anxiety. So, yes. Whatever you want from me, Chase, is yours."

Humbled, Chase slipped his hands up her chest to lovingly curl his hands around her face, studying her eyes. "Thank you." His kisses started out sweet, but quickly heated. Deepened. Intensified to the point they both breathed hard when he finally released her mouth.

He reached for the neckerchief on the dresser. "Blindfold first."

"Like in the movie *9 ½ Weeks*?"

"Never seen it." Chase covered her eyes and secured the knot on the back of her head. He let his lips drift across her forehead, then across her cheeks. Placing his mouth on her ear to whisper, "I don't need anyone else's ideas on how to turn you on, Ava Rose. And sweet darlin', make no mistake. I'm gonna turn you inside out."

She moaned and angled her head, trying to force him to kiss her.

"Huh-uh. Hold still or I won't touch you until you prove you can behave."

"Hard-ass." She bestowed that dazzling movie star smile. "I meant that with the utmost respect, sir."

Chase smooched her mouth. "I like it when you suck up to me. Wrists together." He bound her hands with a bandana, looped his belt through the binding and attached it to the headboard.

"Why are you tying me up? It's not like I've ever tried to get away from you when we're naked."

"And I appreciate that." He straddled her thighs and ran his hands from her bound wrists, down those yoga-toned arms, stopping at those beautiful, plentiful tits. He cupped and squeezed them, loving that his hands couldn't contain all the abundant flesh. "Have you ever noticed your nipples are the same deep pink color as your lips?"

"No. Look, Chase, you don't have to—"

He covered her mouth with his, stopping her protest. Maybe he was wasting his time fondling her breasts because she couldn't feel anything, but he hadn't done a thorough test yet. If he'd attempted a sensual yet intensive assessment without restricting her hands, well, her clever hands would distract him and he'd lose his focus. And this was all focused on her. As soon as he broke the seal of their mouths, he returned to worshipping her chest.

Letting the tips of his fingers caress the outside swells of her breasts, he feathered his thumbs over her nipples, watching the tips draw into rigid nubs. Tempting, to enclose the peak between his lips, getting it wetter with each suctioning pull of his hot mouth. Making it harder. But he didn't. He just stroked and teased.

Chase didn't need verbal confirmation his focused attention was having a positive affect; her body told him everything he needed to know. He took possession of her mouth. Whispering kisses across her passion-dampened skin. Using his tongue to trace the upper and lower bow of her lips while maintaining the slow, steady torment on her nipples.

Only when she relaxed did he mix it up. Following the cords in her neck to the base of her throat, he opened his mouth and sucked the sweet spot by her collarbone the same time he pinched both her nipples. Hard.

Ava gasped and arched.

He was insistent in his attention. Licking, softly kissing, gently biting her neck, then randomly tweaking those taut peaks. Relentlessly and very, very thoroughly.

"Chase—"

He fell headlong into the rush of serving up harsh kisses whenever she opened her delectable mouth. And he knew the exact moment she realized he was one hundred percent in charge and she surrendered to him completely.

Chase murmured, "Good girl," and started on her nipples. The teasing laps and random licks on the tips didn't get much reaction.

But when he sucked strongly and used his teeth, she thrashed beneath him. Normally by the time he'd taken his lover to that point, he'd back down and move to the next step in the seduction process. Not this time. He kept up his assault, immersing himself in the taste of her, the feel of her, taking her someplace new, no matter how long it took.

When he blew a cooling stream of air across the erect peaks and Ava trembled, he pushed her breasts together so closely her nipples almost touched. Tucking his knees beneath her armpits, he slid his shaft into the valley of her cleavage.

Her body bucked beneath his.

Chase groaned at the slickness of her skin and how hot it looked with the head of his cock fitted into the hollow of her throat. "I've wanted to fuck your tits like this since the moment I saw them." He pulled out, then slowly slid back into the tight tunnel he'd created, savoring the clasp of her flesh around his. He added another layer of sensation and pinched her nipples. "Can you feel that?"

"Squeeze them together more. Like that. Touch my nipples harder," she panted. "Even harder than that. You're not hurting me."

He growled at the visual feast before him. Ava bound, at his mercy.

Chase rocked his hips faster, driving his cock against that pliant skin, pinching her nipples in time to his thrusts. When his balls lifted, his hands fell away and almost told her to open up and swallow him to the root. But he stopped.

Too soon. Not about you. About her. She needs this.

Ava whimpered at the loss of contact.

He caressed her cheek as he leaned forward to grab his supplies off the nightstand. "You're beautiful. Incredible. Christ, Ava, you undo me."

She twisted in her bonds. "I want—"

He placed his fingers over her lips. "In time. Now hold still." He scooted back until he straddled her pelvis. Holding open the old-fashioned, spring-loaded wooden clothespins, he simultaneously attached them to her nipples.

When she arched and emitted a surprised cry, he murmured, "Seems you have some feeling there after all." He hopped off the end of the bed. Tapped her ankles. "Spread your legs for me. Wider. Nope wider than that."

"Chase—"

"Come on, yoga girl, I know how flexible you are. Do it."

Her heels slid out until one hung off the bed.

He positioned himself in the space she'd made. He placed an openmouthed kiss on her belly. On each hip. Then he released the clothespins for about ten seconds before he reattached them sideways, so the holes surrounded the tips.

Ava's cries became louder as he settled his mouth on her cunt. She was already drenched. He lapped her honey, pushing his tongue deep inside her, then retreating to trace the folds of her sex. Teasing the skin around her clit, but never coming into direct contact.

She bumped her pelvis, thrashing, her body begging.

Pressing open the fleshy skin protecting that pleasure pearl, he licked. Delicately. Insistently. When her entire body stilled, he zeroed in on her clit and sucked continuously until her pussy contracted against his mouth.

As she came down, Chase scattered kisses up her torso and slid two fingers inside her hot channel, stroking the pillow of flesh on her inner vaginal wall. Then he quickly removed the clothespin from her left nipple, knowing the instant blood returned to the tip.

Ava jerked, whimpering, "It hurts, God, it's throbbing," and flat out shrieked when Chase sucked the distended nipple into the wet heat of his mouth.

She climaxed again suddenly. Violently.

He felt her orgasm pulsating on his tongue as he suckled her nipple. He felt it beneath his thumb as he strummed her clit. He felt it squeezing his fingers as he stroked the inside wall of her sheath. Every part of her body radiated the pleasure he'd wrought from her, brought to her.

It was fucking hot as hell.

His impatient cock, hard as a fencepost for the last thirty minutes, poked into his abdomen, leaving a slick trail.

She twitched with aftershocks and Chase continued to pet her, stroke her. He kissed her temple. "Ava. I'm gonna unhook you from the headboard."

She rubbed her cheek against his and mumbled.

Once he had the belt undone and the bandana off, he put on a condom and patted her hip. "Sit up."

As soon as languorous Ava moved, he snagged a pillow and covered it with a towel. "Up on your knees." Chase repositioned her, pressing a hand to the middle of her back. "On your elbows, so your chest is over the pillow."

Ava groaned. "The towel rubs on my nipple."

"I know."

"Can I take off the other clothespin now?"

"Not yet." He kneed her legs apart to create a wider base. Taking himself in hand, he prodded the entrance to her pussy twice before sliding in halfway.

She automatically arched, trying to force him inside her fully, but Chase covered her body with his. Molding his belly to the soft curve of her ass, pressing the weight of his damp chest against her back, bracketing her arms with his. Boxing her in. Making her wait. She only had movement he allowed.

He pulled out and snapped his hips, plunging in to the root. Every thrust sent her tits swinging and rubbing over that cheap, nubby towel. Every thrust had her crying out. Every thrust brought Chase closer to detonation. He couldn't hold off. He didn't want to hold off. When his balls drew up, he hammered into her without pause. Burying his face between her shoulder blades, sucking in her scent with every ragged breath, he came in a hot, fast rush.

Just when Chase thought that burst of pleasure was over, he felt Ava's contractions start again. Despite his shaky stance, he reached between them and released the clothespin.

Ava bucked as he massaged the tender tip. Her whimper escalated when the blood rushed back to those tissues. He forced her to ride the line between pleasure and pain as her pussy pulsed around his cock.

Her elbows gave out and she fell forward.

Chase peppered her shoulder with kisses, giving her a second to find her equilibrium. A muffled sob escaped, snapping him from smug satisfaction. Panicked, he flipped her on her back, looming above her to see Ava...crying.

His gut clenched. "Ava? Baby? Did I hurt you?"

She shook her head and more tears spilled free.

He tenderly swiped them away. "Then what? Sweet thang, you're killin' me here."

She bit her trembling lip, turning her head toward the wall.

"Look at me." When she didn't respond, he repeated, "Look at me," more sharply.

Those breathtaking eyes connected with his, even as she blinked back tears.

"God. Don't cry. Talk to me."

"No one..." She swallowed hard. "No man has ever seen to me like that. Taken time and demanded patience from me. How did you know that's what I needed and wanted?"

Relieved he hadn't somehow fucked this up by acting too domineering, Chase gave her a lingering smooch. "How did I know you needed more nipple stimulation?" His intent to be flip vanished when he realized sharing the truth mattered more than touting his years of sexpertise. "A combination of instinct and curiosity."

"Really?"

"Can I tell you something?"

Ava ran the back of her knuckles across his cheek. "You can tell me anything, Chase."

"For all my supposed sexual experience, I've always been a taker in bed. No need to work for it when women were vying for a piece of me, vying to please me."

Although she didn't say a word, her eyes and her face echoed total understanding.

"But with you...from the start, even us just bein' friends, I demanded more because I wanted more. Not more to take, but more to give. You bring out something in me, Ava, a side of myself I never knew existed. It's scary shit. Does that make sense?"

"Yes. And no." She smiled. "I can't believe you'd ever be passive in bed. You're so...inventive. And maybe this sexual aggressiveness *feels* new, but it's not new. It's part of your makeup that's been dormant." Her fingertips brushed his whiskers. "I like it. I can't imagine you being any other way."

Humbled, Chase kissed her. Kept it light. Breezy. Not the passionate show of possession his head urged him to demonstrate.

Ava broke the kiss with a heartfelt sigh. "So what's on the agenda today before the rodeo starts?"

He grinned. "I'm definitely thinking I need another ride."

Chapter Nineteen

"Done. You really needed a trim." Ava set the clippers on the table.

After she brushed the remnants of his hair off his shirt, Chase's hands circled her hipbones. Then he tugged her onto his lap. "Put your hands back on my head."

"Why? Did I hurt you?"

"God no. It feels so damn good when you're touching me there."

The deep, raspy timbre of his voice rolled over her. Through her. She placed her palms on his cheeks and slowly slid them up the planes of his chiseled face. Once she reached his hairline, she let her nails scrape over his scalp. Slowly. Thoroughly. Losing herself in touching him at his invitation, without restriction. Loving how the stubbly hair felt beneath her palms and fingertips. Remembering how it felt gently scraping the inside of her thighs. Her belly. Her breasts.

Chase expelled a groaning sigh and pressed his soft, warm lips to the base of her throat. His mouth wandered south to the upper swell of her cleavage. He dragged his goatee across that tender flesh, adding in a lingering kiss here and there.

Ava's thighs tightened around his hips. She allowed her head to fall back, stroking his head as she pleased, wishing her hands could wander. But since Chase's touches never veered out of control, she followed his lead. One of these days she'd step over the line and push him to unleash the wild man he attempted to control. For now, she'd lose herself in his sweet need.

"Ava," he whispered thickly against her neck, below her ear.

"I know you're going to warn me we don't have time for this. But I don't want to stop."

"I wasn't gonna tell you to stop. I was gonna ask you pretty please to go get a condom."

She laughed and kissed his smirk. "Be right back."

"Hurry."

Sweaty and sore, Chase paced in front of the motel room. The pains and twinges in odd places served as a reminder he'd gotten spoiled in the PBR. There was a world of difference in getting on one, two or three bulls over a three-day period, as opposed to PRCA riders, who climbed on one or two bulls each night. Sometimes for several nights running. This time of year shouldn't be called Cowboy Christmas, but Cowboy Hell.

He mopped his face with the bottom of his tank top and used his key card to open the door. The sight that greeted him? Ava, half-nekkid, her flexible body bent backward over her exercise ball, that mouth-watering pussy tempting him from between her toned thighs.

His aches and pains were forgotten. A new ache arose—his cock instantly went hard.

Ava's strong, sexy abdominal muscles rippled as she elevated her torso. "Hey. Great timing. I just finished."

"Perfect timing." Chase dropped to his knees on the yoga mat between her feet. "Take off your bottoms."

"What? Why?" Recognition lit her eyes and a secretive smile appeared. "Really, Chase? Right now?"

"Yep."

"But I'm all sweaty. Can't I take a shower first?"

He growled, "No. Seeing your hot, bendy body stretched out over that ball does it for me in a bad way." Using a single rough-edged fingertip, he leisurely traced the waistband of her yoga pants, low on her hips. But not nearly low enough. "Take. Them. Off."

She stood and peeled the stretchy black fabric down her legs. She began to remove her bra, but he said, "Leave it. Same position you were just in. Arched over the ball, hands on the floor behind you, feet on the floor, legs spread."

With effortless grace, Ava returned her body to its previous pose.

Goddamn she was beautiful like this. Not just her bared body, but also her willingness to cede control to him. His hands skated up the outside of her thighs, still trembling from her workout. Or were they trembling in anticipation? He palmed her hips and squeezed, stopping to stroke the sensitive sweep of flesh between her hipbones until goose flesh dotted her torso.

"This is weird. I can feel you but I can't see you."

Flattening his hands, Chase mapped her quads, his thumbs dragging along the inside of her thighs. He gripped her knees and lowered his head, placing his mouth on her.

Ava sighed.

Chase licked her slowly, savoring the salty tang of her sweat mixed with the musky sweetness of her pussy. That was the extent of his attention at first, his tongue created a repetitive path over the pink slit, from the wet entrance to her sex to the top of her mound. Each pass made her wetter, made that intimate flesh plumper, made her breathing more labored. Made him hotter. Harder.

He fucking loved this. He could spend hours, right here, testing her stamina, his control, and seeing how many times he could make her come with just his mouth.

His hands caressed her outer thighs up to where her leg became the curve of her ass. He loved this hidden, highly sensitive crease, loved that stroking it while lapping her pussy caused Ava to clench her ass cheeks and moan.

And still he feasted on her sex. Nipping, suckling, easing back to blow on her wet skin. With the stiffened tip of his tongue, he rimmed her pussy, from her entrance to her clit and back down the other side.

"Chase."

"Mmm?"

"Blood is rushing to my head."

"That's what I love to hear when I'm eating my fill of this sweet, hot cunt." He shoved his tongue inside her until his teeth pressed into her flesh.

"Oh God."

Chase slid his thumb into her pussy the same time he jammed his tongue in deep. Fucking her with both. Trying to keep her still after she'd begun bumping up her hips, which set the ball bouncing. But then she started thrashing too.

"Ava, darlin', hold still."

"I can't. Please. I'm close."

Keeping his thumb pressed in her clenching channel, he used his index finger and other thumb to separate the skin concealing her clit. Once he'd exposed that swollen pearl, he flicked it with his tongue. No respite. No mercy. As soon as her abdomen and thighs went taut, he sucked directly on it.

Ava detonated. A hoarse cry split the air. Her body vibrated as her orgasm rocked through her and the blood-engorged tissues pulsed against his mouth.

Primal satisfaction roared inside him.

When she shuddered, her wail reverberated through the plastic ball. He wanted to do it again. And again. Bathe in her juices as he swallowed climax after climax. He kept nuzzling her, caressing her, gorging his senses on everything—her taste, her scent, the feel of her body, the sound of her passion.

Her hands stroking his scalp brought him back to earth.

Whoa. He'd never lost himself like that before. He'd hit hazy white space of after orgasm bliss many times, but he'd never reached it by giving pleasure rather than receiving.

Chase lifted his head, meeting her passion-glazed gaze, knowing his own eyes were closer to animal than man.

Ava's shaking fingers lovingly followed the shape of his face. From his scalp, over his forehead to the ridge of his eyebrows. Then down the slope of his nose and the jut of his cheekbones to the broad angle of his jaw.

He stood, bringing her to her feet, teasing her succulent mouth with flirty kisses. After toeing off his running shoes, he shucked his athletic shorts. "Know another yoga pose that drives me out of my mind with lust?"

"What?"

"Downward dog." He scraped his teeth along the cord in her neck, right by her racing pulse. "Maybe I oughta call it downward doggie style. Assume the position." He released her and snatched a condom and the lube from the nightstand.

When he turned around, condom on and slicked up, and saw Ava's perfect ass in the air, he wanted to smack it. Bite it. Bury his cock in it.

Moving in behind her, his greedy gaze pursued the long, strong line of her spine. Resting her body weight on her hands caused the muscles in her triceps and biceps to stand out. His finger forged the same path as his eyes, but slipped past the sexy dimples above her ass, past her tailbone. Down the cleft of her ass. The tip of his finger swirled over the tight rosebud. "Another time, I'm taking your ass like this. Clutching these sweet cheeks as I'm pounding into you. Think you could hold the position, Ava Rose? While I'm fucking your ass hard?"

"Yes." She arched, lifting her head.

Chase reached his ultimate destination, the entrance to her pussy. Oh yeah, Ava was still wet. He widened his stance, rubbing his stiff shaft up the slit of her sex, once, twice, three times, before plunging his cock in to the hilt.

He hissed at the immediate hot clasp of her vaginal walls and the suctioning pull as he retreated. Her innermost flesh stayed pliant as he rammed back in.

Chase closed his eyes for a moment, enjoying every single sensation. Sweat dripping down his back. Ava's taste still lingering on his tongue. His racing heart that sent blood sizzling through his veins. The feel of her firm butt cheeks beneath his fingertips. The cushiony mat beneath his feet. The sheer ecstasy at having this woman naked and willing any time he wanted. Any place. Any way.

"Chase? You okay? You sorta stopped moving."

"Just taking a breather before this." He surged into her. *Slam.* Withdraw. *Slam.* Withdraw. *Slam.*

She emitted a sexy groan.

He noticed Ava hadn't lifted her head. "Tell me what it looks like from that angle," he asked, not missing a single stroke.

"Hot as hell. No wonder you love to take me from behind, if this is what it looks like."

"Oh yeah." Chase picked up the pace, his hands slippery on her damp skin. "It's a fucking turn on to bury my dick so far inside you it looks like we're one person."

"Pretty poetic, McKay. God! Do that again."

"This?" He swiveled his hips when his cock was fully seated.

"Yes! Dammit, I'm done."

She came again. Her body shaking, but she held position.

Which sent him soaring into the abyss. Pulse after pulse of his cock emptying set his limbs to quaking. His eyes rolled back in his head and pleasure swamped him.

When she groaned and said, "I'm getting a cramp," he roused himself from that happy place and pulled out.

She rolled up and gave him a contented look.

He grinned back at her. "You know, Hollywood. This yoga stuff ain't half bad."

Chapter Twenty

If the first two weeks they were together had been about friendship, the last two weeks had been about sex.

They still couldn't get enough of each other. They'd spend all day traveling. Then they'd fall on each other the second they were alone. Usually in their motel room, since Chase wasn't much on public displays of affection. But when that bedroom door closed? It was almost as if her body became an extension of his—their bodies were never apart for very long, whether in rest, in sleep or in passion.

The passion between them...one for the record books. Ava had never been in such an explosive sexual relationship. She'd known Chase's sexuality was an innate part of him, but she'd never understood it was such an innate part of her too.

Yet, for as addictive as their lovemaking had become, the friendship part of their relationship hadn't changed. They never ran out of things to talk about. Silly things. Serious things. She never had to guess Chase's feelings on anything. He threw them out boldly and without apology. The silences between them weren't awkward, demanding conversation.

What she wouldn't give for some silence right now. Total silence. She sighed.

"That's about the fifteenth time you've sighed in the last five minutes. What's wrong *now*?"

Rather than let it go again, she snapped, "Do you have to eat those stupid sunflower seeds every damn time we get in the truck?"

Chase said, "Yup," then spit the spent seeds into his discard cup.

Rattle the bag. Fill his mouth with seeds. Crack the seeds. Spit out the empty shells. Repeat. Sometimes for six hundred miles.

It drove Ava fucking insane.

Sure, it was Chase's truck. But if she had to listen to Mr. Chipmunk Cheeks enjoying his nuts for the next three hours, she might do something rash, and rude, and violent to his nuts.

Needing a distraction, she flipped on the radio, scrolling through static until she found a station that played decent music. Her bare toes tapped in time to Lady GaGa's "Poker Face" as she resituated herself and her laptop.

Click. Off went the radio.

Ava didn't demand he turn it back on. She just reached over and did it herself.

"Shut that shit off," Mr. Chipmunk Cheeks said around a mouthful of seeds.

"I'm listening to it."

"You wanna hear music, listen to your damn iPod."

"I told you my ear buds broke, but you couldn't be bothered to stop so I could pick up a new pair. So deal with it."

He sighed with utter exasperation. "You can have the radio on if you find a country music station."

"No way," she sneered. "I hate that whining, puntastic drivel."

"And 'Poker Face' is what? Pure musical artistry?" Chase sneered right back.

"Yep." Ava cranked the music a notch higher.

He turned it back down. "You're starting to piss me off."

"The feeling is mutual."

How had they survived these last two weeks?

Wait a second. Hadn't Chase told her he'd rarely made it past the two-week mark with any lover? Maybe this was how he intended to end it. By picking fights.

But you started it. Be the bigger person and let it go.

"I wish I had your damn camera pointed at you right now so you could see your diva side, a side which you claim ain't there, because darlin', it sure as hell is." *Spit. Spit.*

That smart comment totally screwed him for her being the bigger person. "I wish I had my damn camera pointed at you right now so you could see how ridiculous you look with your mouth crammed full of sunflower seeds," she mimicked. "Ooh, and the bonus? You'd get to hear how fucking irritating it is when you spit them out."

He smiled at her with sunflower seeds all over his teeth.

"Eww. Gross, Chase, shut your mouth. That's nasty."

"Now you're just bein' mean." He rolled down the window and emptied his overflowing seed cup.

Great. Now when he spit out his spent seeds she'd hear a *ping* against the paper cup after the *pa-tooey* spitting sound.

Next pee break Ava was buying barbecue-flavored CornNuts. The crunch and the smell would be the ultimate payback. "When are we stopping?"

"Not until I need to fill up. Why? You gotta use the bathroom *again*?"

"My bladder is different than yours. Plus. I'm hungry." When he offered her his bag of seeds, she almost grabbed it and chucked it out the window. Which he knew, if the smirk on his face was any indication. "I want real food."

Chase snorted. "Define real food."

"Something that is not battered and deep fat fried. A fresh garden salad with spinach and arugula and butter lettuce, bursting with crunchy vegetables."

"You had a salad yesterday."

"I had chopped iceberg lettuce with a few carrot shavings and one cherry tomato—that is not a salad. And since when is a cup of fruit cocktail topped with sliced bananas considered a side of fruit?"

"Since always. I can pull over and you can forage for fresh crunchy greens in the ditch if you like."

"Oh shut up. Now who's being mean?"

He sighed. "Look, it sucks that it annoys you, but do you want to know why I need sunflower seeds when I'm on the road?"

It'd really piss him off if she didn't ask.

Even when you are dying to know?

Dammit. "Fine. Why do you *need* sunflower seeds?"

"Because I used to chew tobacco. Goin' from event to event, I was chewing a can of Copenhagen a day. When my usage inched up to nearly a can and a half a day? I knew I had a problem."

"So sunflower seeds helped you quit?"

"First I got a prescription for Chantrix. Then I started on the seeds. It's been three years since I quit and I still fucking crave chew. Especially when I'm on a long drive. And I'm usually by myself, so I don't give a shit about how obnoxious it is."

"I'm glad you quit chewing, because it's a disgusting habit." She shuddered, thinking of all the cowboys she'd watched spitting all the damn time. "But you're telling me to suck it up as far as your need for seed."

"Pretty much."

Ava cooed, "Well, darlin', I say the same to you as far as the music. Suck it up." She turned the music a hair louder and refocused on the task on her computer, separating pictures and video snippets into appropriate folders.

Talk about a long, silent, uncomfortable drive.

Because they were hitting another rodeo in Montana that started at noon the next day, they wouldn't need a motel room since they'd—she'd—be driving straight through the night.

Chase parked in the far corner of the lot. He faced her. "You're not coming to tape my rides?"

"I'd better rest up for the drive." She might actually be able to sleep without Mr. Chipmunk Cheeks' constant chomping.

He cleaned up the mess on his side and pulled out a sun shield that fit the entire windshield. "Keep the windows cracked for air. Be glad it ain't a hundred degrees today. Need anything else before I take off?"

A kiss so I know there's no real hard feelings between us.

But for some stupid reason, pride probably, she couldn't ask for it. She shook her head.

"Lock the doors," he warned and he was gone.

Don't obsess. You're together all day, every day. This was bound to happen sooner or later.

Sighing, Ava snagged her pillow, donned her eye mask and drifted to sleep in blessed non-nut-cracking silence.

And she must've slept hard because the next thing she knew, Chase gently jostled her awake. "Hey."

She sat up and blinked at him, standing just inside the passenger door in the glow of the interior light. "What time is it?"

"Almost ten. Ran late because of some annual local awards that took damn near forty-five minutes before the bull ridin' started."

"How'd you do?"

"Rode the first one. Bucked off the second. Didn't place." He unzipped his vest.

She automatically touched his arm. "I'm sorry."

"It happens." When Chase unhooked his chaps, Ava noticed he winced. He seemed to be taking a long time getting upright.

"How hard did you hit?"

"Ain't the buck off that hurt. It was the damn hoof to the ribs and the hoof to my right thigh."

Ava scooted to the end of the bench seat and started on his buttons. "Lemme see."

"Ava—"

"Now."

Chase eased his shirt aside.

A huge bruise was already forming along the inside curve of his rib cage. "Oh, baby. Look at you." Her fingers traced the welt in the center of the bruise. "Is the rib cracked?"

"Nah. Sore as hell. Gonna hurt like a bitch to ride tomorrow."

She couldn't say *Don't ride* because he would anyway. She leaned forward to kiss him. To stroke him. To give him the TLC he needed. "Pretend I'm kissing your owie."

He smiled against her mouth.

"What else can I do for you?"

"This... You..." He struggled and finally sighed. "You're all I need right now, Ava." Chase returned her kiss with such sweetness she felt tears prickle behind her lids. Mr. Tough Guy wasn't always so tough. She really loved that he had no problem showing her his softer, needier side.

"I'm dead on my feet," Chase said. "Can we hit the road?"

"Get in. I'll load up your gear."

"I'll do it."

"Don't argue with me, Chase, you're beat to shit. Just get in the damn truck."

"Fine."

Once she'd programmed the GPS and they were on track to the Big Sky Rodeo, she glanced over at Chase.

His normally bright eyes were dulled by pain. "Will you wake me if you get sleepy?"

No. "Sure."

"Or help yourself to my sunflower seeds. God knows when I eat them they keep you awake. And usually pissed off."

"Ha-ha." Ava brought his rough knuckles to her lips. "Go to sleep, cowboy. I've got your back."

And the next time she looked over at him, he was sound asleep.

About five hours into the drive, when Ava had a hard time keeping her eyes open, she reluctantly reached for the bag of sunflower seeds.

He'd never let her live it down.

Chapter Twenty-One

"You know, for claiming you wanted to see the countryside, you're spending a lot of time looking at your computer."

Ava's fingers stopped clicking on the keyboard. "If you wanted a conversation, Sundance, all you had to do was ask," she said sweetly.

He shrugged.

Clickety-clackety. Musical tones sounded, indicating she'd shut down her computer. She stowed it and turned sideways in the seat to stare at him. Glare at him most likely. "Happy now?"

"Beyond words," he said dryly.

"Let's talk."

"Sure. But I didn't mention your computer work again because I needed conversation. I just hate to see you missing out on this scenery."

Finally she looked out the window. "Oh. Wow."

The Big Horn Mountains stretched along the left side, long rolling prairie on the right. The scale of the area was deceiving. They'd drive toward those mountains for another forty-five minutes before they even reach the base.

"I don't know why I'm surprised to see snow on mountaintops in July."

"Those are about thirteen thousand feet so you'd have to climb up awful damn far to get a handful of the stuff. But it's pretty here. One of my favorite places in Wyoming."

"If that's true, why don't you still live in Wyoming?"

"I did for a while. In a junky old trailer between my folks' place and Quinn's house. PBR events are spread out across the country, and I started flying more. Air travel ain't cheap—" he smirked, "—unless you've got a private jet at your disposal."

"You'll never let me live that down, will you?"

"Nope. Anyway, since Denver is a hub, me'n a couple of guys rent a three-bedroom apartment close to the airport."

"Are the other guys bull riders?"

Chase shook his head. "Dylan is a pilot. He's all over the place. Lance is a troubleshooter for a computer software company. None of us are ever there at the same time. It works well because we're all at the same point in our careers. We basically needed a place to crash, store our stuff and park our cars when we're on the road."

"How'd you meet? Since you all have diverse occupations."

"I graduated from high school with Lance and he met Dylan through a friend." When Ava remained quiet, he said, "What?"

She reached for his hand and threaded her fingers through his. "Is that where you were before you decided to hide out at Ginger and Kane's?"

Yeah. And I felt like a fucking loser the entire time. Sitting alone in a place as impersonal as another damn hotel room. Wishing I could go home, but feeling like I didn't have one. Didn't have anyone I could really talk to either. Not like I've learned to talk to you.

Rather that share that embarrassing memory, he brought her hand to his mouth and kissed her knuckles. "Smart and beautiful. How did I get so lucky?"

Ava laughed. "And wily, because you're avoiding the question, cowboy."

"Oh, I ain't the only one who avoids questions."

"Meaning what?"

"Meaning...why won't you tell me what you're working on so diligently? Since you spend hours on it."

She gazed out the window. "I'm keeping a lid on it because it's something I've never attempted. Being the paranoid type, I'm not sure it doesn't suck. So, it is an ego thing, with a little superstition—talking about a project while it's in incubation stage—thrown in to make it really mysterious." She sent him a coquettish glance. "Plus it wouldn't do to expose all my secrets to you, McKay. You might get bored with me."

"Highly unlikely that'll ever happen." Chase slowed and took the exit ramp for the Ranchester turnoff, pulling to the shoulder past the stop sign. Then he scooted from behind the steering wheel and said, "C'mere," hauling Ava onto his lap.

"Chase! What are you doing?"

"Getting me some sugar." He curled his hands around her neck and brought her mouth to his for a kiss. Nibbling on her lips, he let his thumbs stroke the strong, sexy line of her jaw. When she expelled that sweet sigh of surrender, he swept his tongue into her mouth. The kiss was a hot mix of teasing licks, shared breath and the wet glide of firm lips on soft. This unhurried kiss wasn't a prelude to anything else. Too often when the sexual heat exploded between them, they couldn't wait to get to the naked part, ending this deep connection. Which was a shame, because while the sex rocked his world, this stirred his soul.

He slipped his lips down to smooch her chin, then placed a very soft kiss on the side of her throat.

Ava's head fell back and she whispered, "God."

"Mmm." He set her back in her seat and slid back behind the wheel. About a minute later, Ava reached for his hand and squeezed.

The road up the Big Horns was long and flat—to a point. Then it became a twisty maze of switchbacks as the road ascended. When they finally reached Sand Turn, he found a spot in the parking lot, which was crowded, most vehicles with out-of-state license plates.

"We're there already?" she asked.

"Nope. Greybull is on the other side, but this is a cool spot. The view is great, so grab your cameras."

Heat beat down, but being so high up, a constant breeze stirred the air, bringing the scent of sun warmed pine and chalky dust. Amazing didn't begin to describe the view; you could see for two hundred miles. The sky was a watered-down blue, causing the thin clouds floating by to disappear into the endless horizon like ghostly vapors.

Once they stood by the rock ledge, Ava grabbed his arm. "This is magnificent."

"Thought you'd appreciate it."

He leaned against the wall and alternated between watching people and watching Ava. They'd stopped frequently over the last few weeks so she could film scenery that struck her fancy. Ava behind a camera lens was a different Ava. Focused. Patient. Intent. Her voice even had a more authoritative tone, not the usual soft lilt reminiscent of a Southern belle.

She shot a lot of footage, but she never showed him the results of her hours of labor or asked his opinion on her next subject. She could spend hours marveling at tiny pink flowers blooming alongside a mud puddle. Or an animal track. One afternoon she even taped a beetle climbing a yucca spike for an hour before he forced her away.

Her reaction boggled him. He'd expected a privileged woman like Ava to become bored quickly. When in fact, he'd gotten bored a helluva lot sooner than she had.

She'd become so intent on zooming in on the variance in colors of the canyon walls she nearly missed the big launch. "Ava, there's a hang glider about to take off on your far right side."

Immediately she spun and refocused. Holding on to the bars of the metal cage, the guy raced to the edge of the cliff until he ran out of ground. A collective gasp echoed as he successfully cleared the first group of pine trees. It was bizarre, seeing a hang glider from the top, not from beneath. The glider caught a thermal and began to climb.

Ava's tendency to film reaction to events, rather than just the event itself, amused him. While she had the camera pointed at the sky, he also knew the spectators on the ledge were within her view.

He braced himself for when she aimed her lens at him.

"So, ever had a desire to hang glide? Skydive?"

"Are you kiddin' me? That kinda dangerous stuff can kill ya."

"Says the man who makes his living climbing on the back of two thousand pounds of pissed-off bull."

Chase grinned. "Danger is all in the perspective, ain't it?"

Ava shut off her camera and they walked to the truck. "I suppose so. But you'd never catch me doing either."

"And here I thought you'd be the daredevil type."

"Ha. I'm more the Chicken Little type."

"I disagree. It is daring to leave the comforts of your cushy lifestyle. Hit the road with a guy you barely knew. Immerse yourself in way of life you didn't know existed. Few women would start this journey, let alone embrace it fully, let alone enjoy it without restriction. I find that amazing. I find you amazing."

And for once, he'd stunned her into total silence.

Following slow-moving campers down the narrow, twisting road into the valley put them behind schedule, so Chase's anxiety was high when they finally reached the Greybull rodeo grounds. "I called yesterday and made reservations at Sleepy Time cabins." He pointed. "Right over there."

Ava pecked him on the mouth. "Good luck."

The contestant line wasn't long. He paid his entry fee and headed to the designated area. At some smaller Wyoming rodeos, sponsors fed the competitors behind the chutes in the sponsor tents and Chase was starving. No sign of food.

He hadn't seen Ryan or Taz yet. The thought of waiting around, striking up a conversation with someone he'd have to lie to about who he was didn't sit well with him.

Maybe that's a sign you should be done with this.

Chase had his phone out to text Ava, when he heard, "Chase?" He spun around and was face to face with his cousin Tell.

Fuck.

Tell wore the black-and-white-striped vest designating him a PRCA judge. His cousin tried to grab Chase in one of those awkward man hugs, but Chase didn't want to draw more attention to them, so he smiled and thrust out his hand. "Fancy meeting you here."

"I could say the same. Thought my eyes were playin' tricks on me. Man, you look different. Good, but...wow. I almost didn't recognize you."

Chase gave Tell a once-over and whistled. "Lookit you. All official and judge-like. 'Bout damn time. Uncle Casper can't throw a shit fit that you're off to the rodeo, bein's he ain't in charge no more."

Tell smirked. "And life is good because of it. Brandt is so over the moon happy these days, he don't mind if I take off because he has Jessie has to help out."

"So Brandt and Jessie are doin' good?"

"Yep. Me'n Dalton tease them endlessly about acting all newlywed starry-eyed and shit, but after what they've been through, hell, after what we've all been through with Luke and now Mom and Dad, no one deserves happiness more than them."

"I hear ya."

Tell's gaze landed on the piece of paper sticking out of Chase's duffel bag that served as his contestant number. He frowned. "You're competing in this rodeo? I didn't see your name listed anywhere."

As a supposed star of the PBR, the rodeo promoters would've made a huge deal out of Chase McKay's appearance at the tiny rodeo, hoping to increase attendance.

"I thought the PBR discouraged their top fifty riders from competing in PRCA events," Tell said.

"Management hasn't ever come right out and said *Don't do it*, but that don't mean it ain't heavily implied."

"So you're rebelling?" Tell shook his head. "Why am I not surprised? Good thing I'm not judging bull ridin'."

Chase shuffled his feet. "About that. There's something you oughta know. It's kind of a funny story." He relayed his double life as Bill Chase.

Laid-back Tell vanished. His eyes narrowed and he looked so much like his dead brother Luke that Chase had a serious case of déjà vu. "Lemme get this straight. You've been a fraudulent member of the PRCA...for twelve years?"

"It's not like that."

"Bullshit. You got a pro card under false pretenses. Competed under false pretenses. Took money under false pretenses. Is that about right?"

"Yeah."

"How long you been double-dipping in PRCA events? All along?"

"No. Just the last few weeks after my suspension from the PBR tour. I didn't see the harm. It's not like I'm in it for the money. In fact, I haven't spent a dime of the payouts I won."

"That's not the fuckin' point," Tell retorted hotly. "This is just another example of the almighty Chase McKay thinking he don't have to play by the rules. How cheating is somehow all right if it benefits *you* in the end. Well, fuck that."

He'd never seen Tell so mad. And what sucked is Chase didn't blame him for his fury because Tell hadn't said a thing that Chase hadn't considered.

But you discarded the guilt and did what you wanted anyway, didn't you?

"Look. I'm sorry."

"Goddamn right you should be. Does your family know you've done this?"

He shook his head.

"And why is that?" Tell let the pause linger. "Because you know it's wrong. They'd tell you it's wrong, and they'd kick your ass until you made it right. I look at you and I feel like I don't know you at all." Tell stormed off, stopping when he reached the metal fence by the livestock gate. His fingers curled around the rail and he stared across the arena, his posture vibrated with anger.

Why hadn't Chase considered he might run into his cousin while skipping from event to event in Tell's jurisdiction?

Because once again you only thought about yourself.

Seemed to be a theme.

Chase slumped against the corral and waited for the impending ass-chewing from his upstanding, do-the-right-thing younger cousin. He glanced at the clock. The longest his diatribe could last would be forty-five minutes until the rodeo kicked off.

Tell walked back to him, a grim set to his mouth. "First off, I wish I wasn't wearin' this damn vest because I'd love nothin' better than to knock your dumb ass right in the dirt."

"I'd deserve it."

"But since that ain't the smartest option, we'll go with the other one." Tell paused. "Withdraw from the competition."

His jaw dropped. "What? No. I drove a long damn way. I need to get on some bulls tonight."

"Tough shit. This is how it's gonna be. Either you voluntarily withdraw or I will report you to the head judge and you'll be disqualified anyway."

Without thinking, Chase snapped, "Jesus, Tell, judging power gone to your head or what? Why would you do that to me?"

Tell loomed over him because he knew it drove Chase bat-shit crazy. "To *you?* This ain't only about you. I won't turn a blind eye to this and get myself banned as a judge. I've worked too damn hard. Now that I know that you've been lying and cheating puts me at more risk than you, do you understand that?"

The truth tumbled down on him like a load of bricks. Was he really so single-minded he'd risk destroying his cousin's future in the PRCA just so he could get on another bull?

No. Fuck no. And it made his cheeks burn with shame and his gut churn that he'd even considered it. "You're right. I'm sorry. Christ, Tell, I'm a sorry son of a bitch sometimes."

"No lie."

"I'll withdraw from the competition right now."

"You do that. And while it was good to see you, since you can't be bothered to come home very often, part of me wishes I hadn't laid eyes on you." Tell walked away without looking back.

Chase dragged ass as he trudged back to the check-in table. The secretary agreed to remove his name from the roster, but the fee was nonrefundable.

Now what?

Find Ava and get the hell outta Dodge.

As he'd started typing another text message, he heard his name shouted and Ryan fell into step with him.

"Hey, you're going the wrong way. The contestant area is back there."

"I'm not competing tonight."

Ryan frowned. "Why not?"

Lie. "I'm burned-out and my shoulder is acting up. I thought it'd be okay to ride, but it's not, so I changed my mind and withdrew."

"That sucks."

"Yeah."

"Or maybe it doesn't."

Chase's head snapped up to see a slow grin spreading across the kid's face. "I might actually have a shot at winning tonight?"

"If you keep your chin down, which wouldn't be an issue if you'd wear a freakin' helmet."

Another scowl. "No way. It'd throw my balance off. Just because it works for you don't mean it'll work for me, so quit nagging me about it. Sheesh. You ain't my mom."

"Maybe you oughta rethink that smartass comment, since my ridin' percentage is over eighty after I made the switch and yours ain't close to that."

"Rub it in, why doncha," he grumbled. "Are you at least staying to watch? In case I do win?"

"The last fuckin' thing I wanna do tonight is sit up in the goddamn stands," he said curtly.

Ryan froze. His cheeks flamed and he ducked his head, hiding his face beneath his cowboy hat. "Oh. Okay. Ah, I'll catch ya later I guess." The he spun on his heel and was gone.

Nice going. Maybe you can knock a toddler's ice cream cone in the dirt too.

In his foul mood, it didn't take long to reach the cabins.

Three soft knocks broke her concentration. She glanced up from the computer screen as Chase said, "Ava. Let me in."

She leapt up to disengage the locks. "Are you okay?"

Chase sauntered in and set his hat on the dresser before he plopped into the lone chair in the room. "No, I'm not okay."

"What happened?"

"I ran into my cousin Tell. He's a judge for saddle bronc and bareback. He wondered why I was here, I told him the truth. Then he spewed every shitty thing about me sneaking around the PRCA circuit, which ain't anything I haven't already been wrestling with since I started this trip."

First time he'd mentioned feeling any guilt.

He sighed. "Long story short, Tell demanded I quit the event or he'd report me. I understand where he's coming from. It'll be his ass if anyone finds out he knew I'd been lying to the PRCA about bein' Bill Chase. So I dropped out of the competition. Then I ran into Ryan, and he's confident he has a shot at winning tonight since I'm not competing. He begged me to watch him ride and I was a dick, which is just fuckin' awesome, because for the millionth time in my life I used my shitty mood as an excuse to be a douchebag to someone who didn't deserve it."

Hard, to watch him struggle, but Ava knew from past experience Chase wasn't in the frame of mind to be petted and soothed.

That's when she knew for sure it was more than just sex between road buddies as they killed a couple of weeks during a lost summer. That's when she realized she was completely in love with him. His opening up to her, letting her see the man who struggled, who cared what people who he cared about thought of him, not just the charming bull rider with carefully crafted PC answers, not just the determined lover, but the real Chase McKay.

"What can I do?"

"Do we have any beer?"

"No."

He sighed again. "Just as well. Makes me think it's time to pack it in and cut the rest of this adventure short."

Outwardly Ava managed a bland expression, but inside she panicked. She wasn't ready to end this. Not now that she'd cemented how she felt about him.

"I've been ridin' better than I have in years. I'm ready to go back to the PBR." He expelled a bitter laugh. "But that ain't up to me, is it?"

Ava sauntered over and straddled his thighs.

"What are you doin'?"

"Getting me some sugar," she mimicked his husky drawl and swooped in for a kiss. The same type of soul kiss he'd bestowed in the truck that literally left her breathless. After she'd thoroughly scrambled his brain, she whispered kisses beneath his jaw. "The way I see it, we have two choices for tonight. We can lock the door and engage in wild, kinky, loud sex all night. Or we can go to the rodeo. Cheer Ryan on. Drink beer. Get rowdy. Do all the fun stuff as spectators that you don't get to do behind the chutes. I've been to several rodeos with you, Chase, but we've never *gone* to a rodeo together."

"True."

"Besides, we've already paid for the room, so we might as well stay. And if you're serious about no more PRCA events, you should hang out with Ryan one last time. He'd appreciate it. Especially after your dickish behavior."

Chase rested his forehead against her chest. "Okay. You've convinced me."

Wrapping her arms around his neck, she rubbed her chin across the stubbly hair on his head, loving their wordless connection.

"How soon do you need to be back in California?"

"Why?"

"After we leave here tomorrow, you wanna head to Yellowstone for a few days? No rodeo, just you'n me playing tourist?"

"That sounds like heaven."

"Good." He slapped her butt. "I'm gonna grab a soda out of the vending machine. Want one?"

"Sure."

The phone call from Marnie deflated her good mood. She debated on answering, but she'd rather get it over with because she'd been expecting—dreading—this call for days. "Hey, Marnie."

"Ava, dear, I have news. The Richfield casting agency has gotten you a reading for a new sitcom."

At least Marnie never made small talk. "Is this for a pilot?" There was no guarantee a pilot would be picked up by any TV network and she considered auditioning a waste of time.

"It's not a pilot. It's already been approved and will air on the CW as a mid-season show. Granted, it has a limited episode run, but that works in our favor."

Say no.

Say yes, you idiot. Haven't you had enough time tooling around the countryside with Chase? You need to get back to your real life.

"Ava, sweetie, are you still there?"

"Yes. Sorry. Thanks, but I'll pass on this one." God. Was she making a mistake? How much would Marnie have to cajole her to get her to cave in?

A lot. She wasn't ready to walk away from Chase yet.

"Well. I wasn't expecting that. However, it's your decision. I'll figure out a way to decline the audition, although, you should know I really put myself out there for you, Ava."

"Well, that *is* your job. Take care." And she hung up as Chase entered the room.

"Who was on the phone?"

"Hannah." Fibbing didn't feel right, but Chase would insist she go back to LA. Even when he wasn't the only reason she'd said no. Her gaze flicked to her laptop. She'd made progress on her project and hoped to have something tangible to show Chase in the next week, especially since he'd mentioned her secretiveness about it today.

"Is everything all right?"

"Yes. But save the soda for later. Right now I need a beer."

At the rodeo grounds they scarfed down Indian tacos and drank beer. They chose seats at the top of the bleachers, away from the main crowd.

Chase watched her digging in her bag. "I'm surprised you brought your cameras."

"My cinematography efforts haven't been solely focused on you, you know." She wanted to video Ryan's ride. The long angle from the stands would be a nice contrast to the rest of the footage she'd shot.

She fiddled with the zoom function. *Looky there.* Two well-endowed buckle bunnies, with puffy blonde hair, and skin-tight jeans waiting for cowboys. "Are these painted chickies your type?" She held the camera close so he could check them out.

"They *were* my type."

"You would've taken them both on at once?"

Chase looked at her evenly. "We've talked about my past, Ava. Why the questions now?"

"I was just curious if your preference for girl-on-girl action is out of your system or if..."

"If some night I'll bring another woman into *our* bed and expect you to be all right with getting down and dirty with her just to please me?"

His emphasis on *our* bed sounded permanent. She didn't focus on that, just offered him a shrug. "Maybe."

Then Chase was right in her face. "I'd never demand something from you that makes you uncomfortable. And no one, man or woman, gets to put their hands on you, because in case you haven't noticed? When it comes to you? I. Don't. Fucking. Share."

A tingle heated her blood at his blatant possessiveness.

"Any other questions?" he asked in that rough rasp.

"Ah, no. I'm good." Ava's attempts at taping the rodeo events were half-assed because she kept sneaking looks at Chase. The man she loved. And where her eye went, her camera lens followed.

He sighed. "Will you please get that goddamn thing outta my face?"

"But yours is such a gorgeous face, beyond compare really.

Broody. Masculine. Sexy with that perpetual five o'clock shadow. I love how your hat shades your eyes. And when you're a little pissy, that muscle along your jawbone jumps and I just wanna sink my teeth into it."

"Ava—"

"I can compliment you if I want, McKay, so suck it up."

Chase laughed.

"You know, as I've been taping your handsome self, I realized I have the perfect job for you if you don't get a call back from the PBR."

"And what's that?"

"Movie and TV stunt man."

Chase turned and looked at her as if she'd lost her mind.

"I know some people in the business, if you're interested. I can hook you up."

"Has it escaped your notice that I'm a little on the short side of, oh, not bein' tall, dark and handsome?"

"Now that you mention it, I'm usually too busy staring and drooling over all those eye-popping muscles of yours to worry if you measure up, because you're beyond any standard scale."

"How many beers have you had to get so much honey to drip outta your sweet mouth?"

She knocked into him with her shoulder. "You are forgetting a couple of key points, Mr. Negative."

His lips twitched. "What's that, Pollyanna?"

"Most guys in Hollywood are short. These days few guys are as big as the old action stars like Dolph Lundgren and Arnold Schwartzeneger."

"Yeah? What about Vin Diesel?"

"Don't distract me by making me name specific actors who don't hit the six foot mark."

"I'm a solid five inches below the six foot benchmark, sugar."

"Alls I'm saying is you could find work if you wanted to switch your occupation." Then she looked away.

Chase curled his hand around her jaw, forcing her to meet his blue gaze. "And where would I live if I relocated to LA?"

She didn't hesitate. "With me."

A couple of seconds passed before he kissed her hard. Twice. "I'll take it under consideration." He slipped his hand into hers and tugged her closer. "Now can we watch the damn rodeo?"

When bull riding started, he gave her space to tape.

Taz stayed on and ended up with a score of eighty. Two other riders reached the eight-second mark but scored below seventy-nine. Three riders hit the dirt and Ryan was up next.

Chase got a little fidgety when the gate opened and Ryan and the bull burst into the arena. "Come on," Chase said under his breath. "Follow his switch. That's it. Just a little longer... Yes!" He whistled loudly and faced Ava. "That's about an eighty-two point ride."

Ryan won. He looked ready to cry, vomit and pass out—all at the same time. But he managed to keep his cool at the ceremony when the sponsors awarded the belt buckle, the check and the piece of artwork painted on deerskin that detailed how Greybull had gotten its name.

When the crowd of well-wishers thinned out, Chase and Ava approached him. Ryan was so pumped he picked Ava up and spun her in a circle, oblivious to Chase's warning growls.

"Thanks for comin'! I wish my mom coulda been here to see me win, but she promised to come to the event next week in North Platte."

Chase offered his hand, forcing Ryan to release Ava. "Congrats. That was an excellent ride."

"First time I ever felt I coulda ridden a bull all night. Man. It was awesome." He squinted at Ava's bag. "Did you tape it?"

"Yes, sir. I wasn't close, so I don't know how good it is."

"Can you email it to me so I can show my mom?"

"Sure, what's your email address?"

He scrawled it on a napkin and handed it to her. "Thanks."

"You in the mood to celebrate?" Chase asked.

"Hell yeah. I met a couple of girls earlier and they're taking me to a party."

Only Ava noticed the brief flash of disappointment on Chase's face that Ryan already had plans.

"Sounds like fun." He clapped Ryan on the shoulder. "It's been great getting to know you, Ryan, and good luck the rest of the season."

Ryan looked confused. "Sounds like you're saying goodbye."

"I am." He reached for Ava's hand. "We're leaving tomorrow morning for R&R in Yellowstone."

"But you are competing in North Platte next weekend, right?"

Chase shook his head. "Bill Chase has retired."

"But...it's the rodeo closest to my hometown. I thought we could hang out. You could meet my mom."

Ava couldn't stand to see Ryan's distress. "We'll see how the week plays out and he'll call you, okay?"

"Okay." He was about to say something else, when two girls raced to his side. The brunette said, "There you are! We've been looking for you." The trio got caught up in conversation, leaving Chase and Ava staring after him.

"So now that Ryan has blown us off, is your offer for wild, kinky, loud sex still on the table?" Chase asked.

"Absolutely."

Chapter Twenty-Two

Chase's phone buzzed on the seat.

Ava picked it up and read the text. *Where are you?* She sighed. "How many times has Ryan texted you today?"

"Probably a dozen. Kid's just a little anxious."

"Think he's afraid you won't show up?"

"From what he's told me, that's been a common occurrence and I don't wanna be another guy who disappoints him."

"Ryan does realize how far out of our way this event is?"

He looked at her. "Some other place you need to be today, Hollywood?"

"No. But ten hours in the car is a long haul. Even for old road dogs like us."

Chase laughed. "Admit it. You'd had your fill of nature."

"Maybe forever."

On their Yellowstone trip, they'd spent one night in Cody, checking out the museums, strolling through the town, but they skipped the rodeo. Then they'd driven around Yellowstone for the next three days. He'd even talked Ava into camping one night.

Not a good idea.

While she appreciated the scenery, including the star-filled night sky and the clean mountain air, every noise freaked her out. She'd convinced herself bears would attack them during the night and she didn't sleep, which meant he hadn't slept. She bitched about the cold, rocky ground. She gagged when forced to use an outhouse. Smoke from the campfire made her cough and her eyes water. She burned her hot dog and her marshmallows in the coals. Bugs dive-bombed her head. Glowing eyes stared at her from the tree line. She'd complained from the moment they'd pitched the tiny two-man tent until the next morning when they'd packed up. They'd even skipped spending time in the Tetons because Ava's priorities were a finding a shower, putting on clean clothes and getting a manicure. In that order.

The odd part of the fiasco? Chase hadn't been mad. If any other woman had acted that way? He might've pitched her over a steep cliff. But Ava amused the hell out of him because her comments weren't mean-spirited or snotty, just honest.

While he and Ava spent time isolated, out in nature, he realized that he wasn't a huge fan of the great outdoors himself. Being outside on the McKay Ranch was one thing; he'd always loved that, even when he hadn't been thrilled with the backbreaking work. His brothers never suggested camping outside after chores were done. The same held true for most of his McKay cousins simply because when the workday ended, they wanted to be inside. Where it was cool, or warm, depending on the season. Where snow wasn't blowing or sun wasn't beating down. Where a meal and a conversation waited. That break from the elements was a necessary part of surviving as a rancher.

Once they'd reached Jackson Hole, Chase found a luxury resort and surprised Ava by booking a suite. She'd actually teared up when he arranged for two hours of in-room spa treatments and left her alone to be pampered.

While she was getting massaged, he took his truck for an oil change and called his family to catch up. Maybe it stung a bit, their shock he'd contacted them without prompting. But Chase was determined to prove he could make changes in all areas of his life and stick to them.

"What are you thinking about?" Ava asked.

Chase grabbed her hand and kissed her palm. "How fantastic these last six days have been. Just me'n you seeing the sights. Hanging out with my friend. Then you rockin' my world in bed and out of it."

She permitted a smug smile. "I did, didn't I?"

After driving through Riverton, Ava suggested they drive up to Thermopolis to see the famous hot springs. Then she surprised him and booked a room at a bed and breakfast joint that boasted a small private hot spring. She'd dragged him outside after the other guests were in bed for the night. Talk about a thrill, seeing Ava take control. Rubbing her firm, curvy body slick against his. Her mouth tasting. Her hands roving. Her voice a sexy rasp in his ear as she'd taken him to heaven.

"It went beyond...well, anything for me too, Chase," she said softly, when he realized he'd gone completely quiet again.

What Ava didn't realize was he'd lain awake last night, wondering if that was the beginning of the end for them, because they'd made no future plans after Ryan's event. He still hadn't heard from the PBR. Eight weeks had passed. He might be in limbo, but Ava had a life in California that was more than just a career.

And how fucking sad was that for him?

Chase pulled into a service station. "Need anything?"

"You're buying sunflower seeds, aren't you?"

He grinned. "Yep."

"Fine. You know what I want."

"Red licorice and a Diet Dew comin' up."

Ava had her headphones on when he returned. And she'd fired up her computer, something she hadn't done often the last six days. Nor had she snapped many photos, which didn't make sense, given they'd been in a scenery-rich national park. He'd learned not to question her because it always got her back up.

He'd become accustomed to hours driving in the truck, so he wasn't tired when they reached the fairgrounds. His cell rang. "Yes, Ryan, we're finally here. Where are you?"

"At the beer garden with my mom."

"We'll be right there." He faced Ava to find her staring at him. "You ready?"

"Yes."

Chase stopped just inside the gate to gather his thoughts.

Ava rubbed his arm. "Chase? You all right?"

"Nervous."

That surprised her. But she offered him that sweet, pure Ava smile and tenderly brushed her lips across his. "I imagine he is too."

Ryan leapt up the instant he saw Chase, nearly tackling him. "How slow did you drive? Man. I thought you'd never get here." He wrapped his arms around Ava and lifted her off the ground.

Chase couldn't help but grin. Ryan was like a big goofy pup. No boundaries. Honest affection and boundless enthusiasm.

"Come on. We're sitting over here."

Ryan's mother was a bottle-dyed redhead, somewhere between thirty and fifty, with the rough edged look he'd seen on plenty of single blue-collar mothers. But she had Ryan's big smile and obvious pride in her son, by the way she kept fussing over him.

"Mom. This is Chase. And Ava."

He offered his hand. "Nice to meet you after Ryan has told me all about you."

"Jackie Ackerman. Ryan is such a huge fan of yours. It's been a dream come true for him, getting to hang out and bullshit about bull riding." She turned her gaze to Ava. "Thanks for sending the video of Ryan's winning ride. I really wish I coulda taken time off work to see it live."

"No problem. Do you mind if I tape your rides tonight?"

Ryan smiled widely. "'Course not."

It was difficult to get a word in edgewise with Ryan yammering a million miles an hour. The kid defined nervous energy. Finally Chase put his hand on Ryan's restless fingers and said softly, "Relax. Take it down a notch."

Struck Chase strange that Ava remained behind the camera for the entire conversation. She'd toss out remarks occasionally, but stuck to the observer role. She had changed too, seeming content to stay out of the spotlight.

The five-minute warning for the start of the rodeo echoed across the grounds. Ryan said, "You coming back to help me pull my rope?"

"Sure. If you promise you ain't gonna talk the whole damn time we're waiting for you to ride," he teased.

Jackie laughed and playfully smacked her son's shoulder. "He's got you pegged, Ry-Ry."

Ryan stood, lifted his mom to her feet and squeezed her in a bear hug. "See ya after. Cheer loud for me."

"You know it. Be safe, okay?"

"Love you too, Mom."

Ava slipped on her press pass and entered the restricted area with Chase and Ryan.

Chase loved the buzz around the chutes, but he also felt the odd man out because he wasn't competing. Ryan knew quite a few of the guys. He flitted between chatting up bronc riders to leaning over the fence and talking to timed event competitors. The barrel racers weren't on their horses yet, or Ryan would've been on that side of the chutes, charming the ladies.

He and Taz watched the action in the arena without speaking beyond the occasional remark on the performance. When the Dodge truck drove onto the dirt to drop off the barrels, they headed behind the chutes.

The roster had twenty bull riding competitors. Taz had drawn fourth, Ryan twelfth. He and Ryan helped Taz and watched as the bull landed hard on its front hooves and Taz sailed ass over teakettle until his body smacked into the ground and bounced before stopping.

Taz wasn't moving. The bullfighters watched over him until medical professionals arrived.

Ryan's eyes were huge as he faced Chase. "He's gonna be fine, right?"

"He's tough. They're getting him fixed up. See? He's on his feet."

The kid jumped down a level before Chase caught him by the shirtsleeve. "No need for you to head over there. They'll shoo you out. And Taz will bitch about you wanting to hold his hand anyway."

Ryan nodded. Blew out a distressed breath. Squinted at the scoreboard to see who was up next. Then Ryan went into that quiet time before a ride. Some guys called it psyching themselves up. Others called it getting in the zone. Chase found those minutes leading up to climbing on a bull the hardest. Once he was on and getting a good wrap on his hand, he went through a mental checklist. Once the gate opened, he focused on keeping his seat, staying on, spurring and making that buzzer.

So he paced right along with Ryan. Until they stopped, stared at each other foolishly and smiled.

"Come on, kid, you're up next. Show me whatcha got."

Ryan's bull was a mean bastard. First it wouldn't get up. Then it decided to fight. Chase held the bull rope as Ryan got a fast wrap. Taz held on to the back of Ryan's vest until Ryan shouted, "Go!" and the gate opened.

The bull had a showy style, leaping and twisting like a marlin on a hook. Ryan's hat went flying, but the kid held on.

Chase curled his hands around the wooden rail and muttered, "Almost, come on," and the buzzer went off.

As Ryan reached to release his rope, the acrobatic bull jerked its head, catching Ryan in the face with a horn. Ryan fell back far enough that when the bull's rear legs left the ground, the momentum ejected the kid sideways. He slammed into the solid metal gate head first, and then his body crumpled to the ground.

Confusion reigned in the arena when the bull charged a bullfighter. Then the barrel man. The pickup men cornered the angry animal and dragged it out with ropes.

He looked back, expecting to see Ryan on his feet, but he hadn't moved. What the hell?

Distorted noise echoed through the loudspeaker system, the words garbled and grating.

Get up.

Chase wasn't sure if he'd said the words aloud. His vision became a pinpoint focus on a too-still Ryan lying in the dirt.

Then the bullfighters and medical team erected a human tent around Ryan and he couldn't see a damn thing.

Get up kid. Come on. Shake if off. Don't scare your mama like this. Jesus. Don't scare me like this.

More medical personnel raced over. A stretcher appeared. Then an ambulance. It never looked right, a ghostly quiet emergency vehicle slowly rolling across the arena dirt. No flashing lights, no wailing sirens, no rush.

The sound of spectators clapping as they paid respect to the person leaving via ambulance partially roused Chase from his stupor. Seemed as if he'd blinked and the next rider was up, and the rodeo was back in business.

He turned and literally ran into Ava. "Let's go to the hospital. Ryan is probably freaking out. I imagine Jackie is already on her way." He took Ava's hand and they weaved through the melee of contestants leaving the event. She didn't speak until they were in his truck.

"Will Ryan be okay?"

Chase shifted in the seat. "In small events like these, there are no med techs, so they automatically take injured riders to the closest hospital as a precaution. And Ryan is young. Old timers like Taz refuse to ride in an ambulance and find their own medical treatment. But I doubt a youngster like Ryan put up much of a fuss when they told him he needed to go to the hospital."

"Oh. Okay. That's explains a lot."

They made the drive to the hospital in silence. He parked in the emergency lot, and it seemed to take an hour to walk through those emergency room doors.

Inside the hospital waiting room, Jackie paced in front of the windows. Ava hustled over and hugged her. "Any news?"

"No. They haven't told me anything."

"Did you call someone to wait with you?"

"My boyfriend is on his way. I won't call the rest of my family until I know what's going on. I appreciate you coming. I know Ryan will appreciate it too. It can be a group effort to chew his ass for worrying us once they let us see him."

"Anything I can get you?" Ava asked. "A drink? Something to eat? A blanket?"

Jackie shook her head and continued pacing.

Chase wanted to bust through the swinging doors and get some answers. Shoving his hands in his pockets, he braced his shoulders against the cement wall, his stomach too queasy to pace.

Time dragged. The click of Jackie's heels competed with the beeping machines that echoed from the nurse's station.

Ava left him alone. She left Jackie alone too. The three of them were the only ones in the waiting room, but they might as well have been miles apart.

The doors opened.

"Jackie Ackerman?" a woman wearing blue scrubs asked.

"Yes. I'm here. I'm Jackie."

The woman wandered over. Fatigue lined the skin around her eyes, but her face remained blank. "I'm Doctor Silsbee. I headed the team that worked on your son."

"How is he?"

She paused. "I'm sorry but he didn't make it."

"What? Didn't make it as in...he died?"

"Yes. I'm sorry. He coded twice and our attempts to revive him were unsuccessful."

Every bit of blood drained from Chase's face. He watched the doctor's mouth move, but her words were muffled by the accelerated beating of his heart in his ears.

Silence. Then a switch turned on and sound blasted his

eardrums.

"No!" Jackie yelled at the doctor. "No. It's not possible. Ryan is just a kid. He's tough. He'll pull through. I know it."

"I'm really sorry, Miz Ackerman. The trauma to your son's brain was too severe. I can request a counselor or a clergyperson for you to talk to."

"I don't need a fuckin' counselor, I need to see my son."

Doctor Silsbee appeared to brace herself.

Chase felt himself splinter into two halves. One part stood there stoically, reasonably, wanting to help. The other part let lose a low-pitched wail that escalated into an unending scream.

"How do I know you're not lying to me?" Jackie shrieked. "How do I know this isn't some big goddamn mistake and you've got Ryan confused with someone else's kid?"

"Ma'am, we have verification from the ambulance crew who brought him in from the fairgrounds. I'm really sorry."

"Bullshit. This isn't funny! Take me to him. Now."

Heartsick, and barely hanging on by a thread, Chase stepped between her and the doctor. "You don't want to see him, Jackie."

"Move out of my way."

He curled his hands around her upper arms and said softly, "Look at me and listen."

Something shifted in her. Jackie blinked pain-filled eyes and whispered, "But I have to see him."

"No, you don't. There's no reason for you to do this to yourself. Don't have your last memory of Ryan be what you see lying on a gurney. Because that image will overtake everything, even all the good ones. He's not there anymore. That's not him. He deserves better and so do you."

"He can't be dead." She shook her head so hard her tears splattered his cheeks. "How can he be dead?"

Because he refused to wear a helmet. The stubborn kid might be alive right now if he'd listened to me.

Shame and guilt warred inside him at the ugly and callous words his brain tossed out. God. How could he even *think* that at a time like this? Ashamed, and fearing Jackie might see those thoughts in his eyes, Chase ducked his head and walked away.

A burly biker strode in and Jackie launched herself at him. Her raw sounds of anguish nearly knocked Chase to his knees.

He couldn't move. Couldn't breathe. Couldn't do anything but stand there helplessly and witness Jackie spiraling into debilitating grief.

Goddammit to fucking hell. He wanted to punch someone. Kick something. Hurt himself so the pain on the outside matched the pain on the inside.

Ryan. Dead. Eighteen years old. His life just starting. So full of happiness and joy. Now gone. That light forever extinguished.

He couldn't stay in this hospital another second. He very calmly walked out the door, even as his legs urged him to run. The night air was so thick with humidity it was impossible to suck enough air into his lungs. He felt as if he were drowning. Chase closed his eyes, hating being mired in that special slice of hell called limbo. Time had no meaning.

Ava's voice brought him out of his dark thoughts. "Chase?"

He flinched when she touched him.

"Baby, come on, let go of the railing."

Railing? He looked down at his white-knuckled grip on the metal handrail, then at Ava standing next to him. Tears dripped down her cheeks. His mouth couldn't form any words.

She attempted to pry his fingers free. "Chase. Please. You're scaring me. I've been trying to get your attention for five minutes."

Something about her tone spurred him to act. His fingers uncurled, but he'd been clutching the metal so hard he'd lost feeling in his hands. No. He was numb all the way to the bone.

How long had he been standing there in shock? Absolutely lost in grief and disbelief?

She took his keys and half-shoved him in the truck and slipped into the driver's seat. "We need to find a place to stay tonight."

"Fine. Just find a liquor store first."

"Chase. I don't think that's a good—"

"Find a goddammed liquor store."

Chapter Twenty-Three

Chase had crawled inside a bottle for the past two days. How he hadn't passed out wasn't a testament to his ability to handle his liquor, but a testament to his stubbornness.

Ava had never felt so helpless. She wouldn't mother him. She wouldn't press him to talk. So she curled up beside him on the bed, offering her physical presence while he steadily polished off another bottle of rotgut whiskey.

He absentmindedly stroked her hair while he clicked through TV channels. Occasionally he'd switch out the remote for the bottle. His body temperature was warm despite that he only wore a pair of athletic shorts. He didn't speak. At all.

He hadn't moved either. Not even when her phone rang yesterday and she'd left him to take the call outside.

She hadn't wanted to talk to Marnie—it didn't matter what offer the woman dangled. No way was she leaving Chase alone at a time like this. No way. But Marnie hadn't understood Ava's absolute refusal to listen to the pitch for another audition. Not even after she explained she was dealing with a friend's death. Her agent went on a tirade about sticking her neck out for her client, complaining bitterly about Ava's lack of consideration for Marnie's reputation. Ava half-listened, her mind elsewhere, mainly on the devastated man hiding in the motel room, just out of her reach.

Chase's cell phone buzzed on the nightstand, startling her. He didn't bother to grab it. The buzzing rings stopped for a couple minutes, then the phone began to vibrate again. Ava looked at him. "Aren't you gonna get that?"

He shook his head.

The phone quit ringing.

Five minutes later it started again.

Chase took a swig from the bottle when it stopped.

By the third attempt, she rolled off the bed and picked up his phone. Caller ID read: Ryan Ackerman. She shivered and answered it anyway. "Hello?"

"This is Jackie Ackerman. I'm looking for Chase. He didn't leave me a way to contact him. I found his name on my son's phone, so I'm hoping this is the right number?"

"Yes, it is, Jackie. This is Ava." She felt Chase's gaze snap to her. "Did you want to talk to him?"

"Can I?"

"Sure. Hang on. Let me get him." Ava covered the mouthpiece. "You need to take this."

"I can't." His voice was rough from too much whiskey and too little use.

"You have to." She spoke into the phone. "Jackie? He's right here."

Chase muttered and set aside the bottle to snatch the phone Ava held out to him. "Hey, Jackie. No. It's all right, you're not a bother."

A bunch of "Uh-huhs" followed. Then, "Of course I'll be there. No. That's fine. I'll find it. See you. Thanks for letting me know. Take care." He punched the off button and tossed the phone aside.

Perched across from him on the other bed, Ava waited a minute before she asked, "What's going on?"

He held up the bottle, studying the two inches of remaining liquid. "She gave me the time and place for Ryan's memorial service. Memorial service. The kid had barely begun to live. Is there anything worse on this whole fucking planet than memorializing a promising life cut short?"

The lump in her throat prevented response.

"We all have to fucking sit there, looking at the goddamn picture of him, or the fucking casket, and pretend he's in a better place? That this is some kind of master fucking plan? Wrong. Goddammit everything about this is so wrong I...can't...even..." Chase tipped the bottle up and sucked it dry in three greedy gulps.

Ava wanted Chase to lash out. To act out. To lose control and throw the bottle at the wall as hard as he could, screaming his rage and frustration as it shattered. But he'd closed himself off.

Or so she thought.

Chase lurched to his feet and staggered to the bathroom. Slamming the door behind him. Attempting to keep her out.

Not a fucking chance, McKay.

She leapt up after him, but paused, unsure what to do. Pressing her back against the wall outside the bathroom, listening to him retch. Her belly roiled. Her heart seized with his every distressed whimper. Her tears fell freely as she heard him trying to hold back his sobs.

Time passed in a vacuum of misery.

After she heard the toilet flush for the third time, she curled her palm around the handle, praying he hadn't started locking the door. The door swung open with a loud squeak.

Chase sat on the floor, his face hidden in his hands. He said, "Get out," in that dangerously low tone.

She parked herself next to him, hip to hip. When he didn't bark at her to leave, she placed her hand on his knee, wondering if he'd accept her need to soothe him.

Try.

"You want some water?" she asked.

No answer.

She counted to one hundred. "Chase? Do you need—"

"I don't need anything. Just go."

"I can't."

"Don't you understand? I don't need you."

Ava ignored the sharp pang his words caused. "But I need you."

Chase slowly lifted his head and looked at her with red-rimmed eyes. "What?"

The stark misery had her reaching for him without conscious thought. "Don't turn me away. It's ripping me up to see you like this. I need to help you. Tell me how. Please."

"You can't."

"Can't what?"

"Help me. So just go the fuck away."

She slowly rolled to her feet. He probably thought he'd scared her off. *No way, buddy, I'm sticking.* She filled a cup and held it out, waiting for him to take it. She'd stand there all night if she had to.

Finally, he said, "Fuck, all right, give me the goddamn thing," and snatched it from her fingers.

He could scream obscenities at her if it'd bring him out of his sorrow-filled drunken stupor.

An eternity later, when he figured out she wasn't going anywhere, he started to talk.

"Watching Ryan these last few weeks, before he..." Chase squeezed the plastic cup so hard water shot out the top. "It drove home the point I've had it so fuckin' easy my whole life." He gulped the water, swished it around in his mouth and leaned forward to spit it in the toilet. "I cheated to get where I am today by bein' Bill Chase."

"Whatever name you used didn't get you to the top. Your drive to be the best did."

He couldn't argue with that. But she'd be surprised if he didn't try.

"The guilt is eating at me."

"Guilt that you're alive and Ryan's not?"

"No. Guilt I didn't push him harder to wear a helmet. He'd be alive if he'd listened to me. Banged up, but alive. How can I live with that?"

Pointing out the obvious—there were no guarantees anything

would've saved Ryan—would mean nothing to him right now.

"And here I am, wrecked because an eighteen-year-old kid I barely knew died. But I sure as fuck didn't act this way after my cousin Luke got killed." His head fell back against the concrete wall. "Christ. I grew up with Luke. His death ripped our family to pieces. But I could only spare two days out of my life, out of my precious schedule to go to his funeral? And once I was back on tour, I didn't think of him at all. Even when I knew his brothers were beyond hurting. Did I reach out to them? No. Did I make an extra effort to keep in better contact with my own brothers because I understood how lucky I was I still had them? No.

"In fact, I called them less than before. Same with my folks. Even now, when Jackie lost her only child and she's devastated, I'm sitting here thinking about myself. How *I* feel. How it's affected *me*. How fucked up is that?" Chase squeezed his eyes shut against the tears trickling down his miserable face. "Don't answer that. I'm a cold, self-centered son of a bitch. A shitty son, a shitty brother and a shitty friend."

Ava silently cried along with him, her heart breaking for this man who only saw the worst in himself.

"None of this matters," he said, his tone defeated.

"What?"

"The PBR, the PRCA, bull ridin'. It's all bullshit."

"Chase. You don't mean that."

"I don't know what I mean. In all my years, I've never seen anyone killed on the back of a bull. Seen them hurt? Yes. Seen them seriously hurt and even paralyzed? Yes. But someone I know, someone killed right in front of me and hundreds of other people? That's a first. That's so wrong. So fucking wrong. Ryan's death, and the tragedy of it, will make papers across the country. But it won't change anything. It won't give his mother comfort. Christ. He was her only kid and now she's alone."

Chase broke down. His massive shoulders shook as he cried.

When the worst of it passed, and he'd taken the quiet comfort she'd offered, she stood. "Come on. You're exhausted and need to sleep." She held out her hands to help him up.

"Ava, I'm not three years old."

"But you are three sheets to the wind."

Chase turned his head away. "Sorry I'm such a mess."

"All the more reason for you to let me help you."

An eternity passed before something shifted in him. He struggled to his feet by himself, but allowed Ava to guide him back to the bed he'd barely left for two days.

Once she'd settled beside him, he twined his arms around her, tangled his legs with hers. "Don't go," he whispered thickly against her throat.

"I'm here. There's no place I'd rather be than with you, Chase. You know that, right?"

His whole body relaxed as he expelled a deep sigh and passed out.

She trailed her fingers up and down his spine.

Ryan's death had changed them both. Where did they go from here?

They kept a low profile during Ryan's funeral. But so many people attended it was easy to blend. All in all, the service was nice. Sad.

Ava ran into Taz as cars loaded up for the trip to the cemetery. She almost hadn't recognized him without his cowboy hat. His hair was shorter. He wore a sports coat.

He hugged her with a gruff, "Ava."

"Taz. How you holding up?"

"Not so good." He glanced at the hearse. "Still can't believe it."

"Me either."

"How's Chase?"

"About the same as you." Miserable, blaming himself. Avoiding people.

Silence.

"You been on the road?" *Stupid question, Ava.*

"Nope. I'm done."

"Done?"

"I quit. No more rodeos. No more foolin' myself. I ain't been ridin' good consistently for a couple of years anyway."

"What are you going to do?"

"A buddy of mine bought some land outside Scottsbluff. He's been trying to get me to take over, making improvements on it, for the last year. I wasn't interested until..." He cleared his throat. "I realized I ain't too old to learn something new."

"We could all learn something from this."

Taz glanced around and pulled her off to the side, out of earshot. "Listen, I know you got a lot of footage of Ryan while you were taping Chase. I'd like to see you do something positive with it. Even if it's just for his mom. The kid deserves that much."

"I agree. Is it all right if I use footage of you too?"

"Don't know what for, but sure."

Ava kissed his cheek. "Take care of yourself, Taz."

They were sitting in a diner outside Alliance, picking at a meal neither wanted.

"Chase?"

"Yeah."

"What happens now?"

"I don't know." He glanced up from smashing a pile of peas with his fork. "Why? Did you have something on your mind?"

"Yes. And hear me out before you automatically say no."

"I'm listening."

"Come to New York City with me. Just for a couple of days. We both could use a break. A little bit of pampering. I've spent time in your world, Chase, I'd like for you to spend time in mine."

"Why New York? Why not LA?"

"My assistant mentioned there's still paparazzi lurking around my place. We'd be trapped. In New York...we'd probably be anonymous." She reached for his hand. "Let's park your truck in Omaha, get on a plane and we'll be at LaGuardia in three hours. My family has a standing suite at the Cooper Square Hotel. We can stay there as long as we want."

His eyes searched hers. "Why is this so important to you?"

"I'm not ready to say goodbye. Are you?"

"God no."

His vehemence surprised her.

"Good. I'll make the arrangements. We could use a distraction. It'll be fun."

Chase smiled for the first time in days. "Let's go."

Chapter Twenty-Four

"Ladies and gentlemen, welcome to New York City. The local time is three p.m." Ava glanced out the airplane window as the flight attendant rattled off the usual spiel. She was anxious to get out of the plane and into the city.

Chase leaned across the armrest. "You all right?"

Ava faced him and frowned. "Why wouldn't I be?"

"I dunno. I expect you'll be different now that the city mouse is back in her element."

"What about you?" she countered. "Will you become the country mouse? Afraid of taxis, sirens and the crush of people?"

"I ain't skeered of nothin'." Chase pressed his lips to hers. She'd expected a quick peck, but he cranked the kiss to hot and teasing as his thumb discreetly rubbed the stiff point of her nipple.

She pulled back. "Chase—"

"I missed touching you the last few days," he murmured.

"I missed it too." Ava rested her forehead to his. "Hold that thought, okay?"

"Okay." He gave her a lingering smooch. "Bear in mind that just because we're on your turf don't mean you get to call the shots."

That forceful statement delivered in his masculine growl sent a curl of heat through her. Yes, she'd missed this sexual part of Chase because it was such an important part of who he was. "I wouldn't dream of horning in on your territory."

They exited the plane and wended through the crowd at baggage claim. After Chase hefted their luggage, Ava led him to the area where private transportation companies waited. A man in a black sports coat stepped in front of another guy wearing a gray pinstriped suit. "Miss Cooper?"

"Yes."

"I'm Gino. I hope your flight was enjoyable."

The young man attempted to take the duffel bags from Chase,

earning a dark scowl as Chase increased his grip on the luggage. "I've got it."

"That's fine, sir. The car is this way, please."

The heat and stench assaulted her as they left the cool comfort of the terminal. God. The noise didn't bother her, but somehow she'd forgotten how rank the city smelled in the summer months—garbage, urine, grease and exhaust fumes.

Gino popped the trunk on a black limo at the curb.

Chase stopped by the rear passenger door and looked at her as Gino snuck in and grabbed the bags. "A limo, Ava? Really?"

"It's a compact size, not a stretch limo, and it was the same price as a car service. I thought you'd be happy I comparison shopped."

"I am. But I'm surprised you used that name to book it. What happened to us laying low?"

She bristled. "That name happens to be my name, and it's on the credit card I used. What's the big deal?"

"Forget it." He stepped aside to open the car door for her, only to scowl again when Gino beat him to the punch.

Ava crawled in first and slid across the bench seat. Naturally, Chase didn't allow the distance and scooped her up, settling her on his lap. "Chase."

"What? I changed my mind. I'm scared in the big city."

She rolled her eyes, but she didn't move.

Gino took the wheel and said, "Cooper Square Hotel?"

"Yep. And Gino, buddy, I'd appreciate it if you'd engage the privacy screen and take the long way," Chase drawled.

He nodded and the black glass separated them.

"Not your first time in a limo, is it, McKay?"

"Nope. But it'll be my first time fucking in one." Chase placed a kiss on the center of her throat. "I'm dyin' for you, my Ava Rose."

The man could be so sweet.

"Undo your bra. I want them sugar tits in my mouth."

And...not so sweet. Not that she was complaining. Chase had already untied the bow at the neckline of her sundress and slipped the loosened material down her biceps. She twisted the front closure of her bra and his rough-skinned hands were there, knocking hers away.

"Arch back." As soon as she complied, Chase's hot mouth surrounded her left nipple. He suckled strongly. Purposefully.

That familiar, delicious heat spread. Ava gave herself over to it. Over to him. Reveling in the act of surrender.

Chase knew exactly how to eek out each sigh and moan. He expertly toyed with her mouth, his kisses so maddeningly arousing, so ripe and sensual, so unbearably erotic, she wanted to beg him to stop. Or to never stop.

He whispered gruffly, "Hang tight," below her ear and rolled her, dropping to his knees on the floor of the limo.

Breathing hard, dizzy, wet and achy, Ava rested her back against the plush center cushion. She watched as Chase shimmied her sundress up around her waist. Then he tugged her so far forward her butt cheeks were barely on the edge of the seat. "I'm falling."

"I've got ya." He stretched her left arm to the safety strap on the left side of the car roof, curling her fingers around the leather as he dragged kisses from the cup of her shoulder, across the sensitive bend in her elbow, to her fingertips. And back, to repeat the process on the right side.

Circling his thick fingers around each ankle, he pushed her legs wide, almost in straddle splits and hooked the edges of her low heels into the plastic lip that housed the door handle.

Keeping his eyes locked on hers, he took a condom out of his wallet and held the package in his teeth as he yanked his briefs and jeans to his knees.

"Want me to put that on?" she asked, her focus on his fully erect cock.

He lifted a brow and smiled briefly before his teeth tore open the square package. "You're stretched a little thin." Once he had the condom on, he worked himself inside her, his mouth busy on her throat.

Ava's head fell back and she groaned. So full. So hot. So good, every time.

Then Chase started to move. Endlessly long, deliciously slow, completely thorough strokes of his hot, hard flesh into hers. His cock buried so deeply inside her she felt his balls resting against her ass.

For being in the back of a limo, in New York City, during rush hour, there was no rushing Chase. He made love to her with his usual passion, but this tryst also served as a reminder that he'd have her, his way, no matter where, no matter when.

The rhythm of Chase's strokes increased and he slipped his hand between their bodies to manipulate her clit.

"Yes. Like that. You know just how... God...don't stop."

"I love watching you come," he growled, his eyes on her face as he pumped into her. "You're mine, Ava. No man has ever known you like this. No man but me will ever know this side of you."

No declaration of love, just possession, which maybe was the closest Chase came to admitting love. She smashed her mouth to his, matching the kiss to the brutal intensity of the way he fucked her.

He bottomed out with every thrust. One hand gripping her ass, the other rubbing her clit as he mastered her body with his. As Chase came undone.

Those teasing tingles tightened, coalesced into full power. The orgasm swamped her. She felt the pulses in her clit, in her pussy muscles spasming around Chase's cock, in her nipples. Even her lips throbbed as Chase turned the kiss into a sensual tease.

His body might've stopped moving, but his hands didn't. His mouth didn't. He nuzzled and caressed every section of her exposed skin. This was another thing she loved about him—his reluctance to release her after such an explosive interlude. He uncurled her fingers from the straps, sweetly kissing each knuckle. He unhooked her shoes, massaging her calves, her quads and her inner thighs. He ditched the condom and straightened her clothes before he bothered with his own. Then he gathered her in his arms and held her, like she was precious. Fragile. Like she was his.

And Ava let him.

The intercom buzzed twice, then Gino's voice came on. "We're about four blocks from the Cooper Square Hotel."

They remained wrapped together until the limo stopped. The rear door opened and Ava watched Chase's face as he caught his first glimpse of her family's hotel.

Yeah, he wore the holy-crap expression.

The hotel, situated in the Bowery section of Manhattan was quite impressive, with its seemingly twisted tower, a modern architectural work of art, twenty-one stories tall, comprised of glass on all sides.

The bags were whisked from the car trunk directly inside. Ava waited while Chase shook Gino's hand and slipped him a folded bill.

Chase placed his hand in the small of Ava's back. "Ah yeah, Hollywood, you were definitely slumming with the places we've been staying."

The front door, at least fifteen feet tall and nine feet wide, swung open and she had her personal welcoming committee ushering her inside the postmodern, oriental-themed lobby.

"Miss Cooper! We're so happy to have you back in New York."

"Thank you, Jason." She gestured to Chase. "Jason, this is my companion." Ava purposely allowed Chase to introduce himself, not knowing if he intended to keep up his Bill Chase persona or not. Either way, it was his decision.

He thrust out his hand. "Good to meet you, Jason. Chase McKay."

Ava relaxed slightly. "Jason is the evening manager. The man who can make anything happen."

Jason, a slight man in his early thirties, smiled at Ava after shaking Chase's hand. "The pleasure is mine. We have you set up in the family suite on the fourteenth floor. Chef Delacorte has asked if you have any specifics requests for in-room dining?"

"I'd love a sampler of his latest appetizers, since I'm not sure what our dinner plans are for later this evening."

"Consider it done. Delivery time?"

Ava glanced at Chase. "Are you hungry?"

He shrugged. "I could eat."

"As soon as possible would be great."

"I'll see to it. Also, the bar is stocked with your usual requests." Jason handed Ava a slip of paper. "Here's your access code. The staff is here to fulfill any of your needs, so don't hesitate to ask."

"I won't. Thank you." She slipped her hand through Chase's and led him around the corner to the elevators. Although Chase seemed to study everything, the funky patterns, the light fixtures, the restaurant behind the artfully placed glass partition, he didn't say a word until after they'd entered the corner suite.

The entire space was floor-to-ceiling windows. The enormous bedroom and bathroom were enclosed off to the left. A sitting area faced the city side.

And still Chase said nothing as he stared out the window at the bustling city below.

Ava kicked off her shoes and moved in behind him, circling her arms around his waist, setting her chin on his shoulder. "You okay?"

"Fuck no. This place is... I've never stayed anywhere this upscale, Ava."

Better not tell him this wasn't the crown jewel in the Cooper Hotel chain. "Like you told me when we first started traveling together. It's just a room with a bed."

"Sometimes I'm a fuckin' idiot." He wiggled away from her, pressing his forearm against the curved glass. "The staff fawned over you. Like you're royalty or something."

"How is it any different than sponsors fawning over you?"

He scowled over his shoulder. "Big difference. Trust me."

At a loss of how to deal with his reaction to their economic disparity, she retreated to the opposite sitting area. Less than fifteen minutes ago they were as physically close as possible. Chase had looked her in the eye and assured her he knew her. Were those just babbled words uttered in a moment of lust?

She'd shared every facet of herself with him. Ava never lied about her family background. Could he only deal with her when she was in his world? A transplanted city girl who had to rely on him for everything?

It didn't matter if he didn't want her to be this Ava. Truth was, this was the real her.

Chase had known her family had money.

To think he'd been afraid a Hollywood actress was out of his league? That was a drop in the bucket compared to seeing her as the billion-dollar baby.

He needed a drink. He correctly guessed which cabinet held the minibar and opened it, snagging the first beer he found. Fucking Heineken. He drank it anyway. Damn thing probably cost twenty bucks.

Two knocks sounded and Ava went to the door. "Come in. That looks amazing. Chef Delacorte truly outdid himself."

Chase wandered over to see what type of feast management laid out for a member of the royal Cooper family.

A small Asian man draped a pristine white tablecloth over the table and arranged the first rectangular platter. "Pink sweet potato soufflé topped with tapenade."

Chase waited for the man to serve up more than two spoonfuls.

But he revealed the next plate with a flourish. "Arugula salad with roasted beets, feta and toasted pumpkin seeds."

Beets? The greens looked like wilted dandelion leaves. That whole dish resembled something his mom served when she was cleaning out the fridge.

The Asian man said, "Polenta with shallot dill sauce."

A rubbery yellow disk with what looked like a splotch of ranch dressing and a skinny piece of ditch weed sticking from the center.

What the hell kind of appetizers had Ava ordered? Where were the nachos? Chicken wings? Fried pickles, okra and cauliflower?

"Pulled pork sandwich with ginger mango slaw."

Now, he could eat pork. But calling that one bite wonder a sandwich was stretching it. Chase counted five more covered dishes. Which probably equaled another five ounces of food.

"Bruschetta with heirloom tomatoes and anise-flavored basil."

He snorted softly. Chopped tomatoes on toast.

Ava glanced at him sharply and he gave her an innocent look.

"Spicy yellow fin tuna rolls with lime-pickled onions. And salmon on a bed of black diamond coconut rice."

Two sushi dishes. Fucking awesome.

The waiter lifted the last two lids. "Crimini mushroom ravioli with kale pesto. Baked brie with caramelized fresh fig."

Maybe he'd find a bag of peanuts in the minibar.

Ava gushed, "This looks and smells absolutely amazing. Give my sincerest thanks to Chef Delacorte and tell him I'll pop into the kitchen while I'm here to thank him personally."

"Ah. But he sent you one more token, Miss Cooper." From beneath the cart he presented a small plate and lifted the silver dome. "Your favorite dessert. Lavender-infused crème brulee' with sugared pansy petals."

"Oh. I can't believe he remembered."

I can't believe you don't see this for what it is: a total suck up.

Chase felt somewhat guilty for that thought. How could he fault people for liking Ava so much when he felt the same?

After she let the server out of the room, she picked up a vivid red rectangular plate and scrutinized the food. "There's so much to choose from."

She couldn't be serious.

He hoped the beer would drown out how loud his stomach growled.

"Grab a plate and dig in," Ava said.

"Nah. You go ahead."

Ava faced him. "What's going on with you?"

"Nothin'." He sipped his beer. "That kinda stuff is not really my thing."

"So we have all this delicious food and none of it sounds good to you?"

"First, dime-sized helpings don't qualify as *all this food*. Second, if I don't know what's in something, I don't eat it. Period."

She lifted her chin with a look of determination. "If I fix you a plate, will you at least try some?"

"If you feed me," he said silkily. "While you're sitting on my lap. Nekkid."

"You are such a brat sometimes."

Chase stiffened and turned away.

A minute or so of silence hung in the air.

Then Ava's hand lovingly followed the contour of his spine. "Sorry. Me pushing food on you is bratty. Will you try some of these dishes if I hand-feed you? Could be sexy and fun. Very upscale *9 ½ Weeks*."

She'd finally convinced him to watch that flick on her computer— not that they'd made it to the end. "Fine. But no sushi."

"Why not?"

"Because where I'm from? We call raw fish bait, not food."

Ava rolled her eyes and bit into a tuna roll. "Mmm. More for me. Sit." She began loading a plate.

After she straddled his lap, he curled his hands around her ass cheeks, murmuring, "For balance," as he kissed her strong, stubborn jawline.

"Here. This is your speed." She pinched the tiny pork sandwich between her forefinger and thumb, popping it in his mouth.

He chewed. Swallowed. "Not bad. Coulda been a whole lot bigger. Something that small just pisses my stomach off."

"I know you like cheese." She loaded her fork with a gooey white substance and then dragged it through some kind of sauce. She held the fork close to his lips. "Open."

He obliged, and as soon as he finished chewing, he swooped in for a kiss. "I liked that one. But my favorite part of this is you feeding me."

Her beautiful turquoise eyes glittered with triumph and she waggled the fork at him.

"What's that? Christ. Oh hell no. Food is not supposed to be pink."

"It's sweet potato soufflé."

Chase hoped his gag reflex wouldn't kick in. He closed his mouth around the fork tines, letting the glob sit on his tongue. Swallowing, he withheld a shiver of disgust. "Next."

After he'd appeased her and tried several samples, he carried her to the bedroom. Spreading her out on the thick white comforter, he stripped her to skin.

"I'm still hungry and needing something sweet. So I'm gonna eat my fill of you." His finger followed the creamy slit between her thighs. "And like any fine dining experience, I plan on taking my time. Enjoying the experience."

She moaned.

A lot.

After he'd brought her to the edge three times, he finally sent her soaring. He kissed his way up her trembling body; humbled he affected this woman so strongly. He tucked them under the covers, spooning behind her and whispered, "Thank you."

"What for? I should be thanking you, Chase."

"Thank you for sticking by me the last week. I ain't been the easiest guy to be around." How did he tell her he'd never opened himself up to anyone like he had with her?

"Easy is boring." She turned her head and kissed his arm. "I missed the cocky, bossy bull rider part of you. Although everything that happened with Ryan is beyond tragic and it's still in the forefront of both our minds, I'm really glad you came to New York with me."

Seemed he didn't have to tell her anything. Seemed Ava already knew. And for the first time in his life, that didn't scare him to death.

A nap refreshed them both. Chase would've preferred to stay in for the rest of the night, but Ava kept tossing out comments about the city that didn't sleep.

He stretched out on the bed, watching her get ready, which was a new experience. The Ava he'd traveled with was low-maintenance. This Ava went all out with hair, makeup, snappy clothes. Chase didn't want to know where she'd gotten all the extra stuff.

"The first day we hung out in Sundance, you bought me the world's best chili dog." She rubbed glittery gunk on her cheeks. "So I wanna take you out for the best burger in New York." Her eyes met his in the mirror. "I imagine you're hungry."

"Starving. But you sure the place will be open? It's almost ten o'clock."

"It's Friday night in New York City. The place closes at midnight and we have reservations at eleven."

Chase frowned. How had she known he'd agree? Did she assume he'd just go along with everything she planned?

Ava misread his scowl. "I had Jason make the reservation while you were in the shower."

"This ain't just a place you can walk in?"

"Most of the good restaurants aren't."

Good restaurant. Hah. Probably wouldn't be the type of burger joint he preferred. He envisioned their time in New York entirely different than she did. Was she anxious to be in the spotlight again? Because she sure as hell dressed for a photo op.

Ava Dumond's comings and goings wouldn't necessarily attract attention in a city of ten million, but Ava Cooper's might. Didn't she see that? Or didn't she care?

"Chase? You're quiet."

"I'm quiet more often than you realize."

She lifted a brow.

"Anyway, you sure us going out is a good idea?"

"It'll be fun."

"I'm assuming it's kosher to wear jeans to this burger place? Because I'm low on Armani suits."

"It's fine for tonight. But we can look at adding to your wardrobe tomorrow when we're—"

"Don't say it, Ava. I am *not* goin' shopping with you."

"Why not? We're in the fashion capital of the world. It'll be fun."

"No fucking way in hell."

Ava walked over to sit on the edge of the rumpled bed. "What's going on with you?"

"Nothin'."

"Bullshit. Talk to me."

Chase crossed his arms over his chest. "You wanna hit the pricey stores on Fifth Avenue tomorrow? Fine. That's your thing. Not mine. I'm sure you have girlfriends who'd love to shop with you for a few hours while you're in town. You've probably already lined up a car service. You don't need me. And you shouldn't expect me to trail behind you, carrying your bags and standing around like a fucking idiot while you're pawing though purses."

Her eyes narrowed. "You're too manly for that?"

He rolled to his feet on the opposite side of the bed. "Yes. And you'd be wise to remember I ain't a lap dog like Jake neither." He slammed the bedroom door behind him and grabbed another beer—his third of the night.

Christ. He should've known. Ava Dumond was fine being with a dirty rodeo cowboy in his world, but when it came to Ava Cooper's world, he didn't measure up. She intended to turn him into a slick-haired, suit-and-tie-wearing, shopping-for-fucking-shoes pussy.

Screw that. Just to be ornery, Chase dug out his big Man of Steel championship belt buckle and threaded it through the belt loops of his Wranglers. He'd considered leaving his cowboy hat in the room, but that too, was part of who he was, so on it went.

He'd finished half his beer when Ava emerged from the bedroom. The woman embodied hot sin in tight white pants, a gauzy shirt draped over a cleavage-enhancing silver-sequined tank top. She hadn't worn ankle-breaking stilettos to spite him, which was a plus. His eyes roved over her. "Goddamn you look fantastic."

"Compliments won't negate your shitty attitude."

Chase held his beer bottle aloft. "Booze might."

Ava's laugh was laced with exasperation.

He crossed the room and kissed her soundly. "I don't like fighting with you, Hollywood. Let's go have us a burger."

A car service delivered them to db Bistro Moderne. Ava approached the hostess stand. "Reservations for Cooper."

Of course the reservation was for Cooper.

The host, a scrawny, pimple-faced Mexican kid, grinned. "We're so pleased you've chosen to dine with us tonight, Miss Cooper. I was such a huge fan of *Miller's Ridge*."

"Thank you. That's so sweet."

"Could I trouble you for an autograph?"

"I'd love to sign one. I'll swing by on our way out."

The kid beamed. "Right this way."

From what Chase could see, the restaurant was tiny—ten tables total. The walls were plastered with brightly colored paintings. Music blared but didn't mask the din. The host led them to a table directly in front of the windows. Talk about being in a fishbowl. Since it was the only seating available, it wouldn't do any good to complain.

"Can I bring you a beverage from our bar, Miss Cooper?"

"A Stoli martini, extra dirty."

"Excellent choice. And for you, sir?"

Weird. He didn't know Ava drank martinis. Seemed there was a lot he didn't know about her. "Do you have a beer list?"

"No sir. We don't serve beer."

Chase managed not to blurt, *No beer in a burger joint?* He said, "Chivas on the rocks. A double." Before he opened the menu to check whether this place even served burgers made of meat, Ava placed her hand over the top of his.

"Do you trust me to order for you?"

This was a test. He thought back to the night they'd eaten at the supper club. She'd allowed him to order for her, so she obviously expected the same courtesy. "Sure. But no—"

"Fish. Got it."

She ordered. When their drinks arrived Ava raised her glass for a toast. "To having fun in the Big Apple."

He clinked his glass to hers and drank, but he couldn't tear his gaze away from her face. The lighting gave her an extra golden glow.

"You're staring at me."

"Because you're beautiful."

She blushed.

Goddamn he loved it when she blushed. "C'mere."

She leaned across the table until they were nose to nose. "What?"

"This." Chase angled his head and pressed his mouth to hers, memorizing the shape, softness and taste of her lips beneath his. He let the kiss linger, didn't use his tongue, only parted his mouth slightly and rubbed his lips over hers twice before he eased back.

They didn't speak as they took in the ambiance of the restaurant and gazed out the window. Seemed to take forever until their food arrived. His burger had gooey stuff in the middle that tasted like his Aunt Caro's goose liver spread. The meat was juicy, but the burger would've been better with a layer of mustard, onions and pickles—in his opinion.

Ava only ate half of hers and declined dessert and coffee.

The server dropped the bill at Chase's elbow. He automatically opened it and looked at the damages.

Holy. Fucking. Shit.

"Chase. Gimme that."

He gaped at her. "A hundred bucks? For one hamburger?"

Ava snatched the check from him. "I told you I was buying."

"You didn't tell me you were buying me the most expensive burger in New York."

"It's not the most expensive. I said it was the best. There's a restaurant on Wall Street that has one that costs more than this."

"Seriously? You almost coulda bought a cow for what you paid for two burgers."

"Let it go."

But Chase couldn't help but think... Hell, he had no freakin' idea what Ava was thinking, bringing him here, paying that much for what oughta cost six bucks, max. With fries.

The server returned with her credit card and the receipt.

"You ready?" she asked tightly.

"Yeah."

The outside air wasn't as chilly as her attitude.

Your fault. Fix it.

Chase wrapped his arm around her waist instead and pulled her against his body. "I'm not an ingrate. Thank you for supper, Ava."

"You're welcome."

"But just so you know? Forking out a hundred bucks and change for a burger don't guarantee that I'm putting out for you tonight."

She laughed, called him a redneck, and all was good between them.

But Chase knew it wouldn't always be that easy.

Chapter Twenty-Five

Chase left the room early to work out. She was editing the video images of the first time she'd taped Ryan riding, when her cell rang. "Hey, Han. You're up early."

"Don't remind me. How's New York?"

She stopped resizing images. "How'd you know I was in New York?"

"Courtesy of the New York City newspaper *Talk of the Town*, which contacted me at five a.m. for a comment on Ava Cooper's newest squeeze. Apparently you were spotted out and about last night."

"Shit."

"Yeah. See for yourself. The picture of you and cowboy dude is online."

"Then maybe no one will see—"

"And it's in the print version too. I was already up and headed to Booksoup for all the trade rags."

How had that happened so quickly? Ava remembered Chase's concern last night when she'd mentioned Jason calling for reservations for them. Chase's distrust of Jason wasn't surprising; Chase didn't trust anyone. With good reason. But Ava refused to believe Jason would violate her privacy. Most likely the host or waitstaff from the restaurant had contacted the press. She squinted at the picture of her and Chase, taken through the restaurant window, right when he'd kissed her.

It'd been a beautiful, sweet moment between them. Not something to be exploited. Something else occurred to her. "Did they give his name?"

"Not yet. But it'll only be a matter of time. And everyone in the press knows where you stay in New York. Call me later."

Ava couldn't suggest Hannah leak Chase's identity to end speculation. She wasn't sure which bothered her more. Admitting Chase was right in reminding her they were supposed to lay low? Or that she thrived on the attention and she'd lived in the spotlight so long she missed it when it wasn't an almost daily part of her life.

No. She didn't want to court trouble. Or speculation. She wanted a normal life where no one cared if she kissed the man she loved, in a restaurant in one of the biggest cities in the world.

That truth shook her to the core. In showing Chase her world, she understood she didn't want to live in it all the time anymore. But she'd seen the guarded look in his eye. Would Chase even believe her?

Her phone buzzed in her hand again and the name on the caller ID shouldn't have surprised her, but it did. Ava answered, "Hello, Petra."

"I can't believe I had to find out from a trashy rag like *Talk of the Town* that you're here."

"Our plan to have a quiet couple of days was blown the first night."

"You've been off the grid, darling. People are curious when you resurface. Anyway. How are you?"

"Can't complain. What's new with you?"

"I've volunteered way too much time to my charities, but I simply don't know how they'd survive without me, so I continue to raise money and Arthur continues to complain about it." She laughed. "He's been in California more than you have in the last month."

"I bet that makes you crazy."

"Yes. I don't miss LA at all. Anyway, I assume you're not jetting off today?"

"Not today."

"Good. It just so happens I'm throwing a little cocktail party tonight at the apartment and I'd love for you to come."

Ava nearly snorted. Since Petra lived in a fifteen-million-dollar apartment on Park Avenue, her little cocktail party probably meant a guest list of fifty, a black tie affair with a quartet from the New York Philharmonic providing entertainment.

"As a matter of fact, I won't allow you to say no, Ava."

"Be honest, Petra. How elaborate is this party? And what's the dress code?"

Petra sighed. "Twenty guests. Just appetizers. New York casual. Really, it's practically a barbecue."

Ava laughed at the image of stylish, elegant and immaculately coiffed Petra in jeans and a gingham-checked shirt, serving fried chicken.

"Glad I amuse you. Show up any time after seven-thirty. And feel free to bring the gentleman in the hat. Ta."

The gentleman in the hat might be optional after he got wind of their tabloid appearance.

Almost on cue, the door opened and Chase walked in.

She should be used to his jaw-dropping physique by now. The massive biceps, bulging triceps, thick forearms, bulked up chest, the delts, the quads, the glutes, the eight-pack abs. God she loved his abs. She loved to dip her tongue between the hard ridges of muscle, tracing every work-honed line. Especially after he worked out. Losing herself in the musky, salty taste of his skin.

"What? Do I have pigeon shit on my clothes or something?"

Her eyes snared his. "No. Just admiring the goods. Seeing you half naked...you are a damn beautiful man, Chase."

"You been hitting the minibar first thing?"

"No. I don't tell you enough how unbelievably attracted I am to you. Seeing you like that stops me in my tracks."

"Ava."

She marched over to him, pulling her three-inch height advantage. "You compliment me all the time. Why can't I do the same? You think it's insincere?"

That intense blue gaze never wavered. "No. You ain't blowing smoke up my chaps just to get into them. I just don't know what to say. Everything I think of sounds fucking wrong. And I sure as shit don't want you to think I don't appreciate it, because I do. So I'm left with saying nothin' at all."

As they stared at each other, uncertainty morphed into heat.

Ava bent down and brushed her lips over his ear, waiting for his shiver, because he always shivered—and he didn't disappoint. She nipped his rigid jaw, loving how his stubble felt on her lips. "I want to suck you off. Right now." She lowered to her knees and hooked her fingers in the waistband of his stretchy shorts, then yanked them down. She looked up at him and said, "Shirt. Off."

One tug and it was gone.

She reached between his legs and rolled his balls over her fingers as she suckled the cock head until he was fully erect.

Chase emitted a sound that Ava understood as *more*.

And she didn't tease and tempt. She wanted to drive him to that point of pleasure so hard and fast he didn't know what hit him. She used her hand. Her tongue. The deep suctioning power of her mouth. She loved she could render him as powerless to her touch as he rendered her.

Chase didn't touch her roughly until he muttered, "Fuck," and his shaft tightened. Then his hands gripped her neck, his thumbs pressing to keep her jaw fully open as his hips pumped into her face. Warm spurts hit the back of her throat and flowed over her tongue as she swallowed.

His legs trembled and his harsh breathing sliced the air. He stumbled back and his bare ass landed on the bed. The covers made a *whoosh* as his upper body fell back and he uttered another, "Christ Almighty."

Smiling, Ava untied his shoes and slipped them off. The fact Mr. My-Ticklish-Feet-Are-Off-Limits didn't stir when she removed his socks was an excellent indication of how thoroughly she'd rocked his world.

The bedroom phone rang and she leapt up to get it. "Hello? Oh. Damn. I lost track of time. No, don't let him leave. Tell him I'll be down in ten minutes. Or if he prefers, he can park back by the service entrance so he doesn't have to keep circling the block. Great. Thank you."

She saved her work and shut down her laptop. She twisted her hair and attached a hairclip. Her clothing choices were dismal, but her shopping excursion would fix that. She threw jeans, a white T-shirt and ballet flats into her bag.

Chase rested on his elbows when she returned to the bedroom to say goodbye.

"This is short notice, but my friend Petra called and she's having a cocktail party tonight. I told her we'd go. Which works out because I'd already made hair and makeup appointments at my favorite salon."

"Who's Petra?"

"An actress I worked with when I started out in LA. Petra aimed her goals much higher than acting and snagged a New York financier who dabbled in the movie production biz as her husband. Arthur is thirty years older, and she's very New York high society now, but for some reason she's always kept in touch with me." Ava slung her bag over her shoulder. "Think about coming to the party with me, okay?"

"Fine. But where you goin' now?"

"First to a yoga class near my salon. Then to the salon. Then shopping." She pointed at him. "Don't give me that lost puppy look, McKay. I believe you said *no fuckin' way* when I mentioned shopping yesterday."

He scowled. "I meant it. Any idea when you'll be back?"

"I'll text you." She made it to the door when she found her back pressed against the wall and Chase's mouth insistent on hers.

After he'd obliterated every thought from her mind, he released her. "Have fun today, Hollywood, because now I know how much you really love all that time-consuming girly shit."

It wasn't until she reached the car that she realized she'd forgotten to tell him about the press situation.

Chase wasn't uncomfortable being by himself in New York City. He'd been there a half-dozen times, usually with a group, but any place he needed to get to was a taxi ride away.

He showered and dressed, walking away from the hotel into the shops in the East Village until he found food that appealed. Two slices of pizza would hold him for a while. The sun beat down, heating the pavement, reminding him the city smelled like ass. The tiny storefronts fascinated him. Everyone was in a hurry, except for the bums. Another thing he noticed? He wasn't the shortest man around. Here, his height was average. Maybe even above average.

Much as he hated to admit it, he needed to find something suitable to wear tonight. His clothes were fine for rodeo and travel, but not decent enough for a penthouse cocktail party in New York City.

Once again he was reminded of the differences between them. He didn't blame her for wanting to return to the lifestyle she'd been born into.

None of the shops looked promising for his preferred type of clothing. And he refused to dress in uncomfortable or trendy clothes to impress people he didn't know. Leaning against a shady section of the brick building, he punched up a Google search and skimmed the results. The closest store was twenty-seven blocks away, according to Google Maps. He hailed a cab.

The familiar scent of leather and denim greeted Chase as he stepped into Western Spirit. The store itself relied more on kitschy country chic than plain country. Racks of high-end leather coats filled the aisle. Along the wall were vintage boots enclosed in glass cases. Vintage, another word for discarded and out of fashion. He peered at a beat-up pair of Tony Lamas, nothing fancy except the stitching on the snip toe, and the asking price was seven hundred bucks. A new pair didn't cost that much. Shaking his head, he crossed over to the men's clothing section.

He expected to be left to his own devices. His experience with sales staff in New York hadn't ever been good. So he was surprised when the salesgirl immediately wandered over.

"You have an idea of what you're looking for that I can help you find?"

Chase glanced up from the rack of long-sleeved western shirts and smiled. The Italian girl, who looked to be late teens, gasped, "Omigod. You're Chase McKay!"

Holy crap. He wasn't expecting that. "Good eye...?"

"Angelina. I can't believe bull rider Chase McKay is in our store. I saw you ride at Madison Square Garden for the last two years. That was the most exciting part of the event when you rode Tick Tock for ninety points. My girlfriend Sarah and I still talk about it."

"Well, I'm happy to hear it made such an impact on you, Angelina."

"So has your injury healed enough to get you back on tour?"

This was one of his favorite parts of being part of the PBR, connecting with fans. "I hope so."

She seemed to remember she was supposed to be selling him something. "These shirts are pretty basic. The ones with the custom embroidery are over there. Are those more your style?"

"Actually, I'm wanting something simple. And without sounding boring, I'm looking for white or black."

"Classic choices." She eyed the breadth of his shoulders. The length of his arms and torso. Then pulled out four shirts. Two white, two black. "These are the same brand but the fabric weight is different. Try them on. The dressing rooms are back by the boots."

Chase bit back a groan. Why couldn't he just buy the damn things and be done with it? He hated to try shit on. But he did.

Angelina scrutinized him after he exited the dressing room. "Definitely the heavier weight."

"Sold. Now I need a coupla pairs of Wranglers." He rattled off the size, cut, color and style.

"We have those. I'll take them to the counter."

As Chase dug out his wallet, he noticed Angelina's focus kept drifting to the door. And when she caught him watching her, she blushed. "I don't mean to be rude or nosy, but do you always have photographers following you around?"

"Almost never. Why?"

"One followed you here. He's been waiting in the shadow of that grocery store awning since about five minutes after you walked in."

"No shit?" Chase craned his neck and squinted at the man. "He's pretty well hidden. How'd you see him?"

Again she blushed. "My boyfriend is a journalism major at NYU, so I tend to notice stuff like that because he does."

"I wonder what he's doin'?"

"Probably following up on the picture of you and Ava Cooper in this morning's edition of *Talk of the Town*."

Chase froze. "Excuse me?"

"You haven't seen it?"

How come Ava hadn't mentioned it? "No, ma'am."

"They don't name you, just mention the mysterious man in the cowboy hat. And without sounding all freakish fan girl, when I saw the picture, I thought that might be you."

"Do you have a copy of the paper?"

She shook her head. "My boyfriend uses them for class so it's at our apartment."

Pissed him off that someone had tipped the press Ava was in town. They couldn't even have a dinner out alone like a normal couple without it being news?

The snoopy bastard had probably been lying in wait today. Had he followed him to the gym? Obviously the asshole had followed him from the hotel. Wait. Chase had taken a cab. Had this guy jumped in a cab too? Why? How had he tracked him down in a city this size?

Face it, you haven't seen another man wearing a cowboy hat so you ain't that hard to find.

Didn't matter. By now probably all the media outlets had figured out who he was. They'd already linked him to Ava, so he'd just add another link and hope like hell this would play well with the PBR. "Angelina, is your apartment close by?"

"Within a few blocks."

"And your boyfriend? Is he home now?"

"Yeah. Why?"

"He's got a lot of media contacts?"

"As far as I know."

Chase grinned at her. "Good. How would he like an exclusive with Ava Cooper's New York City companion, Chase McKay? With pictures?"

"Are you serious?"

"Completely."

"But...why?"

"I hate that these bastards have invaded my privacy. Someone is gonna get the story. For once I'd like to control who that someone is and what information they get."

Immediately Angelina had her phone to her ear. "Ryan? Get your camera and come to the store. Now. I've got your first story. The man with Ava Cooper last night." She didn't notice Chase's frozen smile.

Ryan.

Goddamn just the mention of the name made his gut clench with sorrow. He closed his eyes, reminding himself it was a common name. Reminding himself he was here to have fun.

He had his clothes delivered to the hotel. To be ornery, Chase killed a few hours buying gifts and checking out a museum. While his paparazzi shadow thought he was getting a scoop, Ryan had already sold his story to *Talk of the Town's* competitor. He wandered into an Irish pub for a beer and a plate of corned beef before he returned to the room.

Ava texted she was running late. After being with her practically twenty-four/seven the last month, he missed her. Hopefully she hadn't filled all her upcoming days in New York with shopping trips and salon appointments. Hopefully she wanted to spend time with him before they returned to the real world.

Or maybe Ava is sick of your crap attitude as she's showing you her world.

Christ, he had been acting like a jerk. And it wasn't entirely from the lingering sadness of Ryan's death. He was out of his element and taking it out on Ava. He had to buck up, cowboy up and make sure he didn't embarrass her tonight.

His jaw dropped when she blew into the room, an absolute fucking vision—artfully tousled hair, fancy makeup and a lavish skintight turquoise dress that matched her eyes.

"Sorry. I thought about having you meet me at Petra's, but that wouldn't be fair..." Ava's eyes narrowed on him, sprawled in the sitting area, in his boxer briefs, drinking a beer and watching classic ESPN. "Chase? Aren't you going to the party with me?"

"Of course I'm goin' with you."

"Then why aren't you ready?"

He drained his beer. "I am ready. I showered. Shaved. I was waiting to get dressed."

"What are you wearing?"

"Does it matter?"

He watched her struggle with her answer. Finally she gifted him with that mega-watt star smile. "As much as I love to see you undressed like that, cowboy, it is a little informal. So maybe you oughta cover up all those muscles so female party goers aren't drooling on you."

"Such sweet bullshit." Chase retreated to the bedroom and yanked on new jeans, buttoned the white shirt, added his championship belt buckle, slipped on his boots and hat.

All in under two minutes.

"So? Do I pass?"

She nodded, and returned her focus to two pairs of shoes. One pair, four inches high, were a funky shade of shiny yellow patent leather with turquoise stitching. The other pair, were flats, fancied up with flowers, but were nowhere near as hot as the stilettos.

"Problem?" he asked.

Ava fingered the yellow heels. "I love, love, love these Louboutins. They are so perfect with this dress, but..." She looked up at him and put on a too-bright smile. "But these will be fine. I've gotten used to wearing flats the past few weeks."

Damn woman was willing to give up wearing her fancy new shoes so she wouldn't tower over him in public? That's when Chase knew that she loved him.

He pointed at the yellow pair. "Wear them."

"But—"

"Ava. It's okay. I don't mind."

She squealed when she slipped them on. "Have I mentioned how much I love them?"

"A time or two. Let's go."

"Wait. There's something I forgot to tell you. We made the papers today. Evidently someone told the media I've come out of hiding, so there are photographers hanging around."

"I noticed."

"You did?"

"Yeah." He smiled and opened the door. "But I handled it."

A look of horror crossed her face. "You didn't, like, beat them up or anything?"

"I ain't a total redneck," he chided.

Any photographers around the hotel were discreet; he half expected popping bulbs everywhere.

Ava seemed nervous, which was a switch because he wasn't a bit nervous.

He took her hand. "What's goin' on, sweet thang?"

"Although it's been a few months since the thing went down with Jake, this is the first social event I've attended with industry professionals."

"I thought these people were your friends?"

"I guess we'll find out, won't we?" She sighed. "Sorry. I'm sure my poor little rich Hollywood girl whine is getting old."

"Never apologize for how you feel. None of us has to walk in each other's shoes." He smirked and pointed to her feet. "And no fuckin' way do I *ever* wanna walk in them babies."

She smiled. "You always make me feel better. Make me feel normal, no matter what I tell you. I just don't want to spend the whole night fielding questions about the Jake debacle or tell anyone where I've been the last few weeks."

Chase stiffened beside her.

"Not because I'm embarrassed, Sundance. But because our time on the road together was our time. I don't want to share it with anyone."

Her sweetness always caught him off guard. "So don't."

Petra's place was a Park Avenue palace, marble floors, alabaster pillars, gilded wood, velvet and silk curtains, priceless tapestries on the walls and floor. The space screamed filthy rich, but it was cold. Unwelcoming.

So Chase was surprised Petra's house wasn't a reflection of her personality. Petra faked kissed him, cooed over his cuteness and whisked Ava away, leaving Chase alone.

Tuxedo-wearing waiters circled with trays with food that looked as if it'd been zapped by a shrink ray gun. What was this town's fascination with miniaturized food?

He'd knocked back half of a stiff drink when Petra's husband

Arthur introduced himself and several of his friends. The men were fascinated by Chase's occupation. More respectful about it than he'd imagined.

As Chase did more listening than talking, he appreciated the PR training he'd had over the years. This nodding and smiling was actually easier than sucking up to sponsors, trying to charm them out of their money.

Ava was ready to leave before him, but by the time they'd made the rounds, saying goodbye to everyone, he couldn't wait to take a breath of fresh air.

Until he actually inhaled stanky-ass New York City air.

Their driver directed them to the right car, since the all the damn service cars lined along the curb looked exactly the same.

Ava slipped her shoes off first thing and sighed.

He'd never in a million years understand women and shoes. "So that was fun."

"Really?"

"Yeah. Why?"

"Now don't take this wrong, but you didn't have a problem fitting in with that crowd."

"You'd expected I'd put my boots up on their Louis the Fourteenth furniture and challenge Arthur to a bare-chested wrassling match while swigging from a bottle of hooch?"

She laughed. "No. God, no. It just struck me as odd that you were more nervous to meet Ryan's mom than some of the most powerful men in New York."

"Those men have no power over me, Ava. But Ryan's mom? Shit. He'd built me up to be a superhero, to the person who mattered most to him in his life. Meeting her and measuring up? That's humbling stuff."

Ava blinked at him.

Hell, was she...crying? "What?"

"You are such a beautiful man. Inside and out. Thank you for going to the party with me."

"You're welcome." He brought her hand to his mouth and kissed it. "You *are* gonna feed me real food now, right?"

"Poor starving baby. Want to brave the cameras and eat out? Or order room service?"

"How about if you use some of that Cooper clout and get us a table at the hotel restaurant? You look too goddamn good to waste sitting on a bed in our suite." He grinned. "But feel free to leave them shoes on later."

After a leisurely meal, which turned out to be romantic and fun, even amidst a crowd, they returned to their room. Chase led Ava to the bedroom and stripped her slowly. Silently. When she was bare before him, he murmured, "I knew I'd find my Ava under here."

Her eyes, always so expressive, were oddly wary when she whispered, "Am I really your Ava, Chase?"

"Goddamn right you are. The rest of this stuff—country boy, city girl—doesn't matter. You understand that, right? I'm not here with you because you're a celebrity, or because you're rich. I'm with you because whenever we are, whether it's in Wyoming or Nebraska or New York City, it feels right. When I'm with you, Ava, I feel like I'm where I'm meant to be."

"That's not just the wine talking."

"It's me talkin'." Chase inhaled slowly, trying to calm the mad beat of his heart. "Ava. I love you."

A beat passed. She smiled cheekily. "I figured since you ain't the type to wear your heart on your goddamn sleeve that I'd have to say *I love you* first."

He laughed at her perfect imitation of his way of speaking. This woman rarely reacted as he'd expected, which was just another reason he was so crazy in love with her.

"Meeting you is the best thing that's ever happened to me." She started in on his buttons. "I'm not here with you because you're a famous bad boy bull rider or because of your slamming body...okay that might be part of it." She kissed each inch of skin she exposed. "I love everything about you. We fit together in so many ways. I never thought...I'd find someone like you."

Was she really choked up, telling him how she felt? "Ava. You undo me."

"Take me to bed. I'm dying for you."

Yep. Definitely in love with her.

"It says what?" she practically shrieked.

"*The City Star* has an exclusive with Chase McKay. And a picture of him shopping in a western store. Get this, one of his purchases was a...rope. Apparently he was pretty vague on what he planned on using it for in Manhattan."

"Oh my fucking God, I'm going to kill him."

Hannah laughed. "Chill out, Ava. This is funny stuff, because you know he did it to make the reporter for the *Talk of the Town* look like an idiot."

"But why didn't he tell me?" Shit. He *had* told her he'd handled it. And she shouldn't be shocked he'd used a subversive tactic. "What else does it say?"

"*The City Star* says he visited FAO Schwartz and Tiffany's, creating speculation you're knocked up. So they're postulating he's buying you an engagement ring and baby items."

"This is so ridiculous."

"I imagine it is for him too." Hannah giggled. "And he ended his day with a visit to the Museum of Sex."

Ava's thoughts returned to their sweetly intense lovemaking last night and the new things he'd tried that'd sent her into orgasmic overdrive. Twice.

"I don't hear you complaining about *that* one," Hanna said with a *rowr*.

"No comment."

"Then *Talk of the Town* has photos of you guys leaving the hotel last night. Fabulous dress. Vivienne Westwood?"

"Good eye."

"More photos of you leaving Petra's apartment. Lastly a really grainy shot of him feeding you something at the hotel restaurant."

"Steak," she said distractedly. "The man is a meat-eating machine."

"So you plan to go out and tempt paparazzi today?"

"We'll see. He's at the gym. I talked to Arthur a little last night. He was very helpful."

"How far are you in the project?"

"Waiting for her to send me stuff. It's on hold until that point or until..." Ava scrolled over the images on the screen. Ryan smiling and talking to Chase.

When the door opened, she said, "Han, I've gotta go. I'll touch base with you later," and quickly closed the file on her laptop.

Chase flopped into the chaise. "Who was that?"

"Hannah. Bringing me up to speed on today's reporting. Seems *someone* had a very busy day yesterday."

His bottle of water stopped halfway to his mouth.

"Really, Chase? The Museum of Sex?"

He grinned. "Hey, it *is* a museum. I was tryin' to get a little culture while I'm in the big city, Hollywood."

"Not funny. And for someone who was such a fit about going shopping with me, you managed to hit three different stores yesterday."

"First of all, you told me I needed clothes. Then I had time to kill so I picked up a stick horse for my nephew and a stuffed panda for my niece at the toy store. I wandered down the street and saw a fancy crystal vase in the window and knew my mother would get a kick out of a box from Tiffany's showing up in Wyoming. And while I was in there I found a lamp for Ben's desk and a picture frame for Quinn and Libby."

He'd really been shopping for his family? That was so unbelievably sweet. And out of character for the rough cowboy.

"Did you buy anything for me?"

"Nope." He cocked his head. "Did you buy anything for *me* when you went shopping yesterday?"

"Nope. But maybe we can pick out something for each other today when we go shopping together, since I now know you were lying through your pearly whites about hating to shop."

"Ah, well, I have plans today."

"What kind of plans?" *And why didn't you tell me?*

"One of Arthur's friends was talking about corporate sports sponsorships last night and I weighed in. Evidently I didn't come across sounding like a hick idiot because he called me this morning and invited me to lunch and a Yankees game."

Her eyes narrowed. "Who invited you?"

"Bill Dahl."

"Bill Dahl? Who used to work with Donald Trump? Who has box seats at Yankee Stadium invited you to his inner sanctum? God. Billion dollar deals are made in those seats. You realize that, right?"

"No. But it's not a big deal, Ava. Just a couple of guys eating hot dogs and bullshitting while watching a ball game." He popped to his feet. "I better get in the shower. He's sending a car to get me in about fifteen minutes."

"Fifteen minutes? That gives you enough time to get ready?"

Chase rolled his eyes.

"You have clothes, right?"

"No, I thought I'd stroll in buck-assed nekkid. Christ. I can dress myself. Sometimes I think you forget that I've been on TV damn near once a week for the last eight years. So I have an idea how to conduct myself in a professional situation."

Now she felt like a snob. "Sorry. I do forget that."

Without prompting, he said, "I love you," and smooched her on the mouth. "That guy who holds the door said the manager wanted to talk to you in his office as soon as it was convenient for you."

"I'll see you later."

Chapter Twenty-Six

"Come on. I have something to show you." Ava draped a lightweight cashmere sweater over her arm and shouldered her purse. She was surprised Chase took her hand without asking questions.

Jason waited for them at the elevators. "Ready?"

"All set."

In the elevator, Jason swiped a keycard and inserted a small key into the panel before punching in a code. He faced them as the elevator moved. "Everything is set up as you requested. We have an event scheduled for noon, so the cleaning crew will arrive at six a.m."

"Thank you, Jason."

"My pleasure." He stepped aside as the doors slid open. "Enjoy your evening."

"We will." Ava gripped Chase's hand and stopped in the center of the round room.

"You wanna tell me what's goin' on, Hollywood?"

"We haven't spent as much time together on this trip as I'd hoped. So tonight, it's just us."

His gaze scanned the polished wood floors, the glass walls, and the three doors, which were open, allowing a breeze in. "Where are we?"

"The penthouse. It's rented out mostly for parties because...come on. I'll show you." Ava tossed her purse and sweater on the settee. She lifted a brow. "You aren't afraid of heights?"

He snorted.

Holding his hand, she led him out the door and straight to the edge of the wide walkway.

"Holy shit."

That summed it up perfectly. The modified balcony surrounding the penthouse boasted a 360-degree view of the New York City skyline. A waist-high glass partition was the buffer between penthouse and the twenty-one stories to the busy street below.

Neither said anything for several long minutes as they drank in the spectacular view. Ava had timed it so they arrived just before twilight, which allowed them to watch day turn to night as the lights of the most famous skyline in the world came on.

They walked the perimeter, stopping every few feet to gaze across the rooftops and the cityscape beyond. Ava pointed out landmarks. This time of day the light reflecting off the Chrysler Building gave it a pinkish-orange hue.

When they reached the opposite side, Chase said, "Holy shit," again.

"I thought you might like this."

A perpetual breeze blew due to the altitude. Ava's dress flapped around her knees. Strands of hair drifted across her face and she wished she'd tied it back.

Chase rested his forearms on the glass ledge and peered over side. "Long drop."

Ava matched his stance, switching her focus between the activity below and the buzz of helicopters and airplanes in the distance. She glanced at him when he snickered. "What?"

He raised his head and grinned at her slyly. "The little redneck boy inside me wants to spit over the side and see where it lands."

"You can take the man out of Wyoming...but a little tobacco juice always remains."

He chuckled.

They were shoulder to shoulder, enjoying the view when he turned around and pointed to the main space. "What's around the corner?"

"A living area with a kitchen and a bathroom. Behind that, a bedroom with two bathrooms."

"Handy."

"Very." A cool blast of air eddied around her and she shivered.

"C'mere. I'll keep you warm." Chase stepped behind her, wrapping his arms around her middle. When he nestled his chin on his shoulder, he sighed, "Well, that ain't gonna work. You're blocking my view, bein's you're taller than me."

"Do you mind that I'm taller?"

"Not so much anymore. Especially not when I see how sexy them sky-high heels makes your legs look."

"But you still won't dance with me."

He brushed his lips across the shell of her ear. "I don't recall you asking me recently."

"So if I turned on music up here?"

"I'd two-step with you all night." Chase swept his thumbs over her nipples until they hardened. "Well, maybe not all night. I might have time for a little mattress dancing if you play your cards right."

"I'll cheat at cards if have to, to make that happen."

He laughed. "How often have you stayed in the penthouse?"

"Never."

That seemed to surprise him. "Why not?"

"Because it's usually rented with weddings and parties. My visits to New York are spontaneous. As much as I love the penthouse and the view, hanging out up here all by myself is kind of a waste."

"Mmm."

"But I do sneak up if there isn't an event scheduled. There's something very humbling staring across all these high-rise buildings. I get that same feeling when I stare out at the ocean."

"What feeling is that?"

"Insignificance. Here, I'm one of millions of people. On my beach, I'm as trivial as a grain of sand. Seeing proof of my irrelevance puts things in perspective for me, especially when I've been puffed up by my own self-importance and have lost that insight."

"I hope you don't lose that humbleness, Ava. It's one of my favorite things about you."

She snuggled into his arms, wishing she owned the right to be in them every night, fearful of bringing up the "what happens next" question.

Silence lingered as they watched the city lights blaze against the indigo sky.

Chase's hot mouth trailed kisses up and down the side of her neck.

She tilted her head to the side, offering him full access.

He murmured, "You're so beautiful all the time. But especially so tonight in this light. I want you."

A shudder of need rolled through her. "I suppose that means I should show you the bedroom."

His arms tightened. "No. I want you like this. Right here. Right now. With the city lights shining like your eyes."

"But the paparazzi—"

"Won't have a clue what we're doin'." He gestured with is chin to the closest building, half a block away. "Can you see in the windows from here?"

"No."

"Then no one will see us, Ava. We'll look like two lovers lost in each other, admiring the view."

The idea of making love in public, but in a private setting, appealed to her. Yet, she couldn't help but compare it to her last rendezvous at her beach house. The humiliation when an intimacy simply became gossip fodder. She'd never put Chase through that. "Chase—"

"Besides, like you said, who'll notice us in a city of millions?"

It wouldn't be the same at all. Chase isn't like that other guy who wouldn't man up. Even if you are caught, Chase would stand beside you. He wouldn't be embarrassed about anything you do together because he loves you.

His sweetly seductive warm lips brushed the shell of her ear. "Please," he whispered. "I need you."

Need. Not want. Ava turned and caught his mouth in a deep kiss.

He pulled back and his lips curved against her cheek. "I'm takin' that as a yes."

"Yes."

"Lean forward a little and hold on to the partition."

She heard his clothes rustle. Then his rough-tipped fingers were teasing the backs of her thighs as he slowly lifted her dress to her hips. One finger traced the thin strap of her thong down the crack of her ass.

"Move your feet out, tall girl, so I won't have to go on tiptoe to fuck you."

His rough-toned words were the best kind of foreplay. Heat and hardness pressed into her backside. Beneath the silky fabric of her sundress, Chase's hand followed the curve of her hip to the rise of her mound. His finger delved under the elastic band of her thong and stroked her slit. He groaned softly as he discovered she was already wet and ready.

"Cant your hips back, baby."

Soon as she moved, she felt the condom covered head prodding her entrance.

Chase fed his cock into her slowly, his hot breath tickling her ear. "Ever done it standing up?"

"Ah, no."

"Ever done it this close to the edge of a twenty-one-story building?"

"No. But every time you touch me, Chase, you take me to that edge that always makes me dizzy."

"I love this sweet talkin' side of you. I love all sides of you, Ava." That said, he thrust into her fully.

Ava bowed into the solid wall of his chest.

Eroticism bombarded her from all angles. The sights and sounds of the city. The temperate breeze washing over them. His firm grip on her left hip. The perfect friction of his shaft tunneling in and out on a slow glide. Then arbitrarily ramming harder. The teasing flick of his fingertip over her clit. The feel of his mouth tasting her skin from her bare shoulder to behind her ear.

"Chase...I'm already..."

"Christ. It's too goddamn good with you. Every. Fucking. Time. Hold on. I don't wanna push you forward and send us crashing through the glass for the big finish."

She twined her left arm back and gripped his neck as he rammed into her more forcefully.

When he shoved deep and stayed lodged inside her, she shattered.

Chase breathed raggedly against her nape, his pelvis still bumping into her in tiny increments. "Ava."

"I know." She turned her head, rubbing her damp cheek against his.

"Do you?" he whispered.

"Yes."

"Say it."

"You love me."

He sank his teeth into her neck and she squealed.

"Okay, okay. I love you, Chase." She loved his playful side. She loved his passionate side. She loved they fit together, no matter where they were. No matter who they were with. But she really loved just the two of them together.

Chase's voice dropped to a barely discernible growl. "That's what I wanna hear." He scooped her into his arms and carried her to the bedroom.

With pure male heat and hunger, he undressed her, then himself. This wasn't a sensual exploration resulting in an achingly sweet union of bodies. No. This was raw mating. He demanded. Took. Teased. And ultimately gave all of himself with such unending passion, he left her knowing no other man would ever reach inside her like he did.

Sated, spent and sleepy, Ava stretched out on her belly next to Chase as his fingers lazily trailed up and down her spine.

"Was I too rough?"

Did he sound worried? She rolled over to look him in the eyes. "No. Why?"

"I got a little carried away."

"I like that about you." Ava pecked him on the lips. "Every time I think you can't top the last go-round? You do."

"Mmm."

"And because I know you're always famished after you ravage me, I took the liberty of ordering food."

"What kind of food?"

She traced the scar below his collarbone. "You seemed to like it when I hand-fed you, so the chef whipped up two trays of appetizers."

Chase froze.

Laughing, she kissed his nipple. "I'm kidding. I didn't want to be interrupted so we're having steak salad and other stuff that can be served cold."

"This has been great tonight. Just the two of us." He sighed. "You're always thinking of me, so I've gotta admit..."

"What?"

"I'm always thinking of you too, and I lied to you the other day. I did buy you something at Tiffany's. I've been carryin' it around in my pocket because I ain't sure you won't think it's stupid."

Ava perked right up. "A present? For me? I love presents."

"There's news," he said dryly.

"Hand it over."

Grumbling, he moved and rummaged though his jeans pockets.

Her eyes focused on what he'd clutched in his hand when he returned to bed.

"Close your eyes." Something cool and hard landed just above her cleavage and his finger fumbled with the necklace clasp below her hairline. "Okay. You can look. But if you don't like it, won't hurt my feelings if you wanna return it."

Ava glanced down as her fingers lifted the charm. A miniature rose. The twisty stem and tiny leaves were antique silver. The bloom, the size of an eraser, was milky white shot through with pink undertones. Delicate, old-fashioned and absolutely perfect.

"I couldn't find one like your grandpa gave you, and this was the closest I could come. The rose is carved out of rose quartz, which is all over Wyoming."

"So I'll think of you whenever I wear it." *Like I'll ever stop thinking of you.* Ava tried really hard not to cry, but a couple of tears slipped free. The last man who'd given her jewelry had been her grandfather.

"Ava?" Chase tipped her face up. "Ah, hell. Don't cry. I told you that you can take it back."

She made a sound half-laugh, half-sob. "No way am I taking it back, McKay. It's beautiful. Perfect. I love it. Thank you."

The guardedness in his eyes vanished. "You're welcome."

Chapter Twenty-Seven

Chase paced in the hotel room, glaring at his phone. He hadn't minded that the fucker hadn't worked at all yesterday, since he and Ava had spent the whole day in their room, most of it in bed after they'd returned early in the morning from the penthouse.

Dammit. He needed to access his email. Nothing was showing up on his phone. And he'd been in such a hurry to get away from the sorrow in Nebraska he'd accidentally left his laptop in his truck at the Omaha airport.

His gaze landed on Ava's computer on the desk. She'd left it on for a change. It'd take him about two seconds to log on to his account. If Ava were here she'd probably tell him to go ahead and borrow it.

Two programs were running and he minimized them before clicking on her web browser. He typed in his server site, his password and waited while five days' worth of messages downloaded. Four jokes from Quinn. Eight forwards from his father, which made him smile.

When Charlie McKay first got daily computer access, he drove Chase insane with all the crap messages he forwarded. But at some point, Chase figured out those forwards, sometimes funny, sometimes politically incorrect, sometimes sentimental, were his dad's way of showing love. His way of telling his youngest son that he was thinking about him. Now he didn't mind them at all.

He scrolled through the messages. Inquiries from his website from fans wondering when he'd be back in action. A notice from his credit card company about receiving his automatic payment. Same for his cell phone. Same for his rent. The last email, from Elroy, was time stamped roughly two hours ago, a form letter to all riders, regarding changes in the remaining schedule. Nothing new, just standard practice before an event. An event in Wichita he hadn't heard whether he'd be competing in.

What would he do if that call never came?

Go to trade school? Chase didn't see himself working as a mechanic. Or running heavy equipment on a construction site. Or writing speeding tickets as a law enforcement officer.

Think harder.

Chase pushed the chair back and stared at the bubbles popping up as the screen saver. He could ask if his buddy Darren needed an investor and hands-on help for his bull-breeding program in Oklahoma. Possibly Cash and Colby could get their venture off the ground sooner if they had a full-time partner who wasn't ranching. No one could deny he had more current contacts at various rodeos than either Colby or Cash.

Maybe you could try to become a stuntman in Hollywood.

Right. And if he wasn't successful at that, he'd be mooching off Ava.

Ava. The woman turned him inside out. The other night had been nothing short of magical. Standing against the glass partition and looking straight down at the street below thirty stories in the air. Watching day fade to night. Witnessing the lights in the New York City skyline come to life. Dancing with her barefoot across the polished mahogany floor, lights and noise as a backdrop, feeling as if they were the only ones in the world—even amidst a city of ten million. Laughing, carrying her to the gigantic canopied bed, swathed in silk and lace, a bed fit for a queen. Then he'd made love to her, face to face, heart to heart, drunk on the scent of her skin, high on the sound of his name drifting from her sweet lips as a breathy moan, overwhelmed by her. By how much she made him feel.

The computer dinged, indicating a new email. He touched the mouse pad, tapping on the minimized mail icon. The sender was Jackie Ackerman. What? How had she gotten his personal email address? When he opened it and read, *Ava*, he realized he'd mistakenly opened Ava's email program. He should've exited out. But he didn't. He kept reading.

Ava,

Ryan's high school English teacher is pretty computer savvy and she's more than willing to help. I gave her a stack of Ryan's pictures to scan. She's also transferring old home videos into that format you suggested so you can add them to the recent footage you shot. That transfer process might take awhile. Just wanted to give you a heads-up so my portion doesn't hold up production.

Production? Of what?

I'm glad you're working on something that might shed some light on this. I never want to see or hear of another mother going through this. I'll keep in touch. Jackie

What the hell had Ava promised Ryan's mother?

He found her recent history and opened a flash file titled *DOC-WIP current*. His face filled up the screen. "What do I like best about ridin' bulls?" He watched himself scratch his chin. "For those eight seconds we're fighting to see who owns the most determination. Who's got the most try. Even a small man can best a beast."

The frame changed. A squinty-eyed Taz came into view. "What do I like best about ridin' bulls?" He glanced off to the left. "On a day like today, when I've been beat to hell and I can't hardly wrap my hand in my bull rope because it's all swelled up?" Taz raised his right hand into camera view and Chase winced. His entire hand was red and purple, puffed up like a bad bee sting. "I can't tell you nothin' I like about it. But I sure can tell you a whole heap about what I hate."

The frame changed again. A grinning Ryan appeared. Grief sliced through Chase like a scythe through wheat. "What do I like best about ridin' bulls?" Ryan laughed. "Well, mostly that I'm finally old enough *to* ride 'em." He reached in his pocket and proudly whipped out his PRCA card, holding it close to the camera's lens. "I guess what I like is how the experienced riders are around to help out. To offer advice. Like one of my friends said, it's not me versus him in the arena. It's us versus the bulls."

Chase closed his eyes, remembering the day he'd said that to Ryan. Wishing the kid would've listened to his other advice.

Wishing things had turned out differently won't change anything.

He opened his eyes as black letters formed on the screen. *Chasing Eight: The Heartbreak Road To Rodeo Glory.*

Scenery flew by, speeding to super fast until the time-lapse photography made it seem an entire day had passed. Then again the camera was focused on his profile, front lit by the dashboard lights.

Ava's voice, soft and curious, asked, "What makes a champion? Besides winning the big belt buckle?"

Chase's stomach clenched as he waited for his onscreen response. "Winning is the *only* gauge of a champion. Lots of guys want it, they try for it, fight for it, spend years chasing it. If the title was applied to all the great men competing in the sport of bull ridin', just because they're great men? Then the title would be meaningless. A champion is called a champion because he's won. He's proven to be the best."

The next image was Chase receiving his championship buckle and oversized cardboard check at the Man of Steel competition last year. The announcer's words were lost in the thunderous crowd response. The noise and image faded to the next scene, the low fanfare of the Scottsbluff Rodeo win. Two officials shaking his hand. The camera panned the nearly empty stands and then zoomed to the cowboys who didn't win, as they packed up their gear behind the chutes.

A crash sounded onscreen. Although the screen remained blank, he heard his voice. "I'm nekkid here, Hollywood."

"I see that. What do you want me to do about it?" she purred.

The dark screen morphed into a background of a cheap motel room. He watched Ava, fully clothed, crawling across the bed toward him. He tucked a wayward strand of hair behind her ear. His playfulness had vanished. His face was filled with such love, with such wonder, with such longing as he looked at Ava onscreen, that Chase's stomach clenched watching it.

"Chase?"

"To be honest, I'm too beat to shit even for a blowjob." Pain creased his brow. "My head is killin' me."

"Do you want some aspirin?"

"Took it already. Didn't help. Which makes me wonder why am I even doin' this? Putting my body through hell every fuckin' night?"

"You just had a bad buck-off."

He snorted. "Like that's news. The thing that really sucks is none of this matters. The injuries I get on the road trying to prove myself. The PBR will probably flip me the bird and not let me back on tour anyway."

"So quit."

Horror distorted his face. "And do what? Bull ridin' is the only thing I want to do. It's the only thing I can do. It's my life. Who am I without it? Nobody, that's who."

Ava sat back on her haunches. "You're so much more than just a bull rider—"

"No, I'm not," he snapped. Sighing, he let his head fall back against the headboard. "I need them to call me back. And the longer I have to wait, the less likely that phone call becomes."

Chase watched himself onscreen. Christ. Was he...crying with his eyes squeezed shut like that? Fucking awesome. He looked like a whiny-ass baby loser who complained about everything and couldn't even take his girlfriend up on giving him a blowjob.

She moved out of camera range.

His eyes snapped open and his gaze tracked Ava's movements across the room. "Where are you goin'?"

"I need some air."

He reached a hand out to her. "Don't go. I can't..." His voice broke. "I'm sorry I'm an asshole tonight. I feel like shit."

Chase's cheeks burned. She'd fucking taped this? He opened up to her and this was what she did? He thought back to that night. He'd knocked his noggin pretty damn hard when he'd hit the ground. No wonder he hadn't remembered much of the conversation.

Evidently he hadn't realized she'd set up a goddamn camera in their room either.

He hit the pause button, his head spinning, his gut churning, his thoughts focused on one awful thing.

Betrayal.

Yes, he knew she'd been taping all the fucking time, but he had no idea she'd been making a goddamned movie. The whole time they were together. To think he'd invited her to share his experiences on the road. He froze. Wait a second. He hadn't invited her. She'd invited *herself.* Offering a convincing argument about wanting to see real life outside her poor, privileged upbringing.

But Chase sure as hell hadn't encouraged her to creep around, sticking that camera in everyone's face. Capturing their private moments. Having no shame in using them for her own gain. For a woman who claimed to hate the intrusion of paparazzi, she'd become damn good at acting like one of them. She'd promised him she wouldn't show her home movies to anyone.

A new thought chilled his blood. Did Ava have footage of Ryan's last ride? Of his lifeless body leaving the rodeo grounds?

He'd trusted her. After keeping women around for recreational uses only, Chase had opened up to her. Told her things he'd never shared with anyone. He'd fallen in love with her.

Jesus. He was a fucking idiot. She was an actress. She'd probably been acting the entire time.

His bag was packed and on the bed in less than five minutes. Would he leave without explanation? Or stick around to hear hers? As he debated, the hotel door opened. Her voice carried to him.

"Sometimes I cannot believe New Yorkers' rudeness. All I asked for was plain honey for a bagel, instead of that nasty cinnamon honey spread. You'd think I'd asked the girl at the counter to track down a hive and gather a honeycomb herself."

The food bags hit the table. "Anyway. Here's breakfast. Eat at your own risk. I'm half-afraid she spit in the coffee."

When he didn't move from where he leaned against the doorjamb, she prompted, "Chase? You all right?"

"No. I'm trying really goddamned hard not to throw your computer on the floor and stomp it into pieces. But I'm sure a smart cookie like you backed up all the important files, didn't you? So it'd be pointless and I'd probably hurt myself."

"What are you talking about?"

Chase whirled around. "Why didn't you tell me about the movie you've been making since we met?"

Her face, usually so animated, went completely blank. "What were you doing on my computer?"

"Checking my email. Imagine my shock when I accidentally clicked on your account and an email from Jackie Ackerman showed up."

"You had no right."

He was looming above her almost before she could blink. "No, *you* had no right. I had no idea what you were filming would be used for a movie."

"A documentary," she corrected.

"When you offered to help me, I had no fuckin' clue you were really helping yourself, weren't you? Getting some juicy stuff, taping our private moments. Asking those annoying personal questions at every turn. Now I know why."

"You were eager for my help, if I recall. And if I'd stayed focused on Chase McKay all the time—that would've been acceptable?"

"None of this is acceptable. Using me. Using Taz. Using Ryan." Chase stared at her as if he'd never seen her. "You couldn't tell *me* what you were doin' when we've been together every damn day for almost two months? But you told Ryan's mom? How did you get Jackie on board for this exploitation? What scene did you set? Did you promise this 'documentary' will bring her money?"

Her hand cracked into his cheek.

He slowly straightened and backed away.

Ava scrambled after him. "Oh God, Chase. I'm sorry. Let me see—"

"Don't fucking touch me."

"I'm sorry. I've never hit another person in my life. I don't know what got into me."

"You were acting. Playing the part of the outraged woman. Setting the scene. It's all second nature to you."

Again her face rivaled a statue's for stillness.

"Was any of this real?" He laughed harshly. "No. Of course it wasn't. I'm the typical dumb cowboy, believing a beautiful, filthy rich, famous woman like you could fall for a man like me. I probably deserve this. Maybe especially after my womanizing ways over the years. But knocked flat and humbled on camera before millions of people seems a harsh comeuppance."

"I wasn't acting."

"Not when it came to sex. Some things can't be faked."

Ava wrapped her arms around herself and looked away.

Then Chase knew. She couldn't fake her body's reaction to him, but she could set the scene to force his hand. "That first time... Now that I think about it, the loser bar rat in our room. He was a total plant, wasn't he? A guy supposed to drive me into a jealous rage. Force me into taking you to bed before another man beat me to it."

She didn't deny anything.

"I'll take the lapse in judgment. I'll take my licks for bein' played for a fool by you. But I will take them in private."

"What do you mean?"

"After bein' in the PBR for years, I know enough about release forms to remember that I didn't sign *anything* that allows you to use any images of me. No pictures, no sound bites, no videos, no quotes, nothin'. You go ahead and make your documentary, Ava, but leave me out of it. There better not be a single word, a single image or a single reference to me anywhere. And if there is? I will file a lawsuit the likes of which you've never seen. You may have money, honey, but in the court of law, it's all about who has the best lawyer. And I guarantee you the one I have on retainer, from the last unauthorized use of my image incident? Lives for shit like this. He'll make your previous skirmish with the press look like a fuckin' picnic."

"You're wrong, Chase."

"Not about this I'm not."

"No. You're wrong about me. And if you'd stop acting like the wounded male and let me explain, instead of jumping to the worst possible conclusion—"

"Too late," he snapped.

"Will you shut up and listen?" Ava drew herself to her full height and looked down on him. But her eyes strayed to the red mark burning on his cheek. Her face held that delicate thread of a woman about to crumble. "I didn't pull a fast one on you. From the first day I left Denver and stopped periodically to dink around with my cameras, I had no idea what to do with the footage I'd shot. I'd vaguely considered using the scenery as inspiration for a screenplay, which I freely told you the first day we spent together. When I started taping your rides? That changed everything for me. Not because I wanted to exploit you, but everything about your life as a bull rider fascinated me. Scared me. I'd never met anyone like you. That's not me bullshitting you. That's not me acting, for Christsake." She poked him in the chest hard with her perfectly manicured fingernail. "And *fuck you* for thinking what happened between us, either between the sheets or on the road, was acting on my part. It was real. As real as it gets. At least I can admit it. At least I'm not freaking out and backtracking like you are, because you're scared shitless you admitted I'm more than another fuck-and-run encounter."

Damn woman saw too much. "Get to the fuckin' point, Ava."

"After seeing the events at that first rodeo, I thought maybe I was on to something. Especially after meeting Ryan and Taz. The three of you were in different places in your riding careers. The new footage became more focused. I asked questions that would support the images I'd gotten. But my ideas were still being processed. I didn't tell you what I was working on, not because I was creating some big, goddamn, rip-your-life-to-shreds secret video. I couldn't tell you because I didn't know what the hell I was doing." She retreated to gaze out the window. "That changed when Ryan died. I knew some of what I had could be molded into a documentary. A look at Ryan's life and the tragedy of his death. But I'd never do something like that without his mother's consent. Taz approached me at Ryan's funeral about compiling some of Ryan's rides for Jackie. He must've told her about it, because *she* contacted me. So that's where I am. Trying to help a brokenhearted mother put the pieces together."

Her voice caught and Chase fought the urge to go to her.

"So maybe I don't know you as well as I thought I did either. I can't believe after what I've been through you'd consider, for even one nanosecond, I would willingly, gleefully put another human being though that bullshit."

Now Chase was really confused.

His cell buzzed and he plucked it out of his pocket. He put a fake note of cheer in his voice. "Elroy. I hope you're calling me with good news?"

"Yes. You're officially back on the PBR roster and scheduled to compete in Wichita next weekend."

"No kiddin'? That's great." He allowed a tight laugh. "I was getting worried. No word from the powers that be. And then, I've, ah, been in the press the last few days a little more than you'd like, I'm sure."

"To be honest, the coverage of you and Miz Cooper weighed in your favor for a change."

Talk about a shocker. "It did? Why?"

"Because you're finally with a woman who's newsworthy in her own right, and not by virtue of her association with you."

"Did that make sense in your head before you said it? 'Cause that didn't make a lick of sense on my end."

Elroy laughed. "You two are a match made in PR heaven. Even though some tabloid rags are claiming your whole relationship is a publicity stunt." Elroy paused. "Is it?"

"No. And here's fair warning: that is not a topic of discussion. With you. Or anyone else."

"Never thought I'd be happy to hear you say 'no comment' and mean it. Warms the cockles of my cold PR heart, McKay."

"You're a riot. What else?"

"The PBR is picking up your transportation expenses. You're in New York now?"

"Yeah."

"I can't get you to Wichita directly—"

"Book me into Omaha. I left my truck there. I'll drive to Wichita."

"Done. What day you wanna leave?"

"Today. As soon as possible."

Ava stared at him with shock.

"The event isn't for another couple days."

"I'm aware of that. But there are other things I need to take care of first."

Elroy sighed. "Fine. Contact me when you get to Kansas. And I don't gotta remind you no press unless you're escorted by a PBR media liaison."

"I get it. I'll keep in touch."

"Good." Elroy hung up.

Chase returned to the bedroom and picked up his bag.

"You're leaving? Just like that?"

"Yep."

"No discussion. No yelling, no hashing it out?"

"What is there to hash out? You knew I'd be gone the second the PBR called me back. Getting my bull ridin' mojo back was the *only* reason we were even traveling together." Chase held out his bag. "*This* is my life, Ava. Not this." He gestured to the fancy digs surrounding them.

"You told me there were more important things in life than being a bull rider."

Chase looked her in the eye and said, "I lied."

Although it pained him, he shouldered his equipment bag and walked out.

Chapter Twenty-Eight

Ava had been mindlessly staring out the window, crying and wallowing in self-recrimination, when her phone buzzed. Hoping it'd be Chase, she answered without checking the caller ID. "Hello."

"Ava Cooper?"

"Yes. Who is this?"

"I'm calling on behalf of Nina Beal, senior VP of Montieth Associates. Nina is requesting an in-person meeting with you regarding a possible audition for a new sitcom slated to start production next week."

Why were they calling her directly? "This request was approved through my agency?"

"Marnie Driscoll was contacted and gave us this number."

This was Marnie's way of giving Ava full responsibility for declining the audition. "What is the in-place date for the meeting?"

"Thursday. One o'clock. At the Burbank office."

Looked like she'd be home sooner than she'd planned. "That will work."

"Good. We look forward to seeing you then, Miss Cooper."

A casting call. For a new sitcom. She could throw herself into familiar work for the next year and put this summer behind her. Chase had been right about one thing, they both needed to get back to their real lives. And for her, that mean a major overhaul of the way she'd been living. She intended to make changes across the board and start with a clean slate. In both her professional and personal life.

She blew her nose and hoped she didn't sound as if she'd spent the last two hours bawling when she dialed her parent's home number.

"And to what do I owe the pleasure of a phone call from my beautiful daughter?"

"Heya, Dad. I just wanted to talk. I know it seems like the only time I call you is when I want something."

"Do you want something?"

"No. Well, maybe. I want to ask you a question."

"Shoot."

"Does it bug you that I don't take an interest in Dumond Racing? That every time you've asked me in the past decade to come to a race or hang out at an event I've said no?"

Silence. Then, "I know you're busy."

"That's not an answer. Be honest."

"Okay, as long as you asked, yeah, it does bug the crap out of me. It's almost like you're embarrassed that your dad is a former grease monkey."

"I'm not embarrassed. God, I'm embarrassed for myself for being so oblivious to anyone's feelings but my own. You raised me better than that."

"No kidding." He paused again. "Ava, what is this really about?"

His voice was so soft and gentle, more tears fell. "I've had a lot of time to think over the past couple months. I've watched my...friend come to terms with family issues and I saw a lot of myself in him. I realized I haven't been a good daughter, or a good sister, or even a halfway decent supporter of Dumond Racing. I'm so mired in my own stupid, petty problems that I've let important things slide. Important people." She sniffled. "You are important to me Dad, and I love you. And I'm sorry for acting like such a brat. But I can change. I want to change." She took a deep breath. "Can you forgive me?"

"Of course. And I will let you make it up to me in two weeks when you attend the Dumond Racing Team trials at Breakwater Speedway. I'll warn ya. Lots of media. Oh, and your brother is in charge."

"I can handle it. I'm looking forward to it."

"Good. Although, in all fairness, I've gotta point out that you ignore your mother's business just as much as you do mine."

Ava laughed. "Well, she's next on the apology chain."

"I'm right here, sweetie, so there's no need to go through this twice."

"Am I on conference call?"

"Of course. I'm tired of hearing about your life third or fourth hand," her mother chastised.

"Yeah, so why don't you tell us firsthand how in the devil you hooked up with a bull rider?" her father prompted.

She tried to keep things light lest she start bawling again. "I take offense to your term 'hook up' Dad."

"You know what I meant. Start talking."

"I met Chase McKay in Wyoming through Ginger Paulson. I traveled with him on the rodeo circuit for a few weeks and he came to New York with me."

"Bull riding is a damn dangerous job."

You don't know the half of it.

"What's he like?" her mother asked. "Because I'm sure the pictures in the papers don't do him justice. He looks buff. Mysterious."

"Oh, for the love of God, Eileen, really? This is the direction you're taking this conversation?" he demanded.

"If your father is offended by the graphic details you want to share with your mama about that hot cowboy's attributes, we'll kick him off the line."

Her dad snorted. "As glad as I am you called, Daughter, this is where I hang up." *Click.*

Her mother snickered. "Too easy. Now. Spill your guts because this Chase guy. He's the one, isn't he? That's the reason you're keeping him to yourself."

Just like that, Ava broke down. She wished she could crawl through the phone line onto her mother's lap. "I never thought I'd find someone like him. He's the best friend I've ever had and he drives me crazy. He's bossy and so sweet that I melt whenever he touches me even when I want to scream at him. I'm so in love with him it's scary. And funny. And pathetic. And what the hell am I gonna do?"

"Does he feel the same way?"

"He says he did, until... I don't know how to explain because it still doesn't feel wrong to me. I think he's overreacting, but he's pissed off. And he just left."

"Tell me what happened." After she finished, her mother said, "Hmm," not in a good way.

"What?" Ava blew her nose. "Am I a spoiled brat who doesn't think of anyone but myself?"

"Sometimes. But as human beings, we're all like that. I understand why he's upset. You took something very personal and intend to turn it into something public without consulting him. So he's questioning your motives, and he probably fears you've been acting with him this entire time."

Ava felt like she could throw up because Chase had said that very thing. "I wasn't. I love him. I told him I love him. And he took off anyway."

"Isn't that callback from the PBR what he'd been waiting for?"

"Yes, but—"

"This is his career, Ava. You, of all people, should understand that. If the situation were reversed? If your agent had called during the fight? What would you have done? Taken off, the same thing Chase did."

"Don't be so sure about that."

Silence. "Really? Well, that's new. Tell me about it."

Ava talked about what she'd seen and experienced over the last few weeks and how it'd changed her, not only personally but career-wise. It felt good to bounce ideas off her mom, because she defined savvy businesswoman.

"I'm proud of you, Ava. I've always been proud of you even when I didn't understand your love of show business. But I'm happy to hear you've figured out you're more than an actress and want to try other things within the industry. I'd be happier yet if you asked to come to work for me."

Ava laughed and sniffled. "No way. We'd kill each other."

"Probably. Anyway, I'm also happy that you found your other half." Her mom got quiet for a second. "My life would be hollow without your father in it. Having a successful career is great, but being in a loving relationship is even better. So back to the Chase issue..."

"What should I do?"

"Give him time. Don't call him, don't text him, don't IM him, don't email him."

"Mom. I don't think playing games will work."

"Oh, this isn't a game. This is a way to show him what a big hole his life will have without you in it. You've been joined at the hip for almost two months. Let him miss you, sweetie. Let yourself know what it's like to really miss him."

"Okay. Thanks."

"And if that doesn't work? Go with plan B."

Her mother, businesswoman extraordinaire, always had a backup plan. "And what is that?"

"Track him down, tie him up and force him to listen to reason. It helps if you're naked. And holding beer."

"Ah, Mom. I don't think that will work."

"It sure did with your dad. Good luck, sweetie, keep in touch."

Ava packed her bag and booked a commercial flight to LA.

"Why am I so nervous?" Ava asked Hannah, two days later.

"I'll tell you what I think after the audition." Hannah straightened Ava's miniskirt for the third time.

"That's not helping my nerves." She tried not to think that Chase would know exactly what to say to her to calm her down. The door to the conference room opened and a long-legged blond strolled out. "We're ready for you, Miss Cooper."

Ava squeezed Hannah's hand and followed Corporate Casting Barbie into the conference room. Well, at least this production company didn't have the clichéd casting couch. Ava chose the chair directly in the middle, across from the desk of the three executives who were too busy on their phones to acknowledge her.

Finally another blonde met Ava's gaze and smiled coolly. "I'm Nina

Beal. It's a pleasure to meet you, Miss Cooper. I was a huge fan of *Miller's Ridge*. Pity it got cancelled."

"Thank you."

The man sporting a Groucho Marx mustache peered at her over the top of his glasses. "We've cast the two stars of this show. We're casting secondary characters. The part you're being considered for is Mamie's best friend, Sally."

"Sally is the opposite of our quirky, fun-loving, serial dating, always-finding-man-trouble main character, Mamie," the other man, who looked like Woody Allen's younger, nerdier brother, inserted.

So Sally was the stick-in-the-mud sidekick. How fun. "What ages are these characters?"

"Just out of college." The woman studied Ava openly. "She could pass as twenty-two. If we darkened her hair more."

"Definitely put a pair of eyeglasses on her."

The Groucho guy said, "What about brown contacts?"

"Excellent. I'd also suggest taping her chest to downplay the size of it."

Ava clenched her teeth, but couldn't maintain a fake smile.

They talked among themselves. Argued. Gestured to her as if she was part of the furniture.

That attitude didn't used to bother her. But it did now. As an actress, she'd seen herself as a piece of clay. Ready to adapt to the director's vision. Put the right words in her mouth and she could be anyone. Any time. Any place.

But today the clay comparison didn't work. Today she felt like a mannequin.

It became very quiet and all eyes zoomed to her. She cleared her throat. "Excuse me?"

"We're very pleased you agreed to meet with us. Given the issues you've faced the last couple months, it's understandable you're looking to lose yourself in a new role."

That comment sent up her red flags.

"Pity your agent couldn't be here or we could get the details ironed out right now because shooting starts next week."

This was all kinds of wrong. Enough. She was done.

Ava stood. "Thank you for your time and my agent will be in touch." She didn't stop walking until she was through the conference door and standing on the sidewalk.

Hannah snagged her elbow and tugged her around the corner. "Well? Did they offer?"

"Yes, but I don't want it." She looked Hannah square in the eyes. "In fact, I don't want to be an actress at all anymore. There are so many other things I'd rather do with my life."

"Ava, when did this happen?"

"It's been building for a while. Don't tell me the see-all, know-all Hannah missed it?"

Instant skepticism tightened Hannah's face. "How much of this change has to do with the cowboy?"

"Some." Ava folded her arms. "But only because he showed me parts of myself that I wasn't aware of."

"Such as?"

"I can't explain it. I feel more like...me, the real me when I'm around him. Everything was better. Freer. I've been waiting my whole life to feel that way. And I know he felt the same." His words, whispered the last night they were together, when he thought she was asleep, haunted her. *I love you, Ava Rose. Goddamn, what am I gonna do about you?*

"Are you ready to tell me what happened in New York?"

"Chase borrowed my computer and saw the mock-up film I'd started with the footage I'd shot at the rodeos of him and Ryan."

"Is it over between you two?"

"I hope not. There's too much...there. Know what I mean?"

Hannah shook her head.

But the *too much* portion of her comment sent Ava's thoughts spinning. "That's it. I have enough footage to make two documentaries. So I could make one without Chase's image, or approval, not that I want to do that. But if I had something to show him, I could convince him this is a worthwhile documentary."

"And if he still says no?"

Ava looked Hannah in the eye. "Then I go to plan B."

Chapter Twenty-Nine

Meanwhile...outside Sundance...

Gavin Daniels turned down the air conditioning in the rental car. The outside temperature, according to the Lexus XLV, hovered around one hundred degrees. Hot for anyone, except a Phoenix native used to seeing the mercury hit one hundred fifteen degrees regularly in the summer months. He appreciated the heat in Wyoming owed nothing to humidity. Hot and dry he could handle. Hot and wet made him want to peel his soggy skin from his bones.

This trip had been a long time coming. If he was the morose type, he might say all his life. His mother—God rest her soul—had encouraged him to take the journey. As much as he loathed the idea of deathbed promises, that's exactly what he'd done in the days before she'd slipped away forever.

The aftermath of her death was a blur. Grief claimed his attention for several months. After that, he'd dealt with the consequences of neglecting his business while he grieved. Then he'd been waylaid by his daughter's rubber ball tendency—bouncing to whichever parent offered respite from the other parent. Add in his ex-wife's histrionics...that was just another reminder of why Ellen was his ex. Didn't take more than a simple glance at the calendar to know the last eighteen months had been the shittiest time of his life.

When the dust settled, he was faced with the one-year anniversary of his mother's passing. With that shock came the guilt he hadn't accomplished the one final thing she'd requested.

Gavin booked a flight into Rapid City. He'd secured a couple nights at a bed and breakfast between Sundance and Moorcroft. Which was quite a feat, according to the information he'd gathered online, because it was the height of tourist season in the Black Hills around Devil's Tower, a stopping point on the road to Yellowstone. He'd lost track of the number of motor homes and out-of-state license plates he'd passed on I-90.

The female voice on the GPS announced, "Turn left in point one mile. You have reached your destination."

No going back now. Unless once he saw the turnoff he just kept driving right on past it. As the mailbox entered his line of sight, he realized he was unprepared for any outcome in this situation, be it total exuberance, flat-out denial or complete apathy.

That's when Gavin admitted to nerves, to trepidation, to betrayal, to an underlying sense of...wrongness. Add in paranoia and he might as well be thinking about the hours leading up to his disastrous marriage. That made him smile briefly, but he sobered when he recognized the sad truth that hope hadn't surfaced in his emotional turmoil.

When he pulled up to the well-kept ranch house, a couple sat on a porch swing in the shade. Enjoying a normal afternoon. Blissfully unaware.

His heart pounded. Sweat broke out on his brow, yet a clammy feeling slithered down his spine.

The couple stood and started down the steps. Probably wondering what business he had in the middle of nowhere. Probably thinking he was lost.

Gavin ditched his sunglasses and opened the car door. He jammed his hands in the front pockets of his khaki pants, because he didn't know what else to do with them.

The man and woman were equally wary, stopping five feet from him. Waiting.

For what?

For him to be the first one to speak? To explain?

Near as he could tell, they were the ones who had a helluva lot of explaining to do.

He turned his focus to the man. Probably in his early sixties. He wasn't tall; he wasn't short, just average height. Solidly built, not fat, not skinny, not muscular, not wiry, but his carriage and clothing screamed physical laborer. He had a full head of black hair randomly streaked with silver. When Gavin met the man's eyes, blue eyes identical to the ones staring back at him in the mirror every day, he quickly looked away. Which allowed him to direct his attention to the woman.

Again, she was average height. A little on the plump side. Her hair was short, curly as if she'd recently had a perm, a rich dark brown as if she'd recently colored it. She wore her age more obviously than the man did, crinkly frown lines by her mouth, on her forehead and beside her eyes, as if she'd spent her life worrying. Despite Gavin's initial judgment of dowdiness, she wore trendy eyeglasses and dressed in a style he'd call country chic. She appeared the type who'd give out hugs, cookies and advice. She didn't look like the type of woman who'd give away her child.

The man put his arm around the woman's shoulder. "Something I can help you with?"

"Yes. Are you Charles McKay and Violet Bennett McKay?"

They exchanged a look. "Yes, we are. Who wants to know?"

"Me."

"And who are you?"

Gavin took a deep breath. "I believe I'm your son."

Chapter Thirty

The crowd roared behind him, ready to party at the PBR on a Saturday night.

Chase braced himself. The PBR's newest female reporter, a fiery redhead named Lissa, stuck the microphone in his face as soon as he cleared the contestant gate. He'd been expecting it since he'd avoided an on camera interview last night. To ensure his cooperation, the cameraman blocked him in. Bastard.

"We're here with Chase McKay after that amazing ninety-one point ride on Devil's Due. Congratulations, Chase, that's gotta feel good to be back on top."

He focused on the woman and not the camera. "It does. Especially after an extended break and such a poor showing in Dallas."

"Tell us about the ride."

"Well, Devil's Due is an ornery little cuss and highly unpredictable, so I wasn't sure if he'd go into spin mode tonight or hopscotch around. Luckily I was able to stay with him no matter what he did."

"So the past few weeks you've been off the tour to deal with a recurrence of your shoulder injury from last year. Are you still having issues?"

"Not at all. The time off allowed me to find my focus again."

"And how did you accomplish that?"

"I went back to basics. Tried to fix what wasn't working with my ridin'. I was fortunate to have two former PRCA bull riders helpin' me get back on track."

"It appears to've worked, since you're seated first."

"Thanks. The thing I learned, or maybe relearned, is to focus on the bull I'm on and not worry about the next bull or the money or the points or where I might land on the leader board."

"Good advice that's obviously paid off. Two questions. You've come back to the PBR tour more confident and more aggressive. And it's interesting to see you've swapped out your usual black cowboy hat for a safety helmet. Why?"

"This is a dangerous sport, and any time a rider has a chance to protect himself with additional safety equipment, I'm all for it. I've had a couple of close calls in recent years. I've witnessed horrible accidents with other riders that would've been preventable had the rider worried less about appearances and more about safety."

"Spoken like a new convert." Lissa flashed a dazzling smile—a sign she was about to go in for the kill. "Last question, and I'm sure your fans are dying to get the scoop, straight from the source. You've recently been spotted with actress Ava Cooper. Is love in the air?"

"Like my brother Ben has been reminding me, a gentleman doesn't kiss and tell."

She laughed provocatively. "Can you at least say whether there's a chance we'll be seeing Miss Cooper cheering you on in the stands at future PBR events?"

Not a snowball's chance in hell because I'm a freakin' idiot wasn't an approved PR response, so he managed a curt, "You never know who'll show up."

Lissa ended the interview. He scaled the risers to watch the remaining action; aware the cameras would keep cutting to him because he was sitting in first place with only seven riders to go.

He bullshitted with the guys while he waited to help his buddy, Dirk, pull his rope. Other riders seemed surprised he stuck around. Used to be, Chase didn't make much time for riders outside his circle of four or five since he'd been so focused on finding a buckle bunny to hook up with after the event.

Getting to know Ryan, even for a brief amount of time, had changed Chase for the better in so many ways.

Dirk was up next. Chase held the bull rope taut while Dirk rosined his glove. Soon as Dirk had his wrap, Chase and another rider named Reese kept Dirk upright on the bull by holding his vest. Dirk yelled, "Go!" and the gate opened.

Everything went wrong from the moment the bull exited the chute. His massive rear end smacked into the barricade, immediately sending Dirk sideways. Dirk started to right himself on the next rapid fire jump, but the bull's head reared up the same time Dirk's body bounced forward. The side of Dirk's face connected with the bull's skull, knocking Dirk out completely. But his hand was hung up in the rope.

Chase stared in horror as Dirk's unmoving body dangled and was jerked about, his bloody face continually smacked into the bull's side. Twice Dirk narrowly missed the horn piercing his face.

Seemed like an eternity before the bullfighters freed Dirk's hand and got him out of harm's way. But Dirk wasn't moving and the sports medicine team was hustling out.

Just like Ryan.

No, goddammit, this was not happening again. For some reason, Chase glanced up and saw the images of Dirk's bloody, battered face splashed across the big screens.

"Fucking vultures."

Before Chase thought it through, he jumped down from the chute and raced across the arena. The bullfighters didn't try and stop him as he put himself between Dirk and the camera, with a snarled, "Back. Off."

"I'm just doing my job, man. Move."

"No."

"Move."

"Make me."

The cameraman dodged and weaved. So did Chase.

Chase crowded him, so the only thing the camera picked up was an extreme close up of Chase's vest. Which forced the cameraman to shuffle back, which is exactly what Chase wanted.

"Let me do my job."

"Film something else because you're not getting close to him. I'll bust that camera into a dozen pieces and throw it and you in the dirt."

"I'll see that you're suspended for this."

"And I'll see you're fined for exploiting the images of a head trauma. But you wouldn't have as many of these images to splash across the big screen if the PBR stepped up and mandated all riders wear safety helmets."

The cameraman stopped trying to circumvent Chase and kept the camera trained on him.

"Does a PBR bull rider have to die from head injures on camera in full gory detail before changes are enforced? Haven't we learned after what happened to Lane Frost? Only after the shock of his death were protective vests made mandatory for bull riders. It makes me sick to think that another bull rider will have to die before we start protecting their heads as well as their hearts."

"Dirk is a friend of yours?"

"This is not just about Dirk. It's about all bull riders in all professional rodeo organizations. A few weeks back the world lost a promising young man, a friend of mine, because he wasn't wearing a helmet. And now he's..." Chase looked away, fighting the hitch in his voice and squeezing back angry tears. "He's dead. Would a helmet have made a difference? Without a doubt. But no one made him wear it, so he didn't. But he sure as hell had the vest on. Didn't do a damn thing to save his head."

The stretcher was airborne and the sports medicine team hustled out to scattered applause. Chase jogged after them, ignoring the cameraman's shouts.

Once they reached the bowels of the arena where no cameras were allowed, Chase swallowed the lump of fear. "How bad?"

"Concussion. Broken nose. Possibly a shattered cheekbone. They'll know more after he's admitted and tests are run."

A garage door rolled up and an ambulance backed in. Chase forced his feet to move as he headed for his truck. The last thing he wanted was to deal with the other riders and the PBR officials about his impromptu speech. Chances were good it'd been cut out of the TV broadcast. But plenty of people had seen it live. And it wouldn't be the first time his actions ended up on YouTube courtesy of personal video devices.

That made him think of Ava. Everything made him think of her. Christ, he missed that woman. He hated how it ended. So abruptly. With such anger. With such a feeling of betrayal. Although she'd tried to explain, he'd been too irate to listen to her excuses.

Hours later, Chase left the hospital and climbed in his truck. With all that'd gone on, he hadn't checked his phone since before the event. No messages or calls from Ava. Two from Elroy. Four from Ben. That quickened his pulse. Ben never left a message and he'd left...four? Since seven o'clock tonight?

Midnight in Wyoming. He dialed anyway.

Ben answered on the second ring. "Hey, little bro. Thanks for calling me back."

"I know it's late—"

"I figured it would be, with your buddy Dirk getting stomped and your tirade on TV."

"Shit. They didn't cut to commercial?"

"Nope. But I'm not calling you to rib you about that. Something has come up and you need to come home right away."

His heart dropped to his toes. "What happened? Is it Dad? Or Mom?"

Ben sighed. "Both. They asked me to call since you don't always get back to them after they've left a message.

Guilt kicked him in the ass.

"They wanna to talk to us. And they've refused to discuss what it is until we're all in the same room."

"That's goddamn cryptic. What could be so important they can't tell us over the phone?"

"Whatever it is, it came up awful damn quick. No warning, no nothin'."

"So you and Quinn haven't been mulling it over a few days and just decided to contact me?" Not that Chase would blame them for holding back because they knew he preferred no contact until a PBR event ended.

"Nope. Look, we all watched you tonight. Heckuva ride. You

deserve to be in first place and have a good shot of winning the whole event." Ben paused. "I'm sure Mom and Dad will understand if you can't make it."

What Ben was too kind to say? *Mom and Dad will understand because they're used to you disappointing them.*

After hearing the worry in Dirk's brother's voice and his promise to get to Wichita as soon as possible, Chase felt the full weight of his choice to keep his family at arm's length these last few years. If the situation was reversed, and Dirk was making the call to his family, who in his family would hop in the car and drive all night?

Quinn? Yes.

Ben? Yes.

His folks? Absolutely.

And probably any other McKay relation he called.

They were just that way. They might fight like cats and dogs, but when it came down to it, family was everything. And he would do everything to reclaim his place in his family.

"Chase?"

"I'm here. Just figuring the logistics. If I leave now, I can be there by noon tomorrow. Is that early enough?"

"You're really not gonna compete in the final round and you're coming home?" Ben said with total shock.

"Hard to believe, but yeah. I've realized there are more important things than those eight seconds I spend on the back of a bull. I ain't gonna be the one who lets Mom and Dad down."

Ben was very quiet.

"What?"

"You have changed. I'm looking forward to seein' you. Drive safe."

Immediately after Chase hung up he called Elroy.

"You'd better not be calling me to bail you outta jail, McKay," Elroy barked.

"Good morning to you too, sunshine. I'll keep this brief. I have a family emergency in Wyoming and I'm taking off right now."

"Wait. Hold on. You're leaving Wichita? Chase. Did it escape your notice that you're in first place?"

"No, it didn't, trust me. But it can't be helped."

Elroy sighed. "You're looking at your first event win in over a year. On your first tour stop after the suspension. How can you walk away from that?"

"My family needs me."

"That puts us in a helluva bind, especially after the stuff you spewed on live camera tonight."

"Not my problem. I said my piece, I meant what I said and I won't issue a retraction. If the PBR wants to add a disclaimer that I spoke on my own behalf, and not on behalf of the organization, that's fine."

"You sure you're not making a calculated move? Leaving abruptly to build the buzz? And adding to the speculation you're involved with Ava Cooper since she wasn't at the event with you?"

Chase counted to twenty before he spoke. "That bullshit PR spin stuff is suited for your devious mind, Elroy, not mine. I'd rather get on a bull tomorrow afternoon, win the event and pick up a big, fat check than spend twelve hours in my truck driving home to deal with family issues. As far as Ava, she's not a topic of discussion. Ever."

Elroy laughed. "The one time you've actually got a decent hook-up that could be worth great press for months to come, you're telling me...no?"

"I'm telling you *fuck no.*" Chase hung up. He stopped at the first convenience store and loaded up on Rockstar Energy drinks and sunflower seeds. When he saw the bag of red licorice he automatically threw it in the pile, like he always did, only realizing when he reached the truck his licorice-eating copilot wasn't there.

It'd be a long goddamn drive without her.

No, it'll be a long goddamn life without her.

Chapter Thirty-One

Chase pulled into Ben's driveway at eleven a.m. Ace and Deuce greeted him with wagging tails, bumping into his knees expecting to be petted.

Ben opened the door and the dogs beat him inside. "Coffee's on."

"Good." He adjusted his duffel. "Lemme shower and I might feel almost human."

He was down to one clean pair of jeans and one clean shirt. Maybe Ben would let him throw in a couple loads of laundry. The last time he'd washed clothes was with Ava.

During the drive he'd rehearsed everything he wanted to say to her. And he'd say it to her face. In California, depending on what shook loose from this family meeting.

Ben sat at the enormous bar, staring into a mug of coffee. Chase poured himself a cup and joined his brother.

"So you honestly have no idea what's goin' on?"

"No. But I'm thinkin'...wouldn't it suck if Dad found out he has cancer right after he retired?"

"Yeah. My thoughts ran along those same lines."

They drank their coffee in silence.

"So you and Ava Cooper, huh?"

"Seems impossible, don't it?"

"Not really. I knew you were done for when you listed all the great things about her and then swore you weren't gonna drag her to bed the first chance you got."

Chase looked up. "Not banging her is an indicator of...?"

"Come on, brother, say the word. *Love*. You're in love with her."

"No lie."

"Does she know?"

"I told her. But that was before I freaked out and said some stupid shit. Then she said stupid shit back and I left to rejoin the PBR."

"How long ago was this?"

"What day's today?"

"Sunday."

"It all went to hell on Tuesday. Damn. Seems longer than that."

"Time to cool off is rarely a bad thing."

When Ben retreated, Chase looked around. That's when he noticed two items on the far edge of the bar. A short-handled whip and a collar with a chain attached. What the fuck did Ben use those for? Did he even want to know?

Hell yes he wanted to know.

So when Ben returned, Chase said, "What's up with the whip and collar?"

"What?"

Chase pointed. "Over there. Did you forget to put away your bondage toys when you finished with them?"

Ben went very still.

"Come on, Ben. I was joking."

He relaxed. "I know. Guess it's a good thing I didn't leave out the leather restraint straps and the caning set. That really would've made you look at me funny."

Chase stared at him because it didn't seem Ben was joking. And how could he rattle off that type of S&M stuff anyway?

The dogs barked and Quinn stepped inside. "Hey. You guys ready?"

"Ready as we'll be, considering we're goin' in blind."

The drive to their parents' house was filled with nervous chatter. They pulled up behind a Lexus with South Dakota plates.

"I thought this was supposed to be a family only meeting?" Chase said.

"It is. Let's go."

Quinn led the way into the ranch house they'd grown up in. Their parents sat side by side at the dining room table, across from a guy who seemed familiar, but also ill at ease.

"Hello, boys," their mother said. "Have a seat. Would you like coffee?" When she began to get up, Dad curled his hand over hers. "It's okay, Vi. They know where the coffeepot is."

Quinn offered the man his hand first. "Quinn McKay."

The man stood. "Gavin Daniels." He shook hands as Ben and Chase introduced themselves.

Dad cleared his throat. "I—we—appreciate you comin'. Didn't mean to be so cryptic, but this ain't something that can be said over the phone."

"Just be straight with us. Is he your doctor or something?" Ben asked. "He came here to help you break the bad news about whatever is wrong with one of you?"

"No. There's nothin' wrong with either of us. We're both in better health than we've been in a long while. This is about him."

Chase noticed his parents still held hands.

"This is gonna come as a shock, so I'll just say it straight out. Gavin is our son. Your brother. Not half brother, but full-blooded brother."

No one moved. No one seemed to breathe in the crushing silence.

"Forget the goddamn coffee. Break out the whiskey," Ben said.

Almost as if their father had expected it, he pulled out a bottle of Jameson and six shot glasses. And holy fuck, he poured Mom a shot of Irish too. Then he kissed her cheek. "Vi, darlin', go ahead. It's more your story to tell than mine."

"You mean my secret to tell." His mother, his sweet, practical, sometimes judgmental mother, tossed back the whiskey without batting an eyelash. "I won't drag out the details. You boys never knew my father, God rest his soul, and I'm grateful. For being a man of God, Elmore Bennett wasn't a nice man. He ruled his home with the Bible in one hand and a hickory switch in the other.

"I fell in love with your father when I was fifteen years old. I had to see him on the sly because my father believed the McKays were no good. Long story short, I got knocked up at age sixteen. I was scared to death to tell my mother. But I did, and she immediately went to my father. He flew into a rage, called me every horrible name because a preacher's daughter wasn't supposed to get pregnant, especially by a McKay. He swore I'd be eternally damned if I tied myself and a child to that heathen family. To save face, his and mine, he told everyone he'd sent me to finish high school at a Christian academy in Colorado, when in truth, he shipped me off to an unwed mother's home.

"I'll admit to being a brainwashed during my time there. I never considered keeping my baby. My pregnancy was a source of shame. Baby gone, shame gone." She sent Gavin a pleading look. "Please understand times were different back then."

Gavin nodded and drained his shot.

"I had a healthy boy. Then they whisked him away to his adoptive parents. I never knew the details of where he ended up. My folks never spoke of it and I didn't tell a soul."

"Not even Dad?" Quinn asked.

She shook her head. "When I came back to Wyoming, four years later, it was if Charlie and I hadn't been apart. We still loved each other and we married right away. How could I tell him we had a three-year-old son? I'd made the choice to give the baby a better life; there was no going back. No tracking the boy down and taking him from his adoptive parents. I could never do that..." Her voice caught.

Dad leaned over and murmured to her. It took a minute or so for her to regain control.

Chase picked up his shot and his stomach protested when the whiskey hit.

"After a few years, we started having you boys and... Well, my life was busy. Good. Happy. But I never forgot about that sweet baby boy I held in my arms for one short hour. Not a single day went by that I didn't wonder about him. Pray his life was good. Pray he was loved."

Gavin's eyes were on the shot glass he rolled between his fingers.

"So I was shocked when your Aunt Kimi confronted me after your grandpa Jed died. She said one night Jed was loopy on pain meds and he told her that my father told him that I was pregnant. My father bragged to Jed I'd rather give the baby up than have it raised in a godless home as a McKay. Which was a total lie, but Jed must've believed it. After Kimi told me that, I finally understood why Jed never liked me and why he refused to live with us."

"Aunt Kimi never told Uncle Cal?" Chase asked.

"No. But she told your Aunt Carolyn."

Gavin said nothing.

"When did you tell Dad?" Ben asked gently.

"Right after Quinn and Libby got back together." She looked at Quinn. "The day you told me to butt out of your relationship and said my meddling wasn't appreciated and wouldn't be tolerated, I realized I'd been acting just like my mother. It shamed me, the things I'd said, some of the things I'd done, including keeping such a big secret from Charlie."

"Vi. Honey. Take a break. This ain't good for your blood pressure."

She shook her head. "I have to see this through. When I told your father what I'd kept from him, I was scared to death he'd tell me to pack a bag. I expected his fury and everything in my life and my marriage to be over, and I knew I'd deserve whatever I got. But he didn't leave me. My Charlie...forgave me and..." The stalwart ranch woman Chase had seen cry maybe half a dozen times in his entire life completely broke down.

What was equally shocking? Witnessing the loving side of his father. How he automatically pulled her into his arms and soothed her. Maybe it was another sign of Chase's self-absorbedness that he'd never noticed their connection beyond their parental roles. Watching them now, he saw romance. He saw unconditional love. Given the situation, there had to be a whole lot of unconditional forgiveness between them too.

That's what Chase wanted. A lifetime with Ava to learn the ins and outs of love. To be with her every day so they could face whatever curveballs life threw at them together. And he'd do anything and everything to make that happen.

Chase leaned closer to stroke his mother's arm, the exact same time Quinn and Ben reached out to her too. That made her cry harder and blubber.

No one realized Gavin had stepped out until after she'd calmed down.

Gavin hadn't gone far. His back rested against the porch support pole. He stared across the field, hands in the front pockets of his dress pants. He spoke without looking at them. "Sorry. Got to be a little much. It's a lot to take in. I'm still not convinced coming here was the best idea."

"So that's the question, isn't it? What made you seek out your birth parents now?" Ben asked.

When Gavin faced them, Chase was struck by the familiarity of Gavin's features. Same blue eyes. His build was much like their father's. His square chin, like Quinn's. His mouth and nose were the same shape as Ben's. Gavin's hair was dark brown like their mother's, not black like the majority of the McKays.

"I was an only child, and my mother made me promise I'd track down my birth parents after she died." Gavin briefly glanced down at his loafers. "She wanted me to connect with my family." His gaze moved from Quinn, to Ben, to Chase. "I hired a private detective to deal with the adoption records and tracing the whereabouts of the man and woman who gave me up. Didn't take him long to track them since they were in the same place. Never in a million years did I imagine I'd find out my biological parents got married and had three other sons together."

Quinn asked, "How old are you?"

"I just turned forty-one." Gavin crossed his arms over his chest. "I live in Scottsdale, Arizona. I'm divorced and have joint custody of my fourteen-year-old daughter, Sierra. My father was a real estate developer and I went to work for him after I graduated from ASU with a business degree. He had a massive heart attack a year after my daughter was born and I inherited the company. My mother passed away a year ago."

"I hate to be Mr. Obvious, but what happens now?" Chase asked.

"I don't know. No offense, but this has fucked with my head in so many ways." Gavin expelled a quick puff of air. "Don't get me wrong, your parents seem like nice people."

"But?" Ben prompted.

"But that's just it. I see the genetic similarities to them and to you guys, but I don't know what I'm supposed to feel when I see it."

How did any of them respond to that?

Ben, the peacemaker, changed the subject. When they'd exhausted conversation about weather differences and job descriptions, Chase wished they'd brought the bottle of whiskey outside with them.

"Look, Gavin, you wanna come over to my place and have a beer with us?" Ben asked.

Gavin seemed to struggle with his answer, but shook his head. "Thanks for the invite, but I really need to get back to my room and finish some work I brought along."

"Understood. We'll see you tomorrow?"

"Most likely."

Gavin wandered to his car and drove off.

"I don't know about you guys, but I need a fuckin' drink," Ben said.

Chase returned inside to tell their parents they were leaving. But they weren't in the dining room and their bedroom door was shut, so he left them alone.

As soon as they'd bellied up to the bar at Ben's house, Chase said, "A brother."

Quinn kept sliding his coaster on the bar top. "No shit. Never saw that one comin'. Not in a million goddamn years. It's like, Christ. I don't even know Mom. I can't imagine her just handing her baby over to a stranger and goin' on with her life."

Chase knew Quinn was imagining life without his kids after he and Libby tried for so long to have a child. "Can you even fathom how Gavin feels? Finding out your birth mother gave *you* up, but went on to have three other kids with the same guy?"

"Maybe we shoulda checked to see if he had a clubfoot," Ben joked.

"What the hell does that have to do with anything?" Chase demanded.

"History books claim if firstborn sons had any kind of physical defect, the baby would be abandoned. Back then, even a clubfoot would get you a one-way ticket to the woods. The family hoped the next baby would be perfect."

"You're fuckin' morbid," Chase said. "Christ. That's not even funny. Where do you come up with this shit?"

"Try reading something other than *Hustler* some time," Ben shot back.

"Boys," Quinn warned. "Here's where I'm at. I have a hard time believing Aunt Kimi and Aunt Carolyn didn't blab to Uncle Cal and Uncle Carson about this."

"I disagree. Without sounding like a freakin' girl, women keep other women's secrets. Especially when it comes to family stuff," Ben said.

"So do you think they'll break the news to the rest of the family about the forty-one-year-old secret McKay baby?" Quinn asked.

"If it's up to Mom and Dad? Yes. Gavin? No."

Chase sighed. "Think Gavin will...hell. Sounds stupid."

"Will what? Want to be part of our family?" Ben supplied.

"Yeah."

"No."

Quinn and Chase looked at each other, then Ben. "Why not?"

"Was I the only one who noticed he doesn't seem happy? And that didn't have a damn thing to do with him coming here? He's a bunged-up corporate guy."

"I got that impression too," Quinn admitted.

"He's never had siblings. Can't miss what you don't have. He's satisfied his curiosity, done his duty to his late mother, and he'll move on."

"So you sayin' he's done with us? After one meeting?"

Ben passed out another round. "One of us, or all of us, will try and develop this meeting into something. Communication is two-way. Be interesting to see if Gavin reciprocates, or if he'll blow us off."

"That's a fuckin' sad scene you've created, Ben." Scene. Made him think of Ava, always setting the scene.

Ben shrugged. "Calling it like I see it."

Quinn asked, "You think Mom has her heart set on us all bein' a big, happy family?"

"She made her peace long ago. I think she'd like for us to get to know him and vice versa. But she won't push it."

"Dad might. If only for her." Ben lifted his bottle. "To the bright side of today. Neither Mom or Dad havin' cancer."

Bottles chinked together.

Chase raised his bottle. "This is fuckin' sappy as shit, but I just gotta say it. To us. Gavin don't know what he's missing, havin' you guys as brothers. His loss if he walks away because you guys are the best."

Neither Quinn nor Ben gave him shit for being sentimental, probably because Chase never was.

The conversation shifted, but it eventually flowed back to the shock of the day. Chase clammed up when Quinn or Ben asked questions about his future with the PBR or with Ava.

Quinn went home. Chase was surprised he'd stayed as long as he had. Maybe his brothers missed hanging out with him.

But the sleepless night, long drive, and the stress caught up with him. He couldn't keep his eyes open. He mumbled to Ben about finding his cell phone, stumbled to the guest bedroom and crashed.

Chapter Thirty-Two

"I can't believe you're watching this," Hannah said. "Why torture yourself?"

Ava gave Hannah an arch look. "Besides I know how damn good the man looks in chaps?"

"Smartass. But really, what's the point after Chase's meltdown last night?"

Her heart seized, thinking about how Chase had lost it on live TV. She'd wanted to jump through the screen and drag him off to comfort him. Assure him that not every wreck would have the same outcome as Ryan's. Assure him she'd be there for him no matter what.

"I know you can hear me, Ava, so stop ignoring—"

"Ssh... They're giving the injury report on Dirk."

The camera cut to an interview with the head of the sports medicine team. When he finished detailing the bull rider's injuries, the announcer asked his opinion on Chase McKay's comments about mandatory safety helmets. The doctor looked directly into the camera and said, "Helmets save lives. Period."

The camera returned to the main announcers. Their on-air banter circled to rider standings on tour and current matchups with bulls for the final round. When the list of the fifteen riders scrolled on screen, Chase's name wasn't listed.

"What the hell? Why isn't he riding?"

As if they'd heard her question, the camera zoomed to the younger announcer. "After being off tour for two months, Chase McKay made a comeback with a vengeance the last two nights. So it's a pity he won't be riding in the final round this afternoon."

"What!" Ava yelled at the TV.

"That is surprising, since he's seated first," the other announcer said. "Is his withdrawal due to a recurrence of his previous injury?"

"No. My understanding is he returned home for a family emergency. And we wish him, and his family, all the best."

Ava gasped. If that was true, why hadn't he called? She fast-forwarded through the entire program but there wasn't any other news.

Sick with worry, she paced. She should just call Chase. Find out. She scrolled to his name and clicked. One ring. Two rings. *Come on, cowboy, pick up.* Six rings. Then it dumped her over to voicemail.

Maybe Chase was too busy dealing with family stuff to answer. Maybe he was dodging her calls. Dammit. She needed to talk to somebody who knew something.

Ginger? No. Just in case the family emergency only affected Chase's branch of the McKays.

But Ava also knew Chase's entire family watched the PBR, and if they weren't aware there was a problem with Chase's family, they'd know now.

Maybe the PBR had kicked Chase off for his diatribe and used his family as an excuse—they'd done it before with his injury story. Because really. Would Chase McKay give up his big comeback, his chance to win an event, especially riding in first place...to deal with family issues in Wyoming?

The former bad boy Chase McKay might have blown off his family for eight seconds of glory, but the Chase McKay she knew had changed.

That was it. She had to find out. She scrolled through her contact list. God, she needed to weed out about three quarters of these names. Bingo. She had saved his number. She hit *Dial* and returned to pacing until he answered. "It's Ava."

Chase woke completely disoriented. He didn't feel like warmed-over dog crap, so he hadn't been drinking last night. He sat up and looked around. Right. He'd crashed in Ben's spare bedroom.

He squinted at the sun streaming through the window. Was it really late afternoon? He fumbled for his cell phone on the nightstand, only to remember he'd left it at his parents' house. He stumbled into the kitchen.

"Glad you could join me at the crack of five in the afternoon," Ben said slyly.

"Cut me some slack. I slept about two hours out of the forty-eight before I went comatose."

"You're in time to leave for supper at Mom and Dad's with Gavin. Guess he's leaving early in the morning."

Chase scratched his head. His hair needed a damn trim. He'd gotten so used to wearing it short, he wondered if he'd ever go back to longer hair. Especially remembering how good Ava's hands felt on his scalp.

Ava.

He needed her. He loved her. He had to make this right with her. But he couldn't do it from here.

Naturally when he found his cell phone it was completely dead.

Supper was strained. Adam and Amelia made mealtime entertaining, until they both started shrieking and Quinn and Libby took them home.

Saying goodbye to Gavin was awkward amidst half-assed promises of staying in touch, would any of them ever see him again?

Ben sighed as they sat in his pickup in front of his house. "Look, don't think I'm an asshole, but something came up and I'm gonna need you to stay somewhere else tonight."

That fucking blew. He'd looked forward to hanging with Ben. Playing pool. Picking his brain about how to handle the situation with Ava once he reached LA. "It's more a douchebag move than an asshole move, kicking me to the curb at eight o'clock on a Sunday night."

"I'd hope you'd do the same for me if a good woman was involved."

"Probably. It's for the best anyway. I'd planned on driving to Denver in the morning to catch a flight to LA, but if I leave now, I'll get an earlier one."

"You're still dragging ass, Chase. Why don't you head over to Kane's old trailer, get some rest in the peace and quiet? You know you ain't gonna get that at Quinn and Libby's place. Without bein' a dick, Mom and Dad don't need you hanging around tonight."

Kane's place. How hard would it be to stay where he'd met Ava and she wasn't there? But it wasn't like he had another choice. "Will you at least let me plug my phone in for five minutes so I can check my messages?"

"Sure."

Chase had quite a few missed calls, including one from Ava last night. No voice message. Dammit. He stopped at the call from HeadGame, a sports safety equipment manufacturer. They'd only called thirty minutes ago. Intrigued, he kept his phone plugged in as he called the number, expecting to get a recording. But a live person answered. "This is Chase McKay. I received a message from this number tonight." He listened. "Yes, sir. That sounds fine. Actually, I'd planned to be in California tomorrow. Sure. I'll call you in the next couple days after I figure out my schedule. The event in Salinas starts Friday. After blasting my opinion across VERSUS airwaves...I ain't sure they'll let me compete." Chase laughed. "No idea. I'm putting off returning phone calls to my PBR rep until tomorrow. Good enough. Thanks. Talk to you soon."

"What the devil was that about?" Ben asked.

Chase unplugged the charger. "A company that specializes in sports helmets wants to meet with me about possibly becoming a spokesman. Which would be cool, since I've been thinking about putting my...celebrity, for lack of a better term, to good use. Advocate safety in bull ridin'. Some of the older riders ain't ever gonna change. But if I can connect with the younger kids, the ones in high school, or even elementary kids who dream of ridin' bulls, about the need for proper safety equipment, maybe I can save some kids lives. Save some parents from what Jackie Ackerman is going through."

"That's ambitious. And it's great to see you—"

"Acting like a grown up?" Chase supplied with a grin.

"No, smartass. It's great to see you believe in a cause enough to actually do something about it."

"Thanks. I better scoot so your mysterious lady friend can come over under the cover of darkness."

Ben gave him a smug smile. "Don't be a stranger, bro."

He said, "I won't," and meant it.

Chase's mind raced as he drove to Kane's trailer. First he'd book his ticket online. No, first he'd call Ava. He wasn't taking any chance there'd be miscommunication.

Once he was inside the quiet trailer, he caught a whiff of flowers. But this time he didn't attribute it to cleaning supplies. This time, he recognized the scent.

Ava.

His skeptical side warned about wishful thinking, while his optimistic side urged him to hurry the hell up.

Chase threw open the bedroom door. There she was, standing on the bed. Just like before. Except this time she wasn't nekkid. This time Ava didn't look like she wanted to kick his ass.

She looked like she wanted to kiss him.

He hopped up on the bed and kissed her first. "My God, woman, tell me I'm not dreaming."

"You're not dreaming."

"As much as I'm thanking my lucky stars...why are you here?"

"When I didn't hear what constituted a family emergency that had you pulling out of an event you were winning, I called Ben last night. He told me you were here. So I hopped a plane in LA—not a word about me using the family jet—last night and drove over from Rapid City."

His wily brother hadn't been expecting a lady friend after all. "I missed you like crazy."

Ava rested her forehead to Chase's. "I missed you." She tugged him down until they sat on the bed. "What happened with your family?"

"Short version? My teenage mom had a baby out of wedlock with my dad, and I have a brother no one knew anything about. He showed up out of the blue this weekend."

"Wow. That's TV-movie-of-the-week stuff. How's your family taking it?"

"We're in shock. This Gavin guy...my brother...he's pretty tight-lipped."

"So there is a family resemblance," she teased.

Chase smiled. "Maybe." He kissed her knuckles. "Ava. I don't even know where to start to make this right between us again."

"Do you love me?"

"Yes."

"Let's start there." She inhaled deeply and let it out. "First let me say I'm so, so sorry I slapped you. There is no excuse for my behavior but it'll never happen again. I swear."

"I believe you. I'm sorry I left the way I did. I had a lot of time to think between Omaha and Wichita."

"About us?"

"That and some other stuff."

"Like what?"

"I've been thinkin' about safety issues and helmets and all that since Ryan died. And then after what happened to Dirk, I realized I wanna do more than talk about it; I wanna act on it. It's a murky idea right now, but I have an opportunity to make a difference and I'm going to take it." He kissed her just because he could, because she was here with him, where she belonged. "Enough about that. Tell me how long you were in LA, because Hollywood, I was headed there first thing in the morning."

"A couple of hours after you left, I got a casting call for a new sitcom and flew back to LA. I should come clean and let you know that my agent called me three times over the course of our road trip, after she'd lined up auditions. And every time I declined to go back to LA to audition. I didn't know what it meant at the time, besides I didn't want to leave you. But now I understand it was a sign I'm done with acting. Maybe not forever, but definitely for now."

"Are you sure?"

"No." She laughed. "But I feel freer and I'm taking a chance to change the path of my career. Which sounds stupid. I could've gotten off the path at any time."

"Events that force a change ain't always bad," he said softly.

"True. When we met? I really was just using my camera for fun. But after we'd been on the road a couple weeks, I began to see the potential of telling a story from three different sides, from the perspective of three riders at varied stages of their careers. I started cataloguing the video segments and realized I'd shot a lot of footage. I have enough to do at least two documentaries. One with you, one without. I would never exploit Ryan's death. I hope you know I'm not that heartless and willing to do anything to forge this new path."

He kissed her knuckles. "I know."

"But if you say no, Chase, I'll shitcan the whole works and find something else to work on. I'd still like to put together a memorial disk for Jackie so she can see Ryan's happiness being part of the rodeo world."

"I wouldn't ask you to not to do that. This project is important to you." He locked his eyes to hers. "Would you ask me to give up bull ridin'?"

"No. I worry every time you get on the back of a bull, even more now after I saw what happened with Ryan. But it's a part of what makes you, you. I'd never ask you to give it up."

"I've come to the same conclusion. You're talented, Ava. The little bit of your film I saw was amazing. You need to make the documentary however you see fit. If you have Jackie's blessing, and she's the one who's the most affected by all of this, then I'm on board."

Ava briefly closed her eyes and mouthed, "Thank you."

"With a couple of exceptions," Chase cautioned. "I want full veto power on the personal footage you use of us. That was our time, Ava. We fell in love, and we both know it had a lot to do with our conversations on the road, both on and off camera. Since we're both in the spotlight, we have to keep some things private."

"I agree. I'm sorry you saw that segment. And I swear I didn't tape you on a secret camera. I set it down and forgot it was on. I intended to erase it, but in my frantic file switching it ended up in the wrong place."

"That's good to know. Also, if you plan on using the footage, you'll hafta out me as Bill Chase. I don't know what the repercussions will be, as far as how the PRCA will react, not to mention the PBR. But I'm prepared to deal with the consequences no matter what."

"And I'll stick by you no matter what happens." Ava laid her hand on his cheek. "You know that, right?"

"I do now. Look, I'm gonna ride bulls as long as I'm able. There's risk with that. But I'm also looking ahead to what I'll do when I'm done. Maybe I'll open a bull ridin' school. I hear it's warm year-round in California."

She squeezed his hands. "That's an excellent idea. If that doesn't work, I'm sure you'll come up with something else."

"Until that time, I also plan on being very active with safety issues for riders. And to raise money, I want to host a rodeo in Ryan's hometown, in his name. With Jackie's permission, of course."

Ava's eyes filled with tears. "That's perfect."

"Ava. I don't have a lot to offer you. I'm sure the heiress to the Cooper conglomerate could find a much more socially acceptable match than a height-challenged Wyoming bull rider." When she started to protest, Chase put a finger over her lips. "But them other guys? The suit-and-tie and stupid-wearin'-shoes types? They're too late. You're mine now, Ava Rose, *mine*, through and through, and I play for keeps." He let his lips cling to hers in a kiss filled with promise. Then he eased back and smiled. "So. Were you serious about getting married on an island with just your intended and a preacher? Because I'm all over that idea. As soon as possible. Heck, I'm free next weekend."

"Stop right there if that's your way of asking me to marry you, Chase McKay." She poked him in the chest. "First of all, we're going to a Dumond Racing event with my family next weekend."

"We are?"

"Yep." Ava gave him a haughty look. "Be aware that I'm doing this marriage thing once in my life and I expect a real proposal, with a ring, you on bended knee, spouting words of love, holding flowers."

"Always setting the scene, aren't you?"

"Only because you need so much help."

"A lifetime of help."

Author's Note

I've taken quite a bit of artistic license in using the Professional Bull Riders Association and the Professional Rodeo Cowboys Association organizations in this book. Events, actions and persons are entirely fictional and the characters' comments are no reflection on either of these fine organizations, nor the cowboys and cowgirls who compete in them.

About the Author

To learn more about Lorelei James, please visit www.loreleijames.com. Send an email to lorelei@loreleijames.com or join her Yahoo! group to join in the fun with other readers as well as Lorelei: groups.yahoo.com/group/LoreleiJamesGang.

Revenge can be sweet. Forgiveness is sweeter.

Welcome to Paradise
© *2011 Elle Kennedy*
Welcome to Paradise, Book 1

Singing sensation Charlotte Hill can't wait for her high school reunion. She's out to give Nate Bishop—the man who walked away with her virginity—the sexiest ride of his life. Then give him a heaping dose of the same medicine he gave her fifteen years ago.

Stomp all over his heart as she walks out the door.

Nate has never forgotten the green-eyed redhead who set his body on fire, the one girl who saw past his bad reputation. The heat of those memories still warms his thoughts, even after all these years. After he did the right thing and let her go, rather than let his love chain her to a town she despised.

Now she's back in Paradise looking sexier than ever, and Nate finds himself powerless to keep his distance. And Charlotte, in spite of her resolve, can't believe she's so easily falling under his spell. Yet mind-blowing sex doesn't bury the past. It unearths painful emotions too long buried. Emotions that could stamp out rekindled love before it catches flame...

Warning: Contains a reformed bad boy and a newly minted bad girl with revenge on her mind, feuding families, dirty little secrets, and a lot of dirty sex.

Available now in ebook from Samhain Publishing.

SAMHAIN

PUBLISHING

It's all about the story...

Romance

HORROR

Retro ROMANCE

www.samhainpublishing.com

CPSIA information can be obtained at www.ICGtesting.com
Printed in the USA
BVOW070839160412

287769BV00002B/2/P